WHAT HO, AUTOMATA

CHRIS DOLLEY

Book View Café

WHAT HO, AUTOMATA

This is a work of fiction. All characters, pigs, orang-utans, mad scientists, locations, and events portrayed in this book are fictional or used in an imaginary manner to entertain, and any resemblance to any real people, situations, or incidents is purely coincidental.

All Rights Reserved, including the right to reproduce this book or portions thereof in any form.

Copyright © 2014 by Chris Dolley

Published by Book View Café

Book View Café Publishing Cooperative
P.O. Box 1624
Cedar Crest, NM 87008-1624

www.bookviewcafe.com

ISBN 13: 978-1-61138-394-2

The novelette *What Ho, Automaton!* was first published by Book View Café in the anthology Shadow Conspiracy II in 2011

Cover art by Brenda Clough and Chris Dolley
Steampunk Font © Illustrator Georgie - Fotolia.com

First printing, October 2014

Books by Chris Dolley

Resonance

Shift

French Fried

An Unsafe Pair Of Hands

Medium Dead

Magical Crimes

International Kittens of Mystery

How Possession Can Help You Lose Weight

Contents

What Ho, Automaton!

ONE

I think aunts must have come into being on the seventh day when God took his eye off the ball. Let there be light – no quibbles there. Let there be small furry animals – we Worcesters have always been strong supporters of our fluffier friends. But let there be aunts? I think not. They interfere and have 'opinions' which take the form of holy writ. I strongly suspect that Hannibal had an aunt, one who buttonholed him as he was about to set sail for Rome. "Hannibal!" she would have cried. "If you're off to Rome, you must visit your cousin in the Alps. And take those elephants with you. They're ruining my prize dahlias."

Which was why one Reginald Worcester, put-upon sap of this parish, was staring into a stiff drink at the Sloths Club contemplating the inequities of Creation. Not because of elephants – that would have been easy – but because his Aunt Bertha had instructed him to leave immediately for Crandle Castle and extricate his cousin Herbert from an unsuitable engagement.

"Is there any other kind?" I'd asked.

Never attempt repartee with an aunt.

I tried to explain that I was *persona non grata* at Crandle, having once been engaged to Georgiana Throstlecoombe – until the unfortunate incident with the Pomeranian – and that the young lady in question was certain to be at Crandle and would set the dogs – especially the Pomeranians, who have long memories – upon me the moment I crossed the horizon.

Aunts are impervious to both Latin and Pomeranians.

"Why the long face, Reggie?"

I was snapped back to the present by the arrival of one Lancelot Trussington-Thripp.

"What ho, Stiffy," I said, and then proceeded to give him the low-down on the aunt diktat.

"What you need is a Reeves," said Stiffy.

"A Reeves?"

"Yes, we've just found one. He was in a cupboard in the attic."

"Cupboard in the attic?"

My mind boggled on two counts, one, that the club had an attic and, two, that there was a Reeves living up there.

"He must have been there for years," said Stiffy. "He was covered in dust."

My mind reached new heights of boggledom. "Who, or what, is a Reeves?"

"A dashed brainy automaton," said Stiffy, visibly getting excited and shuffling closer. "He's dressed like a fairground fortune-teller and knows absolutely everything. His brain is positively immense. Barmy's trying to get him to tell our fortunes."

"Ha!" I said. "Some of us know our fortunes only too well and would rather not be reminded of them."

"Come on, Reggie. Give it a try. He really does know everything. If there's a way to get out of your Crandle entanglement, Reeves'll know."

I relented. The Worcesters have always had a soft spot for the outsider, and this plan rated a good 100-1 in anyone's form book.

I followed Stiffy to the billiard room where an even more excited gaggle of fellow Sloths were crowded around the far table. No one noticed our arrival. All heads were turned to the figure seated in a chair, which someone had placed upon the billiard table.

Had everyone lost their senses? A chair leg could rip the green baize!

As for the fortune-telling automaton chappie: never had I seen such a morose cove, his giant head topped with a pink turban and his shoulders swathed in flowing robes of pink and orange hues. Machine or not, I felt for the poor blighter. I'd had similar experiences in my childhood – being forced to sit still in the nursery while my older sister, the theatrically inclined Lady Julia, proceeded to dress me up like a prize peacock.

"I say," shouted Stiffy, pushing himself to the head of the throng. "Step aside, Humpy, there's a good chap. This is an emergency. Reggie has aunt trouble."

Like the Red Sea, when confronted by Moses holding a note from his mother's sister, the throng parted.

"Come along, Reggie," said Stiffy, beckoning. "Tell all to Reeves."

I recounted my sorry tale, omitting not a single Pomeranian. The Reeves listened intently, nodding his head in the places a living, breathing son of Adam would have felt like inclining his noggin too. As machines went, this Reeves was of the first rank. One could entirely believe he was human.

"Well?" said Stiffy when I'd finished. "Can you save our Reggie, Reeves?"

"There is a strong possibility that I can effect a positive outcome, sir," said Reeves. His voice was most unmachine-like. Not that I'd ever heard a machine speak, but if I had, I'd imagine it would be redolent of clanking gears and punctuated by puffs of steam escaping from the lips.

I espied not a single puff. This Reeves spoke like an educated cove. Maybe not Oxford, but certainly one of the lesser public schools.

"How?" I asked.

The Reeves took a deep breath. Still no puff of steam, or audible evidence of a piston clanking away in his chest.

"It *is* a most vexing situation, sir. One necessitating the utmost care and coordination. Are you prepared to execute my instructions to the letter?"

"Most certainly. You have the word of a Worcester."

"Very good, sir. You must take me with you to Crandle."

"What?"

My mind reacquainted itself with the outskirts of Boggle-dom.

"My presence at the castle is essential, sir, for I need to see the young gentleman and his intended in order to construct the perfect extrication. One which satisfies all parties, and increases the esteem in which you are held by your Aunt Bertha."

The Worcester lips parted but the tonsil area was bare. I was still mired in Reeves's last sentence. Could he *really* put me in Aunt Bertha's good books? Did she have a good book?

~

And so it came to pass that in the year of our Lord nineteen hundred and three, one Reginald Worcester and his gentleman's gentle-automaton, Reeves – accoutred now in Saville Row's finest valetware – left London for the northern climes of the county of Salop and that ancient pile, Crandle Castle.

We made good time; the Stanley Steamer, my second

foray into the world of the horseless carriage, behaved itself and required only two stops to take on water.

"Do you need to take on water, Reeves?" I'd asked at the first stop.

"Not at this juncture, sir."

"Well, shout out when you do. Coal, water, soothing oils. Whatever you require. I don't wish to return you to the Sloths broken."

"Your intention is to return me to that gentleman's club, sir?"

"Of course. We Worcesters have a code. Return what thou hast borrowed."

"A most excellent code, sir, but ... what if the object in question would prefer not to be returned?"

"Oh."

I cogitated for several minutes as my grey cells struggled with the philosophical niceties. When borrowing an umbrella, one does not expect said *parapluie* to request asylum. *Free me, Reginald, let me fly away to Manchester to join others of my kind.*

"You have an objection to being returned to the Sloths?" I asked.

"If I may be so bold, sir. I did find being locked in a cupboard for fourteen years somewhat less than convivial."

I could see his point.

"How did you come to be locked in a cupboard in the first place?"

"I believe I had been won in a game of cards, sir, the outcome of which was disputed. And, for reasons not divulged unto me, I was confined to a cupboard."

"Where you remained until this very day?"

"Indeed, sir. Young gentlemen can be most forgetful."

My conscience was pricked. Had I ever left a manservant in a cupboard? I didn't think I had, but then if Oxford had been in the habit of handing out blues for memory, the name Reginald Worcester would not have featured.

"Once we've finished here, I shall drop you off wherever you wish, Reeves. The world is your cupboard."

"That is most gracious of you, sir."

~

I parked the Stanley on the gravel drive by the front door and removed my driving goggles.

"Well, Reeves, here we are. Has your giant brain

formulated a plan?"

"I would advise a period of reconnaissance, sir, to ascertain the nature of the relationship between your cousin and the young lady and to posit a theory as to why your aunt would deem her unsuitable."

I was impressed. Just think of the kind of plans he could have come up with if he hadn't spent the last fourteen years in a cupboard!

"If you could engage the happy couple in conversation, sir, I will question the servants. It has been my experience that no one knows more about the activities above stairs than those below."

"Very good, Reeves, and watch out for the Pomeranians. They are deceptively swift."

~

One of the problems with large, stately homes, of which Crandle is one of the largest and stateliest, is that locating people one is looking for is often more difficult than locating people one is trying to avoid. Viz. the Lady Georgiana, whom I discovered, thankfully *sans* hunting pack, on the terrace as I turned the corner.

I was accorded an Arctic glare. "What are you doing here, Reggie? Run out of dogs to kick in Piccadilly?"

"I never kicked your dog, Georgie. It had my ankle in its jaws and I was merely trying to shake the blighter off."

"What rot, Reggie. I saw you!"

"Talking about seeing," I said, seizing the opportunity to change the subject. "Have you seen my cousin and his intended?"

"No, and I wouldn't tell you if I had. Beast!"

Lady Georgiana flounced off across the lawns, tossing epithets such as 'worm' and 'toad' over her shoulder. I thought it wise to beat a hasty retreat in the opposite direction in case she was planning to return with reinforcements.

Espying an open French window, I took refuge within the library. There was little chance of discovering Herbert in such a room – reading being well known to give the poor lad a headache – but I cast a disquisitive eye around the room just in case.

That's when I saw my host.

It is said that Arthur Throstlecoombe, eighth Earl of Twyneham, had never been the same since he lost his wife, having misplaced her at the Newmarket Spring Meeting sometime between the third and fourth race.

Some say she ran off with a jockey. Others maintain that the good lady was the unfortunate victim of an accident involving a runaway Zeppelin. Myself, I rather hope for the jockey. We Worcesters are all romantics at heart.

"What ho, Lord T!"

Lord Twyneham barely registered my existence. He was sitting at a table, poring over a book and muttering.

"It's not right," he said.

"What's not right, sir?"

Lord Twyneham looked up, noticing me for the first time.

"What? Who are you?"

"Reginald," I said. "Reginald Worcester, cousin of one Herbert Worcester, currently feeding at your trough."

If recognition did strike the aged earl, it left scarcely a mark.

"You're not a priest by any chance, are you?"

"No."

"Pity. I'm of a mind to write to the Archbishop of Canterbury?"

"You are?"

"If not the Pope. One of them must know how to exorcise a pig."

Boggledom approached once more. I was beginning to suspect all the roads leading out of Boggledom had been permanently blocked.

"Don't you have a pig man for that?"

"It's not my pig. It's Pomphrey's pig. The Colossus of Blackwater."

"Large pig, is it?"

Lord Twyneham snorted. "Too large. Abnormally large. Demonically large."

I tried to think of something soothing to say – the poor man was obviously out of sorts – but couldn't come up with anything better than, "There are more pigs in heaven and earth, Horatio, than are dreamt of in your philosophy." And Hamlet is never soothing.

"It can't be allowed to win again," continued his lordship. "There has to be a rule against entering devil hybrids in a fat stock show. Do you know the beast is reported to be even larger than last year?"

"I did not."

"The Princess of Crandle cannot be expected to compete

against a devil pig. It's not fair."

Drawing another blank in the soothing word department, I decided it best to take my leave and continue my quest.

~

I located Herbert and his intended in the rose garden, and turned a sleuth's eye upon the pair. She was tall and sporty looking - the kind of girl who would look good on the prow of a ship - while Herbert was his usual stocky self with a neck thickened by years of scrimmaging on the rugger field. If one were considering opening a breeding farm for future England rugger players, I would say, "Look no further."

"What ho, Herbert!"

"What are *you* doing here?"

"Taking the air, admiring the roses," I said.

"What rot! You're here to spy on me, aren't you?"

Herbert gave me the kind of look that had frozen many an opposing scrum half at ten paces.

"Spy on you? No, I often come to Crandle."

"Rot! Which one of them sent you? Brunhilde? Bertha?"

For a man who'd taken a lifetime of blows to the head, Herbert was rather astute.

"I assure you, old bean, I didn't even know you were here. Came as a complete surprise when I saw you sauntering through the rose garden arm in arm with... I'm sorry, we haven't been introduced."

"Josephine Smith," said the mystery girl, proffering her hand.

Now I was up close, I could take better measure of the girl. She was a good hand taller than Herbert, of statuesque appearance, fair-to-middling in the looks department, well-dressed and well-spoken. Not the kind of girl to send aunts reaching for the family blackball.

"Reginald Worcester," I said, doffing the hat. "Would that be the Hampshire Smiths or the Wimbledon Smiths?"

"My family hails from Bristol, Mr Worcester."

She held the Worcester gaze as she spoke. Calm, refined, unexcitable. The girl should have been an aunt's dream.

"Reggie! You *are* here to spy on us. Admit it! All these questions."

"Steady the buffs, Herbert, old fruit. I was only making conversation."

I could tell by the fiery eyeball and the clenched fists that a stronger card needed to be played.

"If you must know, I'm here to see Georgie. We were once engaged, don't you know."

The card was an eyeball quencher. Sweetness and light returned to the rose garden and Reginald Worcester, sleuth, continued his gentle interrogation of the happy couple.

~

An hour later I found Reeves on the terrace and reported all.

"Dashed if I can see anything about the girl that would draw the ire of an aunt. She doesn't smile a lot, but then, she's engaged to Herbert. I wouldn't smile if I was engaged to him."

"Is her family impecunious, sir?"

"Not that I could gather. Have you heard of the Smiths of Bristol, Reeves? I haven't."

"The family is unfamiliar to me, sir, though... I have been removed from society for fourteen years."

"Quite. You know, Reeves, I think the answer to this puzzle may well lie in that ancient seaport. There has to be some black sheep rootling about in the family fold. Something that Bertha knows and we don't. What about your Sherlocking, Reeves? Uncover any sheep?"

"Possibly, sir. One of the chambermaids mentioned something about a tattoo."

"A tattoo?"

"That was what the girl said. A most unusual tattoo, sir."

"The mind boggles, Reeves. Are we talking parrots or declarations of undying love for one's mother?"

"Neither, sir. The tattoo in question is composed of three words. 'Made in Belgium.'"

"What?" I had to have misheard.

"Made in Belgium, sir. It's a small country located between France and Holland."

"I know where Belgium is, Reeves. A bit rummy this though, don't you think? She doesn't sound Belgian. And Smith is not a noted Belgian surname. Is it?"

"No, sir."

"Could it have been a misprint? She says Bristol; the tattooist chappie hears Belgium?"

"I think not, sir. One thought that did present itself – that the young lady may be a mechanical construct like myself – proved unfounded. Several of the serving staff report occasions when she was seen dining at table."

"Not slipping in the odd lump of coal, I suppose?"

"No, sir. The young lady was reported to have a healthy and unremarkable appetite. May I suggest a visit to her room? I believe Miss Smith to be partaking of a game of tennis upon the lawn this hour. A search of her belongings may prove enlightening."

~

The mantle of bedroom sleuth was passed to me, Reeves having cried off with a pressing engagement in the butler's pantry. I affected a nonchalant non-sleuthing air as I followed Reeves's directions to the room in question. I sauntered, I whistled a refrain or two from G & S, I smiled beatifically. The casual observer, had there been one, would have looked upon Reginald and said, "there walks a chap who wouldn't go snooping about in another chap's cupboards."

I arrived at Miss Smith's door the very model of a modern sleuthing general. So far so good. I looked up corridor. I looked down corridor. Not a sausage. I opened the door, and, closing it quietly behind me, slipped inside.

It took longer to search the room than I expected – a person of gentle breeding cannot root about in another person's garment drawer willy-nilly. Particularly if the person in question is a member of the opposite, and reputedly deadlier, sex. Proprieties have to be observed, care taken, eyes occasionally averted. And I have never mastered the art of folding.

Plus there was the matter of what to look for. Clues do not come clearly labelled. I could have been looking for ciphers constructed of dancing men or evidence that the room had been recently frequented by a seafaring orang-utan.

I am not sure how long my slow and fruitless search took but outside the *tempus* was positively *fugiting*. Luckily I heard the footsteps before the door opened and was able to rush to a hiding place behind a small screen by the window.

The door opened.

"I'll meet you on the terrace," said the unmistakable voice of Josephine Smith.

"Right ho," came a distant reply, presumably from Herbert.

I listened as the door closed and prayed for Miss Smith's visit to be a fleeting one. But God, as on the seventh day, must have had his feet up, for I could hear the steady pop of buttons and ... was that the creak of whalebone?

Miss Smith was divesting herself of her clothing! A notion confirmed when one garment was so bold as to fly across the room and drape itself over the top of the very screen I was hiding behind!

I fixed my eyes firmly to the carpet. This never happened to Sherlock Holmes or, if it did, Doctor Watson wisely left those passages out. *Be a good chap, Watson, and scratch that scene with me hiding under Irene Adler's bed.*

As I considered the Great Detective and wondered what he might have done had he found himself in my situation, I was struck with a notion. What if the maid had been mistaken about the tattoo? What if it had said 'Bristol' or 'Belljum' – for was it not possible that the tattoo could be an anagram or a cipher? You can tell that the old grey cells were burning white-hot at this juncture.

I lowered myself onto all fours and sneaked a peek around the side of the screen.

The tattoo was not the only thing that was visible.

There were two screams. One, the louder, from Miss Smith, and the second, somewhat strangled, from Reginald Worcester. Soon there was a third for, I'm sure you have noticed, that whenever there's a commotion in a large stately home, doors fly open and previously empty corridors are instantly teeming with the inquisitive.

My cousin Herbert was more than inquisitive. Espying his beloved wrapped loosely in a towel, he squeezed through the throng in the doorway and placed a cardigan over her shoulders.

Words, always problematical for Herbert, were vaporised before they could leave his mouth. He was incandescent. "R-R-Reggie! Are you *mad!* What are you *doing* down there!"

All reasonable questions. I crouched there, still on all fours, attempting an affable smile while feeling like a guilty Pomeranian discovered next to the body of a dead postman.

Herbert advanced upon me, teeth and fists clenched. I jumped up and said the first thing that came into my head. "I thought this was Georgie's room!"

Firm hands grabbed my lapels and hoisted me towards the window.

"No!" said Josephine. "Herbert, don't throw your cousin out the window."

"Why not?" said Herbert. "It would do him good."

"No! I thought this was Georgie's room! I really did. Awfully sorry, Miss Smith."

If I'd had a hand free I would have doffed my hat, but both hands were busy grasping the walls either side of the window.

"Apology accepted, Mr Worcester. Now do put him down, Herbert."

"I'll put him down all right. I'll put him on the terrace!"

"No!" I tightened my grip. I clutched at straws. "I *told* you I was here to see Georgie. It was an honest mistake. My wits addled by unrequited love and chirping song-birds."

Perhaps it was the song-birds, but something calmed the savage Herbert and he released his grip.

"Now get out!" he said.

Hands free, I doffed my hat and withdrew from the room apace, apologising to one and all. "Awfully sorry. Complete misunderstanding. Too much sun. Surfeit of song-birds."

I fled the castle and hid at the far end of the Yew Alley, close to the wood, for half an hour, contemplating whether or not to write to Sherlock Holmes and ask how the Great Sleuth would have extricated himself from such a situation. I'd just reached the conclusion that the reply would have followed the lines of, "Never have an aunt for a client," when Reeves arrived.

"I believe congratulations are in order, sir."

"I fear your congratulations are misplaced, Reeves. I found nothing in Miss Smith's room, other than to corroborate the existence of the tattoo and the correct spelling of Belgium."

"I was alluding to your engagement to Miss Georgiana, sir. It is the talk of the Servants' Hall."

"What!"

"It would appear that Miss Georgiana was witness to your declaration of love and was much moved. She has spoken to her father."

I slumped against a tree. "I didn't see her there, Reeves." But then I hadn't been looking. I had left the room blinkered and avoiding every eye.

They say that on the point of marriage, one's future flashes before one's eyes. Mine was a terrible sight. First, I saw the church, then... Into the aisle of death strode the R. Worcester. Pomeranians to the right of me, Pomeranians to the left, and a canon in front of me. I was shatter'd and sunder'd before I passed the first pew.

"You see before you a broken man, Reeves. I'm not ready for marriage."

"May I make a suggestion, sir?"

"Suggest away, Reeves."

"If you were to perform a great service for his lordship, he may be disposed to intervene on your behalf with the young lady."

"Make her see reason, you mean?"

"Or forbid the banns."

I could see a pig-sized hole in Reeves's plan. Reason and Lord Twyneham did not enjoy the same relationship as did 'horse' and 'cart.' The ancient relic was likely to forget any service I performed within five minutes, or, worse, reward my efforts by welcoming me into the bosom of the Throstlecoombe family.

"This service wouldn't involve exorcising any pigs, would it, Reeves?"

"Not exactly, sir. The task is one of passing a certain piece of information to his lordship. One that would make the eighth earl regard the messenger with considerable favour."

"Speak on, Reeves."

"Are you familiar with Sir Jasper Pomphrey's pig, The Colossus of Blackwater?"

"We don't exchange cards at Christmas, Reeves, but I have heard of said animal. Is it really a devil pig? Are there chalked pentagrams in the Pomphrey Piggery? Piggery-pokery at Blackwater Hall?"

"Quite, sir. I suspect the animal may be an artificial pig."

"What?"

"An automaton, sir, like myself, though constructed to look and behave as a pig."

"Have you seen the pig?"

"No, sir. I have surmised its nature from information gleaned from conversations in the Servant's Hall."

Now *that* was sleuthing of the highest order.

"Talk in the village, sir, is that Sir Jasper has doubled his coal order and installed a steam boiler in the pigsty. He maintains it is to keep the animal warm in the winter."

"But you suspect otherwise?"

"Indeed I do, sir. Sir Jasper has also recently taken delivery of a substantial quantity of lead."

"Ah, and you deduce it's not for his roofs?"

"I do, sir. A lead-lined pig would be at a considerable

advantage in a fat stock competition."

Of that there was little doubt, but – I stroked my chin pensively – information like this had to be used judiciously. A man delivering porcine tidings of great joy could well be looked upon as prime son-in-law material.

"Pssst!" said Reeves.

"Pardon?" A strange expression had settled upon Reeves's face – one of slack-jawed incomprehension. I followed his gaze, turning to stare into the little wood behind me. Had he seen something? Pomphrey's pig?

"Pssst!" he hissed again. And then fell over.

"Reeves!" I tried to catch him but he was toppling beyond my reach. He fell to the mossy floor like a dead weight. I knelt beside him, patted his cheeks, felt for a pulse but ... I didn't even know if he should have a pulse.

I'd had Reeves for barely a day and already I'd broken him!

Perhaps I'd overtaxed him? No one's at his best after fourteen years in a cupboard.

I had to seek help. Stiffy would know what to do. Ten paces into my dash for the Castle, I was struck by another thought. Lifeless bodies laid out across paths tended to get noticed – questions would be asked, policemen sent for.

I ran back and dragged Reeves over to the trees and propped him up against a trunk. From a distance, it would look as if he were taking a nap.

Ten minutes later, I was in the Castle hallway, stuffing a telegram into the pneumatic capsule and dropping it into the slot by the hall table. *Urgent Stop Come at once Stop Reeves broken Stop Not my fault Stop Reggie.*

TWO

It was dark by the time Stiffy arrived. I flagged him down the second he drove through the gates, having camped out there for the best part of two hours whilst hiding from various fiancées, cousins and imminent fathers-in-law.

I had even missed dinner. Which, for a Worcester, is something not entertained lightly.

I brought Stiffy up to speed with events, omitting, as Watson always did, the scene involving the bedroom.

"Have you topped him up?" asked Stiffy when I'd finished.

"Reeves?"

"Of course Reeves."

"Topped him up with what?"

"*Steam*, you ass! Don't you know anything about automata?"

I had to shrug. "It wasn't on the syllabus at Eton."

Nor, come to think of it, at Oxford. Unless there was a section in Greats I'd missed.

"You've got to plug them into a steam outlet, Reggie. How did you think they took on fuel?"

I shrugged again. "Nuggets of coal with their kippers, I suppose. And I'm not an ass. Steam may be very efficient at keeping parts moving but you can't tell me it fuels the little grey cells. Everyone knows one needs fish to do that."

"He's an automaton, Reggie! He can't eat fish!"

"I think you're mistaken there, Stiffy. I fed him some earlier."

"You did what?"

"I had the cook mash up some turbot with a little warm milk. And I must say he looked a sight perkier afterwards."

"You stuffed turbot in Reeves's mouth?"

"And some milk."

Stiffy's eyes widened to such a degree that I feared for his forehead.

"You *are* an ass."

"No, I'm not."

"Yes, you are. You may have bunged up his works! Quick! Where is he?"

I led Stiffy at a brisk pace across the castle grounds to the Yew Walk, lighting our way with a lantern I'd procured earlier – a lantern that an ass would not have had sufficient forethought to have requisitioned!

I located Reeves and shone the light on his face. His eyes were open but they stared lifelessly ahead.

"Grab a shoulder, Reggie, we need to get him to the Castle."

"Do you think that wise?"

"We need a steam outlet, Reggie. There should be one at Crandle."

"Are you sure?"

"How else would they top up the servants?"

I was staggered. "The servants are automata?"

"Aren't they? Don't all the big houses have automata below stairs these days?"

My mind felt the magnetic pull of the borough of Boggledom. I couldn't have been more stupefied if Stiffy had struck me in the mazard with a lead-lined pig.

"Not the cooks, surely?"

"I wouldn't be surprised."

We hoisted Reeves to his feet and, not without some difficulty, proceeded to half carry, half drag his steamless body down the Yew Walk and back to the Castle. All the time, I couldn't help but wonder how many meals I had consumed in the past ten years that had been prepared by mechanical chefs. Might they have added engine oil to the salad? An easy mistake to make for a mechanical chef one would suppose.

The lights of the Castle loomed into view and I steered a course for the cobbled yard at the back where the door to the servants quarters was. I left Stiffy propping Reeves up by the back door and galloped off in search of Dawson, the venerable butler. No one knew the Castle better than he.

I found him in the Servant's Hall, drinking tea, or, something that looked remarkably like tea. Can one make an engine oil tisane? A half dozen other servants were imbibing likewise. All heads turned at my entrance.

"Ah, what ho, Dawson. Sorry to disturb and all that, but could I have a word?"

We stepped into the corridor, Dawson moving with his usual silent and effortless grace. I had put his near supernatural ability to glide in and out of rooms unheard down to his mastery of the butling arts. But perhaps it was just superior lubricating oil.

"I'm looking for the Crandle steam outlet, Dawson. Where would one find it?"

"Steam outlet, sir?"

"Yes, for ... you know ... mechanical people. Automata."

Dawson shook his head, and added several tut-tuts. "Lord Twyneham would never allow them into the house, sir. He disapproves."

As, by his manner, did Dawson.

"Ah, well ... that's a relief. I didn't think his lordship would have allowed it but, you know, one has to check. One never knows who's preparing one's meals in London. Good to see Crandle still has standards."

I left swiftly.

"Quick," I said to Stiffy as soon as I reached him. "We've got to get Reeves out of here. Automata are *machina non grata* at Crandle."

If any further proof were required viz. the state of Reginald Worcester's mental faculties, we'd no sooner ducked under the small gate of the rear courtyard when an idea, like cupid's arrow slightly off course, struck the Worcester noggin. Pomphrey's pig had its own steam boiler! Now, would an ass have made a connection like that?

"Come on, Stiffy. I know where there's an outlet."

~

I am not sure about the best laid plans of mice, but I nod the head to Robert Burns when it comes to those laid down by men. Mine was half *agley* by the time, huffing and puffing, we reached Stiffy's car. I had no idea where Pomphrey's piggery was.

"You really are ... an ass!" said Stiffy in between deep breaths.

"No, I'm not!"

"Yes, you ... jolly well are."

I had a strong sense of *deja vu*. Had not this very conversation occurred at this very spot less than half an hour earlier?

"It can't be ... difficult to spot." I wheezed. "We'll drive to ... Blackwater Hall ... and take a look."

Blackwater Hall was in darkness, which could be good – if everyone was in bed – or bad – if Lord T. was correct and Sir Jasper was communing with Lucifer in the pig house.

Stiffy parked his car close to a block of outbuildings and, leaving Reeves propped up in the back seat, we set off in search of the piggery. Five minutes and three outbuildings later we were stopped in our tracks by an unusual noise.

"Do automata snore?" I whispered to Stiffy for, the more I listened, the more that's what the noise sounded like.

"I don't know," whispered Stiffy. "Do pigs snore?"

I had no idea. The syllabus at Eton is strangely deficient in these matters.

I turned down the wick of the lantern and we both crept closer to the shadowy building whence the noise appeared to emanate from. I thought I could make out a figure lying by a doorway. We crept closer still, stepping lightly through the long grass. It was definitely a man and he was definitely snoring. I could see a large jug next to him and the air was heady with the smell of beer and pig. He had to be Pomphrey's pig man. It looked like he'd passed out drunk while on pig guard duty.

We eased our way past him and looked over the stable door into what, unless my nose was mistaken, had to be the piggery. I stared into the abyss, holding up the lantern, its soft light beginning to illuminate the low-ceilinged sty...

"Hello," said the pig. "You're not here to feed me, are you?"

I started, involuntarily taking a short step backwards and almost tripping over Stiffy and the supine pig man. Not only was the pig talking but it was enormous! The size of two pigs. Two very fat pigs.

"Hello?" said the pig again, its voice most unpig-like. Not a single oinck or snort. And there was a definite Scottish lilt to its speech. It sounded rather like my old History master at Eton, Donald Farquharson-Fleck.

I looked at Stiffy and he looked at me. We were both marooned in Boggledom.

Presently, I gathered sufficient wits to step forward once more.

"What ho, pig," I said. "Do you mind awfully if we borrow your steam outlet?"

The Colossus looked confused. "What steam outlet?"

I looked once more at Stiffy. He stepped forward. "The steam outlet that feeds you, you know, keeps you topped up?"

"There's my trough," he said. "You can borrow that if you'd like, but I must warn you it's full of the most revolting swill."

I could see the trough at the back of the pen and, raising the lantern higher, I could see the swill.

I gave Stiffy the eyeball once more. "Are you sure automata are fed on steam? It looks to me like this one is doing very well on swill."

"I'm not an automaton," said the pig, shaking his massive head. "I'm a Promethean. There's a difference."

"There is?"

"Oh, yes. An automaton is a purely mechanical construct. We Prometheans are flesh and blood."

"You're a real pig?"

The pig raised a front leg and wiggled a trotter. "Yes and no. I'm made *from* pigs. Sir Jasper collected parts from champion fat stock pigs all over Europe. My head's a Landrace. My left rump's a Black Berkshire. Then he commissioned some mad scientist to sew me together and breathe life into me. I think something went wrong. I appear to have the soul and intellect of a man."

This was rummy. "Do you have any memories of being a man?"

"Vague ones. Ones where I'm up on two feet. Faces that I feel I should know, but don't. Places far away from here, where there are mountains and high moors. Food that wasn't this dashed awful swill."

We Worcesters are not made of stone – nor metal, nor the prime parts of deceased Worcesters.

"You must come with us," I said. "We can take you to Crandle or you can run free in the woods. Whatever your wish."

"Can I have roast pheasant? And some cheese. I'd die for a good strong cheddar. Anything to rid the taste of this vile swill from my mouth."

"You shall eat cheddar. And roast pheasant."

I was feeling much moved by the occasion. As was the Colossus, his eyes were positively moist. I opened the sty door and stood back to let him out.

"Wait," said the pig. "Doesn't one of you need a top up? Sir Jasper has to have something up at the Hall. Most of his servants are automata."

"Isn't there a steam boiler here?" asked Stiffy. "Reggie

said there was."

"It's next door," said the pig. "But I think it's only used to boil swill."

Stiffy and I slipped next door to make sure. The Colossus followed. He was right about the swill. There was a giant copper filled to the brim with the foul smelling stuff, but it wasn't being heated by the boiler. The copper had its own coal fire.

Stiffy took the lantern from me and, turning the wick up, dangled it in front of the boiler.

"Look," he said. "There! A steam outlet. It's the same design as the one my uncle has."

"Your uncle's an automaton?"

"Ass! My uncle has it for his servants."

"So we can plug Reeves in!"

"Once we fire it up." He touched the boiler. "It's lukewarm at the moment. Grab a shovel, Reggie. We need to get the pressure up."

I'd never shovelled coal before. I found it a much overrated experience, and decidedly dusty. If I'd known I was going to spend the evening dashing across fields and shovelling coal, I should have dressed accordingly. The Colossus tried to help, rooting through the pile of coal with his nose and nudging lumps of the stuff onto my shovel.

When the fire was blazing and the pressure rising, Stiffy and I left to fetch Reeves from the car. Five minutes later, the three of us returned.

"Help me stand Reeves in front of the boiler, Reggie."

We hoisted him forward until he was standing a yard away.

"How do we plug him in?" I asked.

"The steam outlet's attached to a rubber hose. We pull out the hose and plug it into Reeves. Now, help me with his trousers."

"What?" I had a sudden and terrible thought. "Where exactly are you going to put that hose?"

"His belly button, of course."

Phew. I helped Stiffy loosen Reeves's belt and pull out his shirt-front. Stiffy undid the bottom three shirt buttons and, *voila*, there was Reeves's belly button. I'd never seen one with a screw thread before.

Stiffy connected him up, and threw a lever. Seconds passed. There were gurgles, a whooshing sound, and...

Reeves coughed and a piece of turbot flew across the

room and struck the boiler.

"I beg your pardon, sirs," said Reeves.

"Never mind that, Reeves." I said. "How are you feeling?"

"Much improved, sir. Though I fear I may be seeing things."

"What kind of things?"

"A giant pig, sir."

"I'm a Promethean."

"Giant talking pigs, sir."

"That's all right, Reeves. We hear him too. He's the Colossus of Blackwater."

I brought Reeves up to speed viz. pigs, Prometheans and Lord Twyneham's opinion of automata.

"I don't want to be any trouble," said Colossus. "But didn't someone promise me some cheese?"

"You shall have a whole cheese, my good pig," I said. "The finest cheddar."

But how were we to get to Crandle? There wasn't room in Stiffy's car for three men and a giant pig. I looked to Reeves. With all that extra steam, and a portion or two of turbot, his little grey cells had to be positively whizzing.

"I believe there is a short-cut to Crandle across the fields," he said.

"Excellent! Reeves. Lead on."

"Alas, sir, I am unaware of its location."

"Do you need more steam, Reeves?"

"No, sir."

"More turbot? A sardine?"

"It's not a question of brain power, sir. It's one of knowledge."

"I know the way," said Colossus. "Sir Jasper and his pig man sneak over to Crandle now and then to spy on the Princess. I've heard them talking."

"Lead on, then, kindly pig."

THREE

We followed the Colossus along a path through a wood. After ten minutes I espied a light up ahead. It couldn't be Crandle, as we hadn't reached the lawns yet, but it could be the gamekeeper's cottage, or maybe the pigsty.

We advanced with caution, dousing once more our trusty lantern. As we approached closer, I recognised the building as Lord Twyneham's pigsty – no one could visit Crandle without being inveigled by his lordship into paying homage to the Princess. The light was coming through the open door, and there, draped bonelessly over the lower half of the stable door, was a figure.

It couldn't be Lord Twyneham – unless he was wearing an ankle length nightshirt. I approached closer, using a clump of bushes for cover to get within thirty feet of the door. It was a woman and, by her height, it had to be Josephine Smith. What was she doing at his lordship's piggery in the middle of the night? Had I stumbled upon the reason for Aunt Bertha's ire – was Miss Smith a pig rustler?

She didn't appear to be rustling. If anything she looked more like his lordship – a pilgrim paying homage at the Princess's shrine.

I inched forward for a better look. A twig snapped.

Miss Smith sprang upright and turned, looking a little shaken. "Who's there?" she said, staring into the night.

This was a situation that needed careful handling. A man last seen hiding in a young lady's room while she was getting undressed cannot afford to burst in upon her a second time.

"It's only me, Miss Smith. I'm with Stiffy."

"You're what!"

"I'm with Stiffy in the bushes."

"Allow me, sir," said Reeves. "I am Reeves, miss. Mr Worcester's man. We are here in the bushes with Mr Trussington-Thripp."

"Good Lord. Are there any more of you in there?"

"Only me," said the pig.

"Who are you?"

"He's Mr Pomphrey's pigman," said Reeves.

I think the turbot had added extra pep to Reeves's speed of thought.

There was a rustle in the shrubbery to my right and, before I could stop him, the Colossus waddled into the clearing.

"Do you have any cheese?" he asked Miss Smith.

Miss Smith was strangely quiet on the subject of cheese, preferring to stare, open-mouthed, at the giant pig as he waddled towards her. But she didn't scream, or faint, or mistake the pig for a love token from Reginald Worcester and regard herself as immediately engaged – as was the habit of most young ladies of my acquaintance. As the initial shock evaporated, she appeared even to warm to the giant pig.

"How are you able to talk?" she asked, circling the Colossus and observing him from every angle.

"I'm a Promethean," he said. "Do you have any food at all? Perhaps a banana?"

Reeves emerged from the bushes.

"Good evening, miss," he said, raising his bowler. "We were on our way to the Castle to obtain food for the Colossus. May I be so bold as to ask for your assistance in this matter?"

"I will help in any way I can." She reached out and touched the Colossus on the shoulder. "So, you're the Colossus of Blackwater, are you? Has Sir Jasper been mistreating you?"

"Have you ever lived for ten months on a diet of swill, swill, and more swill? You don't have an apple on you, do you?"

"If you would be so kind, miss, as to wait here with the Colossus, the young gentlemen and I will fetch sustenance from the Castle."

~

We left Miss Smith deep in conversation with the pig and set off at a brisk pace towards the Castle.

"May I suggest, sirs, that, with the Colossus's escape certain to be discovered upon the morrow, it would be preferable if Mr Trussington-Thripp's car was not found in the vicinity of Blackwater Hall?"

That turbot was working wonders. Reeves said he'd

procure the food while I drove Stiffy back to Blackwater Hall to fetch his car. He even offered to see to the pig himself and carry a couple of hampers out to the woods.

"Young gentlemen need their sleep, sir, and you have had a long and trying day."

Reeves was a valet without peer.

I was feeling dashed pleased with myself as I opened the door to my bedroom that night. I may not have solved the Aunt Bertha problem - yet - but, in the course of my sleuthing, I'd liberated a giant talking pig. Even Sherlock Holmes couldn't say that.

Then I saw the folded piece of paper on the carpet. Someone must have slipped a note under my door while I was out. I picked it up.

"Darling Reggie," it read. "See you at breakfast."

It was signed 'G.'

~

I decided to skip breakfast and take a stroll to the pigsty instead. I got as far as the east terrace when I was accosted by my cousin, Herbert. He was redder in the face than usual and much agitated.

"Can you believe it!" he said.

I probably could. A man who'd conversed with giant pigs could believe almost anything.

"What is it, old chap?" I asked.

"It's Josephine. She's left me. Run off with a pig!"

"She's run off with a pig?"

"Yes!"

"As in 'stolen the pig?'"

"No! They've eloped!"

"What?"

"It's all here in her letter. Look."

He waved the letter in front of me.

"And not only has she left me. But she says here she's not even English!"

"Belgian?" I asked.

"No, not even Belgian. She says she's a Promethean. And I don't even know where Promethea is!"

~

"Well, I didn't see that one coming. Did you, Reeves?"

"I had my suspicions upon observing them last night, sir. I had occasion to converse with them while the Colossus ate his cheddar and roast pheasant."

"Pally, were they?"

"Very, sir. The young lady seemed remarkably well-informed upon the subject of Prometheans."

"Like seeking out like, I suppose. Tell me, Reeves, do you feel any sentimental attachment to other machines? A grandfather clock, perhaps, that might have caught your eye?"

"No, sir."

"How are you for steam at the moment? Need a top-up yet?"

"I think not, sir, though I believe my pressure warning governor needs adjustment. It should have informed me that my pressure was dangerously low."

"Fourteen years in a cupboard can't be good for pressure warning governors."

"Indeed not, sir."

"Do you think Aunt Bertha knew Miss Smith was a Promethean?"

"I could not possibly say, sir."

"Aunts do have extraordinary abilities, you know, Reeves. Aunt Bertha has an inquisitorial eye. One look and she can see right through you. I expect she gave Miss Smith the once over and recognised an arm belonging to a dead relative."

"Quite possibly, sir."

"Reggie, darling!"

The early morning peace was shattered by the piercing soprano of Lady Georgiana, accompanied by a bout of excited, high-pitched yipping.

Dogs! I braced myself, girding the Worcester loins, expecting to be struck from behind by a pack of wild Pomeranians.

"Your fiancée is hailing you, sir."

"Thank you, Reeves," I said, giving him the stern eye.

I, as generations of Worcesters had done before me, then turned to face the enemy with a merry smile and a raised hat.

"What ho, Georgie."

The Lady Georgiana, with dogs at foot, dogs circling, and dogs terrorising the shrubbery, strode towards me with the look of a woman who'd just raised a pheasant and now had him in her sights.

"Have the bags packed and meet me at the car," I whispered to Reeves.

"Sir? Would you not prefer I remain and assist you with your extrication?"

"Leave this one to Reginald, Reeves. I have a plan."

~

"I say, have you heard the news about Miss Smith?" I asked, trying to keep my plan on script while my trousers were being sniffed, rubbed against and slobbered over.

"Is it really true?" asked Georgie. "It's not some tale she spun Herbert, is it?"

"I was there. I saw the pair together. Love at first sight."

"No! When did you see them?"

"Last night as I took my bedtime constitutional stroll around the grounds. Opened my eyes, I can tell you. People running off with animals. Whatever next?"

One of the Pomeranians had discovered my trousers contained a bone - an anklebone - and was trying to get his teeth around it.

"Sebastian! Leave Reggie's leg alone. Go!"

Sebastian gave my ankle a parting nip for luck, then slunk off.

"Mind you," I said. "I think I can understand it. Must be something in the air around Crandle this year. Don't you find the farm animals attractive? A ewe with a well-turned leg? A mare with a firm fetlock?"

She gave me a look. "Reggie?"

"Dashed attractive dogs you have there."

The rummy thing about plans is that they never play out in real life as they do in one's head. Even a perfectly sound one can founder on the smallest rock.

I'd expected Georgie to break off the engagement and flounce off, not set her dogs on me!

Did I mention that Pomeranians were deceptively swift?

Something Rummy This Way Comes

ONE

"It's time you were married, Reginald," said Aunt Bertha.

I blanched. This was going to be one of *those* conversations, the ones where quick footwork and the ability to feign a passable heart attack were essential.

"I've tried, esteemed aunt, but no one'll have me. I don't know why. They're keen enough to get engaged, but no sooner do they come under starter's orders than they pull up or fall at the water jump. I fear Reginald will never see the winner's enclosure of the Matrimonial Stakes."

"Nonsense. Your problem is that you don't try hard enough."

"Trying's not the problem, venerable A. It's the going. For some reason the Matrimonial Stakes is always run on heavy ground."

"Do you talk like this to your fiancées?"

"Like what?"

"Like a blithering idiot."

"I say–"

"No, you will *not* say. You will listen. The new season has begun and there are dozens of young debutantes about to be launched into society who have never heard of you. Time to snare one before they do."

"But–"

"No buts, Reginald. I have discussed the matter with my friends. As of this morning, you have invitations to every ball and dinner party on the calendar. If, for any reason, you fail to make an appearance, I will hear of it. By pneumatic telegram. I have had assurances of this from every hostess in London. You, my boy, are getting married."

There was only one thing to do.

"And *stop* writhing on the floor, Reginald. It fools no one."

~

I believe Armageddon commences in a similar fashion –

with the Aunt of God unleashing The Four Groomsmen of the Apocalypse. 'Go forth and round up every bachelor and march him down the aisle," quoth the Aunt. 'No excuses will be heard and no quarter given. And don't look at me like that, Jesus. You've been single far too long.'

I sighed, and took a long, lingering look around my drawing room. I was immensely fond of my Charles Street flat. Everything about it was perfect – the proportion of the rooms, its location, its size. But if I got married...

Would I have to give it up? Buy something larger? Set up home in the country?

It wasn't as though I was averse to marriage. I had every intention of tying the knot one day and listening to the patter of tiny Worcesters fleeing down the corridor pursued by an irate nanny. But not this year. Marriage was an estate for an older, more responsible Worcester.

"Would you care for a cocktail, sir?" said Reeves, my gentleman's personal gentle-automaton.

"How are you on poisons, Reeves? Know any swift acting ones that mix well with gin?"

"It is not a subject I have studied extensively, sir."

I explained my situation to him at length, ending my sorry tale by showing him the handwritten invitation I'd received to the Duchess of Rutland's ball in Denmark Street.

"It's this evening, Reeves. The runners for the Matrimonial Stakes are in the paddock and I'm about to be well and truly saddled. Know any boats sailing for Botany Bay?"

"I would not recommend such an action, sir."

"Would you not? I suppose there's always America, or the Paris Zeppelin. Are the Foreign Legion still hiring?"

"Might I suggest an alternative, sir?"

"Suggest away, Reeves. Any part of the globe except Denmark Street."

"I was thinking that it may be judicious to acquiesce to your aunt's wishes."

"What? Get married? Steady on, Reeves."

"No, sir. I would never suggest anything as precipitous as that, but ... there may be considerable merit in being *seen* to be trying to get married."

"Aha, feign acquiescence, you mean? Then pull up the Worcester stallion a furlong from home?"

"I would advise a distance considerably longer than a furlong, sir. Having observed your aunt, I am of the opinion that dragging a stallion over a distance of 220 yards is well within her capabilities."

I had to agree. And well within the capabilities of some of the young ladies of my acquaintance too.

"Have you a plan, Reeves? Are those little grey cells whizzing around with turbot-charged vim this afternoon?"

"I do have a suggestion or two, sir. It has been my observation that young ladies are oft times of a somewhat shallow disposition and would look with considerable disapprobation upon a young gentleman who was unfortunate enough to have a blemish upon his countenance."

"What kind of a blemish?"

"A boil springs to mind, sir. It would keep the young ladies at bay without bringing the wrath of your aunt upon you."

"That's as maybe, Reeves, but as you can see, the Worcester face is devoid of boils. I fear you must have dined upon a bad turbot."

"I was thinking of a false boil, sir. With a little theatrical make-up, the results could be quite convincing."

When you have a giant brain even a bad turbot can get it fizzing. I sat upright, thinking hard.

"But how long could I pull it off for, Reeves? Three balls? A week? I can see Aunt Bertha's sympathy for her afflicted nephew running out pretty swiftly. She'd summon a doctor and have us both lanced - the boil first, then me."

"I was thinking that the boil would be no more than a precursor to a series of misfortunes that could thwart your matrimonial prospects, sir."

"I see where you're going, Reeves, but I fear that so would Aunt Bertha. If I appear with boils one week, a hunched back the next, followed by an assortment of blackened teeth and smallpox scars, she would have me committed to a sanatorium."

"Quite possibly, sir. Which is why I would suggest a more subtle approach."

"This wouldn't involve feigning consumption, would it, Reeves? A cough here, a sickly look there? Because I've tried it before and it does not work. The girl takes one look at the dying Reginald and is overcome by the spirit of Florence Nightingale and visions of romantic poets ebbing away in the arms of their beloved."

"No, sir. I was thinking more of garlic."

"Garlic?" I was confused. I'd heard that garlic could ward off vampires, but girls? "Do I wear it about my neck,

Reeves?"

"No, sir. It's for one's breath. If one chews four large cloves of garlic before each ball, and exhales readily in the presence of young ladies, I posit they will yearn to be elsewhere."

Now *that* was a plan.

"If I may further suggest, sir–"

"You have another plan?" I was astounded. "It doesn't involve a crucifix, does it?"

"It does not, sir. It occurred to me that if a rumour concerning your suitability as a son-in-law should come to the ears of the families of these young ladies, your matrimonial prospects would suffer considerably."

I furrowed the Worcester brow. "What kind of a rumour, Reeves?"

"Financial, sir? Perhaps a risky foreign investment that threatens your financial prospects?"

This required some thought. I inclined my head to the right. I don't know why, but I find I always think clearer with a slight list of the noggin to starboard. Maybe it takes the pressure off the left hand grey cells. Maybe it chivvies along the ones on the right. Who knows? I was about to ask Reeves when I remembered the pressing task at hand. That's the problem of inclining your head in thought – it can send your little grey cells rolling away in all directions.

Seconds passed in deep list. I could see the merit of Reeves's plan. A rumour that Reginald Worcester was on his uppers would vastly diminish his marital prospects. But I had a tailor and several bookmakers who looked upon financial insecurity with considerable disapproval.

I shook my head. "Sorry, Reeves. The risks outweigh the benefits. If I'm halfway up the aisle, feel free to pass notes of my imminent bankruptcy along every pew on the bride's side of the church. But, until then, not a word."

"I agree it is a risky strategy, sir. How does one feel about insanity?"

"What?"

"As a subject for a rumour, sir. A suitor with a history of insanity in his family would be at a considerable disadvantage."

Now insanity I could live with. What noble family in England didn't have a great uncle who chewed the occasional carpet or kept newts in his bedroom? We Worcesters had more than our fair share. Of course, most families preferred not to talk about them. Which meant that the person who did would have a clear advantage! Or do I mean disadvantage?

"How would you propose these rumours be spread?"

"Well, sir, if word were to reach the servants of the families in question, I am sure the information would percolate upstairs. If you wish, I could commence this evening. All the families in question will have footmen or chauffeurs waiting to convey them from the ball."

~

I drove the Stanley Steamer to Denmark Street, following for a while one of the new Daimler steam cars – the ones with the super-condenser and heated seats – and cast an envious eye in its direction. Not that I gave voice to my thoughts. Since meeting Reeves, I've been wary of casting opinions on inanimate objects in case they took offence. If Reeves can have feelings, then why not the Stanley? And the last thing one wants on a journey is a sulking car. *You used to look at me like that. Aren't I good enough for you any more?* I wasn't sure if a steam car could sob, but one presumes that if it did, it would play havoc with the boiler pressure.

I left Reeves to park the car and spread rumours – Denmark Street being stuffed to the gills with assorted steamers, Hansoms and coaches-and-four – and found an unobserved spot by an entrance pillar where I swiftly despatched six cloves of garlic. They took some chewing, and considerable inner fortitude, but, compared to the alternative, it was worth the discomfort. Although next time I'd make sure I had a hip flask handy. My throat, already on fire, was beginning to close up.

Within a minute I was penning another mental missive. *Next time take a visiting card with you.* It was bad enough trying to force my name through a burning and constricted throat without the additional pressure of watching the hostess's butler wilt before my very eyes.

"Mr Reginald," he announced, pausing while he leaned back in search of fresher air. "Woo-oorcester."

Well, if nothing else, I had proof of the garlic's efficacy.

A few eyes turned my way as I descended the staircase into the ballroom. There had to be about three hundred guests in the room, all dressed to the nines. The Duchess of Rutland was waiting for me at the foot of the stairs, her gaze somewhat withering. I bowed my head towards her, but didn't stop to chat. When one has a mouthful of a secret weapon, it's best not to exhale inklings within nostril distance of the enemy's spies.

And, besides, if I didn't find a drink soon, I'd choke.

For a full ninety minutes I was the very model of an ardent suitor. I danced, I mingled, I pursued. And, in between the dancing, mingling and pursuing, I talked – at length – recounting the adventures of my good friend Horace Hildebrand Haversham of the Hampshire Havershams, breathily stressing the aitches with such gusto that even a well-exercised fan couldn't waft the foul air away. Two minutes of Horace Haversham and even the most polite young lady found a pressing reason to visit the far side of the room.

This garlic was a deb repellent of the first order!

That is, until it came up against Miss Emmeline Dreadnought. I'd assumed her a retiring wallflower kind of girl. Tall and willowy, she rarely danced and spent most of the evening hiding within large groups, keeping her eyes downcast and barely uttering a word. But one whiff of Horace Haversham and she changed.

"Your breath smells," she said as we waltzed around the dance floor.

"Does it?" I replied. "I hadn't noticed."

"It does. Do you eat a lot of garlic?"

"All the time. You can never have too much garlic is my motto. I have it with herring, halibut, haddock...." I ran out of aitches.

"Hake?" suggested Miss Dreadnought.

"Of course hake. That goes without saying." I was about to launch into a further list of aitches when I was struck by the positive lack of meats and vegetables beginning with aitch. Fish: they were legion. But other comestibles – not a sausage.

"Maybe with a haunch of venison?" said Miss Dreadnought. "Or with ham and a Hollandaise sauce?"

I was taken aback. This tall willowy wisp of a girl had broken the Worcester code! I examined her closer, expecting a smile or a smirk but finding neither. If anything, she had a wan, distant look, as though haunted by some great inner sadness.

Could garlic vapours do that to a girl?

"Admonish me if I intrude, Miss Dreadnought, but ... is

something the matter?"

She looked up, our eyes meeting for the first time.

"I think Amelia Runcible has been kidnapped."

TWO

"Kidnapped?"

"No one's seen her for a week. Her family fear she's eloped, but she wouldn't. Not without telling me. We're the closest of friends and there simply isn't anyone she'd run off with. The season's only just started and no one had caught her eye."

"Have the police been informed?"

"Her father won't hear of it. He's forbidden anyone in the family to talk about it. He thinks the family name will be blackened enough by an elopement without having the police brought in."

"What does her mother say?"

"Very little. She questioned me thoroughly when Amelia first disappeared, asking me if I knew of any young man Amelia was particularly friendly with. But since then, every time I try to talk to her about Amelia, she changes the subject."

"Well that's dashed odd. Do you think the family may have received a ransom demand? 'Pay up or you'll never see your daughter again. And don't tell the police or she dies.'"

Miss Dreadnought frowned. "I hadn't thought of that."

"That's because you don't eat enough garlic, Miss Dreadnought. It's like fish when it comes to adding vim to the little grey cells."

"Is that *all* fish or only the ones that begin with an aitch?" She smiled for the first time. "And please call me Emmeline, Mr Worcester."

~

As much as I enjoyed Emmeline's company – for here was a girl with a quick wit *and* an eye for spotting a kidnapping, a combination one rarely meets outside the pages of a thriller novel – I was not so smitten that I didn't recognise the danger. One minute you're exchanging theories about the best way to crack a debnapping case, the next you're engaged. How it happens is beyond me. Of the eight or so times I've been engaged, I only remember bending the Worcester knee once. The other times it just happened. I assume I stumbled over a troth and gave it an accidental plighting. But what a troth looks like and what exactly constitutes a good plighting, I haven't the foggiest. I suspect few men do.

As for breaking an engagement, that is something a Worcester could never do. It's a matter of honour. A word once given - even if one doesn't remember giving it (see troth and plighting) - can never be taken back. Only the female party of the arrangement, or maybe The Supreme Aunt, can do that.

Which is why, when the arrival of an excited former school friend of Miss Dreadnought, overburdened with news to impart, provided an opportunity, I inclined the noggin to both ladies and left.

I was feeling peckish so I headed for one of the side rooms. I'd seen a buffet in there earlier and a decanter or two of claret.

I was just finishing my second slice of cake when Percy Tuffington-Scrope hove alongside.

"What ho, Reggie," he said. "Didn't expect to see you here. I thought you hated the season."

"What ho, Tufty. You see before you a victim of the eleventh commandment. Honour thy father's and thy mother's sisters: for they are infallible and never miss a stoning."

"Say no more. Got to get married, have you?"

"The shotgun is loaded and pointing between my eyes."

A melancholy look descended upon Tufty's face.

"I did think I was going to get married."

"You did?"

"Yes." He sighed, his face drooping like that of a bloodhound who'd just been informed that dinner was running several hours late. "Then she goes and disappears."

"What? Her name wouldn't be Amelia Runcible, would it?"

"No. Lucretia Anstruther-Smothers. She would have been deb of the year, but no sooner had she come out, than she went back in again."

The hairs on the back of my neck bristled. Could there be two missing debs?

"Has anyone seen her, Tufty?"

"I haven't. Her family won't let me near her. I called upon them last month and they gave me the third degree, asking all manner of strange questions before throwing me out. Now I'm banned from their house and if they see me in the street, they snub me. Dashed if I know why."

"Does Miss Anstruther-Smothers accompany her family on these promenades?"

"No. I think they must have sent her back to their estate in Somerset. I tried to call upon her there, but the servants had orders not to admit me."

"When was the last time you saw Miss A-S?"

"Eighteen days, one hour and far too many minutes ago."

My sleuthing brain was positively whizzing. Two missing debs. Two tight-lipped families. And, if kidnapping was involved, why was this Lucretia still missing after eighteen days? Had the family refused to pay the ransom? Or was something more devilish afoot?

~

I left the ball at a fair lick. This was a problem that needed the attention of a giant steam-powered brain. I found Reeves in the company of a group of liveried footmen and gave him a hearty wave.

"What ho, Reeves. Have you got a sec?"

The footmen stepped back as one and gave me the strangest of looks. I think one of them may have crossed himself.

"Have you mislaid your newts again, sir?" said Reeves, looking at me in a very odd way. "I did think it unwise to bring them with you to the ball."

"What?" Had Reeves gone mad?

I watched, stunned, as Reeves turned and addressed the gathered footmen. "You see how confused he looks. I'd better go to him at once."

Fourteen eyeballs stared my way as Reeves hurried towards me. I stared back, astonished at their impertinence, until the penny dropped. Reeves had been spreading rumours.

Needless to say I was feeling a dashed sight peeved. I guided Reeves out of their earshot and spoke to him tersely. "Is your pressure low, Reeves?"

"No, sir. I topped up before we left."

"Well, you better have a good reason for your behaviour. I thought you were going to spread rumours about insanity in the *family,* not cast *me* as chief carpet-chewer!"

"That had been my intention, sir, but I fear I was forced to raise the stakes."

"Why?"

"The incidence of insanity within the great families is much higher than we anticipated."

"It is?"

He nodded gravely. "I was matched uncle for uncle, sir. Every story I recounted was met with its equal. I ... I fear it is something to do with my programming, sir, but I felt a compulsion to fulfil my allotted task."

"And so you threw down your trump card – Reginald, Jack of Newts?"

"Precisely, sir. It will not happen again. I will add a sub-routine to my programming."

"I should think so. Are your little grey cells otherwise un-impaired?"

"Yes, sir."

"Good. Because we're going to need every one of them."

I told Reeves all – the missing debs, the families closing ranks, their failure to involve the police.

"There is something rummy in the state of Denmark Street, Reeves."

"So it would appear, sir, though I suspect your estimate of two missing debutantes may be on the low side."

"You do?"

"From the discourse I have had this evening with the assembled footmen and chauffeurs, I suspect we may be able to add Miss Hortensia Effingham-Blinding and Miss Philomena Brackett to the list."

"Any hint of a ransom demand?"

"No, sir. The impression I received was that the families in question were shocked and baffled. They seem to have adopted the view that their daughters must have formed an unsuitable liaison and eloped. Though, in both cases, that opinion was not shared by the young lady's maid."

"Have none of them gone to the police?"

"It would appear not, sir."

This was most disturbing. And strangely exhilarating. Four girls were missing, and no one was looking for them! Probably more than four. There couldn't have been more than 400 people at the ball. How many other families were sitting at home, pining for a missing daughter, yet unable to seek outside help for fear of scandal?

It was then that I decided to become a consulting detective. I, Reginald Worcester, would take up the pipe and deerstalker – maybe not the violin, though I wasn't ruling it out – and Sherlock for England, Harry and the flower of British womanhood that had been so untimely ripp'd from the bosom of their families.

~

The next morning I rose with the lark – the kind of lark that has been up all night swotting over detective novels and likes to keep his beak under the covers until well into the afternoon.

"I'm looking forward to this detective business, Reeves," I said over my breakfast kipper. "I think I may have found my calling. Does God call people to become consulting detectives, do you think?"

"I see no reason why not, sir."

"Because one never hears about it. Vicars, they're always talking about being called. Missionaries too. But I've never heard a policeman mention a celestial tap on the shoulder, and Doctor Watson is surprisingly quiet on the subject."

"Perhaps Mr Holmes asked him to omit that particular passage, sir."

I ruminated upon the possibility as I chewed. And then my thoughts, as if nudged by a celestial force, switched to the matter of the missing debs. How were we to proceed?

"About these debs, Reeves, could there be any truth in this elopement theory?"

"One would have thought there would be more evidence of the young ladies having a pre-existing relationship with a young gentleman, sir."

"And those young gentlemen would have disappeared too, what? Has there been a spate of missing suitors, Reeves?"

"Not that I have heard, sir, though young gentlemen tend to go missing at all times of the year."

That was true. The call of the continent was only an aunt's withering look away.

"I think we shall go visiting today, Reeves. Thanks to Aunt Bertha I have an open invitation to every deb's home in London. With you sleuthing below stairs and me above, we'll soon get to the bottom of this mystery."

I flicked through Debrett's, jotting down the London addresses of the missing debs' families and making notes. I looked up Emmeline Dreadnought's entry too. It would help to have an ally, and the more I thought of it, the more I believed I might need one. Playing the prospective suitor may gain a fellow admittance into homes that still housed a debutante, but what about those where the young lady had gone missing? Would they close their doors to me? Give an order to the butler that the family were at home only to close friends?

I posed the question to Reeves and his giant brain concurred.

"If Miss Dreadnought is agreeable, sir, I would suggest the two of you first visit the home of Miss Runcible."

~

I left Reeves in the Stanley and trotted up the steps to the Dreadnought abode in Audley Street.

"Mister Worcester, sir," announced the butler, standing back from the drawing room door to make room for my entrance.

I sauntered in to find a veritable fleet of Dreadnoughts moored in the drawing room. The rear admiral, the mother, Emmeline, and – if Debrett's were correct – a possible sighting of a grandmother, two aunts, four cousins, and an uncle as well. All of them regarding me somewhat inquisitively.

"What ho, Dreadnoughts," I said, breezily.

Silence reigned for a nautical second or two before recognition dawned upon the mother, one Clotilde Dreadnought, a matriarch of generous proportions, who spoke.

"Ah, yes," she said. "You're Bertha's nephew, aren't you?"

"We met Mister Worcester at the ball yesterday evening, mama," said Emmeline.

"Did we?" said her mother. "You must forgive me, Mister Worcester. We meet so many people these days. Emmeline is *such* a popular girl."

She gave me a look. One that I had difficulty in deciphering. It may have been disapproving, or it may have been quite the opposite. Whichever way, it appeared to convey a warning. Either 'keep away from my daughter, she can do better' or 'hurry up and make an offer, suitors are circling.'

Emmeline looked embarrassed.

"Ever been in the Navy, Worcester?" asked the rear admiral, taking his turn to cast the inquisitorial eye my way.

"Is that the public house in Haymarket, sir?"

"What? What did he say, Emmeline?" said the rear admiral, cupping his hand to an ear that was part obscured by the starboard portion of a wayward pair of mutton chop whiskers.

"He said he's never been in the Navy, papa."

"Then why's he here?"

"I've come to kidnap your daughter, sir." The words had barely bid farewell to my tonsils when I realised my mistake. "No! Not kidnap. Borrow. I don't go around kidnapping daughters. Or sons. Or anyone for that matter. Would never even think of it. But, if I could just borrow your daughter for an hour or two... I'll give her back. I promise."

I decided to stop talking and smile as broadly and as affably as I could, clutching the rim of my hat to my chest as though my life depended on it.

A roomful of Dreadnoughts stared back. Some had their mouths open.

"What *is* he talking about?" asked a confused rear admiral.

"A stroll around Hyde Park," I said, rather louder than intended due to the excitement of actually finding something cogent to say. "The sun's out, birds are positively tweeting their little hearts out, and I was wondering if Miss Dreadnought would like a jolly old promenade around the park."

"The park *is* very pleasant this time of year, mama," said Emmeline, sitting up and looking at her mother. "I'm sure Mister Worcester would have me back in good time to dress for the Arbuthnots' dinner party tonight."

"Of course," I said. "Punctuality is synonymous with the name Worcester."

"Are you sure, Emmeline?" asked her mother, looking first at her daughter and then, rather pointedly, at me. "Mister Floss-Trussock may call at any minute."

"Then Mister Floss-Trussock will have to call another day, mama. For *I* shall be in the park."

~

"I'm surprised to see you, Mr Worcester," said Emmeline as we trotted down the steps outside her house. "The speed with which you withdrew last night, I thought I'd frightened you off."

"Not I, Miss Dreadnought."

I glanced back to make sure the drawing room curtains weren't twitching.

"There's something I have to tell you," I said, leaning closer in.

"Don't tell me. You've given up garlic and we no longer have to walk around a park beginning with aitch."

"No, though you're spot on about the park. Tell me, have you read any Sherlock Holmes?"

"I adore Sherlock Holmes! I've read every story."

"Then you'll know what I mean when I say 'the game is afoot.' Amelia Runcible is not the only deb to have gone missing this season. We suspect there are at least four."

"We?"

"Reeves and I. He's my Watson, except he's not a doctor, and he does have a giant brain. Think of him as a cross between Mycroft and Watson. He has Mycroft's brain and Watson's legs. Not literally of course. That would make him a Promethean. Which he isn't. He's an automaton. Give him a bunker of coal and a freshly-steamed turbot, and there's no problem he can't solve. He's over there in the Steamer."

I pointed at the Stanley parked on the other side of the road.

"He doesn't look like an automaton," said Emmeline, peering on tiptoe.

"He's a superior model. One look at Reeves and they broke the mould. One can examine him with a magnifying glass and still not tell he's a machine. As long as one doesn't look at his navel. It has a screw thread, don't you know? So he can be connected to a steam outlet and brought up to pressure."

"Is that how it's done? I'd never thought to ask."

"Neither had I. Until I met Reeves, I didn't even know what an automaton was. Now, Miss Dreadnought, will you help a sleuth in a hole? We need to gain access to Miss Runcible's house, and I thought if you accompanied us...."

"I'll help on one condition."

"What's that?"

"You stop calling me Miss Dreadnought. My name is Emmeline."

THREE

We drove to the Runcible house, Emmeline insisting that she sit on the small single seat at the very front of the car and screaming with excitement every time we turned a corner or bounced off a pothole in the road. I suspect it was her first outing in a horseless carriage.

"May I enquire as to your plans for the forthcoming interrogation of the Runcible family, sir?" said Reeves, one hand grasping the seat arm, the other holding onto his bowler.

"You may, Reeves. And feel free to chip in. My plan is more embryonic than fully-fledged. I'm not sure whether to employ stealth, or to come straight out with it and declare myself a consulting detective offering his services for free. What do you think, Reeves?"

"I think it safer to err on the side of caution while you gauge the family's likely reaction to an offer of assistance from an outsider."

"You think they may clam up?"

"They may well be sensitive to the dissemination of family business to a stranger, sir. I would recommend that Miss Dreadnought lead the conversation and steer it gently towards the following subjects: One, have the family received any unusual visitors or communications in the days leading up, and subsequent, to Miss Runcible's disappearance."

"Are you listening to this, Emmeline?"

"I'm hanging on his every word."

I decided to stop the car and take out a pen and paper. A detective cannot afford to dry up in mid-interrogation. *Awfully sorry about this. It really is on the tip of my tongue, you know. Something about a thingamajig. Or was it a whatsit?*

One suspects that even Sherlock Holmes kept a notepad with him at all times.

"Hang on a minute, Reeves, while I write that down."

"Two," continued Reeves once I'd caught up. "What was the young lady's disposition in the days immediately preceding her disappearance. Was she unusually excited or withdrawn?"

"I think I can answer that," said Emmeline. "She'd only come out three weeks previously. Everything was new and exciting. Balls, dinner parties, young men. She was as excited on the night she disappeared as she was on the nights preceding it."

"Which brings me to the third question, miss. When and where was the last time she was seen. And who saw her?"

"Is that three *and* four, Reeves, or is three a two-parter?" I asked.

"I would lean toward the latter, sir, as by determining one, the second is revealed."

I crossed out '4' and replaced it with '3b.'

"Four, what is the demeanour of the family? Are they as distressed today as they were on the day they learned of her disappearance? And is every member of the family equally upset?"

"You suspect the family, Reeves?"

"I believe it is the detective's mantra to suspect everyone, sir. But, in this case, it is less suspicion and more a question of 'Has someone received news of Miss Runcible since her disappearance.' A note, perhaps, from the young lady to her mother or a family confidante to say that she is well and not to worry."

This was brainpower of the first order. What could be more natural than the girl writing to her sister and spilling all with a quick note not to tell the parents?

"I don't think she has any family confidantes," said Emmeline. "She has no sister, and her brother's an ass. She may have written to her mother, though."

"Any more pearls of wisdom, Reeves?"

"No, sir. I have a number of other questions, but they are best answered by the servants."

"He really does have a giant brain, doesn't he?" said Emmeline.

"You should see him after a lightly braised halibut. His grey cells turn positively white-hot with all the extra vim and vigour."

"I thought automatons couldn't eat?" said Emmeline.

"That is correct, miss. Mr Worcester, however, is of the opinion that a brain cannot function without fish. I have tried, but I cannot disabuse him of that notion."

"Ah, but I've seen the evidence with my own eyes, Reeves. You're a dashed sight brainier on the days you're in the kitchen preparing fish. Don't tell me you don't sneak a morsel or two of halibut while you're dishing out my meals."

"You see what I mean, miss?"

~

I didn't think the butler was going to allow us past the Runcible threshold such was the firmness of his eye and the resolution of his speech. But Emmeline Dreadnought proved to be a very persuasive young prune, and her threat to chain herself to the front railings proved decisive.

"I shall see if Mrs Runcible is at home," said the butler, looking much put out.

"She is," said Emmeline. "I can see the back of her head through the drawing room window."

The butler grimaced. It was only a fleeting grimace, but it was there, and I felt for the poor blighter. No one likes having their authority challenged and, being a man recently accused of attending a ball with a pocketful of newts, I empathised.

Steeling himself, the aged butler spun slowly on his heel and proceeded inside at a funereal walk. I took hold of Emmeline's arm in case she decided to follow and chivvy him along.

Presently, the butler returned and, without glancing once at Emmeline, conducted us to the drawing room where Mrs Florence Runcible and her son, Aloysius – who I vaguely recognised from a scone fight at the Sloths – were sitting.

Mrs Runcible put down her embroidery and rose from her chair. "Emmeline. What's the meaning of this? Chivers said you threatened to chain yourself to our railings." She paused, noticing me for the first time. "Who is *he*?"

I stepped back, discerning something of the Aunt Bertha in Mrs Runcible – her look, her bearing, the steely glint of her eye. They might have been chiselled from the same iceberg.

Emmeline stood her ground. "I'm sorry, Mrs Runcible, but this *has* to stop."

"What has to stop?"

"*This.* It's not right. Have you heard from Amelia?"

So much for erring on the side of caution and gentle persuasion. It was like two giant icebergs meeting at dawn, stalagmites drawn. I thought Mrs Runcible was going to explode. Young Runcible was on his feet too. I stayed by the door, smiling affably.

"I must ask you to leave," said Mrs R. "You are *not* yourself, Emmeline."

"No!" said Emmeline, stamping her foot. "Amelia is *not* the only missing girl. There are at least three others! And *no one* is looking for them because each family is closing ranks and refusing help. It *has* to stop!" She stamped her foot again. "Mr Worcester here is a consulting detective and he's promised to help."

All eyes swung my way.

"What ho," I said, just above a whisper, and adding only the tiniest of waves – a slight finger waggle of the right hand.

Mrs Runcible turned upon Emmeline. She was incandescent, which is not good for an iceberg. "You brought the *police* to our house?"

"He's *not* the police! He's a consulting detective like Sherlock Holmes."

"You're babbling, girl. Who, pray, is Sherlock Holmes?"

"He's a fictional detective, mater," said young Runcible. "His stories appear in the Strand magazine."

"Exactly," said Emmeline. "And Mr Worcester is just like him."

"Mr Worcester is a fictional detective?" asked Mrs Runcible, her face radiating confusion and distaste in equal measure.

"He's Bertha Worcester's nephew," said Emmeline.

Recognition appeared to dawn over the ice floe.

She raised a lorgnette to her eyes and gave me the once-over. "Which one? He's not the strange one, is he?"

"No," I said, wondering if Reeves's newt tale had reached the Runcible household. "That would be my cousin Clarence. A confirmed carpet-chewer. Fear not, Mrs R, your carpets are entirely safe with me."

Mrs Runcible turned to Emmeline. "Why is he talking about carpets?"

"Detectives like Sherlock Holmes and Mr Worcester don't think as we do," said Emmeline. "Their brains are differently wired. It's how they can solve mysteries that leave the rest of us dumbfounded."

I hadn't thought of it like that, but Emmeline was right. It did take a certain type of brain to make sense out of a knotty case where reason appeared to have taken a holiday. The police were perfectly capable of collecting evidence, but it needed a Sherlock Holmes to make sense of it. Even Reeves, with his giant brain, couldn't think the unthinkable. Whereas I did it all the time.

"Oh," said Mrs Runcible, giving me another appraisal through the lorgnette.

"I can assure you, Mrs R," I said. "Not a word of your situation will reach ears outside of this house. Tact and good manners are my middle names."

"Hmm," said Mrs Runcible, evidently undecided. "I shall have to ask Mr Runcible."

"The pater won't be back from Dover until tomorrow," said Aloysius. "I really think you should take Mr Worcester up on his offer. If Amy had eloped we'd have heard something by now."

"He's right," said Emmeline. "Every day we wait is a day wasted."

"And if Amy hasn't eloped," said Aloysius. "She may have been taken by white slavers!"

"Or a eunuch," I added. "Anyone spot any eunuchs in the vicinity. Big chaps, foreign looking, usually bald?"

"Eunuchs?" said Mrs Runcible.

"Out collecting for his master's harem," I said. "An Arab Sheikh or a Turkish Sultan. Anyone spot any sheikhs recently?"

"You can't think my Amelia has been taken off to a harem!"

"It's the first rule of detection, Mrs R. Rule nothing out. Mr Holmes swears by it. First you have to eliminate the impossible, then, whatever's left, however rummy, has to be the truth."

Mrs Runcible had to sit down. I took out my notebook and glanced down at the first page.

"Now," I said. "Did anyone see anything or anyone unusual in the days leading up to Amelia's disappearance? Any orang-utans spotted in the vicinity? Large dogs? Seafaring midgets with one less leg than might otherwise have been expected?"

Following the wise example of Doctor Watson, I have decided not to recount the details of the subsequent five minutes. They don't advance the story and no party comes out of it well. Suffice to say, things were said – some in haste, and some involving newts.

I skipped question two, Emmeline having already provided an answer on the drive over, and moved swiftly to question three. "When and where was the last time anyone saw Amelia?"

"I last saw her around midnight at Lady Fraser's ball," said Emmeline.

"I didn't go to the ball," said Aloysius. "I saw her earlier that evening then I went to the Sloths. I don't know what time I came back but the house was empty."

All eyes turned to Mrs Runcible, whose arms were folded and mouth firmly set.

"Please, Mrs Runcible," implored Emmeline.

Mrs Runcible sighed. "I saw Amelia at the ball *after* midnight. She came to tell me that she was going on to the Harcourts' for supper. *She said* that Lady Harcourt had invited her especially."

"Did you talk to Lady Harcourt?" I asked.

"Of course I talked to Lady Harcourt! I went to see her the next day as soon as I discovered that Amelia had not returned home. Lady Harcourt was *most* surprised. She told me that no such invitation had been made, and that she'd never spoken to Amelia that evening."

My heart began to race. "What was Lady Harcourt's demeanour when you asked her about Amelia? Did she look shifty? A bit pale around the gills?"

"Emmeline, dear, what *is* he talking about now?"

"I think he wants to know if Lady Harcourt was at all nervous when you saw her."

"Why should she be nervous? She's Lady Harcourt. You can't think that she has anything to do with Amelia's disappearance."

"A great detective suspects everybody, Mrs R. Besides, if Lady Harcourt is telling the truth, then it means your daughter wasn't. Is Amelia in the habit of lying to you?"

"No, Mr Worcester, she is not."

~

I exited the Runcible household feeling pretty pleased with myself. I was a natural at this detecting game.

Reeves was waiting by the Stanley. "Might one enquire as to how the interview went, sir?" he asked.

I was about to tell all when Emmeline interrupted in an excited gush.

"He asked Mrs Runcible if she'd seen any orang-utans or

seafaring midgets with one less leg than might otherwise have been expected."

"Indeed, miss?" said Reeves, pointing a disappointed eyebrow in my direction.

I felt moved to defend myself.

"I have it here, Reeves, from your very lips," I opened my notebook and proceeded to read a short extract. "*Point one: Have the family received any unusual visitors or communications in the days leading up, and subsequent, to Miss Runcible's disappearance.* That's precisely what I was doing – enquiring about unusual visitors!"

"I was not alluding to apes, sir."

"My dear Reeves, if you had read as many detective thrillers as I, you would know that these are exactly the kind of questions a consulting detective has to ask. It's always the seemingly inconsequential events that turn out to be important. Something that a witness doesn't think to mention or slips their mind."

"Such as an orang-utan at the door, sir?"

"Precisely! The police wouldn't ask 'Seen any large monkeys recently' and no witness would dream of mentioning it, as how could an orang-utan be germane to the crime?"

"My thoughts exactly, sir."

"But they invariably are! If you read Doctor Watson or Mr Poe you'll see that a large proportion of crimes are committed by animals – be they venomous snakes, large dogs, apes or what have you. Think how quickly they'd have solved *The Murders in the Rue Morgue* if someone had had the forethought to ask about ape sightings from the get go."

"His brain really is differently wired," said Emmeline, looking not a little awe-struck. "Don't you think so, Reeves?"

"Indeed, miss. I don't think I have ever encountered one quite like it."

Honour satisfied, I gave Reeves a précis of what we'd discovered, giving special prominence to the Lady Harcourt revelation.

"How about you, Reeves? Was your sojourn below stairs as fruitful?"

"I had a long talk with the young lady's maid, sir. She is convinced that something ill has befallen her mistress."

"She didn't see a eunuch, did she, Reeves? A large, bald chappie loitering about outside, watching all the comings and goings."

"No, sir. It was the fact that none of the young lady's clothes or possessions were missing. There was a brooch that Miss Amelia was particularly fond of. The maid swears that her young lady would not have left that behind had she left willingly."

"She's right," said Emmeline. "I know that brooch. It was her grandmother's."

Reeves went on to report that no unusual visitors had been admitted to the house, no strangers – domestic or foreign – were seen lurking in the vicinity, and that no unusual letters had been delivered.

"Did you ask about orang-utans?" I enquired.

"I am afraid I did not, sir."

"No matter. You can always ask later. Now, does anyone know where Lady Harcourt lives?"

"Might I be so bold as to suggest we visit another missing young lady's family first, sir?"

"Why?"

"To seek confirmation, sir. At present we have two possibilities. One, Lady Harcourt lied about inviting Miss Runcible, and, two, Miss Runcible lied to her mother. It has been my experience that even young ladies of a truthful disposition are not averse to the occasional falsehood if it helps facilitate an assignation with a young gentleman that may otherwise be forbidden."

"He's right," said Emmeline. "If Amelia had been invited somewhere she didn't think her mother would approve, Lady Harcourt's just the name she would have dropped."

I was torn. Reeves's logic was, as usual, unassailable. But we consulting detectives are men of action. We like to beard our adversaries the moment we discover the location of their den. Although ... the more I thought of it, the more I began to think that maybe bearding Lady Harcourt in her drawing room could turn unpleasant – she might be innocent – and we Worcesters can't abide unpleasantness. Reeves was right. More proof was required.

"Perhaps if Miss Emmeline was to look at the names of the other missing girls, sir, she may find a family with whom she is acquainted."

I handed my notebook to Emmeline.

"Philomena!" she cried out after barely a second's perusal. "I went to school with her! We'll have to go there first. I know Mrs Brackett. Oh, *poor* Philomena. I thought it a while since I saw her last."

~

Our visit to the Brackett household provided just the kind of proof I was looking for. Miss Brackett was last seen by her mother at the Countess of Bute's ball. *And* she'd told her mother not to wait for her as she'd had a personal invitation to supper from Lady Harcourt.

Time, I thought, for a bearding.

"Two out of two is pretty conclusive in my form book," I told Reeves as we conferred on the pavement outside the Brackett house. "Do consulting detectives have the power of arrest, Reeves?"

"I would advise caution in this instance, sir. Lady Harcourt is not a personage without influence. Princes and Prime Ministers dine at her table."

"But are any of them missing, Reeves? That's what I'd like to know. Have we mislaid a Prime Minister recently?"

"No, sir. According to this morning's *Times*, Mr Balfour is still very much with us."

"Do you really think Lady Harcourt is behind this?" asked Emmeline. "I can't think why she'd do it. She's the premier hostess in London. She has oodles of money. Why risk all that for ... whatever she's doing with the girls."

She had a point.

"Could someone be impersonating Lady Harcourt?" I said. "A eunuch maybe, dressed up in all the finery and inviting impressionable young girls to supper?"

"I should think it unlikely, sir."

To a consulting detective, the word 'unlikely' was synonymous with the phrase 'precisely the kind of ploy the astute criminal mind would come up with.' One does not become a criminal mastermind by doing the obvious. One uses guile and the unexpected. And eunuchs would have access to a haremful of the finest female fashions.

Reeves would not be moved. "A more likely possibility, sir, is that the abductor is a gentleman of persuasive talents. Someone who convinces the young ladies that he has talked to Lady Harcourt about them and received, on their behalf, a personal invitation to a supper that her ladyship is hosting after the ball."

I am not sure if trilemma is a word, but if it is, I was speared upon its horns. Three theories and three sexes – a man, a Lady and a eunuch. Even Sherlock Holmes would have recognised this as a three pipe problem.

There was no point asking Reeves for an opinion as he'd

already pronounced judgement. And if the 'persuasive gentleman' was the logical suspect then it would undoubtedly be the incorrect one. Crime cannot abide Order.

Which left me between a eunuch and a Harcourt. The eunuch had the motive, but how was I to find him? Debrett's didn't have a eunuch directory, did they?

"Is there a Guild of Eunuchs, Reeves? A handy tome where one could look them all up?"

"Not that I have heard, sir."

Which, by a process of elimination, left Lady Harcourt.

"Anyone know Lady Harcourt's address?" I asked.

"I do," said Emmeline. "It's in Clarges Square."

"Then let's get going."

Reeves coughed.

"Are you all right, Reeves? Your pressure's not running low is it?"

"No, sir. I was wondering if you could be persuaded to delay your visit to Lady Harcourt until later this evening."

"Why?"

"I fear a direct approach to her ladyship at this juncture would not be productive, sir."

"Why ever not?"

"If her ladyship is guilty, sir, she will deny any knowledge of the affair. If she is innocent, she will do the same. And, if she is indeed guilty, your visit and your questions will make her aware of your interest. She would become more circumspect."

As ever, Reeves had a point. Turning up unbidden at Lady Harcourt's door asking questions about missing debs would tip our hand.

"So why counsel delay until later this evening?" I asked. "Is twilight a more auspicious time to conduct an interview?"

"It is my belief, sir, that Lady Harcourt hosts dinner parties most evenings during the season–"

"She does," said Emmeline, interrupting. "But they're very exclusive. It's not just society, she invites all sorts – industrialists, scientists, actors, poets. It's very hard to get an invitation. None of this year's debs have managed it."

I gazed with admiration upon that giant steam-powered brain.

"You're thinking of Aunt Bertha, aren't you, Reeves?"

"Indeed, sir. Do you think your open invitation to every dinner party in London extends to Lady Harcourt's?"

"I don't see why not."

Emmeline's eyes widened. "You have an open invitation to *every* dinner party in London?"

"So my Aunt Bertha assures me. She thought it would improve my matrimonial prospects."

"I must go home and change at once!" said Emmeline. "Will it be formal? Or is it modern? I don't want to wear the wrong dress!"

Emmeline clapped her hands and bounced on the spot.

"I thought you were dining with the Arbuthnots this evening," I asked.

"Hang the Arbuthnots. I'm going to Lady Harcourt's!"

I looked at Reeves, hoping he was about to spring to my aid. He appeared to find something interesting over the road to look at.

"I don't know if I can swing a second invitation at this short notice," I told Emmeline, watching the excitement drain from her face. "If these Harcourt bashes are as exclusive as you say, I might not be able to go myself."

Emmeline glared at me. "You can't ditch me in the middle of an investigation! Besides, I'm your cover."

"I don't need any cover."

"Yes you do! Reeves said it himself. People will wonder why you're there and Lady Harcourt will be on her guard all evening - especially if you start asking her about Amelia and Philomena. But if I'm with you, you can tell everyone you're there as my smitten escort. And *I* can ask the questions. Amelia and Philomena are my friends, after all. Why shouldn't I mention them in conversation?"

"That's all very well but this dinner party won't finish until late. Won't you need a chaperone?"

"I don't need a chaperone."

"Your father may think otherwise. What if he keelhauls me?"

"Sherlock Holmes wouldn't worry about being keel-hauled."

"I rather suspect he might. Watson doesn't publish everything that happens, you know?"

"If you don't take me with you, I'll ... I'll chain myself to your car."

"You don't have any chains."

"I'll ask Reeves to fetch some."

"He will not."

"Yes, he will. Reeves, fetch me a chain. Medium gauge will do."

"I would not advise it, miss."

"Then I shall make my own chain. I'll rip my petticoats and knot them together!"

"No!"

There comes a time, as the Runcibles' butler had discovered earlier, when the wise tree bends before the irresistible force. And I had a feeling that a girl tied to one's car by her petticoats was probably viewed as a legal contract of marriage by some of the more excitable cultures.

"Enough," I said, holding up a hand in surrender. "I'll have a word with my aunt. If she can swing it – *if*, mark you – then you *shall* go to the ball, Cinderella Dreadnought. But you'll have to square it with your family."

FOUR

I thought it best to leave Emmeline outside in the Stanley with Reeves while I talked with Aunt Bertha.

"It's for your own safety," I told Emmeline. "The Aunt B. is descended from a long line of Mastodons. One wrong word and she can stampede all over you."

I found the venerable aunt in the drawing room looking at maps of Europe – probably planning which country to subjugate this coming August.

"What ho, Aunt B. Lovely day and all that. Birds singing in the trees. Squirrels squirreling and so forth."

"What *are* you wittering about, Reginald? Are you engaged yet?"

"Not yet, esteemed aunt, though, on that subject, I was wondering if your standing invite to dinner parties extended to Lady Harcourt's."

Aunt Bertha closed her Atlas and gave me one of her appraising stares.

"Why would *you* want to go to one of Lady Harcourt's dinner parties?"

I felt somewhat nettled by her tone.

"Why shouldn't I go?"

"I would have thought they were too intellectual for you. They keep their food *on* their plates. They don't throw it at each other."

Aunts, like Mastodons of ancient yore, have memories that go all the way back to the prehistoric plains. One throws a single bread roll at a dinner party and, years later, it is regurgitated – the memory that is, not the roll.

"I'll have you know that Stiffy cast the first roll. I was merely retaliating. Besides, the Duchess should have ducked."

"Duchesses should not *have* to duck."

"And neither will they. I am a changed Reginald these days, Aunt B. And if I am to get married, I need to be at the

Harcourt bash this evening."

Aunt Bertha's demeanour changed in an instant.

"You're going there to meet someone?" she asked, her surprise self-evident.

"Actually, I'd like to take someone with me. You know what these debs are like. They get it into their heads that a dinner party with Lady Harcourt is what they want and then that's it. Nothing else will do. Emmeline has exacting standards."

"Emmeline? Emmeline who?"

"Emmeline Dreadnought."

Aunt Bertha inclined her head to one side and ruminated, looking not unlike a Mastodon chewing on a particularly toothsome prehistoric branch. "Naval family?" she asked.

"That's the one."

"I'll expect to meet her."

"That was Emmeline's other wish. 'When can I meet your aunts,' she said."

Aunt Bertha flung another appraising look my way, making me feel that perhaps I was over-egging the 'Emmeline as aunt's delight' ploy.

"Hmm," she said. "I will send a telegram to Lady Harcourt at once. You *do* promise not to throw any food?"

"You have the word of a Worcester."

~

With dinner for two confirmed, next stop was to take Emmeline home so she could change.

"You *will* be coming for me at eight thirty this evening, won't you?" asked Emmeline as I escorted her to her door.

"You have my word."

"Because you know where I'll be at eight thirty tomorrow morning if you don't?"

"Chained to the railings outside my flat?"

Emmeline smiled. "You know me so well."

The Stanley's pressure was getting low so we stopped at Jessop's garage on the way back to the flat to take on water and have the paraffin reservoir topped up.

"Do you need topping up, Reeves?" I asked as we watched Jessop's boy attend to the Stanley.

"I am running a little low, sir, but I have sufficient pressure to last the journey back to Charles Street."

As the boy disconnected the water hose and went off in search of a paraffin can, I began to contemplate the evening ahead. Emmeline was right about Lady Harcourt lacking an obvious motive. Eunuchs had harems to fill. But what would Lady Harcourt want with a gaggle of debutantes?

"Do you think we may have been hasty dismissing the elopement theory, Reeves?"

"I think not, sir. One or two young ladies may elope during the season, but they generally make contact with their family within a week. To lose four - possibly more than four - in less than a month is abnormally high. Even the summer of 1870 never saw such attrition."

"Refresh my mind, Reeves. 1870?"

"The Franco-Prussian War, sir. It clashed with the Paris season, forcing a large section of French society to relocate to London, bringing their sons with them."

This was something I'd heard about. With Paris under siege and nothing but five courses of rat for dinner, who could blame them?

I was struck by a sudden and grisly thought.

"Were all those girls in 1870 accounted for, Reeves? None of them could have been eaten, could they? Only ... all those stories about starvation and rat dinners. What if some of those *garcons* were feeling a bit peckish?"

"No, sir. All the young ladies were accounted for."

Well, it was an idea.

I don't know about you, but I find that ideas are not unlike cucumbers - you have one at lunchtime and it stays with you for the rest of the day. So it was with this culinary idea.

"What do orang-utans eat, Reeves?" I asked when we were back at the flat.

"Fruit, I believe, sir."

"Not debutantes?"

"No, sir."

I pondered further. Lady Harcourt was well known in society as a woman of wide and eclectic tastes. If there was a new fad in town, Lady Harcourt would want to know about it. If there was a new actor or poet, she'd have to invite them to one of her parties. She was just the kind of person who would have an orang-utan for a pet.

"These orang-utan chappies, Reeves? Are they at all like magpies?"

"In what respect, sir?"

"Do they share a penchant for stealing the glittery stuff? Imagine the scene, Reeves. Lady Harcourt has a pet ape. Said pet, having a fascination with all that glitters, takes one look at the debs in their tiaras and necklaces, and feels compelled to swoop. He's only trying to grab the jewellery, but the deb screams. This frightens the creature, who then runs amok and kills the deb. Lady Harcourt then swears all her guests to secrecy."

"One would think, sir, that after the first death, her ladyship would have taken measures to ensure that ape and guests never came into close proximity again."

Even at low pressure, Reeves's brain could still spot a fatal flaw from twenty paces.

"Are you coming sleuthing with us tonight, Reeves?"

"No, sir. I was planning to visit the Jolly Footman public house this evening. It is the preferred meeting place of all the local servants. I am hoping I may find a footman who remembers seeing one of the missing young ladies on the night they disappeared. Whoever abducted them may have departed in a carriage."

I took out my notebook and hurriedly began to write.

Does Mrs Harcourt have a carriage? Question footmen about who they brought home from each ball.

"The Harcourt footmen won't have the evening of a dinner party off, will they, Reeves?"

"Unlikely, sir. They would be expected to wait at table. My plan, with your permission, was to call upon them tomorrow, depending on how your investigation proceeds this evening. I consider the Jolly Footman the richer vein of information tonight as I can enquire there about other missing girls. I suspect the number to be considerably higher than four."

~

I'd had Reeves prepare me a kipper before I left so my brain was positively whizzing as I drove to pick up Emmeline. I wondered if Sherlock dined on fish the night before an important meeting. One would think so but – if memory serves and, with all that fish coursing through my veins, one would think it might – he seemed to prefer his pipe. Just think of the cases he could have solved if he'd had the benefit of a piscine pick-me-up!

Emmeline was not so chipper. I found her sitting in the Dreadnought drawing room, arms folded and lips in full pout.

"We are to have company," she said. "Mama insists I have a chaperone."

"What? I don't think I can swing a third invite."

"You won't need to," said Emmeline. "It's mama's maid.

She'll sit with the servants."

The maternal Dreadnought's maid proved to be a stern creature of hawk-like appearance. She didn't like me, and she didn't like the Stanley.

"Don't you have a carriage?" she said as she stood on the pavement looking down her beak at my faithful Steamer.

"This *is* my carriage," I replied.

"*This* is not a carriage. *This* is an abomination."

"Agnes!" said Emmeline. "I think you forget yourself."

The maid narrowed her eyes and pointed the pair of them at Emmeline. "I forget nothing. Your mother has instructed me to watch over you as I did when you were a child. And watch over you I shall."

I half expected Emmeline to threaten to chain the elderly maid to the Dreadnought railings, but she was surprisingly subdued, lowering her eyes and walking away.

"I shall take the front seat," Emmeline said, unlatching the foot plate and seat cover and swinging them into place.

"You can't sit there!" said Agnes. "What if you fall off? It's far too dangerous. Your mother would have a heart attack."

"Then you'll have to sit here," said Emmeline.

"I will not!"

"Then where will we sit? There are only three places!"

"We'll sit at the back. Mr Worcester can sit in front."

I let Emmeline point out the flaw in Agnes's logic. I find it good policy not to interfere in heated discussions between two members of the opposite sex.

"Mr Worcester has to *drive* the car, Agnes. He can't do that from the front seat."

"Then we will all have to share the back seat," said Agnes.

I don't know if you've ever ridden in a 1903 Stanley Steamer, but it's usually described as a two-seater. The foldaway seat at the front is something of an extra. And there is not room for three people on the bench seat. Even if one of them resembles a hawk.

Emmeline looked at me imploringly, semaphoring the words 'Do something!' with her eyebrows.

I looked at Agnes. She stared back, defiant, her right toe tapping on the pavement. It may have been Morse Code, and, if it was, it was tapping out the phrase 'Just you try!'

I wondered how long it would take to walk to Clarges Square. Too long, I feared. And Emmeline's dress would pick up a peck and a half of dirt from the streets.

"Ladies," I said, gesturing with an outstretched hand towards the rear seat of the Stanley. "If you'd like to take your seats."

As she climbed on board, Emmeline gave me another look – something to do with men and mice.

I climbed on last, squeezing into what was left.

"*Do* be careful, Mr Worcester," grunted Agnes. Emmeline said not a word. She stared straight ahead, felling passers-by with the daggers that shot from each eyeball.

I drove all the way to Clarges Square like a hunchback, my shoulders bent forward, my feet often finding another foot on the very peddle I was trying to press, and my left arm being repeatedly grabbed by Agnes whenever I attempted to turn the steering tiller. It was a wonder we didn't have an accident.

With conversation impossible, my mind began to wander, wondering if Lady Harcourt could be persuaded to kidnap Agnes. From there it wandered into deeper, darker places. The combination of kipper and compressed fetlock twisted the little grey cells into thinking the unthinkable. What if there were a pie shop next door to the Harcourts?

It was a black thought, but ... it would explain the missing debs. And provide a motive for Lady Harcourt, the demon hostess of Clarges Square!

I parked the Stanley with difficulty. It's not easy to pull back the parking brake when one is bent forward and the lever is hiding somewhere behind your flailing right hand.

I sprang from the car at the first opportunity and gave my spine a goodish stretch.

"Aren't you going to help me down?" demanded Agnes.

I looked up at her and, for a brief moment, felt a strong desire to say something stern – if not witty and scathing. But, possibly due to good breeding, or maybe some form of brain atrophy brought about by Agnes's hawk-like stare, I couldn't come up with anything better than 'Big nose.' Which is not something a Worcester would say, however crippled he was.

I held out my hand and helped her down. Emmeline joined us on the pavement and we walked the remaining sixty yards to number fifteen, an imposing pile with a Palladian portico.

"If you'd arrived earlier, Mr Worcester, we could have parked closer and wouldn't have had to walk so far," observed Agnes. "Look at all these splendid carriages. Their masters didn't cut it fine."

I was a good four feet away from Emmeline but I could feel the steam of suppressed rage hissing from her ears. I wondered if Agnes realised she was barely a second away from spending the night alfresco in Clarges Square, wrapped in a chainlink blanket.

"I think the servants' entrance is down there," said Emmeline, nodding at a flight of steps descending into the bowels of number fifteen.

Agnes peered into the abyss, and the abyss, not surprisingly, refused to peer back. "Hmm," she said. "I thought it would be grander." And, with those words, she began to descend.

"That woman!" said Emmeline as soon as we'd moved under the portico and out of earshot. "I don't know why mama puts up with her. She's insufferable. She used to give me nightmares when I was a child. I'd dream she was a crow perched on the end of my bed waiting to peck my eyes out."

I could imagine.

The Harcourt front door was open so we strolled through into a rather grand entrance hall – sweeping staircase, marble floor and a scattering of Italian sculptures. A butler and two footmen were taking people's coats. We waited our turn.

"May I take your coat, sir?" the butler asked presently.

I handed him my topcoat but instead of folding it over his arm and beetling off, he remained where he was, looking not a little uncomfortable.

"Your newts, sir?"

"Pardon?"

"I think your newts would be happier in the kitchen, sir. They will be attended to most thoughtfully."

I'm not sure if automata have spines, but, if they do, I hoped Reeves felt a sudden shiver down his, for I sent an astral presentment of displeasure winging all the way to the snug bar of the Jolly Footman. Was I never to be free of this newt calumny?

"That's frightfully good to hear," I said, thrusting both hands into my trouser pockets and pulling the linings out between finger and thumb. "But look! Not a single newt. I am a man *sans* newt this evening."

The butler looked relieved. "Very good, sir," he said and moved off to attend another arrival.

Emmeline drew alongside. "Why do people think you have newts in your pockets?"

I shrugged. “Dashed if I know.” Then swiftly changed the subject. “Remember, Emmeline, tact and cunning are tonight’s watch words. No threats to chain yourself to the dining table.”

“Understood. Do you think the Prince of Wales will be here? I’ve heard he brings Mrs Keppel with him.”

“*Tact*, Emmeline. We’re not here to draw attention to ourselves or point at royalty. We’re here to observe and, when the wine begins to flow, to ask the pertinent question.”

“I will be the soul of discretion. I just hope my dress is all right.”

I turned a sleuth’s eye to my surroundings, looking for anything untoward as a footman conducted us to a drawing room on the far side of the staircase. But I saw no padlocked doors, and the marble floor was devoid of poorly cleaned bloodstains or half-eaten bananas.

The drawing room was already heaving with guests and over the next twenty minutes Lady Harcourt, dressed rather exotically in what looked like a dazzling blue and silver silk Kimono, introduced us to them all. There were close on fifty guests of whom I only knew a handful. A couple I’d been at Oxford with and three I recognised from the stage – Gabrielle Ray, Lottie Collins and The Great Mephisto. The others consisted of a former Minister for War, a foreign ambassador or two, assorted factory owners, university dons, lawyers, men of letters and the wives and daughters thereof. I’d forgotten half their names before the drinks came round.

“Doesn’t The Great Mephisto make people disappear?” asked Emmeline, nudging me in the ribs.

She was right. I’d seen him do it several times on stage. His assistant would step inside a wardrobe thingy and re-appear ten seconds later in the audience.

“You don’t remember seeing any strange looking wardrobes at those deb balls, do you?” I asked.

“No.”

I took my notebook out of my jacket pocket and jotted down a quick entry: *The Great Mephisto – wardrobes!*

~

I was seated next to Emmeline at dinner and not a little disappointed to find that both Lady Harcourt and The Great M. were at the far end of the table. Our gentle interrogation would have to wait until after dinner.

When everyone had taken their place, Lady Harcourt rose and addressed the table. "I have a surprise for you all tonight. As many of you know, Doctor Pelling is renowned throughout the Empire as one of the leading designers of automata."

A few wise heads nodded. Not mine, as I'd never heard of the chap.

"Well, tonight," continued Lady H. "I think you will agree that he has excelled himself."

An expectant hush descended over the table. A few heads, mine included, began to turn this way and that. Were we supposed to be looking at something? I hadn't expected a show.

Lady Harcourt clapped her hands. "Bring on the first course."

The double doors at the far end of the room opened and there was a gasp.

It was at least seven feet tall, had a bright blue face and ten arms. It was like that Indian Goddess. Harry Llama? Kali? You know the one I mean. The one with all the arms. Except this one was carrying plates of food instead of swords.

At least I hoped they were plates of food.

The dinner guests reacted as you would expect any dinner party to react upon the unexpected entrance of a seven-foot, ten-arm, blue-faced waitress. Some clapped, some coo-ed, some I-say-ed and some screamed. One woman, Lady Dormer, fainted and at least three glasses went flying.

One of those glasses was mine. Its contents went flying across the table in a fine arc until they found the face of the Duchess of Arran, seated opposite.

Duchesses never duck.

Of course I apologised profusely and the Duchess took it all in good sport, saying that being splashed in the face was all that had kept her from fainting dead away on the carpet.

Meanwhile, in the doorway, Kali began to move. She walked with a dancer's grace, her arms constantly in motion, her red eyes blazing. It was rather hypnotic just watching her as she danced towards the table, gracefully stepping over the supine body of the Lady Dormer. Then she started serving, depositing plates on the table at a speed no mortal waitress could match, blue arms a-blurring. We guests – the ones not lying on the carpet in full swoon – froze in place, not daring to move as blue arms flew either side of our ears.

She was soon joined by a second Kali, and a third. They'd

dance into the room, waft plates past our ears, then sinuously depart, returning with a new set of plates. And when they'd finished, all three of them formed a chorus line in front of the fireplace and continued their gyrations until Lady Harcourt dismissed them with a clap of her hand.

I'd never seen anything like it. Even at the Sloths, where Dress-up Friday can get a little outlandish, I'd never experienced the like.

"Do you think all Lady Harcourt's parties are like this?" asked Emmeline, looking not a little awestruck.

I shrugged. "I would think it difficult to top this."

"We've got to come again," said Emmeline. "We simply have to."

Once Lady Dormer had been brought back to verticality, conversation around the table set off at a fair old buzz. Everyone was most impressed with the Kalis, though a few wondered if they came in a smaller size. There's something about a seven-foot tall servant that disconcerts. And a few of the guests had country properties with those inconveniently low ceilings.

The former Minister for War saw another use for the Kalis. "One day we will have armies like that," he said. "Imagine that waitress with ten swords in her hands. Or ten pistols."

For a second it was even money that the Lady Dormer would become reacquainted with the carpet. Her face turned white at the thought of all those knife-wielding arms, and she swayed slightly in her chair.

"I thought the Treaty of Paris banned the use of automata in warfare," said Lord Carfax.

"A piece of paper," said the former M. of W. rather dismissively. "Germany's pumping millions into automata research. You can't tell me none of that's going into military applications. I blame the Kaiser. He has the whole country on a war footing. Mark my words, there will be war soon between our two countries."

"There I must disagree with you," said Lord Carfax. "I know for a fact that the Kaiser has a very deep affection for our dear queen. She is, after all, his grandmother. He would never bear arms against us."

"Not while the queen lives, perhaps. But she is eighty-four, and the Prince of Wales and the Kaiser do not get on. They detest each other."

"That's true," said Lord Willoughby. "And the Queen is not in the best of health. I have it on the highest authority that she would have died in 1901 if it hadn't been for Doctor Tregorran, her new surgeon. All the family had been summoned to her bedside – the Kaiser included. No one thought she'd survive the day. And then the Prince of Wales sent for Doctor Tregorran and, as some of you know, he modified her."

"Modified?"

"Removed her legs, didn't you hear? She'd lost the use of them anyway. I'm not a medical man, but I was told the removal of her legs was necessary to take the strain from the rest of her system. The good doctor then replaced her legs with mechanical ones. It gave her a new lease of life. But for how long?"

Well, the things you learn! I wondered if the Queen's legs were steam-powered. And were they the same length as her old ones? I rather fancy I'd ask for a pair a little longer if I was under five feet tall.

Conversation began to fragment after that. One can't limit a table of fifty to a single conversation. I thought I'd casually introduce the subject of this season's balls into the conversation at our end of the table to see if any of our neighbours had been in attendance. None had. Which just about skewered any hope of advancing our investigation.

But I did have a thought. The old M. of W. had been spot on when he'd mentioned what a fine soldier Kali would make given a sword or ten. What if she malfunctioned? It could happen to the best of machines. Even Reeves had recently found an overzealous subroutine. What if Kali developed a taste for prime debutante?

This was a variation on my earlier orang-utan notion – the one that Reeves had shot down. But what if Lady Harcourt wasn't worried about Kali preying on her guests? What if, and here my little grey cells reached new heights in pursuing the unthinkable, what if Lady Harcourt was a cannibal? She *had* lived in Africa for five years. She might have developed a taste for human flesh while she'd been out there!

And what could be more succulent than a debutante?

I cast an eye around the table, gauging everyone's succulence. Emmeline won by tasty margin.

I leaned closer to Emmeline, preparing to whisper a warning in her ear, but pulled back. How would I phrase it? *Be careful, Emmeline. You may be returning to the Harcourt table a lot sooner than you expected. As next week's third course!*

Needless to say, these thoughts cast a pall over my enjoyment of the food. It's difficult to appreciate the culinary arts when one is forever on the lookout for pieces of debutante lurking beneath the Brussels sprouts.

I counted seven courses that night, each of them brought to the table by a different species of automaton. Kali had been but an appetiser. These later machines didn't look the least bit human. Some were simply bizarre – looking more like mobile works of abstract art with arms. Every one of them was striking, both in colour and design. One looked like a giant chicken. Lady Dormer was spending so much time on the carpet I thought someone might set a place for her there.

By the sixth course I began to have doubts about my chair. I half expected it to sprout arms and grab my knife and fork.

Eventually Lady Harcourt rose and signalled that the time had arrived for the ladies to repair to another room. I touched Emmeline's arm. "Be careful. Remember you're a deb in a house where debs have a habit of disappearing."

Her eyes widened. "Oh. I hadn't thought of that."

I watched the ladies depart, two of them supporting Lady Dormer as the giant chicken returned with the gentlemen's port. I don't think I could get used to having a giant chicken around the house. I would be forever wondering if I'd shrunk. And what would one do with the eggs? They'd take hours to boil.

I did my best to circulate and play the sleuth, trying to steer the conversation debwards whenever I could. But each attempt was a dead end. Most of my fellow guests hadn't been to a ball in years, and those who had didn't recognise any of the names I so carefully dropped.

I even asked Lord Harcourt what the food was like in Africa. "Pretty rummy I should guess, what?"

To which he reeled off a list of various antelopes, crocodiles, elephants and buffaloes that he'd hunted and eaten, but not one mention of debutante or native bearer.

I wondered if Emmeline was having better luck.

After half an hour the ladies returned. I watched them file in, looking out for Emmeline. She wasn't in the first group. Or the second. Then I saw her and I could breathe again.

I fairly shot across the room. "Any luck?" I asked.

"I couldn't get close to her," said Emmeline. "Every time I tried she turned away or decided she had to mingle with a group on the other side of the room. I think she knows. Why else would she be avoiding me?"

Emmeline looked worried. I didn't feel too hot myself. Even Moriarty never had a household of Kalis at his disposal.

But cometh the hour, cometh the Worcester. We weren't in a dark alley, we were in a room overflowing with the cream of society. No harm could befall us with so many witnesses.

"Follow me," I said. "People are always trying to avoid me. I have learned a few tricks."

I don't wish to boast, but when it comes to buttonholing, I have been trained by aunts and can button with the best. A firm eye, a cheery 'what ho!' and cut off all means of retreat.

I sent Emmeline circling to the right on a flanking movement and closed in on Lady Harcourt, who was standing by the fireplace with Lord Carfax and his wife.

"What ho! Lady H. Dashed fine supper, what? And that Kali – never seen anything like it. Do they come in any other colours besides blue?"

"Kind of you to say, Mr Worcester. Why don't you ask Doctor Pelling? He's over there."

Lady Harcourt pointed to a spot over my shoulder. Of course, I knew better than to turn and to look. If I had, Lady H. would have taken the opportunity to exit fireplace right. I'd used the manoeuvre myself on several occasions.

"Really?" I said. "I must talk to him later. Yes, indeed, first class party. Just what Miss Dreadnought needed."

Lady Harcourt's eyes began to wander and I suspect her feet felt a certain itchiness too. But as she turned to her right in preparation to flee, she found Emmeline dug in and blocking her way.

"Ah, there you are Emmeline," I said. "I was only this second telling Lady Harcourt what a fillip this supper has been for you. What with your recent bad news."

Emmeline took her cue and ran with it.

"It *has* been upsetting. Amelia's my closest friend. Goodness knows what's happened to her."

"Which Amelia would that be, dear?" asked Lady Carfax.

"Amelia Runcible," said Emmeline.

I was watching Lady Harcourt, waiting to see how she reacted. I'd been expecting a tinge of guilt, or possibly a tongue gliding over the lip if the memory had been particularly toothsome. I was not expecting such a strong reaction.

"Runcible?" she said, her eyes unglazing in an instant.

"Good God, I had her mother banging on my door last week. She thought *I* had the girl. I don't know what you debs are up to this year but it's about time it stopped." She turned to Lady Carfax. "Would you believe I've had *four* visits this month from distraught mothers asking where their daughters were."

"Why ever would they call on you?" asked Lady Carfax.

"Because these silly girls tell their mothers I've invited them to an after-ball supper at Clarges Square. Or, if not me, someone else." She stopped talking and craned her neck, peering around the room. "Ursula! What was the name of that deb you were accused of harbouring last month?"

The Duchess of Arran replied from across the room. "What? Oh, *her*. I can't remember her name. One of the Anstruther-Smothers brood."

Lucretia Anstruther-Smothers! That was Tufty's missing girl.

"See," said Lady Harcourt. "Never used to happen in my day. I wouldn't have dreamed of stopping out all night. And I *wouldn't* have involved an unwitting third party in such a deception."

Well, this was one in the eye for my 'Lady Harcourt, cannibal mastermind' theory. And it raised the number of missing girls to at least five. Part of me wanted to ask Lady Harcourt for the names of the other three girls she'd been accused of harbouring, but I felt we'd already drawn enough attention to the subject. We consulting detectives are pretty hot on secrecy and, even if Lady H. was innocent, one of her guests might not.

I caught Emmeline's eye before she could threaten to chain herself to the fireplace. "Emmie, I think Lady Dormer's trying to attract your attention."

Lady Dormer wasn't, of course. She was standing by the windows as far away from the door or any piece of furniture which looked as though it might sprout arms. But she had a haunted, vigilant look which could be mistaken for someone desperate for a word. I waved to her and we detached ourselves from the group.

The rest of the evening passed off somewhat uneventfully. I'd run out of questions to ask and there were too many people within earshot to discuss the case with Emmeline. I had hoped that Lottie Collins and the Kalis might be persuaded to give us an impromptu performance of 'Ta-ra-ra Boom-de-ay' but Miss Collins said her throat was too sore to do it justice.

~

“So,” said Emmeline as we were waiting in the hall for our coats. “What’s the plan for tomorrow?”

I didn’t have a plan for tomorrow. I had a plan for tonight – confer with Reeves – and that was about it.

“You do know there’s a ball tomorrow?” said Emmeline.

“Is there?”

“Yes. I think we should watch every deb and make a note of who they’re dancing with.”

I wasn’t so sure. Watching every deb and writing copious notes sounded more like police work, something Inspector Lestrade would suggest. We consulting detectives preferred to observe and deduce. To ponder the imponderable over a pipe or two in the comfort of our favourite armchair. It was a more gentlemanly approach to solving crime.

But it did make sense to attend the ball and keep an eye on the debs. With Emmeline and me inside and Reeves without, one of us should be able to spot someone up to no good.

We’d just agreed to meet at the ball when our coats arrived. Closely followed by Agnes, who looked like she’d spent the entire evening sucking a disagreeable lemon.

“What ho, Agnes,” I said, putting on a breezy smile in an attempt to lighten her mood.

It didn’t work. She gave me a dismissive look before turning her beak towards Emmeline. “You’re ready then?” she said. “I thought we’d be leaving earlier.”

Emmeline didn’t reply. Stern-faced, she continued buttoning her coat and then strode for the door, pushing past Agnes in the process. “Come along, Agnes, do keep up,” she said over her shoulder.

I followed, taking the opportunity to have a final stretch of the Worcester spine and shoulders before it was time to reprise my role of Quasimodo the chauffeur.

Emmeline made straight for the front seat of the Stanley and unlatched the footplate.

“What are you doing?” snapped Agnes.

“Doing what I should have done earlier,” said Emmeline. “I don’t care what you say. I’m sitting up front and if you don’t like it, you can stay here all night. I’ll tell mama you refused to chaperone me on the way home.”

“Emmie!”

"Don't 'Emmie' me, Agnes. I am not a child any more. I am eighteen."

It may have been June but there was a distinct, and very localised, frost all the way to Audley Street. Not a word was spoken. Agnes managed a handful of disapproving grunts whenever the Stanley hit a bump in the road or turned unexpectedly, but the rest of the time she clung to the seat with both hands and glared resolutely ahead. Emmeline was remarkable quiet too, emitting not a single girlish scream – even when I had to swerve to avoid a dog that, mesmerised by Agnes's Medusa-like glare, had run out right in front of us.

FIVE

It was with relief that I drove back to the flat. Reeves was waiting for me. He'd uncovered another two missing debs - Adele Cholmondeley-Chudleigh and Hortencia Hervey-Turvey. At this rate there wouldn't be a deb left by Christmas!

"What *is* going on, Reeves? How many debs does this person want?"

"It is a puzzling question, sir."

I told him about Lady Harcourt, the Duchess of Arran and the Kalis.

"Do you think Lady H. and the Duchess could be in cahoots, Reeves? A secret society of cannibals looking to spice up the supper menu?"

"I think not, sir. Miss Hervey-Turvey informed her mother she had been invited to supper by the Countess of Winchelsea."

Yet another society hostess!

"And," continued Reeves, "the Countess of Winchelsea's footman was most adamant that *no* young lady accompanied his mistress from the ball. The only occupants of her carriage that night were the Count, the Countess and their son."

"So it's definitely a ruse - these supper invitations. I don't suppose any of the other footmen remembered taking home an extra girl, did they?"

"No, sir. I canvassed extensively. I had hoped that someone may have seen the young ladies leave. One would have thought a young lady expecting a ride in her hostess's carriage would have been surprised to be offered an alternative ride home. One would think she may have said something. Or acted with alarm. But none of the footmen present witnessed such an event at any of the balls in question."

Curiouser and curiouser. "Which makes one think all these girls left willingly."

"Indeed, sir."

Well, if this wasn't a three pipe problem I didn't know what was. Not having a pipe, I thought I'd try a three cocktail variant and asked Reeves to fetch the gin.

While I could envisage one deb - or even two - climbing into a strange carriage without a word. I couldn't envisage six. Debs know their carriages. It's one of the things they're taught. They'd know a duchess or a countess would have a coat of arms on their carriage. And they'd know which coat of arms was which.

"There is also the question of chaperones, sir," said Reeves as he handed me my drink.

"There is?"

"Yes, sir. A debutante leaving a ball unchaperoned in the company of a young gentleman would be noticed. Their ball gowns, having to be white, make them very distinctive, and the younger footmen tend to pay particular attention to the comings and goings of the young ladies."

This man must have been dining on fish the entire evening!

"Were any unchaperoned debs spotted?"

"None, sir."

Well, that about put paid to the 'persuasive young gentleman' theory. Even on the darkest night, no deb could sneak out of a building in eight yards of voluminous white.

"So what does this mean, Reeves? Are we dealing with a woman?"

"Possibly, sir. Or an older man - one who could pass for her father - or indeed a gang."

"A gang?"

"One with a female member, sir, who could put the young lady at her ease."

"Or a eunuch!" I said, nearly spilling my cocktail. "Dressed as a woman. Never forget the eunuch, Reeves. He's the only one with a cast iron motive."

"Quite, sir."

~

The next day I was up with the lunchtime lark and feeling pretty braced.

"I shall dine on nothing but fish today, Reeves," I said over my breakfast kipper. "For tonight we catch our man - or woman, or, indeed, our eunuch. Whoever they are, they'll be at the ball tonight and so shall we. Vigilance, Reeves, shall be our watchword."

"Indeed, sir? Might I enquire if you have a plan?"

"Vigilance, Reeves, that *is* the plan. You shall be stationed outside, watching the doors vigilantly. Miss Dreadnought shall be inside, watching for debs preparing to leave. And I'll be sitting quietly in a corner of the ballroom, observing all. Nothing shall get past us. I dare say I'll have spotted our man, or gang, or whomsoever, long before midnight. They'll give themselves away. They always do. Many of them have a limp, you know?"

"Quite. If I may make a suggestion, sir, on the off chance they don't give themselves away by limping during the evening...."

"Speak on, Reeves. Even the best plan can benefit from an injection of your steam-powered logic."

"I think we should compile a list of every debutante who attends the ball and note with whom she leaves. If one of the young ladies should subsequently go missing, we would then know whom to investigate."

This sounded suspiciously like police work again but, the more I mulled it over, the more I began to see that it never hurt to have a plan B.

"What if we don't recognise the person they left with?" I said. "I doubt I could put a name to every face in society. On a dark night, one set of mutton chops looks very much like another."

"I had anticipated that contingency, sir. My intention was to walk along the line of carriages and engage the footmen and chauffeurs in conversation. That way I will know people's identities by the carriage they drive off in."

"Ah, but what if, like me, they drive their own car?"

"Then I will make a note of the type of car, sir, and give it special attention. I had considered taking a stick of chalk with me and making a mark on the underside of such vehicles so that, if needs be, we could identify said vehicle later."

If Reeves's brain was not one of the seven wonders of the world then I did not know what was. Would the Collossus of Rhodes have come up with such a plan? I think not.

"To aid our endeavours, sir, I have this morning purchased *Milady's Debutantes Guide 1903*, the illustrated edition."

"There's an illustrated guide to debutantes?"

"Yes, sir. It contains the names, photographs and lineage

of most, if not all, of the debutantes coming out this year. It will certainly aid our identification of the young ladies."

"Is this guide a modern innovation, Reeves? I don't remember hearing of it before."

"I believe it was first published last year, sir. Such was its popularity that a companion edition, listing the form of young gentlemen, was launched earlier this year."

I put down my fork. "A form book of young gentlemen? Am I in it?"

Reeves looked decidedly sheepish. It was one of the few expressions he had – impassive, disapproving and sheepish. And that instant he was showing a good deal of wool.

"Well, Reeves? Am I?"

"Yes, sir. I took the liberty of purchasing a copy on your behalf. I had thought of writing a letter to the editor requesting an amendment to your entry to improve your odds of remaining single, but ... it would appear that that will not be necessary."

"Not newts, is it?"

"No, sir." He withdrew a slim volume from his jacket pocket and handed it to me. "Page fifty-three, sir."

I flicked through the pages pretty swiftly, then began to read:

FF/PF-KF **Worcester, Reginald** Well-bred, expensive colt but lazy, needs strong riding as tends to give up if going gets heavy. Has run nine times. Never finished. Prone to bolting.

It read like a dashed racing guide! It even had the results of my last six outings – fell, fell, pulled-up, fell.

"What does 'K' signify, Reeves? I didn't kill anyone did I?"

"No, sir. There is a key to the abbreviations at the front. The 'K' in question stands for 'Kicked Dog.'"

That would be the Throstlecoombe girl. She knew full well I never kicked her Pomeranian. Though I ought to have. The beastly hound was attempting to remove the marrow from my anklebone at the time. But I hadn't. I'd merely shaken the blighter off.

"Looking on the bright side, sir, any young lady with matrimonial intentions would view this entry as a discouragement."

"I fear you do not know the female mind, Reeves. Few do,

so don't despair. But this is just the kind of entry to encourage the sort of girl who considers herself a strong rider. The kind who likes a challenge. They are aunts-in-waiting, Reeves. Proto-aunts who see men as clay to be moulded and fired. Not to mention glazed."

"Perhaps a stiff letter to the publisher, sir?"

"Saying what? Carries newts in his saddlebags? Insanity in the bloodline?"

"I was thinking of broken-winded, sir, and prone to lameness."

~

I'd recovered my earlier vim by the time we departed for the ball. I was full of fish, and had the distinct impression that I was standing a good two inches taller than normal. A casual observer, had such a cove been standing outside my Charles Street flat, would have felt not a little awed.

We arrived a good hour before the ball was scheduled to begin and parked right in front of the entrance. It looked as though we were the first to arrive, but I thought it best to make sure.

"I'll go in and have a quick look around to make sure there are no debs inside," I said.

The Piccadilly Palais was a large, modern affair – a tearoom by day with a ballroom upstairs that was hired out for tea dances and receptions, with the occasional ball thrown in during The Season. The tearoom was closed and I passed through the foyer to a wide red-carpeted staircase ascending to the ballroom.

There was no one on the ballroom door and, it not being locked, I gave it a push and poked my head inside. Empty, except for two waitresses in their black and white uniforms checking that the chairs and tables along the side walls were placed correctly.

I returned to the car.

"All clear," I said. "No one's arrived yet."

We then had a final run through of The Plan. One, Reeves would list all the debs as they arrived. Two, Reeves would catalogue all the carriages and, by cunning means, discover whom they belonged to. Meanwhile, three, Emmeline and I would spend the evening observing the debs and looking out for eunuchs and suspicious behaviour – i.e. people with a limp, Sultans and Arab sheikhs.

At the stroke of midnight, Emmeline would switch to door

duty, observing any debutantes who looked like they were leaving and give their companions the thoroughest of appraisals – eunuch, check; limp, check; cannibal, check...

Reeves coughed, his expression veering to one of distinct disapproval.

"I thought we had agreed, sir, that it was not possible to identify a cannibal from their appearance."

"Ah, but that was before I had that poached salmon. Second thoughts have been had, Reeves. Would Sherlock Holmes throw in the deerstalker if called upon to spot a cannibal? I think not, Reeves. And neither will I. I fancy a cannibal might drop a little something on his tie. Or look at a deb as a starving man might look upon a leg of roast mutton."

Reeves's look of disapproval did not lift. If anything it deepened.

"It is my recollection, sir, that we decided a far more efficacious use of Miss Dreadnought's time would be to look for debutantes whose companions did not appear to be family members. Miss Dreadnought, either by direct knowledge, or by comparing facial characteristics would, in that fashion, determine which debutantes were in danger, and attempt to attract your attention. If, for some reason, your attention was impossible to attract, she would follow the young lady outside and inform me."

"Well, yes, I do recall something along those lines."

I still felt Reeves was playing too solid a game. His logic was faultless, his technique superb, but ... where was the flair? We consulting detectives are pretty enamoured of the hunch. And stains on ties, for a stain can tell a thousand words to those with the attuned eye.

However, I decided to agree with Reeves for the nonce, as I did not care for his disapproving face. I'd make sure he was out of earshot when I had my little chat with Emmeline about what to look for.

I moved swiftly to item four of the plan. To spare Reeves from being overwhelmed by the number of departing debs, I would step outside and assist when the ball began to break up. Emmeline would remain inside, watching the door, until the last deb departed, whereupon Emmeline would accompany her out. All three of us would then confer.

As for the contingency of what to do if Emmeline identified a deb in danger, that was a simple one. We would follow the deb in the car, then play it by ear.

"You don't have a service revolver on you, I suppose, Reeves."

"No, sir."

"Pity. Doctor Watson swears by his. Can you buy a service revolver this time of night, Reeves?"

"I think not, sir."

"Well, add it to your shopping list for tomorrow."

Twenty minutes later, guests began to arrive and I followed them inside. The Dreadnought fleet steamed into port shortly afterwards and I whisked Emmeline away to give her her instructions.

"You want me to be on the lookout for eunuchs?" she said.

"I do."

"What do they look like?"

I had to think about that one. Most of the eunuchs I'd seen had been on the stage, dressed up in colourful costumes and dripping in greasepaint.

"Large, fat, and foreign looking, I think. And, if they begin to sing, listen out for a lilting castrato voice."

Hours passed. Dances were danced, and the Great Detective, braced by a couple of stiff ones from the bar, observed all. I must say having all the debs dressed in white made things a dashed sight easier. One could spot them a mile off. I kept the hawk-like trained upon them, watching who they danced with and with whom they talked.

Emmeline reported back at intervals.

"Pinky Pinkerton has a limp," she said, still breathless from a vigorous two-step. "He says Minerva Beaufort stepped on his foot repeatedly during a Polka, but Minerva is such a fine dancer I don't think she would."

Pinky Pinkerton went straight into my notebook.

"And Georgie Stafford Brooke Warwick was humming to himself just now."

"Humming?" I had a quick glance at my notebook. I didn't think I had humming down as a mark of criminal proclivity.

"A high-pitched hum," said Emmeline.

"Aha! How high-pitched? Castrato high?"

"I've never heard a castrato sing. But it was higher than a tenor."

I wouldn't have marked Georgie Stafford Brooke Warwick down as a eunuch. But, as we consulting detectives know, that was probably the strongest reason for believing he was.

"Anything more?" I asked.

"Prince Otto is a little odd. He offered to buy me a pony."

"Did you ask for a pony?"

"No. He just came straight out with it. 'Would you like a pony, little miss?' He is foreign though."

"Is he large and fat?"

"No, he's small and slim."

He didn't sound like a eunuch. But he *was* foreign and a tad too free with the ponies for my liking, so I added him to the book.

"Anyone else?"

"Lord Craven has a limp but he's over seventy and can't walk a step without a stick."

"I already have him in the book. I'll try and get a closer look at his stick later. I wouldn't be surprised if it was one of those sword-canes."

Midnight arrived and the first guests began to depart. I caught up with Emmeline before she took up her station near the door.

"Have you cleared things with your mother about staying on?" I asked.

"Yes, I told her Lady Harcourt had invited me to supper."

"She bought that?"

"She did when I told her a very important personage, whom I could not name as I'd been sworn to secrecy, was going to be there with his two unmarried sons."

Emmeline Dreadnought would make a dashed fine criminal mastermind.

With Emmeline watching the door, I decided to wander the tables and see what snatches of conversation I could pick up. I'd made a note of the lame and the high-hummers. Now was a time to seek out the gangs - a furtive brother and sister act, an artful mother and son, or a predatory father and daughter. If they were here, now would be the time they'd be making their last minute preparations.

I sauntered along the row of tables, my ears turning like a fine hunter chaser to every whispered snatch of conversation, listening for the words 'deb' 'harem' or 'tasty.'

It was a fruitless journey, though I did pick up a good tip for the Cesarawitch: Billy Bass's horse, Grey Tick. They reckoned he'd start at thirty-three to one!

I returned by way of the other side of the room, sauntering back to join Emmeline by the door.

"Any luck?" I asked.

"Not yet. The girls I know were all with their families. No

one has looked at all furtive."

I decided to pay a visit to the bar. A stiff one helps jolly up the reticent little grey cells that a fish might have overlooked.

Suitably jollied, I ran the eye over the denizens of the bar. Most of them were male and most were talking very loudly about all manner of topics except kidnapping debs.

I returned to the ballroom and executed another circuit or two. The evening was beginning to feel a little like police work. All this walking and waiting. Sherlock wouldn't have stood for it. He'd have taken his violin into a quiet corner and fiddled until the sea-faring midgets arrived.

I joined Emmeline for a minute or two – she still had nothing to report – and then went outside to give Reeves a hand.

"What ho, Reeves. How goes it?"

"Tolerably well, sir. Thirty-one debs have exited and fourteen remain inside. All thirty-one have driven away with their respective families."

I took charge of the debs illustrated guide and read off the names to Reeves as the girls came out. Reeves followed each deb's progress, his neck craning to peer through and over the crowds so that he could identify their carriage. Sometimes he had to run after them to get a better look. I'd never seen Reeves run before. I wasn't sure he could. He had a darting gait, very much like a spider but with fewer legs. He'd go from stationary to brisk dash in the blink of an eye and stop just as smartish. And all done with the minimum of noise. Not a single clank, puff or slap as his feet hit the paving stones. Reeves was as well-oiled as they came.

The crowds began to thin and the line of carriages diminish. We were down to the last two debs. I saw a cloud of white silk appear in the foyer. The last deb was coming out. Emmeline would be close behind.

Except she wasn't.

I waited ten, twenty seconds.

"Is it possible you miscounted the number of debs, Reeves?"

"No, sir. I was most meticulous."

"Was one of the older ladies wearing a white gown?"

"Not that I recall, sir."

I went inside. Emmeline was not where I'd left her and I couldn't see a single white dress anywhere in the ballroom. I ran to the bar. No Emmeline there either. I tried the cloakrooms, asking the dowager Countess of Ilkley if she wouldn't mind checking the lady's cloakroom for me as it was an emergency.

She returned a minute later without Emmeline. The cloakroom was empty, she said.

As was the gentleman's cloakroom.

I ran back to Reeves.

"Have you seen her?" I asked.

"No, sir. I tried the tea room door. It is locked and bolted from the inside. The only other exit from the building is the staff door on the far side of the building. I noticed it earlier during my perambulations."

I hadn't thought to observe the staff. Could one of them have smuggled Emmeline out of the ballroom? It didn't sound likely. A girl in a voluminous white gown is difficult to smuggle anywhere.

"Might I suggest, sir, you watch this door while I investigate the staff entrance?"

"Be swift, Reeves. Run all the way."

Reeves darted off in a blur of valetware, leaving me deep in thought. How could Emmeline have disappeared? She'd been by the door in plain sight of scores of guests. No one could have overpowered her and dragged her away. And she would never have gone willingly. She was on the lookout for suspicious characters. No one could have tricked her into leaving the ballroom by a back entrance.

The little grey cells boggled. No amount of fish or alcohol could coax an answer to this conundrum.

Presently Reeves returned, at pace and alone. He spoke without showing the slightest hint of breathlessness. "The kitchen staff are adamant they never saw Miss Emmeline, sir. The cook was on duty the entire evening and never left the kitchen. There is no other way out. The staff door opens directly into the kitchen."

"Then she must still be inside."

We ran up the staircase and into the ballroom. The orchestra were packing up and the waiting staff were starting to clear the tables. A few die-hard guests were dotted around the room and a fair buzz of conversation still echoed from the bar.

Not a sign of Emmeline anywhere.

We asked a waitress if she'd seen a girl in a white dress in the last ten minutes. She shook her head.

"Could she have wandered through the wrong door and got lost?" I asked her. "Are there any staff exits up here?"

The girl pointed to a door at the far end. "It leads to the kitchens, sir."

"Are there any other exits from this room, miss?" asked Reeves. "To a store room or a cupboard?"

"No, sir."

We hastened across the dance floor to the far side. As we approached the door I noticed something white on the floor and stooped to pick it up. It was a dance card. *Emmeline's* dance card. Her name was at the top, followed by a list of her dance partners.

I showed it to Reeves.

"She was here, Reeves. She must have dropped it as a clue so we'd know to follow."

I opened the door and peered through. It was a dimly lit stairwell with concrete steps going both up and down. The kitchens would be downstairs. Was there an attic upstairs?

"This way, Reeves."

I positively flew up the first half flight of steps then slid to a halt. There, by a window, was a white handkerchief and two large white feathers. I recognised the feathers at once – they came from Emmeline's headdress. I bent down to retrieve the handkerchief, and saw the initials 'ED' sewn into a corner. Emmeline Dreadnought.

"The window is locked, sir," said Reeves, pointing to the latch that secured the upper and lower parts of the sash window.

I trousered the evidence and took the next half flight up, and the next. More windows, but no more evidence of Emmeline. The steps continued for another couple of half flights before ending at a door.

"Can you see any more dropped clues, Reeves? I can't." The light may not have been good but Emmeline had had *three* feathers in her headdress and a white feather would have stood out even in this gloom.

I opened the door and a cold breeze blew against my face. We were on the roof! A large flat roof with a brick parapet a yard high to my left. I peered into the gloom and gradually my eyes became accustomed to the dark. I couldn't see Emmeline.

"I'll search this side, sir," said Reeves, striding off to my right. I took the left, leaning over the parapet every now and then to see if there was another way down. There wasn't.

Reeves and I must have covered every inch of that roof but we found no sign of Emmeline. If she had been brought here, how did she get down? There were no ladders and the neighbouring buildings were the width of a street away.

"Can you make any sense of this, Reeves?"

"I would like another look at that window, sir."

We left the roof and walked back down to the window where I'd found Emmeline's handkerchief and feathers. Reeves unlatched the window, opened it, and leaned outside.

"A long ladder could have been placed against this window sill, sir."

I had a look for myself. "It would have to be a dashed long ladder. It's a good thirty or forty feet to the ground." It was then that I noticed the drainpipe. It ran from the roof to the ground, passing within a yard of the open window. Like Saul at the Gates of Damocles, I was hit on the noodle with the lightning flash of revelation. I knew exactly how Emmeline had left the building. And I knew who had taken her.

"The orang-utan!"

Who else could it be? My instinct had been right all along!

"I beg your pardon, sir. Did you just say orang-utan?"

"I did, Reeves. Who else could have pulled it off? You've seen Miss Dreadnought in action. She wouldn't go out without a fight. Can you see anyone carrying her down a long ladder? I can't. But an ape wouldn't even need a long ladder when there's a perfectly serviceable drainpipe less than an arm swing away. And he'd have the strength."

Reeves had the look of someone struggling to find the right words. People often do when in the presence of genius.

"An orang-utan," I continued, feeling the fire of inspiration burning white-hot between my ears. "Or, perhaps, a gorilla. Do you think I should add gorillas to the list, Reeves? I always see gorillas as being rather sombre and law abiding, whereas orang-utans have that furtive sort of look, don't you think?"

"I've never speculated upon the comparative mendacity of the Simiidae, sir."

"No? Well, perhaps you should."

"Might I suggest an alternative theory, sir?"

"A chimpanzee?"

"No, sir. I was thinking of a way Miss Emmeline might have been subdued without the need for brute strength."

"How?"

"Chloroform, sir. It is an anaesthetic much used by the medical profession. A few drops applied to a handkerchief, and then that handkerchief pressed against the young lady's face, would render her unconscious within seconds."

I untrousered Emmeline's handkerchief and was about to give it a good sniff when Reeves stopped me.

"No, sir! Allow me."

He took the handkerchief and raised it to his ear.

"Is your pressure running low, Reeves?"

"No, sir." He cocked his head to one side and closed his eyes. I considered this not a little rummy.

"Are you sure you're all right, Reeves? It's not past your bedtime, is it?"

"No, sir. I am endeavouring to smell the handkerchief."

"With your ear?"

"Yes, sir. It's where my olfactory sensors are located. My nose is only for emergencies."

The mind boggled. "What kind of emergencies?"

"Pressure emergencies, sir. It is a vent. And Miss Emmeline's handkerchief contains no trace of chloroform."

"Well, that's how it goes, Reeves. Nice theory, but not all theories can be right."

Reeves returned Emmeline's handkerchief to me. "I do not consider my theory disproven, sir. The chloroform could have been applied to the abductor's handkerchief. As you said yourself, Miss Emmeline would not have gone quietly. Ape or no ape, she would have cried out at the top of her lungs."

Reeves had a point. Lady Dormer might have swooned at the first sight of an orang-utan, but not Emmeline. She would have yelled all the way down the drainpipe. We would have heard her.

"Furthermore, sir, I deduce there were at least two people. If you recall, this window was latched from the inside. The person carrying Miss Emmeline could not have latched the window from without. We are looking for an individual – a guest or a servant – who lured Miss Emmeline to the stairwell, and an accomplice who was stationed outside with a ladder. Or possibly a rope."

"You miss the obvious, Reeves. It's as Emmeline said the other day. Your brain, immense as it, is too perfectly wired to think the unthinkable. Unless, of course, you'd dined on a bad herring, which I wouldn't recommend. You, seeing this window, immediately think of ladders and ropes, whereas

Reginald Worcester, he thinks orang-utans. It's what marks his brain out as special."

"Indeed it does, sir."

"And, while we're on the subject of furthermores, Reeves, who's going to carry off this long ladder of yours? The accomplice is already carrying Emmeline. He can't carry both."

"He may have a carriage below, sir. He could stow Miss Emmeline inside and lash the ladder to the roof."

I shook my head. "Did you see any carriages tonight with long ladders on their roofs? I didn't. Far easier to employ an orang-utan. No need for ladders at all. Our furry friend could scale the drainpipe and hide out on the roof until his master opened the window and whistled for him. Said ape then waits in the carriage with Emmeline until his master arrives and they drive off."

"I think we should call the police, sir."

"Why? This is beyond them, Reeves. The constabulary can deal with simple matters of affray but the police mind cannot cope with orang-utans."

"That is as maybe, sir, but they have resources we do not. I fear Miss Emmeline's life to be in very real danger. This action tonight has caused me to reassess my hypothesis concerning these abductions."

"Because of the orang-utan?"

"No, sir. Because of the nature of Miss Emmeline's abduction. We had assumed that all the young ladies had left willingly with their abductor. But Miss Emmeline did not. No one leaves a ball willingly by an upstairs window. And no one uses an upstairs window to abduct a young lady if they have an alternative. Why, I ask, did the gang not use the door?"

"Because of the orang-utan?"

I received a glimpse of Reeves's disapproving look.

"No, sir. Executing these abductions takes a considerable degree of planning. They have someone on the inside who is persuasive and able to place the young ladies at their ease. But they can only have one such person, otherwise, why don't they leave by the front door?"

I considered bringing up the obvious again, viz. our friend, the ginger-haired ape, but Reeves fixed me with a look.

"The use of the window tonight, sir, was not a spontaneous act brought about by the unexpected intervention of Miss Emmeline. There was insufficient time to get everything in place. The associate *had* to be outside with a ladder waiting for a signal. Which means, in all likelihood, that a similar method was used in the other abductions."

I was still at a loss to see where Reeves was going this. Windows, doors – what did it matter. An abduction was an abduction. The salient point was the involvement of the orang-utan. Sherlock Holmes would have known which part of the world orang-utans sprang from and set about compiling a list of all the foreign potentates in that region with a harem a tad on the sparse side.

Reeves disagreed. He was in danger of wearing out his disapproving look.

"I don't think the young ladies are being abducted for that purpose, sir. A foreign potentate abducting the cream of British society to fill his harem would not be a potentate for very long. Word would get out, and a gunboat would be despatched forthwith. I fear the man we are dealing with is a very dangerous individual whose motive we can scarcely imagine."

A wise detective knows that sometimes there is no arguing with one's subordinates. The subordinate mind is too closed, too ordered, to encompass a world where potentates do rummy things, and eunuchs are hand in paw with orang-utans.

I changed the subject.

"Let's have a word with the staff. One of them might have seen our chap behaving oddly on the stairs."

~

I left Reeves to question the kitchen staff while I returned to the ballroom. I was hoping I might catch the orchestra before they dispersed. The stage wasn't that far from the door to the stairwell. Some chap might have seen something.

No luck with the violins, but the second cello came up trumps – a young ginger-haired man with an inordinate number of freckles. "Yes, I saw her," he said. "Girl in a white dress standing by the door listening?"

"Listening?"

"That's what it looked like. She had her ear to the door for a good ten seconds before she opened it and went through."

Aha, so Emmeline must have seen something suspicious and decided to play detective. "Did you see anyone come out of the door later?"

"I wasn't really looking."

"What about before the girl got there. Did you see anyone by the door?"

The second cello shrugged. "I only noticed the girl. Bit of a looker. I watched her walk across the dance floor. I didn't notice the door until she got there."

This is one of the frustrating aspects about being a consulting detective – rarely do you meet a witness who sees everything. One of them sees the girl, another spots the eunuch, another sees the orang-utan. But no one ever sees all three together.

I questioned the waiters and waitresses next, asking if anyone had seen any guests using the door to the kitchen stairwell. No one had.

"See anything rummy going on back there? Any chaps hanging about on the stairs or going up to the roof?"

No luck there either.

"Anyone spot any large monkeys?"

I don't recall anyone making fun of Sherlock Holmes when he was making enquiries about large spectral hounds. One suspects the amount Doctor Watson omits from his journals is considerable.

I met Reeves on the kitchen stairs as I was on my way to join him. He said he hadn't had any luck in the kitchen, but at least no one had laughed at him.

"What I don't understand, Reeves, is what persuaded Emmeline to leave her place by the front door and beetle off to the far end of the room to listen at the stair door. If she spotted something rummy, she should have come and fetched us."

"Young ladies can be unpredictable, sir. And Miss Emmeline *is* rather headstrong."

Reeves, as ever when pronouncing on non-simian matters, had spotted the nail and had given its head what for with a hammer. I could see why Sherlock Holmes never took Mrs Hudson with him on a case.

"Well," I said. "Unless you can think of anyone else to beard tonight, I think we should head home."

"There is a police station in Vine Street, sir."

Sometimes you have to be firm with your manservants. "No, Reeves. We've already discussed this. The police are the last people one would involve."

"As you say, sir, but will the Dreadnoughts concur?"

The Dreadnoughts! I'd completely forgotten about the

Dreadnoughts. They thought Emmeline was supping with Lady Harcourt. Mrs Dreadnought would be banging on Lady Harcourt's door straight after breakfast. Ten minutes later she'd be banging on mine!

"What are we going to do, Reeves?" I couldn't think of a thing. The fish must have worn off.

"You are adamant about not involving the police, sir?"

"I am."

"Then we will have to send a pneumatic telegram."

"Saying what?"

"Saying that Miss Emmeline has been invited to the country for a few days. I will consult Debrett's to ascertain a suitable personage who does not attend The Season."

I'd been premature in my dismissal of the fish for, at that very second, an idea sprang fully formed from between my ears. "No!" I cried. "I've got it. Scratch 'suitable' and make it 'very important personage.' Emmeline used those exact words to her mother."

I took out my notebook and began to write:

Dearest Mama, I am invited to the country! The Very Important Personage - whose name you will know very well indeed, but I am sworn not to speak of it - has invited me to spend a few days at his castle in the company of his sons and daughters! I will telegram every day! Remember, secrecy is essential! Emmeline.

I showed it to Reeves. "Do you think there are too many exclamation marks?"

"It has been my experience, sir, that a young lady can never use too many exclamation marks."

That's what I thought. I'd send the telegram from the flat the moment we arrived home.

SIX

I spent a disturbed night tossing and turning. I should never have involved Emmeline. She might be dead. She might be up a tree, held hostage by an enraged orang-utan. Or she might have chained herself to said tree. Headstrong girls did not make good prisoners.

Maybe I *should* involve the police. Reeves's giant brain thought so. But consulting detectives were universally scathing in their opinions of the police when it came to solving really knotty cases. And this case had to be the knottiest. Even Sherlock Holmes would have worn out a pipe.

I awoke with a single purpose – to find Emmeline and free the girls before another day passed. I'd double my fish intake and even get up early for breakfast.

By the second kipper my plan was hatched.

"Is there a ball tonight?" I asked Reeves as he poured my second cup of Earl Grey.

"The Royal Caledonian, sir. I have laid out your kilt."

I took a deep breath. Some conversations can turn dashed awkward, and I was about to ask Reeves to perform a task that few employers request of their manservants.

"Talking of kilts, Reeves. I have decided upon a bold plan of action for tonight."

"Indeed, sir?"

"Indeed, Reeves. I think the situation calls for a bold plan and, as bold plans go, this one's up there with the boldest. Sacrifices, Reeves, have to be made and the unthinkable has to be thought. Don't you agree?"

"Possibly, sir." I could tell Reeves's disapproving face was only a muscle twitch away. I pressed on.

"What do hunters use, Reeves, when they're out to catch some dashed cunning prey?"

"Guns, sir?"

"No, not guns, Reeves. Bait. That's what they use. They lay a trap."

"Are you proposing we use a young lady as bait at the ball tonight?"

"No, Reeves. We've already lost Miss Dreadnought. I'm not going to risk losing another. You'll have to do it."

The muscle twitched and there it was – the disapproving face. "I think not, sir."

"But it's the obvious plan, Reeves. Sherlock's always donning disguises. It's part of the consulting detective's code – always be prepared to dress up. I can borrow clothes and theatrical make-up from the Sloths. We have an astonishing array of women's clothing for the larger figure. Our Dress-up Friday sessions are the talk of the town."

"It will not work, sir."

"Why ever not?"

"I am unable to dance, sir. A debutante who cannot dance will not be satisfactory bait."

"Can't you learn? I could teach you the steps."

"Alas, sir, it is not the steps that are the problem, it is my gyroscopes. One fast spin and I wouldn't be able to perambulate straight for a week."

This cast one of those spanner thingummies into the works. "You can't spin at all?"

"No, sir. It would disorientate me. I fear I would pass out."

I tilted my head to one side and had a good ponder. This meant a substantial change to my plan. I couldn't risk asking a real debutante to help out. She'd construe my request as a proposal – spotting a troth somewhere between the lines and assuming it came ready-plighted.

There was only one thing for it. I'd have to take on the role myself.

"You can put away my kilt, Reeves. Reginald the deb will be wearing white tonight."

Reeves coughed.

"What is it, Reeves? You object to my plan?"

"I foresee a problem, sir. A young lady cannot turn up at a ball unaccompanied and say she is a debutante. First, she has to be introduced into society. She has to come out. And someone has to present her."

He was right. The Reeves eye for detail was as sharp as ever.

"What if I pretend to be one of the missing debs?"

"I would not recommend it, sir. The young lady in question will have friends and relatives at the ball who will recognise you as an impostor. And the person whom we are attempting to catch, having already abducted the original of that name, would regard you with the highest suspicion."

The man must have been snacking on haddock all night!

"Come on, Reeves. Put your giant brain to work. How can Reggie go to the ball?"

"Well, sir. You cannot be introduced at the Royal Caledonian as it does not allow introductions, but ... there is another way to introduce a young lady into society."

"There is?"

"Yes, sir, by presentation to Her Majesty."

"The Queen?"

"Indeed, sir. I happened to glance at the court circular in today's Times and Her Majesty is receiving a number of presentations this very afternoon. As is her custom on the day of the Royal Caledonian."

This sounded a positive winner. If I could swing an invite. I wondered if Aunt Bertha's writ ran as high as the Palace. She had said I was invited to every gathering during The Season.

Reeves coughed again. I hoped he wasn't coming down with something.

"To be presented to Her Majesty, sir, one needs a sponsor – a former debutante who, herself, was presented to Her Majesty."

Another tool lodged in the Worcester works.

"I fear this enterprise is too complicated, sir."

Consulting detectives laugh at complications. The more complicated a plan, the more likely we are to choose it. And, already, I could see the ghost of possibility.

"The dowager Duchess of Tintagel!" I cried. "She was a deb back in the day before her self-imposed rustication. No one's seen her for years. Not since the Duke died, and she buried herself in the far end of Cornwall."

She'd make the ideal candidate. A person who everyone had heard of but no one remembered what she looked like.

"You could play her, Reeves. No one would expect the Dowager Duchess to dance. She's in her sixties. What do you say?"

"I think we should call the police, sir."

"Nonsense. You couldn't ask a bobby to dress up as a duchess! Have you seen the average bobby's face? Chiselled out of the primordial cliff they are. And they'd insist on keeping their boots on."

"No, sir, I was suggesting we hand the case over to them.

Your plan has too many dependencies, sir. If one falls, they all fall."

"That sounds suspiciously like defeatism, Reeves. If Sherlock Holmes took that attitude there wouldn't be a single person left alive in the county of Devon. Their bones would lie bleaching on Baskerville Moor!"

"If I may be so bold, sir, I don't recall Mr Holmes requesting that Doctor Watson should dress up in women's clothing."

"Are you saying that Watson wouldn't if asked? I must take issue. 'Pass me the petticoat, Holmes,' he would have said. 'After you with the rouge.'"

"I think not, sir."

"Is this Reeves speaking? The Reeves I rescued from a cupboard?"

"My recollection is that I had already been extricated from said cupboard, sir."

"But how long would that have lasted? You said yourself that young gentlemen are forgetful. I dare say someone at the Sloths would have put you back in a box before the day was out. And, Reeves, refresh my mind, what were you wearing when I first saw you?"

"A fairground fortune teller's costume, sir."

"A fairground fortune teller's costume. And were you telling fortunes, Reeves?"

"Questions of that nature were being put to me, sir."

"Until the intervention of one Reginald Worcester, the man who saved you from a life of cupboards and fortune telling. The man who gave you your own room and all the steam you could eat. And don't forget the fish, Reeves – unlimited supply. And the wages. How many automata are paid, Reeves?"

"Very few, sir."

"And yet you refuse this simple request? I am disappointed, Reeves. Very disappointed."

I caught a glimpse of Reeves's sheepish face before he replied. "It would appear you have a point, sir. It would be churlish to refuse."

I slapped him on the shoulder. "Stout fellow, Reeves. I knew you wouldn't let the side down."

~

We left soon after. I didn't want to give Reeves time to change his mind and I wanted to catch Cicely – aka fellow

Sloth, Claude Sissinghurst - before he disappeared for the day.

Cicely was a man of theatrical inclination. There was nothing he didn't know about costumes and dressing up. Be it *tableaux vivants* at the *Gaiety* theatre or Dress Up Fridays at the Sloths, Cicely would be there, overseeing all.

I rapped on Cicely's door and was surprised to see it opened by a young man who appeared to be dressed as an explorer - I'd never seen so many pockets. I assumed the chap was Cicely's new butler. He changed them so often it was difficult to keep up. The first flush of youth may have deserted The Honourable Cicely but he made up for it by surrounding himself with youth, making it a rule never to employ a servant over the age of thirty. Most of them were barely out of their teens.

"Is Cicely in?" I asked.

"I shall enquire within, sir. Whom shall I say is calling?"

"Reginald Worcester, and tell him it's a matter of the utmost."

Half a minute later Cicely emerged, dressed in similar attire to his manservant. "Reggie, dear boy!" he effused. "And this must be Reeves. I've heard so much about him. Does he really tell fortunes?"

"No, sir," said Reeves, looking not a little put out.

"What's with the clothes, Cicely?" I asked. "You're not off to Africa, are you?"

"No, this is the latest fashion, dear boy. What do you think?" He twirled on the doorstep. "I bought it from that new emporium in Saville Row, *Forty-Seven Ginger-Headed Tailors*."

I'd seen the shop only last week. I'd been meaning to drop in. "Do they really have forty-seven ginger tailors?"

"I only saw two, but both were as ginger as they come. I expect the others were in the back."

"Quite." One would imagine having all forty-seven on show at once would prove somewhat distracting for the casual customer.

"Where are my manners?" said Cicely. "Come in, come in! You absolutely must see my new decor. I've had the entire house refurbished. Arts and Steamcraft, dear boy. Top to bottom."

We followed Cicely inside. The last time I'd visited had been during Cicely's Japanese period - all black lacquer, *papier maché,* screens and oriental vases. The year before that it had been Roman – with all his manservants dressed in togas – and before that he'd dabbled in Gothic. The least said of which the better.

"William Morris wallpaper," continued Cicely. "Stained glass door panels by Tiffany, and a central heating system crafted by the Keswick School. Just look at that radiator."

I gave it the eyeball. It looked like an exquisitely patterned copper plaque hanging on the wall.

"Just wait 'til you see the drawing room."

The Worcester mind is used to boggling. In my book, a day without a good boggle is a very dull day indeed. One look at Cicely's drawing room and I was transported to the fields and pleasant thoroughfares of the fair county of Boggledom, for there was a giant boiler where one would have expected something a little less metallic – like a sideboard or a dresser.

"Is that meant to be there?" I asked. It was enormous, and ostentatious. A gleaming monument of polished brass and copper. And it was in the drawing room, not hidden away in an outhouse.

"Isn't it magnificent?" said Cicely. "The very essence of what Arts and Steamcraft is all about. Craftsmanship, dear boy. Look at the detail! Look at the workmanship! How can anyone hide such a magnificent structure away in a closet? Artistry deserves to be celebrated. Flaunt it, I say."

I was still boggling. If Jules Verne ever took up interior design, this would be his drawing room. The whole room looked as though it could take off into the clouds or dive towards the centre of the earth. There was so much brass and copper pipe and pressure dials, the furniture looked like an afterthought.

"But that's enough of me," continued Cicely. "What are you doing here, dear boy? I'd heard you'd gone over to the dark side."

"The dark side?"

"The Season, dear boy. Deserting us poor bachelors for those dashing debs."

"Aunt's orders, I'm afraid. It was The Season or the Foreign Legion, and I've never liked deserts."

"All that sand," said Cicely making a face.

"Quite. But talking of debs and what not, I have a bit of a rummy request to make of you, Cicely, old chap."

"You're not going to ask me to marry you, are you? I don't think your Aunt Bertha would approve."

"No, nothing like that. I need you to dress me up as a deb. The full works – white gown, tiara, wig – spare no expense. And I need it by this afternoon."

"Really?" said Cicely, stepping back to give me the top to toe once over. "I think blue would suit you better, dear boy. White is so anaemic."

"Sorry, Cicely, I've got to be able to pass muster as a real deb. White it has to be."

He stroked his chin with his right hand and circumnavigated the Reginald. "You're much the same size as Archie Segrave. I did a white gown for him last year. I should be able to borrow it."

"I knew you'd come up trumps! While we're on the subject of dresses, I have another request."

"I'm all ears."

"Reeves here needs to be dressed up as a duchess."

Cicely's left eyebrow – always the more expressive of the two – rose a good half inch. "The deb and the duchess?" he said, his eyes taking on a distant vacant look. "I've never heard of that one. Is it a re-enactment? A tableau vivant perhaps?"

"Not quite. Which brings me to my third and rummiest request, Cicely, old bean. Can you swing an invitation to the palace for me and Reeves this afternoon? I need to be presented to Her Majesty, and Reeves here, has to be my sponsor. He's the dowager Duchess of Tintagel."

The request was too much for Cicely's right eyebrow. It rose even higher than his left and was pursued towards the hairline by his upper lip. If the Tableaux Vivants society handed out prizes for the best surprised haddock tableau, Cicely would have won hands down.

"It's for a good cause," I added. "I need to catch a eunuch."

I hadn't thought it possible, but Cicely looked even more surprised.

"If I may explain, sir," said Reeves, addressing the startled haddock. "Mr Worcester has recently become a gentleman's consulting detective and is at present engaged in a case involving the abduction of debutantes. Seven of the young ladies have gone missing in the past six weeks, and it is Mr Worcester's desire to pose as a debutante at the Royal Caledonian ball this evening in order to entrap the abductor who may, or may not, be a eunuch."

"Don't forget the orang-utan, Reeves."

"I fear it would be impossible to forget the orang-utan, sir. It is etched deeply in my memory."

The startled haddock regained his composure. "Should I ask about the orang-utan, Reeves?"

"I would not recommend it, sir."

"Well, Reggie, dear boy, you *are* full of surprises."

"Needless to say this is all hush-hush, old chap. Not a word to anyone. I don't want half the Sloths turning up tonight to watch."

"My lips are sealed. I don't think I could do the story justice if I tried."

"So, how about it, Cicely? Can you swing it at the palace? I remember you talking about some acquaintance or other you were chummy with at Buck House."

"That'll be Torquil. He's the Queen's equerry. It *is* rather short notice, but he is very efficient. I'll give him a buzz. What name shall I say? Regina Worcester?"

I'd decided on the way over, in consultation with Reeves, that I'd have to be American. It would be too risky to try and pass myself off as British – people would wonder why they'd never heard of me. But an American heiress, with oodles of money, could enter society from nowhere. I was going to be Millicent Boston, daughter of a cattle baron. Or maybe a railway magnet, whatever a railway magnet was – presumably someone attracted to railways. Whatever he was – magnet or baron – he'd hit upon the plan to send me to Europe and had written to his old friend the Dowager Duchess to ask her to put me up.

Five minutes later Cicely returned. "It's on," he said. "Four o'clock sharp. Now, what's your curtsy like? You *do* know Her Majesty insists on the full court curtsy?"

I gave it a go, bending the old knee and trying to look demure and stately with my hands posed balletically.

"No, no, no," said Cicely. "That'll never do. It's a *deep* curtsy with your knee almost touching the floor. Like this. And whatever you do, don't wobble."

We spent the next ten minutes practising. I'd never realised curtsying was so hard. According to Cicely, debs spent years practising. And it wasn't just the one curtsy, one had to curtsy to all the royals present, then walk backwards out of the Queen's presence in a floor length gown with a three yard train.

"Are your gyroscopes up to curtsying, Reeves?" I asked. "You'll have to do one too."

"I think a little extra oil for my knee joint may be judicious, sir. I should not like to squeak in the Royal presence."

~

Cicely said he'd need a couple of hours to collect the dresses and shop for all the extras. Apparently there's quite a dress etiquette for presentations to the Queen. Feathers are in, tiaras are out. And one needs a veil and train. Not to mention shoes of an appropriate size.

I thought it best to have an early lunch and meet Cicely back at his house afterwards. In the meantime, Reeves and I would practise curtsies, deportment and female elocution.

We Worcesters are not ones to boast, but I thought my American accent was top notch. I'd spent a month in New York the previous summer and modelled my voice on an actress I'd met at the Lyceum.

"Your turn, Reeves," I said. "Did I mention the Dowager Duchess has a broad Cornish accent?"

Reeves's disapproving facial muscle twitched. "You did not, sir."

"Didn't I? Must have slipped my mind. Yes, it was one of the reasons she left society. You'll have to speak like a pirate, Reeves."

"I think not, sir."

"Verisimilitude, Reeves. If that's a word. Is it a word, Reeves?

"It is, sir."

"Well then, that's the word – verisimilitude. It's the reason I must speak like a cowgirl and you as a pirate. Actors do it all the time."

"I am not a thespian, sir."

I thought it time the young master put his foot down.

"Is this Reeves speaking?" I drew out the Reeves syllable and put a little emotional timbre into it for effect. I'd seen Rose Le Clerq do something similar as Lady Bracknell at the St. James's Theatre in '95.

"Yes, sir. It is Reeves, not a pirate."

Lady Bracknell having failed, I resorted to pleading. "But why? It's not your gyroscopes again, is it?"

"No, sir. It is a matter of good taste. As no one in society has seen – or heard – the Dowager Duchess for a good many years, I think it entirely possible that Her Grace would have obtained elocution lessons from a visiting thespian and would now speak like this." Reeves twitched his neck and his voice changed instantly. "Is this an acceptable voice, sir?"

Except for the fact it sounded remarkably similar to my Aunt Bertha, it was. Though I have to admit to a certain degree of disappointment. The prospect of watching Reeves's timbers being shivered as he introduced me to the Queen with a merry, 'Ooo, arrr, Vicky, me 'earty. This 'ere young maid be Millie from yonder Americky,' would have been a pleasant one.

~

I dined on smoked salmon and caviar. I wasn't sure if caviar rated as fish or eggs when it came to brain food, but one would think it would add a little extra vim to the grey cells - maybe help with those embryonic thoughts that are not quite all there.

The trough emptied of its last morsel, we drove over to Cicely's to find that he'd converted his dining room into a dressing room. His Regency dining table was covered in dresses and petticoats, and he had two footmen in attendance to help us get in and out of them.

"We'll do the fitting first, dear boy," said Cicely. "I'm sure there'll have to be one or two adjustments made. I'll pin the dresses and James and Edward here will do the taking in and letting out. Who's first? Beauty before steam?"

I stripped down to my undergarments and was rather surprised to be handed a corset.

"Is this really necessary, Cicely?"

"Essential, dear boy. Your body has to go in where it has never gone in before. And we have to take at least five inches off your waist."

I looked at Reeves and wondered if wearing a corset ranked up there with talking like a pirate.

"Reeves won't need one," said Cicely. "A dowager duchess is allowed a modicum of leeway. But a deb's body has to be trained with whalebone."

As James the footman, his knee pushing into the small of my back, strapped me into that ancient instrument of torture, I couldn't help but wonder how large these whales would be if it weren't for their bones keeping them in.

Next came the shoes, the petticoats, the dress, the veil, the train and the wig. Somewhere below me, there was so much dress in the way I couldn't see, Cicely pinned and primped and measured until he was satisfied that Millicent

Boston passed muster.

Reeves took his turn stoically, uttering not a word - other than the occasional 'I think not, sir.' His transformation was remarkable. A bit on the stern side, but then dowager duchesses have a lot to be stern about.

It took almost as long to undress as it had to dress. James and Edward took our clothes away to alter and Reeves and I became men again, except for our footwear, which Cicely insisted we leave unchanged.

"You have to get used to walking in heels. And you simply must, dear boy, learn how to walk like a deb. Keep your head straight at all times and glide. Like this."

He glided across the floor, keeping his head erect and motionless, then glided back.

"Now you, Reggie."

I gave it a go.

"No, no, no! You're positively bouncing, dear boy. Your head is bobbing up and down like a ship at sea. Less bounce, more glide."

It was all very well for Cicely, but we Worcesters are natural bobbers. We are born with a bouncing gait. And I'd recently dined on salmon, who are natural leapers.

Reeves took his turn and, whether it was down to superior gyroscopes or the quietening effects of spending fourteen years in a cupboard, he glided like a deb born to it. His head remained erect and motionless, his feet slid over the Axminster as though it were ice.

My turn again. And again after that. I wouldn't say I emerged from the exercise as an expert, but I did emerge.

Next came the make-up

"Will Reeves's skin take rouge?" asked Cicely "Or do I need to apply some sort of undercoat?"

"I believe my synthetic skin is formulated to accept cosmetics, sir, though I would appreciate it if such additions were kept to a minimum."

"The barest, I assure you, dear boy. I just have to make you look older. What age is the Dowager Duchess, Reggie? Sixty?"

I must say that when it comes to costumes and make-up, Cicely ranks up there with the best. He was transforming Reeves before my eyes. With the addition of the wig and gown, I couldn't have told Reeves from a real dowager duchess.

I only hoped my transformation was as good.

As soon as the final touches were applied, it was back to deportment class.

"Remember, Reggie, glide and keep your head straight. Remember those three feathers in your hair. Her majesty insists on all debs having them arranged in the Prince of Wales style - erect - not flopped over."

One thing to be said about being strapped into a corset - it certainly helped take the bounce out of the Worcester gait. I was having too much trouble trying to suck air into my lungs to bounce.

After the gliding came the curtsy and the walking backwards. The latter I'd been dreading. How can anyone walk backwards in a floor length gown with a three yard train?

"Don't worry about stepping on the train, dear boy. The trick is to catch it. The Palace has a groom whose job it is to step forward and pick up your train as soon you're ready to depart. He'll throw it up into the air and it's your job to catch it with your left arm and let it drape there."

This sounded a rummy way to run a presentation, but as the poet says, 'ours is not to reason why, ours is but to catch and glide.'

We ran through the entire presentation several times. Cicely played the Queen and sat on a dining chair at the far end of the room. Reeves glided in, curtsied and spoke his lines. I beetled in, gliding in between breaths, curtsied to all the chairs, kissed Cicely's ring, then threw out my left arm before proceeding backwards and hoping James had thrown my train within catching distance.

I only fell over the once. And that was James's fault for throwing the train in the air so that it fell over my head.

Twenty attempts later, I had it down to a tee.

"How are you arriving at the Palace?" asked Cicely. "Have you booked a carriage?"

"No need. I have the Stanley outside."

"What! Not that two-seater? You can't drive yourself to the Palace in a two-seater. You'll ruin the dress! I'll call for a cab. James call Fotheringay's immediately."

The cab arrived and an emotional Cicely, flanked by James and Edward, waved us off.

"Good luck with the eunuch, dear boy. And don't worry, you'll be the belle of the ball."

SEVEN

There was a row of carriages outside the Palace and I instructed our cabby to pull in at the back. Reeves spotted a deb and her family making their way towards the Palace and we did a spot of fast gliding to catch up with them. Luckily it was neither raining nor windy, for one strong gust of wind under my gown and I feared Reginald would have glided all the way down Pall Mall at tree height.

Once inside the Palace we were conducted to the St. James Gallery, where eight other debs were nervously fanning themselves and being offered soothing words by their sponsors.

"Can you see anyone who looks like a Torquil, Reeves? Cicely said he'd be here to meet us."

"I think that gentleman over there is trying to attract your attention, sir."

Reeves, as ever, was spot on. We glided in the equerry's direction, to a quiet location at the other end of the gallery.

"Millicent?" he asked as we hove to.

"That's me," I said, slipping into my cowgirl accent. "Torquil?"

"My word," said Torquil, casting an appreciative eye. "Cicely *has* surpassed himself. I'd never have known you weren't a deb. Anyway, here's your card. I've filled it in. All you have to do is hand it to the Lord Chamberlain when it's your turn to enter the drawing room. He's the one that looks like a walrus."

I took the card.

"You'll go in last," said Torquil. "Debs are presented in order of precedence and Cicely said your father would be a colonial so you'll be at the back. And, whatever you do, *don't* look at the Queen's feet."

"Why not?"

"She has four of them, which makes her a little sensitive on the subject."

"Four?" I'd heard she'd had her legs replaced but one would have thought they'd have given her the right number of feet.

"Yes, she had to have stabilisers added last month to help her balance."

If the fair county of Boggledom had a palace, I was there – sitting on the terrace in a bath chair, contemplating feet.

"May I ask if that was Doctor Tregorran's work?" asked Reeves.

"Yes. You know of him?" said Torquil.

"I have heard of him, sir," said Reeves.

"He's a regular miracle worker," said Torquil. "He fitted an implant for the Prince of Wales yesterday. I believe the Prince is trying it out on Mrs Keppel this very moment."

~

As four o'clock approached, we took our position at the back of the line. Nine debs waited, dressed in floating islands of white, their sponsors at their sides, and a hoard of butterflies flapping away inside each and every stomach. Then an aide barked a command and the line began to glide forward.

"Steady the buffs, Duchess," I said to Reeves. "Here we go."

It took an age for the line to move. I listened intently. Names were called and dresses rustled, but I didn't hear a single rip or scream.

It's at moments like this when people turn to God. Or possibly drink. I certainly could do with a fortifier. It's not every day one's presented to a Royal quadruped while dressed as a woman.

The line of debs in front of me dwindled. Soon there was only one, and then off she toddled too. I shuffled forward to allow myself a peek around the corner into the drawing room. It may not have been etiquette, but I wasn't going into that room blind. I watched as the deb's sponsor curtsied, then peeled off from her charge and took up a position to the side of the drawing room. I could now see the Queen. She was a small round figure dressed in black, looking not unlike a Christmas pudding – though with less holly and more feet. She was perched on the throne next to what looked like a hookah. I could see puffs of steam wafting from the top. Then my view was blocked by the deb.

No sooner had the deb stopped curtsying than a liveried

aide stepped forward and lifted her train, waiting until she started her backwards glide before tossing the train high above her head. She caught it on her arm without moving her head in the slightest. This would be a tough act to follow.

My turn came and I was out of the traps like a good 'un. I may not have had the grace of a trained deb, but I had pace. I launched myself towards the Lord Walrus and handed him my card.

"Her Grace, the Dowager Duchess of Tintagel, and Miss Millicent Boston," announced the Lord Chamberlain.

Reeves had a good turn of foot too, for a sixty year-old. He curtsied to the Queen and was off, executing a perfect peeling glide towards the line of courtiers milling on the right.

I waited for an aide to straighten out my train before pointing the right hoof queenwards and sliding forward into a glide of epic proportions. Thinking back it was more of a tango glide as I fear I led with my right shoulder. But I did keep my head still and feathers erect.

Then down I went into a court curtsy, first to the Queen, then to all other royals present, and I suspect a footman too. Stepping forward, I averted my gaze from the Queen's many feet and fastened both eyeballs to her ring, to which I pressed the Worcester lips before springing back into another curtsy.

I don't know if it was the heat or the tightness of the corset, but all that curtsying was beginning to take its toll. I felt decidedly light-headed and, as I straightened up for my backward glide, I started to sway. Suddenly everything went hazy. Not because I was about to pass out, but because my wobble had positioned my head under the falling train. I was veiled, and my feathers probably flattened. But I kept going, executing a fast glide shuffle as far and as speedily away from the Queen's presence as I could. There's nothing like panic to chase away any thoughts of fainting. As soon as I saw the veiled outline of a door, I was through it and, lifting my gown, I legged it down the corridor.

When Reeves caught up with me, I'd removed the train from my hair and made a passable attempt to resurrect the feathers. I'm not sure if debs can be struck off, but I wasn't taking any chances.

"Did anyone say anything, Reeves?" I asked. "I don't have to do it again, do I?"

"No, sir. Your regrettable accident was put down to your

colonial upbringing. I mentioned the fact that there were very few good schools for young ladies in the state of New York and how hard you had been trying since your arrival in England."

~

Back at the flat I managed to grab a few hours of corset-less bliss before Reeves strapped me back in. One wonders how debs make it through the season. And whether their stomachs ever find their way back home. Mine was still hiding somewhere in my rib cage.

I spent my corset-less hours stretched out in deep reflection upon my chaise longue, a stiff cocktail in one hand and my chin in the other. Preparation was something we consulting detectives were pretty hot on. Most of our cases were solved in the armchair, not in dark alleyways.

After ten minutes of deep thought the only conclusion I'd come to was that my second drink should be a Manhattan. My little grey cells, after their earlier bout of light-headedness, needed a change of stimulant.

"Any ideas about tonight, Reeves?" I asked as he poured the thought-restorer.

"I was thinking about the psychology of the individual, sir."

"Did it do any good?"

"From the little reading I have managed on the subject, sir, it would appear that criminals are widely held to be creatures of habit."

"Well this one certainly is. He steals one deb and can't stop."

"Indeed, sir. I was speculating more along the lines of pattern. Does he abduct a particular type of young lady? Those with fair hair perhaps. If he did, we would know which young ladies to pay special attention to tonight."

If any doubt still lingered about Reeves's brain's rightful place amongst the Seven Wonders, this just about skewered it.

"Reeves, fetch the debs illustrated guide."

I flicked through the pages, searching for the missing debs and studying their pictures. I couldn't believe it. If ever a theory deserved to be right, this one did. But some girls were fair and others were dark. I looked for other similarities – the schools they'd attended, their looks, their names, their shape. Not a sausage. It looked like the eunuch was taking potluck.

I handed the guide back to Reeves and took a long disappointed drink.

"I do have another idea, sir."

"You do?"

"Yes, sir. It concerns the abductor's *modus operandi.* We know that he, or she, has a habit of not leaving by the door."

"He, she, or *it*, Reeves. Don't forget the orang-utan."

"Quite, sir. Therefore I would suggest we arrive late for the ball and take a drive around the building, paying special attention to any ladders, loiterers, or carriages parked somewhat away from the others."

Reeves had done it again. The man was a veritable Phoenix. Set fire to one plan and up he pops with another!

"Should we check the roof for orang-utans?"

"Unfortunately, sir, the venue for the Royal Caledonian this year is the Hotel Cecil."

Reeves didn't have to say any more. The Hotel Cecil was the largest hotel in the world, with four vast wings covering several acres, and roofs that resembled a minor mountain range running along the Embankment skyline – all domes, spires, chimneys and dormers. A whole army of orang-utans could hide up there for a week without being spotted.

And I could see other problems.

"Are you sure it's at the Cecil?"

"Positive, sir. I checked *The Times*."

"Well, this is going to make things dashed difficult tonight, what? The place is a labyrinth. There have to be several hundred windows."

"Seventeen hundred, I believe, sir."

"You amaze me, Reeves. How do you know all this stuff? One would think a person who'd spent the last fourteen years locked in a cupboard would be a trifle out of touch viz. hotel windows. Wasn't the Cecil built during your incarceration?"

"It was, sir, but newspapers are surprisingly informative these days, and I like to spend a couple of hours each day at the library of the British Museum."

I continued my deliberations while Reeves disappeared into the kitchen to prepare a light meal. As usual my thoughts ran wild and free. Which is the problem with a brain used to thinking the unthinkable – it can take the devil of a time to get anywhere, preferring to take the scenic route via the inconsequentials. Like 'would having one's stomach pushed up under one's ribs mean it was closer to the brain, so shortening the time it took for the beneficial effects of a lightly grilled turbot to reach the little grey cells?'

Or 'would having one's stomach constricted reduce the amount of brain-restorer that could be taken on?'

I was flapping about on the horns of that very d. when another thought gambolled past. How would one bait a hook to catch a eunuch? A deb was the obvious answer but, with a ball full of debs, how could one make Millicent Boston irresistible?

I poured myself another Manhattan from the pitcher Reeves had left on my side table and pondered some more. I hummed a few verses from G & S. I considered the correct form of address when hailing an orang-utan, and I traced the pattern a small fly was making as it slowly circumnavigated the chandelier above my head in a series of angular circuits.

It came to me on the seventh circumnavigation. Not the fly, but the idea. Patterns and the psychology of the individual. Every deb had told their mother they'd been invited to an after-ball supper. That had to be something the eunuch had specifically told them to say. Which meant if Millicent Boston went around nonchalantly dropping hints that she'd never been to an after-ball supper and was all for ditching the Dowager Duchess and taking off for one if ever she received an invite, she'd be prime eunuch bait.

My brain may not be as large or as wondrous as Reeves's, but there are times, and I think this was one of them, when, pound for pound, it stands comparison with the Seven Unthinkable Wonders of the Modern World.

~

Ruined dress or no ruined dress, I decided to drive the Stanley to the Hotel Cecil. We might need it later for, in a chase, it was a good deal faster than a Hansom.

Reeves gave the Steamer a bit of a clean first, removing any trace of oil or grease from the pedals and the foot well, then we hitched up our skirts and arranged them as best we could. I would not recommend driving while under the influence of a corset, but when needs must...

I slowed the car as we reached the Strand. Time to start sleuthing. I could see the Hotel Cecil up ahead.

"Shall I watch the right, while you scan left, Reeves?"

"That would be my recommendation, sir."

The Hotel Cecil loomed above us to the right – nine floors

running for 300 feet along the Strand. I slowed the Stanley to a crawl. The pavements were pretty lively with people walking this way and that. A group of footmen were having a convivial smoke in a doorway. A dozen or so carriages were parked on the roadside. But no ladders or obvious loiterers.

I turned right into a side street and eyed the Cecil's east wing. It was as long as the Strand wing, but a couple of storeys lower. And the pavement was less busy. If I were a loiterer, this would be the spot I'd choose.

"Anything?" I asked Reeves.

"We do appear to be approaching a carriage, sir, which is parked well away from the others."

I couldn't see a driver – either on the carriage or standing nearby. And as we passed, I noticed that the curtains were drawn. It was impossible to see if anyone was inside.

I kept driving, as that was the consulting detective's way. A policeman would have shouted "Ho!" pulled on the brake and rapped on the carriage door with a truncheon. Which, though admittedly bracing, would be exactly the wrong thing to do, as it would put the criminal on his guard. One has to catch the criminal red-handed – when he has the deb in his carriage, not when he's having a pre-ball snifter.

"Well?" I asked when we'd driven out of earshot. "Should we wait here and see who leaves the carriage?"

"I would not advise it, sir. The carriage may be empty. He, she, or, indeed, *it*, may have already left for the ball."

With difficulty I twisted around to take a look at the hotel frontage opposite the parked carriage. No ladders, but there was a drainpipe ascending all the way to the roof.

I tried counting the windows from the drainpipe to the corner on the Embankment, but gave up in the low twenties. The inside of the Cecil was designed along the lines of the Cretan labyrinth, presumable with the idea of preventing the guests from escaping. I'd never be able to find my way to the correct window.

We repeated our investigation along the Embankment and then back up another side street to the Strand. A line of carriages ran the entire stretch of the hotel's Embankment wing. Two carriages, fifty yards apart, were parked in the westerly side street. Neither had their curtains drawn, and both appeared to be empty.

I took the Stanley around for another half circuit, passing the mysterious carriage with the drawn curtains for a second time, before parking at the bottom of the side street, as close to the Embankment entrance as I could.

~

When we arrived at the Cecil's Victoria Hall, the ball was in full swing, and very Scottish it all looked – men in kilts, ladies with tartan sashes, all of them reeling and yipping energetically. And in the midst of all the tartan were fifty or so debs dressed in white.

Reeves handed our card to the Duke of Atholl's butler and, once announced, we were presented to the Duke and Duchess.

"So good to see you again, Esmeralda," said the Duchess to Reeves. "What have you been doing all these years?"

I froze in mid-curtsy. This was not in our plan. I'd chosen the Duchess of Tintagel because she was a recluse. I didn't expect her to meet an old friend!

Reeves appeared unruffled. "Well, I have the spent the last fourteen years in–"

I started to wobble. If Reeves said a cupboard the game was up!

"...Penzance," continued Reeves. "I'm the patron of a school for young ladies there. We have a most excellent elocution master – a Captain Flint – perhaps you have heard of him?"

"I don't believe I have," said the Duchess.

I had. Wasn't he the parrot in Treasure Island? I recovered my balance with a little difficulty and bobbed back up.

"And you, my dear, must be the American girl, Millicent," continued the Duchess. "Do you know any cowboys?"

"I know them all, Your Grace. My father being a railway magnet, the Wild West is like a second home to me. Annie Oakley, Capability Jane, Billy the Buffalo."

Reeves coughed. "I believe, having corresponded with your father – the railway mag-*nate* – that the gentleman's correct nomenclature to be Buffalo Bill, Millicent."

"The gunslinger?" I said, giving Reeves a puzzled look. "I think not. Though it is easy to get them all mixed up – the Wild West is simply teeming with Bills. Why there's even one called Wild Bill Hiccup. And wouldn't you be wild if your life were blighted by constant hiccups. I know I would."

"Oh, look," said Reeves. "I believe Lady Harcourt is hailing us. Constance, you must forgive us but I have a matter of extreme urgency to discuss with her ladyship. We must have a long talk later. Come along, Millicent."

Reeves took my arm and positively dragged me into a fast glide away from our hosts. I think the strain of lying on the hoof while dressed as a woman was getting to him.

"Don't worry, Reeves," I said. "Forget about parrots and use your giant brain to sniff out all the exits and spot the unusual. I'll start mingling."

I detached myself from my dowager escort and took out Emmeline's dance card. I'd hunt down every cove on the list and drop subtle hints that Millicent Boston was up for an after-ball supper. I'd buttonhole the suspects from my notebook too – all the limpers and high hummers. One of them had to be our eunuch.

The first suspect I came across was The Honourable Rollo Dingwall-Herries. I floated in front of him, giving him a sideways glance from behind my fan. Whether The Honourable Rollo was shortsighted or just slow on the uptake, I couldn't fathom. So I reverted to plan B and reversed straight into him, giving him a substantial nudge in the gentleman's area with a stout bustle.

I had his attention.

"I am *so* sorry," I said. "I didn't see you there."

"Quite all right," said The Hon. Rollo, his eyes watering and his spine somewhat inclined forward.

"I'm new to these parts," I said, holding out my hand. "Millicent Boston, of the Wild West Bostons."

"Oh," said Rollo, his eyes clearing. He took my hand and bowed, remaining in the stooped position for a good three seconds longer than etiquette demanded. "Rollo Dingwall-Herries, of the Perthshire Dingwall-Herries, at your service, Miss Boston. How are you finding London?"

"Confusing, Mr D-H. I'm a simple country girl, brought up to stalk buffalo and ride shotgun on my father's trains. I'm not used to society. Though I was told by my good friend Billy the Buffalo that while in London I simply had to attend an after-ball supper. 'Millie,' he said. 'There's nothing like it. First chance you get, dump the duchess and get yourself an invite to the swankiest after-ball supper going. You won't regret it.' Do you know of any after-ball suppers, Mr D-H?"

The Hon. Rollo's eyes – which had been myopic, then watery, then clear – were now positively shining.

"I'll ask around. I'm sure I can find one."

"That is most gallant of you, Mr D-H. I can't wait."

"Would you like to dance, Miss Boston?"

"I would *love* to dance, but I think you have a business matter to attend to, do you not, Mr D-H?"

"I do?"

"A certain supper invitation?"

"Oh, yes! Rather!" He bowed and beetled off into the crowd.

That, I thought, went exceptionally well. I'd studied the art of male manipulation at the feet of masters. Aunt Bertha, Lady Lucretia Goshawk, Great Aunt Boadicea. And one doesn't endure eight – or is it nine? – engagements without learning a thing or two.

Now I had to bait and hook the other suspects.

I was halfway through my list when I heard my old friend Percy Tuffington-Scrope hailing me from starboard. "Miss Boston!" he said. "Wait up."

Waiting up was the last thing I wanted to do. I'd known Tufty man and boy, and, more to the point, he'd known *me* man and boy. Would he know me man, boy, and woman? If anyone was going to recognise me, it'd be him.

I covered as much of my face with my fan as I could and turned. "Yes?"

"Would you care to dance, Miss Boston?"

"Unfortunately, my card is full, Tufty."

"Tufty? You know my name?"

"No!" I said, louder and a bit deeper than expected. Steady the buffs, Reginald! "Just a lucky guess. Is your name Tufty?"

"Lucky guess? More like fate. Do you believe in fate, Miss Boston."

This was getting worse. Tufty's face, moon-like at the best of times, was now moonstruck as well. I recognised the look. The man could fall in love at the drop of hat.

"No, Mr Tufty, I do not believe in fate. I was only telling Mrs Anstruther-Smothers the other day...." I waited, expecting Tufty to interject the moment he heard the name of his kidnapped beloved's mother dropped into the conversation, but he didn't say a word. I don't think he even registered her name. He just stared at me with rapt puppy dog eyes.

"Are you all right, Mr Tufty?"

"I'm more than all right, Millie. May I call you Millie?"

"If you must."

"I must. It's such a beautiful name. Millie. I shall compose a poem."

"Steady on." I've heard Tufty's poems. I believe the recent Treaty of Paris had them outlawed.

"Oh, Millie," he said clutching his heart. "I feel as if I've known you for years."

I began to look around for Reeves. This was exactly the time a gentleman's personal automaton, even if recently elevated to the peerage, should race to the aid of the young master.

Not a dowager tiara in sight.

"Isn't that Lucretia Anstruther-Smothers over there?" I asked, peering into the distance.

"Who?"

"I heard she was the most beautiful deb in London."

"She couldn't be. Not while you're here."

I wasn't sure how much more of this I could take. I couldn't even feign a heart attack. Tufty would undoubtedly attempt to revive me and there would be face slapping and clothes loosening.

"Miss Boston! There you are. I've been looking for you everywhere." The Honourable Rollo, flushed and out of breath, appeared out of nowhere, his initial smile fading as he caught sight of Tufty. "Oh. Who are you?"

"Percy Tuffington-Scrope. Who are you?"

"Rollo Dingwall-Herries. Is this man bothering you, Miss Boston?"

"*Millie* and I were talking, Mr Dingbat-Herring. In *private*. I think you should leave."

"I think *you* should leave."

"I will not!"

"I think you will!"

It was like watching two well-dressed stags locking velvet. I took a step back. Maybe I could slip away before they noticed?

The Hon. Rollo turned a pleading eye my way. "I have the supper invitation, Miss Boston. Tell him to go away."

"How dare you!" said Tufty. "If anyone's inviting Millie to supper, it's I."

"No, it isn't!"

"Yes, it is!"

It was at that moment that the thought-fuelling powers of a lightly-grilled turbot, which had been migrating upchannel through my constricted ribcage towards the spawning grounds of the Worcester brain, kicked in. I had an idea, and, rising to my full height – including heels – channelled

Aunt Bertha at her most intimidating.

"Gentlemen! Desist immediately."

A pair of stags, however well-dressed, are no match for a Mastodon in full cry. They unlocked their antlers and wilted.

"Is this what passes for manners in London? Arguing in front of a lady? Billy the Buffalo wouldn't stand for it, and neither shall I. Good *night*, gentlemen."

And with that I turned and, head held high, set sail for the far end of the ballroom.

I found Reeves on his own standing by a table and moored alongside. "You have to protect me, Reeves. I am being pursued."

"By a eunuch, sir?"

"Anything but."

EIGHT

I told Reeves all, starting with the good news – that I was halfway through my list of suspects – and ending with the bad – that the odds on Millicent Boston becoming engaged before the end of the ball were shortening by the second.

"I don't know what it is about me, Reeves, but I appear to be some kind of engagement magnet. Do you think this is why Sherlock Holmes smokes a pipe? To put people off?"

"It is not a theory I have heard, sir."

"I mean, it's dashed difficult interviewing suspects if you're worrying all the time they might whip out a troth and give it a good plighting."

"Indeed, sir. Perhaps that is why Doctor Watson is wont to carry a service revolver about his person."

Once again Reeves had sighted the nail and given it what for with his giant hammer. I would send out for a service revolver first thing tomorrow morning.

"Enough of my troubles, Reeves. How goes it with you? Any suspicious characters spotted. A Sheikh in wolf's clothing looking for a harem?"

"I do have suspicions about Prince Otto von Smith, sir."

The name was familiar. I checked Emmeline's dance card and there it was. Prince Otto von Smith, the cove profligate with the ponies.

"What kind of name is 'von Smith,' Reeves?"

"An unusual one, sir. It is not a family I am familiar with."

"German do you think?"

"He does have the look of a Prussian, sir. In both bearing and choice of upper lip ornamentation. But one would think his name would refer to a town or principality."

"Perhaps his mother married a Smith?"

"That is one possibility, sir, though I suspect he may not have had a mother."

I was astonished. "You think he was raised by wolves?"

"No, sir, I–"

"Orang-utans!" The notion came to me in a flash. It would explain everything. "He's not looking for a harem, Reeves. He's looking for a family! Sisters and playmates and the like. All those years denied human society have given him a craving, not to say dented his perspective somewhat. I expect it's his foster family who are helping him get the debs down the drainpipes."

Reeves coughed. "An imaginative interpretation, sir, but what I was about to say was that I suspect Prince Otto to be an automaton."

"What?"

"An automaton, sir. I noticed that he has the habit of blinking one twentieth of a second before he begins to speak. I observed him for a full five minutes and the interval was always one twentieth of a second. A human being would not exhibit such accuracy or regularity."

"You can measure time to one twentieth of a second, Reeves?"

"I have that ability, sir. I believe my creator had Swiss ancestry on his mother's side."

"No cuckoos though?" I eyeballed Reeves's forehead looking for signs of a trap door. "Your forehead doesn't spring open on the hour and bring forth cuckoos?"

"No, sir. One would suppose that would defeat the object of making me appear human."

Reeves, as always, had a point.

"But what does all this mean, Reeves? If Prince Otto's an automaton, where does the orang-utan fit in? Did the ape find Prince Otto in the jungle?"

I was still attached to the idea of a man raised by apes – even a mechanical one. It fitted the facts so neatly.

"I was thinking, sir, that the presence of an automaton might remove the need for the family *Pongo*. If Prince Otto is an automaton with augmented climbing abilities, he'll be able to climb down a drainpipe whilst carrying an unconscious young lady."

I thought of Kali and the bizarre collection of automata I'd witnessed at Lady Harcourt's. Reeves was right. Prince Otto might very well kick off his shoes and reveal a set of prehensile feet!

"But why would he want to abduct debs?" I asked Reeves. "Has he gone doolally?"

"It is possible that his programming has begun to malfunction, sir. Equally it is possible that someone has programmed him to behave exactly the way he does. We may be looking for a second person."

"A sultan or a sheikh," I said.

"Or, indeed, a person involved in the manufacture of Prometheans, sir. You recall our encounter with Miss Smith and the Collossus of Blackwater?"

I could scarcely forget. It's not every day one meets a giant talking pig. "But why would such a person abduct a herd of debs, Reeves? Aren't these people grave robbers, on the lookout for spare parts to reanimate?"

"I was reading an improving book on the subject the other night, sir, and ... it would appear the best results are achieved when the body parts are fresh."

"Oh."

This was not something Reginald Worcester wished to dwell upon. Or even consider. It has been my experience that coves who spend their lives mired in gloom, expecting the worst, invariably find it. Whereas chaps like me - who go through life with a song in their heart and a firm expectation that every cloud has silver linings to spare, are invariably proved right. I was sure that Emmeline and the other debs were alive. In danger and under imminent threat, undoubtedly - but alive. And we'd find them before the night was out. Any other thought was too dark to contemplate.

"So, what's the plan, Reeves? Shall I track down Prince Otto and bring up my deep desire to experience an after-ball supper?"

"That would be the first item on my list of recommendations, sir."

"You have more?"

"I would like to test my theory that Prince Otto is an automaton, sir."

"How do you propose to do that?"

"Well...."

Reeves's voice trailed off and his expression changed from dowager duchess to dowager sheep.

"Well, what, Reeves?"

"No, sir. I couldn't possibly say."

"Why not?"

"It is...." He paused for a lot longer than a twentieth of a second. "...a delicate matter."

"Go on, Reeves. I insist. We're both men of the world. Well, I am. Your fourteen years in a cupboard may have sheltered you somewhat."

"Well, sir. The gentleman *is* wearing a kilt, and the Eightsome Reel is a particularly lively dance, and centrifugal force, being what it is, hemlines will undoubtedly rise...."

I was astonished. "Are you suggesting I look under his kilt?"

"I would never recommend it as a rule, sir, but ... you may be afforded a glimpse of a nozzle."

"A what?"

"A nozzle, sir. Unlike British automata, which have female connectors located in the navel for attachment to the life-giving steam outlet pipe, German automata have male connectors."

"Nozzles?"

"Precisely, sir. These nozzles are located a little lower than the navel and–"

I shook my head. "No, Reeves, there will be no nozzle glimpsing. We Worcesters have a code, and that code draws the line at bending down and peering up kilts looking for nozzles."

"I did mention I was hesitant to raise the matter, sir."

"I'm not surprised."

~

"Prince Otto is over there, sir," said Reeves, inclining a tiara towards a group by a pillar. "He's the gentleman with the medals."

And what a lot of medals. His chest positively shone with gold and silver. He even had a gold star on his sporran. Stout calves descended from his kilt, and if he were hiding a pair of prehensile feet beneath his brogues, he was hiding them well.

Did he look Prussian? He had the waxed moustache and an upright, shoulders back, military bearing. But he looked more Italian to me – the medals, the slicked-back dark hair, the olive complexion. He looked more like the kind of cove that would inhabit a Parisian Tango club.

And he was talking to a deb.

"I'll nip in close and listen," I said to Reeves. "If you see Tufty or anyone looking like an Honourable Rollo coming my way, head them off."

Before I could reach the Prince and his companion, the next reel was announced, and the pair of them oiled off onto the dance floor.

I watched from the sidelines. The Prince cut quite a dash

and, as he spun and reeled, his kilt began to lift. I started to feel somewhat uncomfortable. A wayward piece of turbot – for where else could such thoughts originate? – kept coming up with all manner of ways to accomplish a furtive nozzle glimpse.

I decided to leave the *environs* of the dance floor post-haste and wait until the reel concluded. As soon as it had, I pounced, detaching the deb with a whispered message that the Prince of Wales was desirous to meet her, and was waiting for her on the terrace with what looked like the largest diamond brooch I'd ever seen. She left in a blur of white.

I curtsied to the Prince and lowered my eyes.

"Hello, little miss," he said. "Would you like a pony?"

I wasn't sure how many ponies this Prince had or where he kept them all, but one had to wonder how the man was going to get through the season. Had he bought a job lot and was anxious to dispose of them all?

"Not at this juncture, your highness," I said. "Though thanks awfully and all that. Back home I travel pony express all the time. When I'm not riding shotgun on my father's trains that is."

"Your father, he is with you tonight?"

"No, he's back in America watching over the trains. Or having supper with Billy the Buffalo. Talking of supper...."

I launched into my after-ball supper pitch, keeping a close eye on the Prince's face as I did so. I wanted to see his reaction.

I don't know if he blinked one twentieth of a second before he spoke, but his left eyebrow leapt like a hairy salmon at the mention of my desire to ditch the duchess at the first opportunity.

"You have adventurous spirit, little miss," he said. "I too have adventurous spirit. Would you like a ride in my Zeppelin?"

"You have your own Zeppelin?

"I have latest model – two-seater sports Zeppelin. He is parked on the roof."

Like Saul reprising earlier events at the Gates of Damocles, I was once more struck by the lightning bolt of revelation. A Zeppelin on the roof! That's how he was doing it. No need for ladders or orang-utans. He had his own carriage.

"Are you feeling unwell, little miss?"

"No, not in the least. I think someone just walked over my grave. Not that I have a grave. I've never been dead. Or re-animated. No, siree. Not me. I'm one hundred per cent alive. Isn't a Zeppelin a bit big to park on a roof?"

I may have teetered for a while, but I think I got away with it.

The Prince paused before replying. "Not the new two-seater sports model. He is only fifty feet long. Very compact. German engineering at his best."

"Well, in that case, I'd love to take a spin, your highness. Do you always park it on roofs? Or does your home have a hangar?"

"I have hangar for when she is windy. But do not worry, little miss, there is no wind tonight. Perfect night for the flying. I can show you your house from air. Maybe park on your roof, yes?"

"Indeed. Talking about houses, whereabouts is your house over here? You do have a house over here, don't you, your highness?"

"I have many houses. Come, we dance, yes?"

"Rather."

I followed the Prince onto the dance floor, the little grey cells working furiously. If I could find out where he was keeping the debs, Reeves and I could hop in the Stanley and get there before the Prince. The alternative was allowing myself to be chloroformed and taken there as an unconscious prisoner.

Call me old fashioned, but I preferred option one.

It wasn't going to be easy. I had to question him without arousing his suspicion. If ever a consulting detective was in need of Reeves's giant brain, this was that moment.

And I don't recall Sherlock Holmes ever questioning a suspect while attempting a Foursome Reel. It had been years since I'd attempted a Foursome, and with all the swinging and figure-of-eight-ing and swapping partners, I was having a hard enough time remembering the steps. All the cogent questions were lost to centrifugal force and light-headedness – for which I blame the corset. How one is supposed to dance energetically and breathe at the same time when your lungs and stomach are occupying the same space is beyond me.

As soon as the dance ended, I marshalled what little grey cells I had left and launched into my first question. "What time are we leaving?" I asked.

"The night she is still young, yes?"

"Indeed."

I struggled to find the next question. I wasn't sure if Prince Otto was being deliberately evasive or he was just foreign. Every question I raised seemed to be brushed aside or answered with another question.

"Do you hunt, your highness?"

"Hunt?"

"To hounds. Billy the Buffalo told me everyone in England hunted and, if I got the chance, I should give it a go. *Do* you ride to hounds, your highness?"

"No, I have never done that. Perhaps I will."

I had been hoping he'd say something like the Quorn or the Pytchley – a hunt I could attach a locality to. Perhaps the time had come to be blunt. I was a gauche American after all.

"Tell me where you're staying and I'll ask someone where the closest hunt is."

"Good idea, little miss. We will talk later but, you must excuse me, I have promised next dance to Lady Boscombe."

And with that he bowed, clicked the heels of his brogues, and was off. I thought of pursuing him, but decided a consultation with the giant brain was the better option.

I found Reeves, took him aside, and spilled all.

"A Zeppelin, Reeves. Can you credit it?"

"Most surprising, sir. I had not realised they came in smaller models. I think I may need to increase the number of improving journals I read each week."

"That's all very well, Duchess," I said, lowering my voice as a group of guests sauntered by. "But what do we do now? I don't much like the idea of taking a snootful of chloroform."

"Now that we know his means of egress, miss, we could return to the automobile and await the Zeppelin's departure."

I liked this. But would we be able to see the Zeppelin? It was night, and there were two acres of roofs split between four wings. If the Zeppelin was on the Strand wing, one couldn't see it from street level on the Embankment even in daylight. Ditto for the other wings.

"We'd never spot it the dark from down there, Reeves. We must get to the roof and look for it."

"May I suggest we look from an upper window, sir? We are not suitably attired for clambering over roofs."

"You certainly may, Reeves. Lead on. I believe I saw a lift by the entrance."

We'd scarcely made ten yards when I felt a tug on my gown.

"Where do you think you're going?" said an irate voice from behind.

I turned and found myself confronted by an enraged deb.

"You've got some nerve," she said. "Spinning me that line about the Prince of Wales so you could move in on Prince Otto."

Recognition dawned. The blur in white had returned.

"Miss Boston is American, dear," said Reeves coming to my rescue. "She thinks that every distinguished gentleman with a beard is the Prince of Wales. I have tried educating her but, alas, it is difficult when one has so little to work with."

I don't think I'd have used those exact words - had I been consulted, which I had not - but they went some way to dimming the deb's ire.

"What about the diamond brooch?" she said. "And why did she say he wanted to see me?"

I thought I'd pass those excellent questions over to Reeves. In the meantime, I'd play the role handed to me and smile witlessly.

"I believe, from what Miss Boston relayed to me, that the gentleman in question said he had a brooch for the most beautiful debutante in the room. Miss Boston, not realising the gentleman was paying her a compliment, took upon herself the mission of finding the most beautiful debutante in the room and informing her of the brooch. I can see that she chose wisely."

This was oil of the *premiere cru*. The deb was transformed from charging rhinoceros to simpering cat.

"Oh," she said, flushing slightly. "Well. Yes. In that case...."

While she was still struggling for words, I thought it best to take our leave.

"Awfully nice to have met you," I said. "Sorry, must dash."

We left the ball at speed, found the lift and rode it to the top. I spotted a window on the landing overlooking the central courtyard gardens but it was difficult to see out - there was too much light in the landing. Even opening the window didn't make much difference.

"Can you see a light switch, Reeves?"

"I can see several, sir. The staircase is extremely well lit."

Reeves set about switching off everything in sight – the chandeliers, the sconces, the recessed wall lights – until a twilight gloom descended. A small aura of light percolating up the stairwell from the lower floors.

I leaned out of the window and let my eyes acclimatise. There was a three-quarters moon shining out from behind a patchwork of silver cloud. I could just about make out the roofline of the far wing and I was looking down on the roof of the west wing. But I couldn't see any Zeppelin. I looked for the tell-tale cigar shaped outline. Or would the sports model be squatter? I peered and strained but all I could see were chimneys, spires, domes, masts and dormers.

"We'll have to try the building on the Strand, Reeves."

We took the lift down and beetled outside. I thought we might be able to catch a glimpse of the Zeppelin from the street but we couldn't.

"I think we may have to park the Stanley on the far side of the river, sir. The view should be better from there."

As long as the moon didn't disappear behind one of those clouds.

We hoisted up our skirts. The pavement didn't look like it had been swept in weeks and I didn't want to return the gowns to Cicely with frayed and grubby hems. We made our way towards the Strand and from there, courtesy of another of those express lifts, to the ninth floor of the Hotel Cecil's northern wing.

"Might I suggest that I look out the window this time, sir? I believe my night vision may be superior to yours."

"By all means, Reeves. I'll get the lights."

I plunged the landing into darkness and waited. After a short while, just long enough for me to hum the opening lines of "Three Little Maids," Reeves spoke.

"I see it, sir. It is located in the central section of the Embankment wing's roof."

I switched the landing lights back on and checked my pocket watch. It was twelve thirty. The ball would probably run for another two hours. What should we do? Go back to the ball and keep an eye on Prince Otto or drive the Stanley across the river and watch the roof from there?

I posed the question to the giant brain.

"It is a difficult one, sir. We do not know if Prince Otto is acting alone in this matter. If he *is* a procurer of young ladies for a second party, it is possible that the second party is present at the ball. He, or she, may even have a hand in selecting the young ladies."

"Do you think so? The Prince didn't say, 'What ho, little miss. I'd like you to meet my good friend X.' I'm using X to specify accomplice or accomplices unknown, Reeves. In case you were wondering."

"I surmised as much, sir."

We decided to give the ball another go. The clincher being that it served drinks and I was in need of a fortifier.

~

Suitably fortified with a large single malt – all that tartan having nudged my choice of fortifier north of the border – Reeves and I found a table where we could keep an eye on the Prince. He was talking to another deb.

"Have you seen him talk to anyone who isn't a deb, Reeves?"

"I have not, sir. The foreign gentleman does appear somewhat single-minded."

"You don't think a deb could be X, do you? By X I mean–"

"The unknown accomplice, sir. Yes, I had considered the possibility. A young lady desirous of removing the competition perhaps. But I dismissed the idea as unlikely."

"You did?"

"Yes, sir. A young lady resourceful enough to kidnap seven other young ladies using an automaton and a Zeppelin, without attracting the attention of a single policeman, is not a young lady who would have difficulty with competition. She would find an easier way to achieve her desire."

I don't know how Reeves does it. He sees a knotty problem and untangles it in an instant. All I see are more knots.

I watched the Prince and pondered some more.

"Should I talk to him again, Reeves? He did offer me a ride in his Zeppelin."

"From what you told me, sir, I think it possible the Prince may have had second thoughts about the arrangement."

"It would help if he were clearer. Am I or am I not about to kidnapped? That's what I'd like to know."

"Indeed, sir. He is a most inexact kidnapper."

The next dance was announced – The Reel of the Ginger Gordon Threesomes. The Prince took the deb's hand and ... escorted her away from the dance floor.

"What's he doing?" I asked Reeves.

The pair threaded their way through the crowd and I lost sight of them.

"He may be leaving, sir," said Reeves rising from his chair. "I recommend we split up and follow."

I glided one way and Reeves glided another. The pair of us headed off in a pincer movement to keep an eye on the Prince. I wove my way between the groups and couples. At least the Prince was easy to spot, but was he heading for the bar or an exit?

He wasn't heading for the bar. He was heading for a door which led to the main hotel. He looked over his shoulder and I dodged behind a group in military attire, finding a particularly large mutton chop whisker to hide behind. When I looked again, they'd gone.

I hurried to find Reeves. We had to leave immediately.

And ran slap bang into Tufty as he was coming out of the bar.

"Millie! My angel!" He exclaimed, his voice veering towards slurred and his gait somewhat unsteady. "I thought I'd lost you! But Fate once more has thrown us together."

"No, it hasn't," I said. "Fate is waiting for me outside. Now, please, I have to leave."

He blocked my way, falling unsteadily to his knees and grasping my left hand.

"You've stolen my heart," he said.

"Please get up. You're embarrassing yourself. And if that's a troth in your pocket, put it away. This lady's not for plighting!"

NINE

Reeves and I hurried along the embankment, all the time looking up towards the roof. I couldn't see the Zeppelin, or even hear it. There was too much noise coming from the Worcester heels as they clattered upon the pavement.

We reached the Stanley and I took a bit of a breather before starting her up.

"Can you see it, Reeves?" I asked.

"No, sir. I think you will have to drive across Waterloo Bridge to get a better view."

When it comes to speed the Stanley is no slouch. It can outrun a horse and, with R. Worcester at the tiller, it can corner on two wheels. We reached Waterloo Bridge in record time, the wind whipping into our faces.

"Can you see it yet, Reeves?"

Reeves was twisting in his seat whilst holding on to his wig and tiara.

"Would it be possible for you to slow down, sir? There is rather too much vibration for me to be certain."

I gave the brake lever a good pull and the Stanley shuddered to a fast walking pace. Reeves almost flew over the front wheels, but I had my hand ready to grab him and pulled him back.

"Thank you, sir," he said.

We both swivelled in our seats and peered hotelwards. I thought I could see something moving on the roof though it was difficult to be certain. The moon was half obscured by a layer of thin cloud and the light wasn't that good.

"I see it, sir," said Reeves. "It's heading east, following the river."

I stopped the car and took the opportunity to light the Stanley's two oil lamps. The roads wouldn't be as well lit as soon as we moved away from London's main thoroughfares.

We followed the Zeppelin for miles. Luckily it appeared to be following the river and not travelling that fast, so whenever we lost sight of it, or our road veered away from the river, we were able to make a good guess as to where we would see it next.

"You don't think it's going to Germany, do you?" I asked Reeves. Its present course was certainly heading that way.

"I would be surprised if a Zeppelin of that size had the range, sir. I think it more likely he is heading for a warehouse in one of the docks."

"You think he's shipping the debs out of the country?"

"I very much hope not, sir. But it is a distinct possibility, given his course."

I'm not sure what the collective noun is for docks – a lamentation? A herd? A hickory-dickory? Whatever it is we passed a large one. The Royal Docks, all the Surrey Docks, Millwall Dock, West India Dock, East India. And where there wasn't a dock, there were wharves. On several occasions we lost sight of the Zeppelin – once we thought we'd have to turn back – but, after a minute or two, Reeves would spot it again, slowly chugging its way across the northern sky.

As we approached Blackwall we had another problem. The Blackwall tunnel was the last river crossing. If we stayed on the south bank and the Zeppelin turned north, we'd lose it. Ditto if we chose the northern bank and it headed south.

I posed the question to the giant brain.

"A difficult one, sir. The Prince does appear to be favouring the northern shore."

One does not argue with a giant brain. I took the turning for the tunnel and crossed beneath the Thames.

An hour or more passed as we snaked this way and that, following the closest road we could find to the riverbank. Sometimes these roads petered out into a swampy field or ended at a wharf and we had to turn around. At Canvey Island we had to turn a long way inland and lost the Zeppelin altogether.

"What do we do now, Reeves?" I asked.

"I fear our only recourse is to take the Southend road, sir, and hope we reacquaint ourselves with the Zeppelin further along the estuary."

It was a long way round but the Stanley could reach 60 m.p.h. on a good road with a following wind.

"We'll have to remove our tiaras, Reeves. It's going to get breezy."

"I think it wise to remove our wigs as well, sir."

I opened up the Stanley and pointed her at the dim glow

that was beginning to appear in the northeastern sky. Sunrise couldn't be much more than an hour away. I'm not sure if we reached sixty m.p.h. but it felt like it. The wind in my face was so strong I had to stop and put my goggles on, and the road – the light grey line surrounded by a mass of slightly darker grey – was coming towards me so fast it was beginning to blur.

At Leigh-on-Sea we picked up the coast road again and I was able to slow down. I found a spot with an excellent view up and down the estuary, stopped the car and removed my driving goggles.

Then began the long wait. Had we overtaken the Zeppelin? Had it landed on Canvey Island? Had it turned inland while we'd been going too fast to notice?

It must have been ten minutes before Reeves spotted it heading our way. It may have been my imagination but I thought I detected a slight twitch of a facial muscle that may have been an embryonic smile.

"I think it would be wise to extinguish the Stanley's lights until the Zeppelin passes over, sir. It is heading directly for us."

I agreed and we sat in the twilight gloom, our heads craned starwards watching the craft pass overhead. The night was so quiet I could hear the whine of its engine.

As soon as it had passed I lit the Stanley's lamps once more and drove off after it.

"Are you sure it's not heading for Germany?" I asked Reeves. "If my geography serves, we're nearly at the North Sea."

"I may be wrong, sir, but one would think there was insufficient capacity aboard to carry the requisite amount of fuel for such a long crossing."

I hoped Reeves was right. We were running out of coastline.

We drove through Southend and then on to Shoebury Ness where the coastline turned northeast. Would the Zeppelin head east for Germany or continue following the coast?

It followed the coast. But only for three miles before turning inland. And it was dropping lower in the sky. It was looking for somewhere to land!

"I recommend we hang back, sir. Our lamps make the Stanley very noticeable from the air."

I looked to seaward, the glow on the horizon was growing.

Already a little colour was seeping back into the world. The grey fields and woods were becoming flecked with greens and browns.

I stopped the car and extinguished the lights. There was enough light to drive by as long as I drove slowly and with care.

The Zeppelin was just above tree height now about a quarter of a mile ahead of us. And then it disappeared behind a line of trees. I followed the road as it bent and twisted through the landscape, slowing the car every time we came to a break in the hedgerow and peering through. Then I saw a wall up ahead and a gate. I stopped the car. The night was so still the hiss and clatter of the Stanley's engine would certainly carry.

"Come on, Reeves," I whispered. "We'll go the rest of the way on foot."

Reeves handed me my wig and tiara. "In case we're seen, sir." The man is a perfectionist.

We crept along the hedgerow. As much as two people with twenty yards of crinoline between them could creep. I couldn't see another property for miles. Whatever was behind the wall up ahead had to be the Prince's hideout.

We came to the gate - one of those ornate jobs in wrought iron standing between two brick gateposts - and I peered through. There was a gravelled drive heading towards a substantial grey shape that looked like one of those rambling Georgian rectories. I couldn't see the Zeppelin. It wasn't on the roof or the grounds at the front. But there were some lights on inside the house which, at a quarter to four in the middle of night, had to count as unusual.

I listened, but couldn't hear a thing. No voices on the wind, no feminine screams.

I opened the gate carefully and the pair of us sneaked through.

"I would recommend we eschew the gravel path, sir, and utilise the lawn," whispered Reeves.

We gathered up our skirts and followed the line of a rhododendron hedge that appeared to run the length of the property. It took us level with the house and then into the gardens at the back.

I stopped the moment I saw the Zeppelin. It was parked on the back lawn. I could see ropes or cables holding it down. They were tied to four bollards placed in a square around it.

And there were more lights on at the back of the house.

"What do we do now? Call the police?" I whispered.

"I fear that would be problematic, sir."

"You do? I thought you were all for calling the boys in blue?"

"Indeed, sir, but the situation has altered somewhat. I suspect a village sergeant might balk at searching the house and grounds of a Prince, if said Prince refused permission."

I could see Reeves's point. Prince Otto would bar his doors and threaten the sergeant with a telegram to the Chief Constable. One glimpse of all those medals and the sergeant would be unmanned.

"We need to find evidence that the young ladies are on the property, sir, in order to convince the sergeant to ignore the Prince's entreaties."

We scouted the property, furtively searching the handful of garden sheds and outbuildings. Not a single sign of a deb or a prison. If they were anywhere, it had to be inside the house.

It's not easy to sneak furtively in a corset for an extended period of time, but I persevered, creeping up to the house with a straight back and a ribcage packed to the gills with organs. As I neared the back of the house I could see a series of half-light windows to what must have been a cellar running along the length of the entire property. All the windows were barred and whitewashed on the inside.

"Dashed suspicious," I whispered to Reeves.

"Indeed, sir."

A light came on inside four of the cellar windows. I froze, then had an idea.

"Do you think you might be able to hear anything from inside?" I said, surmising that if Reeves could have superior night vision his hearing might be up to a similar standard.

Reeves slipped his left hand between the bars of one of the windows and pressed the tips of his fingers against the pane. After what Reeves had told me earlier about his nose being in his ear I wondered if I'd now discovered the location of his missing auditory organ.

Reeves didn't move for a good half minute. Then he turned and whispered. "I have a plan, sir. If you would return to the safety of the rhododendron hedge, I will join you shortly."

I exited, geranium left, sneaking a look back at Reeves now and then to see what he was doing. He appeared to be searching the flowerbed and shrubbery by the cellar windows.

I waited for him to return. "Well, Reeves?"

"The Prince is in the cellar, sir. He is not alone. There is at least one man with him and, I would think, several others within the house."

That made sense. Prince Otto would need men to guard and feed the debs, and to look after the house and grounds.

"Are the debs with him?"

"The one he abducted this evening is, sir. I do not know about the others."

"So what's the plan?"

"We need a distraction, sir. Something to entice the Prince and his henchmen to vacate the house at speed."

When it comes to thinking up distractions, Reginald Worcester is your man. I'm always distracting people. It was but the work of an instant to come up with an idea.

"We'll start a fire! Nothing gets people out of a building faster than a few puffs of smoke and a baritone yell of 'Fire! Fire!'"

"I would not recommend such an action, sir."

"You wouldn't?"

"Fire is a most unpredictable medium, sir. And if there are eight young ladies locked inside the house–"

"I wasn't thinking of a big fire, Reeves. A couple of faggots piled up against a back door."

"If I may make a suggestion, sir, I think a safer and swifter approach would be to untie the ropes holding down the Zeppelin."

"I don't follow, Reeves."

"One would think that the potential loss of something so essential to their scheme would cause the occupants of the house to exit forthwith and give chase."

"You're not proposing we fly the thing, are you, Reeves? I don't know if I could."

"No, sir. My suggestion would be too untie the cables and let it float away. That way it would travel slowly, ensuring the pursuers could see it, while, at the same time, keeping it annoyingly out of reach, thus maximising the amount of time that we would have to search the house in their absence."

I could see one giant flaw in Reeves's plan. "What if they don't notice the Zeppelin floating away?"

"That is why one of us will have to knock on their front door and tell them."

I feared the late hour was affecting Reeves's cognitive powers. "Is your pressure running low, Reeves?"

"It could be higher, sir, but I have every confidence in my plan."

"Well you'll have to do the knocking, Reeves. If the Prince answers the door he'll recognise me straight away."

"That was my intention, sir. I would suggest that you position yourself in the shrubbery by the window I was listening at and await an opportunity to break in through the back door. I will endeavour to effect entry at the front."

"Let me get this right, Reeves. You're going to knock on the door in full evening dress and tiara and say, 'Excuse me, have you a lost a Zeppelin?'"

"Yes, sir. There are times when a direct approach is preferential."

It is a sad thing to witness the decline of a giant intellect. A fully pressurised Reeves with a snootful of turbot would have whizzed off a plan of stunning sagacity. No one would have knocked on any doors and the Prince would have run out of the house begging forgiveness. But ... one cannot abandon a chap just because he's lost the odd marble or two.

I followed Reeves across the lawn to the Zeppelin and helped him untie the ropes. I took the opportunity to give the Zeppelin the once over while I was at it. It was fifty feet long with a two-seater capsule suspended beneath it – one seat sitting behind the other. The capsule had two wheels at the back and one wheel and a propeller at the front. I was about to cast an inquisitive eye over its controls when Reeves spoke.

"Stand back, sir. I'm releasing the last rope."

I stood back and watched as the Zeppelin slowly rose, a slight breeze taking it away from the house at a sedate pace.

"If you would take your place in the shrubbery, sir, I will attend to the business at the front door."

I positioned myself in the shrubbery, in between the wall of the house and a substantial flowering shrub. The Reeves of three hours ago would have known the species. I dreaded to think what the Reeves of an hour hence would make of it. A woody thing with leaves, probably.

I waited, listening intently for Reeves's dowager duchess contralto. It didn't come. I waited some more ... and heard an unexpected rustle in the leaves a few yards to my right. Something was moving. Something that was coming up out of the ground. An outside light came on, spreading a swathe of light along the back wall of the house, and illuminating the object that was now staring back at me.

It was a head. A masculine head with short hair and a soup strainer moustache. It was poking out of the mulch.

"They're here!" he shouted. "I've found them!"

He started to pull himself out of the ground. I don't know about you but, when faced with a strange man emerging headfirst from a flower border, Reginald Worcester is inclined to run first and ask questions a good deal later. I burst out of the shrubbery, hitched up the crinoline, and legged it across the lawn.

I could hear cries behind me. Several men giving voice – some in English, some in what could have been German. *After her! Don't let her get away! Can you see the others? Wo ist der Zeppelin?*

Realising I was running in the same direction as the Zeppelin, I swerved left and headed for a gap in the hedge where I espied a gate. Surely some of my pursuers would veer off to chase the Zeppelin!

I reached the gate, threw it open, kicked off my heels and sprinted into the adjoining field. I didn't look behind me. I could hear several men running and calling. But Reginald Worcester, winner of the Melbury Regis Preparatory School potato race two years running, only had eyes for the grassy meadow ahead. There's nothing like the fear of an imminent thrashing to spur one on, corset or no corset.

I couldn't have covered more than a hundred yards when I heard a distant rumble. It was coming from behind the crest of the small hill I was running up. It sounded like hooves. It couldn't be horses – the hunting season was months away. Could the sight of a Zeppelin have frightened the local cattle into a stampede?

The answer came almost immediately when a line of riders broke across the skyline. Seven of them, all dressed in white, their tiaras twinkling in the first rays of morning sunlight. The missing debs! But how?

Like the Assyrian horde dressed in eveningwear, the debs spurred their mounts into a charge and descended like the sparkly wolf upon the fold.

The ground began to vibrate.

I stopped running and breathlessly turned to see how things stood with my pursuers. Herr Soup Strainer had stopped too. As had his two colleagues. All were looking nervously up the hill.

A terrifying ululation rent the air. It sounded like something out of Billy the Buffalo's Wild West shows. The thundering of the hooves grew louder, and Herr Soup Strainer and his compatriots turned as one and fled.

I glanced uphill. All the debs had their whips out and with cries of 'View Halloo' 'Tally Ho' and 'No Quarter' were in full cavalry charge. Emmeline Dreadnought was front and centre.

I stood stock still and let them thunder past either side of me, then hitched up the crinoline once more and hurried after them.

Herr Soup Strainer was the first to feel the whip; a glancing blow on the back of his head upended him like an inebriated skittle. The other two soon followed - one from a whip and one from a strong nudge in the back from a horse's shoulder. None of them showed any strong inclination to get up.

Emmeline wheeled off from the charge and came back to see if I was all right. Her face, dress and hair may have been smudged and streaked with dirt but, to me, she shone like one of those angels proffering good news to shepherds.

"It's me!" I said. "Reggie. I've come to rescue you."

"Reggie?" To say Emmeline Dreadnought looked surprised would be an understatement. "But you're... Why are you dressed as a deb? Is there something you'd like to tell me?"

"I'm a decoy, Emmie. It was the only way I could find out who kidnapped you and where you were being held."

"Didn't you find my dance card?"

"Of course. I used it to narrow down the suspects."

"But didn't you see I underlined Prince Otto's name? I scratched two lines under it before I followed him onto the stairwell."

"I thought you did that because you found him suspicious."

A cry came up from one of the other debs. "It's the Prince! He's getting away!"

I turned to look. She was pointing at a figure in the distance running after a Zeppelin.

"I must go," said Emmeline, wheeling her mount. "Come on, ladies! Let's get him!"

Off they galloped, ululating wildly and waving their whips. Which is when I realised that I was somewhat on my own - except for the company of the three n'er-do-wells who, two minutes previously, had been chasing me all over field and dell.

They didn't look too perky at the moment – sitting on the ground rubbing heads and necks – but moments have a habit of being fleeting. Had I been in possession of a service revolver I may have lingered and kept watch over them. But I wasn't, so I legged it back to the house to find Reeves.

I found him by the front door in the company of a police sergeant.

"Don't worry, miss," said the sergeant. "We've got 'er."

"Got whom?"

"This one. My constable discovered 'er inside the 'ouse trying to 'ide."

TEN

I could barely look at Reeves. Three hours ago his brain was knocking on the door of the Seven Wonders. The Collossus of Rhodes was packing his bags and The Hanging Gardenias of Babylon were pulling up their roots. Now he was knocking on doors enquiring about missing Zeppelins and having his collar felt by a village bobby.

When the mighty fall, they fall a dashed long way.

"No, sergeant," I said. "You've got the wrong person. The real culprit is Prince Otto von Smith. He's the cove running over the field at the back chasing a Zeppelin whilst, in turn, being chased by the deb cavalry."

The sergeant stared at me blankly. Perhaps I could have phrased my explanation better.

"Excuse me, miss," he said. "But ... are you a man?"

"Of course I'm a man. Ah. Oh, these!" I suddenly realised I'd been using my normal voice, which jarred somewhat with my appearance. "Yes, well, I can explain. Reeves?"

"Sir?" said Reeves using his butling baritone.

The sergeant let go of Reeves's collar and jumped a good foot to the side.

"Is... Is 'e a man too?" he asked, stabbing a finger Reeveswards.

"No," said Reeves at the exact time I was affirming the opposite.

"What?" said the sergeant. "Is 'e or isn't 'e?"

"It's a philosophical question," I replied. "He is and he isn't. It depends what you mean by man."

"Inspector," said Reeves for some reason addressing me. I imagined his eyesight was going the way of his little grey cells. "I think the sergeant here has penetrated our disguise."

"He has?" I said.

Reeves turned to address the sergeant. "I'm Sergeant Reeves and this is Inspector Worcester of Scotland Yard.

We're here in disguise watching this house which we believe to be the centre of a kidnapping ring. We are in these particular disguises because the victims are debutantes and, as you well know, sergeant, society ladies are not happy about inviting members of the constabulary to their balls."

The sergeant nodded. I wouldn't say he looked totally won over by Reeves's explanation, but he looked part way there. As was I. The giant brain might have been a marble or two below par, but it was still a thing of wonder.

"Earlier this evening," Reeves continued. "The inspector and I were attending the Royal Caledonian Ball – in disguise – when we observed one Prince Otto von Smith abduct a young lady from the premises and bring her to this very house. I believe she is still inside. I was attempting to locate her when I was detained by your constable. May I ask, sergeant, how you and your constable come to be present at this property?"

"Ah, well, you see, it was like this. We got one of they pneumatic telegrams from a Miss Emmeline Dreadnought. She said she and six other girls 'ad been 'eld prisoner at this 'ouse and 'ad just escaped. They'd made it to Snetherton Farm and raised the alarm. We come running over as soon as we could. Southend Police are on their way too. They're bringing a charabanc to take the girls home."

There was a sudden commotion by the door and a constable appeared supporting a deb upon his arm.

"I found her locked in the cellar, sarge," said the constable. "She said she'd been drugged."

"It was Prince Otto," said the deb, her feet far from steady. "He drugged me and had his men lock me in that awful cellar down there."

"You see, sergeant," I said. "Just as we said. Price Otto's your man and he's currently capering about in the back field."

I was about to expound further when Herr Soup Strainer and his two friends came running around the side of the house. They sped up when they saw me, and skidded to a halt when they noticed the custodians of the law.

"May I introduce the Prince's gang, sergeant," I said. "Have at them and don't spare the truncheons."

~

Reeves found a chair for the recently drugged deb and we sat her on the porch where she could await the return of Her

Majesty's Finest. In the meantime, the game still being afoot, there were questions waiting to be answered.

"I found some items of considerable interest within the cellar, sir," said Reeves.

"You're sure you don't need a sit down too, Reeves?"

"No, sir, I believe I am still functioning within acceptable parameters. If you will follow me to the cellar, sir. It is through here."

I followed the giant brain through the house and down a steep wooden staircase into what looked a most unusual cellar. All the cellars I'd known had been dark forbidding affairs – home to cobwebs, spiders, shadows and small rooms where one had to stoop. This one was spotless, well-lit, high-ceilinged and huge. This room alone must have run half the length of the house. Pillars supported the ceiling, electric lights were everywhere, a line of whitewashed windows ran along the top part of the walls to the front and back, and a long stack of boxes covered the gable wall. Plus there were three doors – two closed, one open – leading to the other half of the cellar.

"They're in there," said Reeves, pointing to one of the closed doors.

"What are?"

"The automata, sir."

I had been about to open the door but swiftly withdrew the Worcester hand from the doorknob. "Are they dangerous?"

"They are not currently functioning, sir. I checked."

I gave the doorknob a manly twist, pulled the door open and...

...Entered the market square of the fair county town of Boggledom.

Emmeline Dreadnought was staring back at me, flanked by six other debs – all of whom I recognised from their pictures in the debs illustrated guide. I was looking at the missing debs, and they looked so lifelike.

I walked over for a closer look. They weren't dressed in ball gowns any more. They were dressed in daywear – the standard garb that a young lady of gentle breeding would put on to travel.

"One assumes," said Reeves. "That the object of the abductions was to replace the young ladies with these replicas."

"But why, Reeves?"

"That I cannot say, sir. The automata appear ready to go, but no one has switched them on."

"Are you sure they're automata and not the real thing?"

"They're not breathing, sir. But, if you wish to be certain, you could always loosen their clothing and look for a nozzle."

I raised the Worcester palm. There would be no clothes loosening or nozzle searching. This was England.

"What's in the other rooms?" I said, feeling that I'd be more comfortable elsewhere.

Reeves led the way into the room with the open door. It was a large room L-shaped room with two brass beds, five packing crates and a lot of extra bedding strewn haphazardly about the floor. Sitting on the crates were plates and cutlery and half full jugs of water.

"This is where they kept the young ladies, sir," said Reeves.

I wouldn't have liked to have been holed up in that room for any length of time. There was another door leading off. I looked inside and found a bathroom. At least they had some comforts.

"Here is how they escaped, sir," said Reeves from under one of the windows. "They must have loosened the bricks and dug a tunnel up into the flower bed."

I gazed into the mouth of the tunnel. The wall was double-skinned. They'd had to remove the bricks from two walls.

"Remarkably resourceful, the British female, don't you think, Reeves? Or do they teach jail breaking at finishing school these days?"

"I don't believe it to be on the syllabus, sir."

We checked the third room and once more I was transported to that fair county of B.

"What on earth is that, Reeves?"

Two chairs practically filled the small room. Two chairs with helmets suspended above them. Demonic helmets with all manner of wires and metal protuberances poking out of them. Were they torturing the girls?

"It appears to be some sort of electrical device, sir. Given what we already know, I would suspect its function may have something to do with the transference of memory."

I took a closer look. One would think that a machine built for the purpose of transferring memory would have a label of some sort. 'Thorogood's Memory Transferor, patent pending' or such like. But I saw nothing. Not even on the large metal box between the chairs that appeared to control the process.

It had a lever and two dials, the latter surrounded by numbers from one to nine.

"This is rummy, Reeves. We have a room to the right of us full of ready-to-go automata. We have a machine here ready to swap memories at the flip of a switch. And in the room to the left we had a collection of kidnapped debs – some of whom had been in residence for several weeks. Why the delay? Why not complete the plan and transfer the memories?"

"Perhaps they did, sir."

"What?" It was late, the turbot was wearing off, and my little grey cells had been deprived of alcohol for at least three hours. What was Reeves saying? That the debs had already been drained of their memories? Were they dead, alive, wandering the Earth without any idea who they were? And who had led the debs' cavalry charge – the real Emmeline or an automaton Emmeline?

A gentleman should not be faced with such questions at half past three in the morning.

"We may find the answer in the other room, sir. There is a considerable area that has not been searched."

I followed Reeves back into the room at the bottom of the cellar stairs, my mind circling the outskirts of Boggledom. The Emmeline I'd talked to just after her epic cavalry charge had seemed very real to me. But then, so did Reeves.

"These boxes appear to be of German origin, sir," said Reeves standing by a long stack of corrugated cardboard boxes – each box measuring about two feet along each side.

"How do you know they're German?"

"The writing, sir. My knowledge of the German language is rudimentary at best, but I believe the text to indicate a number of months. This stack is labelled 'two months,' this stack 'three months,' and the remaining stacks rise in one month increments until they reach 'nine months.'"

I still had one foot residing in Boggledom.

"Open one up, Reeves," I said.

Reeves opened the top box from the 'two month' stack and pulled out something pink which was loosely wrapped in tissue paper. He removed the wrapping and...

It had a belly button with a screw thread.

"It appears to be a prosthetic, sir."

"A what-thetic?"

"Prosthetic, sir, it's an artificial addition to the body, covered in synthetic skin, designed to give the impression –

one would deduce by the label on the box – that the wearer was two months with child."

The second foot was veering towards Boggledom.

"Why...." I left my mouth open on the off chance something cogent would find a way past the tonsils but, like a certain cupboard I'd heard of, the tonsil area was bare.

"The screw thread indicates that these prosthetics, though manufactured in Germany, were designed to be used in this country. One imagines by the automata in the adjoining room for the purposes of feigning pregnancy."

"Is there a box with a baby automaton in it?" I asked.

Both Reeves and I scanned the room. There *were* no extra boxes.

"This is dashed odd, Reeves. What was supposed to happen at the end of the automaton's confinement?"

"It is most confusing, sir."

Reeves opened the 'nine month' box and gave the prosthetic a good shake just in case an auto-baby was packed inside. It wasn't.

We gave the rest of the room the eagle eye and found a wooden desk in the corner. The top was bare but a search of the drawers yielded a book – a journal – its hand-written pages written in some kind of cipher.

"How are you at reading ciphers, Reeves?"

"It is not a cipher, sir. It is German. And not a neat hand."

I heard footsteps on the stairs and turned to see who it was.

Emmeline waved. "Reggie! I thought I'd find you here. That's not Reeves, is it?"

"Good morning, miss," said Reeves doffing his tiara.

But was it Emmeline? How could one tell if the figure approaching was machine or flesh and blood?

The answer came to me in a flash. An automaton wouldn't have a pulse!

"Emmie," I said. "May I have your hand?"

"This is all rather sudden, Mr Worcester. Shouldn't you ask my father first?

"What?"

"To ask for my hand. I've never been proposed to before. Do I get a ring?"

I don't know if beads of sweat broke out upon the Worcester forehead, but they certainly drenched my little grey cells. I was speechless. One loose sentence and out slips a troth!

"Are you going to be best man or best woman, Reeves?" continued Emmeline.

"I couldn't possibly say, miss."

Emmeline favoured me with a playful punch to the right arm.

"Don't look so worried, Reggie. I was only joking. Though in some cultures you'd have to marry me, seeing as I saved your life out there."

Blood returned to the Worcester face. "As I remember it, Emmie, I was several lengths ahead and in little danger. And it was *I* who was in the process of rescuing *you*."

"But I'd already escaped. *And* I captured Prince Otto. We tied him to a tree in the garden using our reins."

"What about the Zeppelin?"

"Last I saw it, it was heading out to sea. Did you see our tunnel? It's amazing what you can do with whalebone and a brooch pin or two. It took us days to loosen all that mortar."

"May I have your wrist then?" I said, suddenly remembering my original plan.

"What for?"

"I want to make sure you're all right."

"Oh, Reggie, you are a sweetie. Don't look at my nails though. Digging tunnels has been very hard on them."

She proffered me her wrist and I took it, placing two fingers across the vein and waiting anxiously.

I felt it almost immediately. A pulse – strong and fast. She was real!

I felt something else too – a strong desire to give Emmeline a hug. But ... when one's troth has already slipped out once...

"Prepare yourself for a shock," I said to Emmie. "Come and have a look what we found over here."

I showed Emmeline her automaton and heard the sharp intake of her breath.

"It's so lifelike," she said. "And the others! I couldn't tell them apart from the real thing."

She walked around the room, touching the faces, the hands, the clothes.

"Do you know what they were going to do?" she asked. "I overheard them talking. They didn't realise I spoke German. They planned to replace every deb in the country with machines like these."

"You speak German?" I asked.

"I spent a year at school in Switzerland."

I exchanged a look with Reeves.

"Would you care to read this journal for us, miss? It is written in German."

~

"It says here," said Emmeline, tracing the writing with her right index finger. "That this is the journal of Herr Doktor Frank Epstein. He's the one in charge. I heard him talking to the Prince yesterday morning about having to return to Germany. He was in quite a state."

"About what?" I asked.

"A missing part, or was it a faulty part? Something to do with a machine they needed to get the automata working. They couldn't get it to work. Berlin kept promising that a new part was on its way, but every time the boat arrived it wasn't on it."

"There's a boat?"

"It sounded as if it came every other day with supplies. Sometimes with passengers. Some of the girls were forced to sit for photographs and be measured for clothes by a dressmaker. You do know what the object of all this was, don't you?"

"To replace all the debs with automata."

"That's only half of it. The real object was to replace the entire British ruling class with Germans."

"What, by abducting them and replacing them with automata too?"

"No, by marrying off all the men to these Prussian automata. Then, within a year, these mechanical brides present their husbands with a bouncing baby Prussian boy."

"Real or mechanical?"

"Real. That's another of the reasons Doctor Epstein was going back to Germany - he was worried about some breeding programme - something about needing more Prussian girls to ensure the purity of the stock. He's quite mad, you know. His goal was to groom these boys to take over all the high offices of state within the next fifty years."

"Wouldn't the fathers notice? I mean to say if I was presented with a new born baby sporting a waxed moustache, I'd suspect something was not quite right."

Emmeline giggled. "Especially if it was a daughter."

I joined in the laughter. "What do you think, Reeves? Can one groom a child to bend to one's will? Aunts have been trying it for years, but with mixed success, I'd say. Oft times the more one is forced to bend, the more likely one is to rebel."

"Very true, sir. Though I imagine Herr Doktor Epstein may have envisaged a far stricter regime during the child's formative years. A Prussian 'mother,' a Prussian nanny, and, most likely, a special Prussian boarding school too. I would not be surprised if a contingency existed to replace the boy with an automaton, should he stray from his allotted path."

I shuddered at the bleak future Reeves was painting. The flower of British society all listening to Wagner and wearing *Lederhosen* within fifty years.

"Oh," said Emmeline. "This is interesting. There's a page here about Prince Otto."

"What does it say?"

"It says...." There was a long pause while Emmeline read ahead. "Something about Prometheans. What's a Promethean?"

"People made out of bits of dead people and then reanimated."

"Oh, can you do that?"

"Not personally, but this Doctor Epstein sounds like the kind of cove who could. What does it say?"

"Something about making the ideal lure – the most desirable man on earth."

"Prince Otto? Have you read that right?" I leaned in to take a closer look at the journal.

"That's what it says here," said Emmeline. "It's a shopping list of all the parts they'd need. The legs of a Russian ballet dancer, the torso of an Argentinean tango instructor, the right arm of an Italian rake, the left arm of a Spanish bullfighter, the head of a Prussian count. The ... Oh, that can't be right."

"What can't?"

"It says here one part comes from a donkey."

"What part?"

"It doesn't say."

"The ears, do you think?"

~

We were still skimming through the journal when the police sergeant arrived.

"Ah, there you are, miss. The charabanc to take you back to London's arrived."

"Thank you, sergeant," said Emmeline. "I must go, Reggie.

Mama will be beside herself with worry."

Reeves coughed. "I don't believe that will be the case, miss."

"What?" said Emmeline. "Why ever not?"

I was as confused as Emmeline. Was Reeves about to unmask the Dreadnoughts as the masterminds behind the German plan? It's usually the way it happened in books. Just as you're sure the cove holding the bloody knife is the murderer, the detective turns to someone who last appeared on page thirty-six and points the accusing finger.

"If you remember, miss," said Reeves. "You told her you were going to Lady Harcourt's for supper after the ball."

Emmeline's hand flew to her mouth. "I did, didn't I?"

Now I could see the reason for Reeves's cough. I'd forgotten about my telegram.

"There's more," I said. "I had to come up with a plan to stop your mother dashing round to Lady Harcourt's the next day accusing her of your kidnap. So I sort of sent your mother a telegram saying I – that's you – had been invited to spend a few days at an important personage's castle in the country."

"Oh," said Emmeline and I think that summed up the situation pretty well. How were we going to reunite mother and daughter without opening a hamper of worms?

Reeves reprised his earlier cough. "If I may be of service, miss. I would suggest you tell your mother that Prince Otto sent the telegram, and that he also lied to you about the supper at Lady Harcourt's."

"Reeves, you are a marvel," said Emmeline, and I had to agree with her. To think I'd begun to doubt him.

"You must call on me later today and tell me everything that happened whilst I was languishing in the cellar," said Emmeline. "Promise? If nothing else I want the name of your dressmaker."

I promised. "And you can tell me where you found all those horses at short notice."

"That's easy. Snetherton Farm has extensive stables. As soon I saw the horses I knew what we had to do. All of us girls learned to ride before we could walk."

"Emmeline!" came a female shout from upstairs. "We're all waiting out here. What's taking you so long?"

"Coming!" shouted Emmeline. "I must go. Don't forget to call. I want to hear about everything."

I watched Emmeline ascend the stairs, thinking all the

while that *if* – and the 'if' cannot be stressed too loudly – one had to get engaged to a girl, then one could do a lot worse than Emmeline Dreadnought. Naturally, I kept these thoughts to myself as troths have a nasty habit of springing from one's person unbidden and ready-plighted.

"Well," I said to Reeves. "What happens now? If this were a book, we'd have the denouement scene. But the Herr Doktor's in Berlin and Prince Otto's tied to a tree. Doesn't seem fair to beard a chap while he's tied to a tree and tell him how he did it. We already know how he did it and so does he."

"One could pass a full account of our investigation to the police, sir, but I fear that may invite difficult questions."

"Such as?"

"One that springs to mind, sir, is our impersonation of Scotland Yard officers. I believe Her Majesty's Constabulary takes a very dim view of it."

"Ah."

"As indeed may Her Majesty should she learn the true identity of Millicent Boston and the Dowager Duchess of Tintagel."

I could see why we consulting detectives preferred to keep our work quiet. 'Let others take the glory,' we say. 'Our reward comes from having played the game and bested our foes.'

"Time to beat a hasty retreat, do you think?"

"I think it advisable, sir. We can post the journal and a short explanatory note to Scotland Yard later today."

"Reeves you are a marvel."

"I endeavour to do my best, sir."

"Except for that one wobble earlier – viz. the 'knocking on the door in the middle of the night enquiring about missing Zeppelins' – your conduct has been faultless. Sherlock Holmes couldn't have done better. Any idea what caused the mid-season wobble? A sudden loss of pressure? A subroutine upset by the saltiness of the seaside air?"

"I really couldn't say, sir."

"I didn't even hear you knock on the door. You did knock on the door, didn't you?"

"I cannot recall, sir."

"What?"

With the Reeves countenance beset by a sudden outbreak of sheepishness, Reginald Worcester began to think the unthinkable. Reeves hadn't been very forthcoming about what he'd overheard at the cellar window. And the moment he told me to leg it for the rhododendrons, he'd started poking about in the flowerbed where the tunnel was. And he'd distinctly asked me to hide in the shrubbery a few yards from the tunnel entrance.

"Did you know the debs' tunnel came up in the flowerbed, Reeves?"

"What tunnel, sir?"

"You know very well what tunnel."

"I fear the drop in pressure is affecting my memory, sir."

"Very convenient. I shall ask you again tomorrow when you're fully charged."

"I fear that will not do any good, sir. Once I lose a recollection, it is lost forever."

"Reeves!"

"Who is Reeves, miss?"

Reggiecide

ONE

It is a truth universally acknowledged that a chap in possession of a suffragette fiancée is in need of a pair of bolt cutters.

"Which railing is she chained to now, Reeves?"

"The Houses of Parliament's, sir. Miss Emmeline and five other ladies are protesting in Parliament Square."

"Have the police been summoned?"

"I fear their arrival is imminent, sir. Shall I fetch your driving coat?"

I positively shot out of the door. Reginald Worcester does not dawdle when a damsel is about to be distressed by the long arm of the law. Especially when said damsel happened to be Emmeline Dreadnought who, like Queen Elizabeth when confronted by the Spanish Armada, would not go quietly. And there was nothing that irked a magistrate more than a person who would not go quietly. She could get fourteen days!

I pushed the Stanley Steamer to its limits, turning into Piccadilly on two wheels.

"How's the brain, Reeves? Up to pressure and full of vim?"

"It appears to be functioning within acceptable parameters, sir."

Reeves's steam-powered brain was one of the Seven Wonders of the Victorian World. If anyone could save Emmeline from fourteen days of embroidering mail sacks, Reeves was the chap.

"Can you see her?" I asked as we swung into Parliament Square.

"I believe," said Reeves, holding onto his bowler with one hand and the side of the Stanley with the other, "that that is Miss Emmeline by the main gate, sir. It does not appear that the constabulary have arrived yet."

I swerved the car towards the small outcrop of humanity

clustered around Parliament Gate. Emmeline was on the far right of a line of six ladies. I don't know if there's a dress code for protesting, but these ladies would not have looked out of place in the Royal enclosure at Ascot – except for the placards and chains. The Ascot stewards take a dim view of both.

"Votes for women!" they chanted in unison, waving placards conveying a similar message. *Emancipation Now! Votes For Ladies!*

A small group of onlookers had stopped to watch the protest. I aimed the car to the right of them and pulled hard on the brake lever. The Stanley stuttered to a complaining halt a few yards short of Emmeline.

"Good morning, ladies," I said, rising from my seat and doffing the old driving cap. "Sorry to interrupt and all that but ... Emmeline! Quick, jump aboard. The rozzers will be here any second!"

"Good," said Emmeline, affecting a surprisingly haughty tone. "Let them come. Votes for women!"

"What?"

I climbed down from the Stanley and attempted to reason with the young firebrand.

"I don't think you quite understand, Emmeline. The police take a dim view of the Queen's peace being disturbed. Especially when it involves people chaining themselves to the Palace of Westminster's wrought ironwork! You'll go to *prison*."

"Perhaps I want to go to prison. Votes for women!"

"No one *wants* to go prison. It's much overrated. They don't serve tea until well after six and there are positively *no* cocktails. Come on, Reeves. Cut those chains."

"Reeves!" commanded Emmeline. "Stay where you are!"

"If you wish, miss, though ... might I suggest you reconsider your current plan of action?"

"Don't listen to him, Emmeline. He's a man," said one of Emmeline's sisters-in-chains. I'm not sure if Valkyries had aunts, but if they did – and they were partial to large hats and ostrich feathers – this woman could have been a stand-in for Brunhilde's on her days off.

"Actually, he's not a man," I countered. "He's an automaton. A dashed brainy one at that. And if Reeves says reconsider, I'd jolly well listen to him."

Emmeline would have none of it. "This is not a time for listening, Reggie. This is a time for action."

Reeves coughed, one of his mildly disapproving coughs. He'd aired it earlier upon discovering a pair of duck egg blue spats I'd hidden at the back of my wardrobe. "Would not your arrest, and subsequent incarceration, miss, severely limit your ability to protest?" he said. "If you accompany us now, you can protest again tomorrow but, if you are imprisoned, you will be unable to demonstrate for fourteen days."

"Fourteen days of hard embroidery," I added.

"Ah, but I'll have my day in court," said Emmeline. "It's time we took our fight to the judiciary and showed them that women will no longer put up with injustice. Votes for women!"

Four contralto voices echoed Emmeline's call.

This was not going well.

"Why don't you take my vote, Emmie? I never use it."

"That's very sweet of you, Reggie, but I should have a vote of my own. All women should. It's outrageous that it's Nineteen Hundred and Three and women *still* don't have the vote."

"I think you'll find that most aunts have had their husbands' vote for years. I know Aunt Bertha has. I'm pretty sure she has the gardener's too. One glare from Aunt B and one toes the party line."

"I say," boomed a male voice from somewhere to my right. "Aren't you Reginald Worcester, the gentleman's consulting detective?"

I didn't recognise the chap. He looked like a taller and less menacing version of my old house master at Melbury Regis – Stinker Stonehouse, a man who viewed the protection of the school larder from the nocturnal predations of small boys as the highest possible calling.

"Well this *is* a rare piece of luck," said the newcomer. "Scrottleton-Ffoukes is the name. I've mislaid a relative and I need to get him back pretty smartish."

"Have you looked in all the usual places?" I asked.

Reeves coughed, not one of the disapproving genus this time, more of the 'I have an observation to make, sir, but am far too well-mannered a valet to interrupt' variety.

"I'm afraid in this case," said Mr Scrottleton-Ffoukes, a man obviously unfamiliar with Reeves's oesophageal lexicon. "That there *are* no usual places. I had wondered if I might find him here, but am rather relieved I have not. I say, could we go somewhere private? This is a most unusual and delicate matter."

Reeves coughed again.

"You have an observation, Reeves?" I asked.

"Only that this appears to be a most interesting case, sir, and what a pity it is that Miss Emmeline is otherwise engaged."

Reeves had done it again! The man must bathe in fish oil. His brain was positively turbot-charged.

"Indeed," I said, catching Emmeline's eye. "Are you sure you won't reconsider? I know how much you love a good mystery."

Emmeline wavered. She looked at her chains. She bit her lip. She sighed.

"Don't listen to him," said Aunt Valkyrie. "It sounds like a ruse to make you abandon the protest."

"I'm sorry, Reggie," said Emmeline, looking down at her feet. "I've got to see this through."

"But Emmie–"

"My mind is made up."

"I don't wish to intrude," said Mr Scrottleton-Ffoukes. "But this *is* a matter of great urgency. I cannot involve the police. I need your assistance this minute."

I looked once more at Emmeline and realised it would be pointless to try again. Once Emmeline had made up her mind, she was resolute.

"Don't forget to use a false name, Emmie. I'm rather partial to Nebuchadnezzar Blenkinsop whenever I'm up before the beak. You could be his sister, Nefertiti."

~

We toddled over the road into the lawned central area of the square and found a quiet spot under that new statue – the one by Eckstein.

"I believe we would be safer over there, sir," said Reeves, indicating a spot by Westminster Abbey. "If we remain here I fear the police may think us guilty of vandalising this statue."

I gave the Eckstein a swift perusal. "Are your eyes malfunctioning, Reeves? This statue looks tickety-boo to me."

"The female personage – if indeed it *is* a female personage, sir – would appear to have three eyes. And is orange."

I tutted. Fourteen years locked in a cupboard had given Reeves a very narrow view of what is and what is not art. Our opinions had clashed several times.

"It's modern art, Reeves. And who is to say the model was not orange ... or indeed three-eyed. One should never jump to conclusions these days. As the bard said to Lord Nelson, 'There are more things in heaven and earth, Horatio, than are dreamt of in your philosophy.'"

Reeves put on his disapproving face – and made a show of shielding his eyes from the offending statue by placing his right hand hard against his brow – whilst Mr S-F presented his story.

And what a story it was.

"Have you heard of Prometheans, Mr Worcester? Corpses assembled from many parts and brought back to life by the introduction of electrical energy?"

"I should say so. I've even conversed with a couple. Thinking about it, I was almost related to one once – until she ran off with next door's pig."

"Pig?"

"A Promethean pig, assembled from a collection of Europe's finest porkers. And a Scotsman. Although I'm not quite sure how the Scotsman got into the mix. Do you recall, Reeves?"

"No, sir. I fear that will remain one of life's little mysteries."

"Oh." Mr Scrottleton-Ffoukes appeared somewhat non-plussed, an effect I often have on people. I believe Sherlock Holmes generates a similar effect. Emmeline says it's because our brains are differently wired. Our thoughts skip and gambol along paths that the general populace doesn't even know exist.

"Well," he continued. "I have been financing a study into Necrometheans – that is the reanimation of long dead corpses. *Very* long dead corpses."

"How long?"

"300 years."

I whistled. "Three hundred years? Isn't there a problem with um ... you know ... the condition of the specimen?"

"That was one of the first things Mr Snuggles worked on."

"Snuggles?"

"He's the scientist fellow I've been financing. A veritable genius. Anyway, to cut a long story short, yesterday we re-animated an ancient relative of mine and this morning he's gone. We can't find him anywhere."

"Are you sure he's gone and not just ... dissolved into a

pile of dust? If someone left a window open last night his ashes may have scattered."

"I assure you, Mr Worcester, my relative was very much alive when he left the room for he broke the lock on the laboratory door! I fear he has a strong dislike of confined spaces."

"Three hundred years in a coffin is wont to do that to a person."

Mr Scrottleton-Ffoukes began to look a little sheepish. "I fear it is more than that," he said. "He was ... somewhat ill-used before his death. And I think he may be seeking revenge."

"Upon whom? Mr Snuggles hasn't re-animated any other 300 year-old corpses, has he? The Jacobean Scrottleton-Ffoukes weren't involved in a blood feud with the Capulet-Smythes, were they?"

"I fear it is not so much a person that he intends to harm, as an institution."

Institution? The Worcester brain boggled.

"Perhaps if you gave us the name of your relative, sir?" asked Reeves.

Mr Scrottleton-Ffoukes looked down at his brogues and shuffled. "Er ... Guy Fawkes."

You could have struck me across the mazzard with a wet halibut.

"*The* Guy Fawkes?" I asked. "The Gunpowder Plot Guy Fawkes?"

"Yes, though I am sure he is innocent. I have read a great deal upon the subject and am quite convinced the plot was orchestrated by Robert Cecil. He wanted to ingratiate himself with King James *and* convince the King of the Catholic menace."

"Really?" I said. History had never been one of my strong subjects. I knew King James had written the Bible, and what schoolboy hadn't heard of the Gunpowder Plot? Bonfire Night was one of the highlights of the school year – all those fireworks and the weeks beforehand spent constructing your Guy to toss onto the bonfire.

But this Cecil cove had passed me by.

"It was to clear his name that I had Snuggles re-animate Guy – so he could give his side of the story. I have a son, Mr Worcester, and I do not want him to suffer the same humiliation I had to suffer at school. Every November the Fifth it was *my* effigy the boys placed on the bonfire in the quad. It's about time the world knew the truth."

"Quite," I said. "Did your ancient relative have much to say upon the matter?"

"He was not entirely coherent. He was frightened at first – which was not surprising as his last memories were ones of torture and execution. Then he became angry, and later violent. It took two of us to hold him down while Snuggles administered a sedative. We hoped a night's rest might calm him down."

"But he broke out instead. What do you think, Reeves?"

"Perhaps if we were to visit the location Mr Fawkes was last seen, sir. There may be evidence of a trail."

I wasn't sure what kind of trail a three-hundred year old reanimated corpse would leave but, that aside, Reeves's steam-powered logic could not be faulted.

TWO

Mr Scrottleton-Ffoukes conducted us to a fourth-floor attic in a Georgian house off Great Smith Street in Westminster. The attic door looked undamaged at first sight. It wasn't until our host pushed the door open that one could observe the splintered wood around the lock on the doorjamb.

"Are Prometheans noted for their prodigious strength, Reeves?" I asked. Both lock and door looked on the heavy side to me. And yet Guy had wrenched the door clean open.

"Not that I have read, sir," said Reeves, bending down to give the door a thorough eyeballing.

I left Reeves to his sleuthing and toddled inside after our host. It was one of those large attics lit by several skylights – the sort much favoured by artists, except this one was pervaded by a strange smell as though someone had been experimenting with cocktails and had mistaken a bottle of floor cleaner for gin.

I don't know what I'd expected a Promethean laboratory to look like: maybe lined with shelves full of jars containing spare knees; or giant electrical machines buzzing and belching forth sparks of electrical energy; or grave robbers lining the stairs with today's special offers in a sack.

I *was* right about the electrical machines, but they were neither buzzing nor sparking. They towered over a plinth-like bed whilst three large leather straps dangled from the plinth's sides.

"Was Guy strapped to that plinth?" I asked.

"Only during the reanimation," said Mr S-F. "When we left him he was unfettered."

Reeves coughed from the doorway. "May I make an observation, sirs?"

"Observe away, Reeves. We are agog with anticipation."

"I do not believe Mr Fawkes to be responsible for the forcible opening of this egress, sir."

"Why ever not?"

"Because the door was forced open from the outside, sir. One can observe the faint outline of a boot upon the lock rail. A size eight right boot if I am not mistaken."

"Someone kidnapped Guy?" said an incredulous Mr S-F.

"Someone with at least one leg," I added.

"One leg?" said Mr S-F.

"That's all we can deduce from the evidence so far. We consulting detectives are pretty hot on deduction. Any sign of a left boot, Reeves? On the landing, perhaps? An outline in a patch of rare silt of tropical origin, tracked in on the sole of our mystery man's boot?"

"No, sir."

"What about a circular indentation from a wooden leg? Sherlock Holmes rarely investigates a case without finding at least one one-legged man."

"Not that I can observe, sir."

"Well, there we have it. A person, or persons, with at least one leg between them. Now, who else knew that your relative was here?"

I think Mr S-F was pretty impressed by my demonstration of the deductive arts, for he took a moment to reply, his mouth agape in obvious reverence. "Er ... Who else knew? No one, except for Snuggles and myself. We were very careful. Neither of us wished for news of this event to leak out before we were ready to tell the world."

"So," I said, embarking on a spot of pacing. I always find pacing aids the detecting process. Well, that and gin. But as our host hadn't offered the latter, the former had to suffice. "No unexpected callers in the last couple of days? Or anyone showing an unusual interest in your activities?"

"Not at all."

This sounded to me like a three-cocktail problem and there I was without so much as an olive!

I paced some more. In *The Woman in Taupe*, Inspector Lapin of the *Sûreté* solved the case by examining the psychology of the victim. What did I know of Guy Fawkes other than he'd been burned at the stake?

Wait a minute!

"How can Snuggles have reanimated Guy if his body had been burned at the stake?"

"He wasn't burned," said Mr S-F. "He was hung, drawn and quartered."

"Are you sure? If he wasn't burned, why do we burn effigies of him every Bonfire Night?"

"One supposes, sir," said Reeves. "That Hanging, Drawing and Quartering Night would not convey the same message of festive family fun as Bonfire Night."

Reeves, as ever, had a point.

"I have a colour photograph," said Mr S-F, his right hand reaching inside his topcoat. "Mr Snuggles likes to keep a record of his work and took this with his Autochrome just before the reanimation began. You can compare it to contemporary drawings of my unfortunate relative. It is definitely he. A year after his execution, the family collected all his remains and had them interred in our vault at St Stephen's."

I had a look at the photograph. It showed a tall, stocky man with a bright orange complexion and strands of reddish brown hair emanating from his scalp, upper lip and chin.

"Was his face always that colour?" I asked.

"Having one's head impaled on a spike and exhibited on London Bridge for three months is wont to be hard on the complexion, sir," said Reeves.

"That's all very well," I said. "But he's bright orange. His hands, too."

"That's the revitalising skin cream," said Mr S-F. "Guy's skin was grey and cracked, and as dry as dust when we exhumed him. Unfortunately the most efficacious skin revitalizer, though a marvel of modern skin care for the departed, has an artificial tanning agent. It *is* French."

"Should be easy to spot then, don't you think, Reeves? Large orange man in tattered Jacobean clothing."

"That's what Snuggles and I thought. But not *one* of the local traders has seen hide nor hair of him."

Our conversation was interrupted by a clattering of feet upon the stairs, shortly followed by the arrival of a middle-aged cove with an abundance of long, lank, black hair. He stopped dead in the doorway the moment he saw us.

"Oh," he said, his startled expression giving way to an oily smile. "Mr. Scrottleton-Ffoukes, sir. And you are accompanied. May I inquire as to the identity of these gentlemen?"

"This is Mr Worcester, the gentleman's consulting detective, and his man. They're here to help us find Guy. Have you had any luck, Snuggles?"

Back came the startled expression. "You've told them about ... him, sir?"

"Of course. We need expert help and Mr Worcester is the

soul of discretion."

"It's a consulting detective's middle name," I said. "Sometimes *I* don't even know what I'm investigating."

"In that case, sir, I can report that I have travelled as far south as the Old Vauxhall Bridge and as far east as Victoria station, and no one reports seeing anyone fitting your illustrious ancestor's description."

Snuggles smiled unctuously, reminding me of a used Zeppelin salesman I'd once been seated next to at Henley.

While Mr S-F brought Snuggles up to speed viz. doors and boots, I gave the latter the once-over with a consulting detective's deductive eyeball.

Snuggles' hair was long, which spoke of a bohemian nature. It was greasy and unwashed, which meant - I struggled there - was that the mark of a cove who'd fallen upon hard times or a bachelor? His suit looked old and worn which could support the former theory. And he had no flower in his buttonhole which could, again, mean hard times or, equally, a falling out with his florist.

This deduction lark was not as easy as S. H. made out. Snuggles had no walking cane or pocket watch that I could examine, and I felt uncomfortable about asking him to remove his shoes.

Snuggles inhaled sharply. "Someone kidnapped Mr Fawkes? But that's impossible ... unless..."

"Unless what?" asked Mr S-F.

"No," said Snuggles, shaking his head. "I'm sure it's a coincidence."

The moment I heard the word, I knew it had to be an important clue. We detectives take a very dim view of coincidence. Murgatroyd of The Yard refuses to believe such a thing even exists, and has been known - notably in the *Mysterious Body Part in the Butler's Pantry* - to take his walking cane to any of his underlings who suggest otherwise.

"What coincidence?" I asked.

"I thought I was being followed yesterday, sir. An erroneous notion, I'm sure, but ... what struck me as odd was that the gentleman in question had an orange hue to his skin."

~

"You were being followed by a Promethean?"

"I thought I was being followed, but I could easily have been mistaken."

If ever a consulting detective needed a bracing restorative this was that time. My little grey cells were as parched as they were boggled. Who was this other Promethean and why was he following Snuggles?

"Did you recognise the Promethean?" I asked.

"No."

"He couldn't have been one of your former..." I struggled for the word. Was there a word for a Promethean one had made earlier? A reanimatee? A patient? "Someone you reanimated last month perhaps? In disguise and pining for his maker."

I wasn't sure if a Promethean could pine, but I didn't see why not. One hears of ducklings imprinting upon the first soul they see when they pop their shell. Couldn't a Promethean feel the same?

Suddenly I could see a motive. A jealous Promethean discovering Snuggles had a new charge!

Snuggles' next sentence threw a bucket of cold Perrier over my excitement. "I haven't reanimated anyone for over a month," he said. "And this man must have been reanimated within the last three weeks."

"What makes you think that?"

"Because the orange hue begins to fade after that. The makers of ReVitaCorpse recommend daily applications of their cream for a maximum of fourteen days. Beyond that, its effects are deleterious and can lead to inflammation, boils and atrophy."

Reeves coughed. "If I may ask Mr Snuggles a few questions, sir?"

"Of course," I said.

"Is the use of this orange unguent widespread?"

"I would not call it widespread. It's very expensive and has only been available in England for a few months."

"Indeed. Is its use recommended for all Prometheans or only for those, like Mr Fawkes, who have been long dead?"

"It's recommended for treating any part that has been deprived of life for more than 48 hours. Fresh body parts are notoriously difficult to obtain these days. Even the teaching hospitals have tightened their procedures."

Reeves paused and for a moment I was concerned his pressure might be dropping but, no, back he came with another question. "Are all your jars of ReVitaCorpse accounted for? Mr Fawkes' abductor may have seen fit to take some with him. One would imagine that thirteen additional applications would require a considerable amount of ointment."

Snuggles scurried over to a shelf and ran his fingers along the assorted row of pots and jars before returning with what looked like a large, decorated, ointment pot.

"They are both there. A full one, and this one I opened yesterday," he said, handing it to me. "I bought them both from Fortnum's Promethean Essentials department. I believe they are the only stockist in London."

The pot must have weighed several pounds and there was a slight odour which I couldn't quite place. I read the label on the front:

REVITACORPSE
BY
ESTÉE MORGUER OF PARIS

IS YOUR CORPSE SUFFERING FROM HARD-TO-GET-RID-OF NOOSE LINES? OR UNSIGHTLY PATCHES OF MOULD? USE ESTÉE MORGUER'S TWO-IN-ONE BLEMISH REMOVER – WITH REVITACORPSE-666 – THE ULTIMATE TREATMENT FOR DRY, MOULDERING SKIN.

NOW WITH ADDED PINE OIL TO GIVE YOUR CORPSE THAT FRESHLY DUG SMELL.

AS USED ON PRINCE ALBERT.

"Prince Albert's been re-animated?" I said.

"Not our Prince Albert, sir," said Snuggles. "The Belgian one. He's the nephew of King Leopold. I am told it took years off him."

"Related to the Prince of Orange, is he?" I said, rather pleased at the speed of the Worcester wit.

"No, sir. He's Belgian, not Dutch," said Snuggles.

Even the best *bon mot* is lost on some people.

"Wouldn't that play havoc with the succession?" I asked. "I mean there you are one day King of all the Belgians and next day up pop five late uncles and a bright orange great grandfather. Who's the king?"

Snuggles shrugged. "That would be one for the lawyers, sir. Though some might argue that that particular problem is peculiar to monarchies. A meritocracy would have no such problem."

"Quite," said Reeves. "May I suggest, sir, we visit Fortnum's and inquire about recent purchases of ReVitaCorpse?"

"All in good time, Reeves," I said. "First we have to complete our examination of the scene. Now, Snuggles, do you notice anything missing? A spare tonsil removed from its jar? Or something present that shouldn't be? Criminals are always leaving clues. They try not to, but they always do. A muddy footprint, cigar ash, a length of rope with an oddly shaped knot. Speak out if anyone sees anything unexpected."

We searched the room thoroughly, examining jars and pulling out drawers. Then, as I was crawling under a desk, I noticed something small, wrinkled ... and orange.

"What ho, what ho, what ho," I said. "There's something under here."

I picked it up and brought it out into the light.

"What is it?" said Mr S-F.

"It's a bit shrivelled but ... is it a finger?" I hoped it was a finger.

Mr. Snuggles had a look. "It's a finger all right. And it's definitely from a recent Promethean. The tissue is healing but you can still see the damage."

"And it's orange," I added.

"Might I suggest, sir," said Reeves, "that we seek canine assistance. The bloodhound is well known for its ability to track a person by their scent."

"Do we know any bloodhounds, Reeves? We don't have time to drive about the country looking for off-duty bloodhounds. Won't any dog do?"

"It is true that all canines possess a remarkable sense of smell, sir."

"Then I think I know just the chap."

THREE

Binky Binghampton was the man to see viz. our canine friends. If it had four legs and surveyed postmen with a frosty disposition, Binky knew of it.

"Before we leave, sir, might I suggest that Mr Scrottleton-Ffoukes return home in case he has been sent a ransom note? And that Mr Snuggles inquire of his fellow reanimators as to whether there have been any similar abductions in recent weeks?"

I've said it before and I'll say it again. Reeves's brain is a marvel. Maybe it's all that steam – blowing all the cobwebs away – that gives him such clarity of thought.

Reeves and I left Great Smith Street and ankled it back to the Stanley.

"Can you see Emmeline?" I asked as we neared Parliament Gate.

"No, sir. Miss Emmeline and her companions appear to have been removed."

Indeed they had. Six broken chains and a bedraggled ostrich feather were all that remained. I gathered up the rightmost chain and stowed it in the Stanley. I knew Emmeline wouldn't want to lose her favourite chain.

"Do you think we should drive to the police station and post bail?"

"I fear Miss Emmeline would decline, sir. She did appear intent upon pursuing her cause to the courts."

I climbed into the Stanley, glanced momentarily in the general direction of Bosher Street Magistrate Courts, then set course for Binky's flat in Audley Square.

As luck would have it we arrived just as Binky was returning from his morning constitutional around Hyde Park. He was accompanied by an odd-looking canine of uncertain parentage.

"What ho, Binky," I said, jumping down from the Stanley. "How are you on bloodhounds? On first name terms with any of the local specimens?"

"What ho, Reggie. What do you want a bloodhound for? You're not thinking of getting a dog, are you?"

"Only to borrow. I need a four-legged friend who can follow a scent. I have a missing person who needs to be found."

"Well if it's a tracker you want, you can't do better than old Farquharson here. He has the finest nose in all of London."

"He does?"

I surveyed Farquharson and one of Farquharson's eyes surveyed me. The other appeared to move independently and was more interested in the lamppost. One didn't have to be a trained consulting detective to notice that there was something rummy about Farquharson. He looked like an ancient bulldog that had been badly stuffed by an ill-tempered taxidermist. He had lumps where one would not normally expect a lump to be. And his body was covered in scars – one was still puckered and showing signs of recent stitching.

"Are you sure he's up to it?" I asked. "He looks like he's been in the wars."

"He may be old, but he has the heart of a young dog. Literally. He's a Promethean, don't you know? I couldn't bear to lose old Farquharson, so I had him reanimated. It wasn't cheap, mind you. Cost me an arm and a leg – not to mention the heart and lungs."

"Does he talk?"

"Talk? He's a dog, Reggie. Dogs don't talk."

"Are you sure? He doesn't bark with a Scots accent by any chance?"

"Have you been drinking?"

"I believe Mr Worcester is recalling the pig, sir," said Reeves.

"Pig? What pig?"

"A Promethean pig, sir. We encountered a specimen last month who could speak."

"Really?"

"With a Scots accent," I added.

"Well I never."

All three of us looked at Farquharson in case he wanted to comment, but nothing, except a lolling tongue and a prodigious string of drool, escaped his lips.

"Are you sure you don't know any bloodhounds?" I asked.

"I don't want to overtax the poor chap."

"You could never overtax Farquharson. He loves his walks. And there's nothing he loves better than following a scent. He'll have your missing person treed in no time."

I took another long look at Farquharson. "What do you think, Reeves?"

"I think this is a case of 'needs must,' sir. One would suspect that the scent trail will soon begin to dissipate."

~

Stowing Farquharson in the Stanley was problematic. He kept escaping from the foot well and climbing up onto our laps. And driving whilst having one's ears cleaned out with slobber was far from pleasant.

Farquharson didn't appear to handle stairs well, either. Climbing the three flights to Snuggles' attic laboratory took much cajoling, some pushing, and a modicum of dragging. By the second flight I understood why very few consulting detectives include a dog on their staff.

At the top I pushed open the door to the lab and the three of us entered, one at speed and one - Reginald Worcester, consulting detective - dragged along behind on the end of its lead.

"Sit. Stay! Reeves!"

Farquharson not only didn't talk, he didn't listen, either. It was only when his lead became entangled with a table leg that our progress was halted, allowing Reeves to grasp the animal securely by the collar.

Time, I thought, to give Farquharson the finger.

I handed the lead to Reeves while I rummaged in my coat pocket. "I'll let him have a good sniff, then we'll see where he leads us."

I held the finger close to Farquharson's nose and wafted it back and forth. He gave it a good sniff then ... lunged forward and ate it.

One swallow may not make a summer, but it was more than enough to remove our only clue!

"He's eaten it!"

"So I observed, sir. Most unfortunate."

"What do we do now?"

"I hesitate to say, sir."

"But me no hesitations, Reeves. Now is the time for all good men to come to the aid of the party."

"Well..."

"Come on, Reeves. Spit it out."

"I did observe that Farquharson swallowed the finger whole. One could await nature to take its course and ... retrieve the finger."

Even steam-cleaned brains have their off days.

"Reeves," I said. "I fear one of your sub-routines has developed an unpleasant malfunction."

"I did hesitate to mention it, sir."

"Not long enough."

Farquharson, who had been largely silent since the finger incident, suddenly began to retch, his chest heaving in increasing amplitude until...

Bleugh!

Out flew a finger, landing forlornly on the floorboards.

"Is it *the* finger?" I asked, leaning forward for a closer look.

"One would suppose it unlikely that Farquharson had previously partaken of another finger, sir."

"I'm not so sure. He has the look of a dog with unusual appetites. This could be all that's left of a postman he encountered earlier."

Farquharson kept his own counsel, sitting very still and looking pensive. He could have been on the verge of coughing up a kneecap, or he could have been debating a second go at the finger.

Reeves bent down and retrieved the digit. "It *is* orange, sir. I believe it would be a safe assumption that this is the same finger you discovered earlier."

We gave it another go. I held Farquharson by the lead and collar while Reeves carefully wafted the orange digit in front of the dog's nose.

This time it must have taken, for Farquharson started sniffing excitedly and turned his attention towards the floor. I let go of his collar and let him sniff and snuffle his way around the attic ... and out the door.

Farquharson descended the stairs considerably swifter than he'd climbed them. As, unfortunately, did I. Reeves caught up with us while Farquharson was distracted by an ambrosial lamppost.

"Your turn," I said, puffing hard as I handed over the lead.

Dog and valet proceeded to shoot off in the general direction of the Houses of Parliament, Farquharson pulling and wheezing while Reeves did his best to slow the animal down. I followed, growing more and more impressed with the nasal powers of our four-legged sleuth, until he dragged Reeves into a butcher's shop just off Parliament Square.

"Get that dog out of here!" shouted the butcher, a large, red-faced man wielding a meat cleaver.

I have always found it a wise policy to heed the words of large, red-faced men wielding meat cleavers. A philosophy not shared by Farquharson. It took two of us to drag him out of the shop the first time. Three were required for the encore. After that the door was closed and a boy positioned there to stand guard – with orders to call for the police if Farquharson felt like going for the hat-trick.

With difficulty we manoeuvred the struggling Farquharson towards a lamppost and tied him there. Still he continued to strain and pull in the direction of the butcher shop. I didn't know what to make of it. Was it the scent of Guy or several pounds of sausages that affected him so?

I looked closer at the produce in the butcher's window ... and wondered. Could the butcher be selling Promethean pie?

~

I could spend several pages relating the unfortunate events that occurred during our attempt to return Farquharson to the bosom of his master, but I have been advised by my solicitor, and the doctor treating the unfortunate clergyman, that some events are best not written down.

Suffice to say dog and master were reunited, and Reeves and I drove back to the flat for a restorative cocktail.

"What do you think, Reeves?" I said as I sipped my second restorative. "Would a butcher fill his pies with Prometheans if his business was about to go belly pork up?"

"Ordinarily one would suspect not, sir, but I believe there are persons who pay considerable sums for the ground flesh of Egyptian mummies. Perhaps they would pay a similar sum for such an ancient Promethean as Mr Fawkes."

"How extraordinary." I knew that some people liked their meat well hung – but drawn and quartered as well?

"It's believed to be medicinal, sir," said Reeves. "Some sources ascribe rejuvenating properties to it."

I took another sip of my own rejuvenator. "Would they turn orange, do you think? All that ReVitaCorpse has got to go somewhere. And if these chaps are munching away on prime Promethean one would expect at least a tongue to turn orange."

"It is my understanding, sir, that only very small quantities of the ground flesh are ever consumed."

"Oh well."

Bang went my idea to stake out the butcher's shop and look for a steady stream of orange-faced customers. But that's a consulting detective's lot. We're trained to think the unthinkable, and the problem with the unthinkable is that they're often long shots that fall at the first water jump.

I nibbled on a moody olive.

A tinkling of the hall bell heralded the arrival of a pneumatic telegram. Reeves brought it to me. As expected it was from Mr Scrottleton-Ffoukes. It read:

No ransom note. Snuggles can find no report of any other missing Prometheans either. Awaiting instructions.

"Well," I said. "What do you make of that, Reeves? Rules out kidnapping, don't you think?"

"Possibly, sir. Or it may have begun as a kidnapping and then Mr Fawkes escaped his abductors. He was reported to be confused and violent when last sighted."

I pondered upon this. If he had escaped, where would he go? London would look a dashed sight different today than it did 300 years ago. And all his friends would be six foot under ... or impaled on spikes. He'd have nowhere to go.

"Wouldn't someone spot him? I mean, he's bright orange, dressed in tattered clothing and probably violent. Not the sort of chap who would blend in easily."

"One would suspect, sir, that he has found somewhere to hide. An empty building or a cellar perhaps."

Yes, I could see that. "One supposes that he'd have to come out to find food. He'd have no money, so what would he do? Beg? He's certainly dressed for it."

"I believe one should study the psychology of the individual, sir. Contemporary accounts describe Mr Fawkes as a man of action. I posit a man of action in his situation would be more likely to steal food than to beg for it."

"So we should be looking for reports of food thefts in the vicinity of Westminster?"

"That would be my suggestion, sir."

I dashed off a telegram to Mr S-F informing him of our progress and advising him to stay where he was. One does hear stories about mail going astray and just because a ransom note hadn't arrived by the morning post, it didn't mean that one wasn't imminent.

After a light lunch, Reeves and I took the Stanley for a spin around Westminster and Victoria looking for empty buildings and reports of food thefts. There were plenty of the former but none of the latter. Then we had another look at Farquharson's favourite butcher's shop.

"Do you think I should toddle inside and ask if they have any ground Jacobeans, Reeves?"

"I would not recommend it, sir. Mr Holmes generally recommends stealth."

"Very true. And disguise. Maybe I should buy a false beard and a large hat."

"If you must, sir," said Reeves, exhibiting his disapproving face. "But it *is* nearly closing time and my pressure is getting low."

"Tomorrow then. What do you think about an eye patch?"

~

Back in the flat that evening I was sipping a postprandial port and feeling in a reflective mood when Reeves came into the study with extra logs for the fire.

"I'm not sure if I'm in favour of it, Reeves."

"What are you not in favour of, sir?"

"Prometheans. Reviving much-loved pets I can understand. But one has the feeling that the sort of people who'd insist on having their clogs unpopped would be exactly the sort of people whose clogs should be buried with a 'Do Not Unpop' warning. Aunt Bertha for one. Could you imagine Aunt Bertha being reanimated in perpetuity? I shudder at the very thought!"

"The process does appear to be open to abuse, sir."

"Three score and ten – that's what the bible says, doesn't it, Reeves? Nothing about three score and ten per innings."

"I believe Methuselah was reported to have lived for 969 years, sir."

"A Promethean, do you think?"

"The Bible makes no mention of it, sir."

"I expect King James glossed over it."

FOUR

The next day had barely arrived when Reeves appeared in my bedroom.

"Miss Emmeline is at the door, sir."

"What?" I said, poking an inquisitive nostril above the sheets.

"Miss Emmeline, sir. She's at the door and requesting your immediate presence."

I sat bolt upright. "Has she escaped?"

"She didn't say, sir. But she *is* most insistent."

I dressed swiftly – not even stopping to choose a flower for my buttonhole – and ran downstairs to the door to the street.

"What is it, Emmie? Are you on the run?"

"Ha!" she said. "I'll tell you about that later. No, it's you I'm worried about. Have you seen your door?"

I hadn't until then. A note was pinned there by what looked like a poker. The handwriting was crude and the paper was blackened where the poker had pierced it.

> Mr Fawkes doth not concern you. Stay away if you know what be good for you.
>
> M.

"Is it to do with your case? It sounds a corker if they're already threatening you."

Reeves appeared at my shoulder.

"Have you seen this, Reeves?" I asked.

"No, sir. Most disturbing."

"Who's M?" asked Emmie.

I had no idea. "Do we know any M's, Reeves?"

"Not that I recall, sir."

"Well that's dashed odd. And why's he using 'doth?' He's not another ancient Promethean, is he?"

"Your case involves ancient Prometheans?" asked Emmeline.

I brought Emmeline up to speed viz. the case, omitting the full details of the scene between Farquharson and the reverend gentleman on the grounds of good taste and possible legal action.

"Do you think Guy Fawkes will try to blow up the Houses of Parliament again?" asked Emmeline.

I hadn't until then.

"The Queen will be there tomorrow to open Parliament," she continued. "Just like in 1605. I bet this 'M' is one of his co-conspirators."

"Mr Snuggles is of the opinion that no other Prometheans of a similar age exist, miss."

"Ha!" said Emmeline. "That's what *he* says. I bet his first name begins with an M."

I made a mental note to find out.

But why sign the note at all? Threatening letters were traditionally unsigned. Unless...

"What does that note tell you, Reeves?" I asked, thinking the moment opportune to give a masterclass in the art of deduction.

"That someone does not wish us to continue our investigations, sir."

"Exactly! But what else, Reeves?"

"One would surmise that the person in question has strong feelings upon the matter, sir."

"You see, Emmie, this is where the brain of a consulting detective comes into its own. Reeves sees the note, I see the mind of the person who penned it."

"You do?"

"We consulting detectives have an eye for such things. The man, and it must be a man that wrote this note, is a criminal mastermind."

I could see that Reeves was about to cough, so I raised a palm to stop him.

"Sherlock Holmes would agree with me, Reeves. What kind of chap leaves a note skewered to another chap's door with a poker?"

No one could answer.

"Your common or garden criminal would wrap the note around a brick and toss it through the window. Or send a threatening telegram. Or *nail* the note to the door. But *who* uses a poker? It's not the first thing that springs to mind. Which means..." I paused for effect. "The poker has to be a clue. And only criminal masterminds leave clues on purpose. Everyone else tries their darndest *not* to leave clues. Ipso Whatso we're being warned off by a Moriarty of the underworld."

"Whose name begins with M," said Emmeline. "Oh! You don't think..."

I hadn't until then. Could Moriarty have made it back alive from the Reichenbach Falls? Or been resurrected in orange?

Reeves coughed.

"It *is* widely held, sir, that Professor Moriarty is a fictional character."

"So he'd want us to believe," I said. "Next you'll be telling me that Sherlock Holmes is a figment of Sir Arthur Conan Doyle's imagination."

Reeves and Emmeline exchanged glances. One could tell they didn't have an answer.

~

We decided to take the note and the poker upstairs for further investigation. As Reeves was extracting the poker from the door, he noticed the oddest thing. The wood around the hole the poker had made was singed. And the blackened marks on the paper were scorch marks. The tip of the poker must have been hot when it was thrust into the door!

Curiouser and curiouser. Who walks around London with a hot poker *other* than a criminal mastermind?

I quizzed Emmeline while Reeves made breakfast.

"Time to come clean, Emmie. Are you on the run or not? I'm buying a false beard and an eye patch this morning. I can easily buy two."

"That's very decent of you, Reggie, but I'm not on the run. The magistrate refused to imprison us."

"Well, that's a stroke of a luck."

"No, it isn't! You weren't there, Reggie. He treated us like children. He told us to go home to our husbands and fathers and reflect long and hard upon our futures."

"Have you reflected?"

"I have. Then I looked up the magistrate in *Who's Who* and found out where he lived."

This did not bode well.

"I was going to chain myself to his railings this morning

but someone stole my chain!"

"No they didn't. I saw it lying by the gate and rescued it for you. It's in the hall closet. Your best padlock too."

"Oh, Reggie!"

Nothing says love more than twenty feet of quarter-inch Tiffany chain.

~

After breakfast, feeling full of vim and kippers, I pulled down a copy of *Who's Who* from the bookshelf and began looking for M's.

Ten minutes later I'd discovered that Scrottleton-Ffoukes was an Edward George and Snuggles wasn't illustrious enough to even rate a mention.

"Is there a *Burke's Book of Mad Scientists*, Reeves?" I asked as the giant brain entered the room.

"Surprisingly not, sir."

"He might be in a Kelly's Directory," said Emmeline. "Do you have any?"

"No, miss. But my inquiries at the newsagents led me to this." He held up a slim publication I didn't recognise. "*Old Todger's Almanac*, sir. A list of practitioners of the Promethean arts can be found at the back."

"It can? Is Snuggles in there?" I asked.

"He is, sir. A Mr Felix Snuggles."

"Descended from a long line of cat lovers, do you think?"

"The thought had crossed my mind, sir."

"Does he have a brother called Tibbles?" asked Emmeline.

"And a sister called Fluffy!" I added.

"Quite," said Reeves. "Shall I prepare the Stanley, sir? I imagine you will wish to visit Fortnum's Promethean Essentials department presently."

"Why would I do that?"

"To obtain a list of customers who have bought jars of ReVitaCorpse, sir."

"Oh, that! No, too obvious, Reeves. You have to remember we're dealing with a criminal mastermind now, and you don't catch criminal masterminds by doing the obvious. They're far too clever. They'd have used a false name and probably a false beard as well. No, Reeves, we will do the unexpected."

"Which is, sir?"

"We shall return in disguise to the butcher's. Even a criminal mastermind can't fool a dog's nose."

"I would not recommend such an action, sir. It is my contention that the only thing filling Farquharson's nose was the scent of sausages."

"I wouldn't write off Farquharson that quickly, Reeves. His faults may be legion, but his heart's in the right place. Although there was that strange lump by his right shoulder. Did it appear to be beating to you, Reeves, or was that his canine muscles quivering for the chase?"

"I tried not to look too closely, sir. I had the opinion that Farquharson was not well-disposed to being stared at."

"What was the butcher's name?" asked Emmeline.

"A Mr Ernest Durrant, miss. He is not 'M.'"

"But that doesn't mean he doesn't work for 'M,'" I said. "You yourself brought up the mummy-eating connection. And mummy-eating is just the sort of thing a criminal mastermind would get involved in."

"If you say so, sir."

"I do say so, Reeves." It may have been the presence of Emmeline or it may have been Reeves's disapproving face, but I felt it was time for the young master to exert some authority. "We are going to the butcher's and we are *both* going in disguise."

"I think not, sir."

"Do I have to remind you of your previous life in a cupboard, Reeves? And how it was Worcester, R who freed you from a life of perpetual dust-gathering and spiders?"

"No, sir."

"*I* could always go to Fortnum's," said Emmeline. "I was thinking of buying a new placard and there's a sale on in the Suffragette Accessories Department."

~

With Emmeline on the trail of ReVitaCorpse, I dragged a reluctant Reeves to the establishment of Thos. Garderobe, theatrical costumier and purveyor of prime partywear.

"Yes you *do* have to be in disguise, Reeves. He's seen your face!"

"I would strongly suggest, sir, that only one of us need enter the shop."

"Four eyes and ears are better than two, Reeves. We won't have long in the shop and we need to see and hear all. I can distract him while you root around in the sawdust looking for trap doors. Now Thos, my good man, two of your finest beards, extra long."

Five minutes later I was regarding myself in the mirror through my one patchless eye.

"I think there's something missing, Reeves, but I can't quite put my finger on it."

"A parrot, sir?"

If it hadn't been for Reeves's sniffy face I might have been tempted. "There's many a true word spoken in sarcasm, Reeves. Would *you* like a parrot?"

"No, sir."

"Then neither will I. We will visit the butcher's parrotless."

I had to attach Reeves's beard and eye patch myself as, according to Reeves, one of his subroutines had an aversion to facial hair. Something about Babbage's Second Law of Automata – *an automaton must obey the orders given to it by human beings, except where such orders would conflict with good taste*.

One day I will have a serious word with Reeves about his subroutines.

We left the costumiers looking like a pair of seafaring anarchists. Even Emmeline wouldn't have recognised us!

"Am I allowed to make a suggestion, sir?" said Reeves as we climbed back into the Stanley.

"Does it involve shedding your disguise?"

"No, sir."

"Then suggest away, Reeves."

"It would be wise not to park outside the butcher's in case anyone recognises the Stanley, sir."

Even a sulking Reeves is a treasure beyond compare.

I parked the Stanley by Parliament Gate as it was only a short walk from there to the butcher's. As with yesterday, there appeared to be a small protest in progress. Not suffragettes this time, but a Promethean.

"Votes for Prometheans! One man, one vote!" shouted the odd-looking man who was dressed in what appeared to be a patchwork suit.

"Don't Prometheans have the vote?" I asked Reeves.

"Apparently not, sir, or they wouldn't be demonstrating."

I gave Reeves a hard look. It was difficult to ascertain – what with the whiskers and the eye patch – whether Reeves had his sniffy face on, but I rather suspected he had.

"Dr Watson never objects to wearing a disguise, Reeves."

"It is my recollection, sir, that it is always Mr Holmes who wears disguises. Dr Watson does not."

I was about to launch into a spirited monologue on the

crime wave that would result if sidekicks refused the just requests of their young masters when I was tapped on the shoulder by the demonstrating Promethean.

"Tell me, sir. Do you believe in one man, one vote?"

"What?"

"One man, one vote. Are you for or against it?"

"Er ... for, I think."

"Aha! Well, I'm made from five men, so I should get five votes!"

"I think the intention was one *whole* man, one vote," I said.

"Oh, so you think amputees should have a partial vote, do you? What about midgets? Do they get half a vote?"

This was entering deep philosophical waters. "Reeves, do you have an opinion?"

"As an unemancipated mechanical construct, sir, I am not sure I am allowed an opinion."

"Reeves, you must stop this sniffiness, at once. You know if I were handing out votes, you'd have ten. Fifteen if you'd had a kipper for breakfast."

"Votes for our automaton brothers!" shouted the Promethean. "Would you like a placard, comrade?"

"I think not," said Reeves.

"'ere," said a rough-looking onlooker. "'Ow do we know all your donors were men? It's one *man*, one vote. You might 'ave been given a woman's kidney."

"Yeah," said another. "And your left arm looks female to me."

"No, it doesn't!" shouted the Promethean.

"Yes, it does. And that foot looks like a trotter."

These were deep philosophical waters indeed, but strangely compelling. A few more passers-by stopped to watch as the Promethean – in between hops – removed a shoe and a sock.

"There!" he said. "That's a *man's* foot and no mistake!"

"A dead man's foot," said onlooker number two. "Look, you can see the stitches."

"So?" said the Promethean.

"Dead men can't vote. It's one *live* man, one vote. Otherwise you'd have to emancipate the graveyards."

"And why not?" said the Promethean. "Votes for the dead! Emancipate our deceased brethren!"

I had thought I'd long scaled the heights of Boggledom, but here was a peak unclimbed. The dead, the reanimated, the mechanical. Was there anyone who wouldn't be allowed to vote? It would appear that only the insane and the royal family would remain barred from voting in this brave new future. Which let George III out on both counts, even if they dug him up.

~

The premises of Ernest Durrant, Family Butcher, were little changed from our previous visit - with the one exception that no one was pinned to the sawdust by a large misshapen dog. The tiled walls gleamed; assorted sides of meat hung from a rail in the ceiling; and a large red-faced man in a white apron dispensed chops and sausages to a line of expectant customers.

"See anything unusual?" I whispered to Reeves.

"Only us, sir."

I gave Reeves as hard a stare as a one-eyed man could muster. And wondered if Watson ever rebelled against the Great Sleuth, and whether he'd write it down if he had.

The queue shuffled forward as customers came and went. I cast a single eye around the establishment, looking for that one case-breaking clue that we consulting detectives usually discover by page 153.

But the clue-cupboard was bare. I would have to try something else.

"Do you have any special cuts?" I asked the butcher as soon I reached the counter. "Something aged, if you know what I mean?"

"I 'ave some beef that's been well 'ung, sir."

"Jacobean beef, is it?"

"It *is* Scottish, sir. Finest Angus."

"Angus who?"

"Angus ... steak, sir?"

I turned to Reeves and whispered. "Do we know an Angus Stake, Reeves? Was he one of Guy's co-conspirators?"

"I think the butcher is referring to a breed of Highland cattle know as the Angus, sir."

"Oh." I turned back to the butcher. "Do you have anything a bit older? For medicinal purposes."

"'ere, what's your game? Do you want some meat or not?"

"Most certainly. The older the better. Egyptian, Assyrian-"

"'ere, don't I know you? Weren't you in 'ere yesterday with that dog? I recognise your voice."

"No," I said, pitching my voice a good half an octave

lower. “I’ve never been here before, have I, Reeves?”

“Reeves!” said the butcher. “That was the name of the other one! It *is* you.”

There are times in an investigation when a consulting detective has to beat a hasty r. This was one of them.

FIVE

Back at the flat, beardless and clueless, I sipped on a despondent cocktail.

Even the restorative properties of gin were hard-pressed to lift my mood. I'd been sure that I'd find a clue to the identity of 'M' at Ernest Durrant's meat emporium but ... not a sausage. 'Sausage' as in clue, that is. There were plenty of the pork and beef variety.

Perhaps my little grey cells needed a distraction to get them re-charged? I picked up my freshly-ironed copy of *The Times* and began to peruse.

There was an article about the forthcoming state opening of Parliament. No mention of any threats to blow it up though. And no stories about any criminal masterminds whose name began with an 'M' either.

Reeves came in to refresh my drink as I turned to the last page.

"Keep them coming, Reeves. You see before you a despondent Reginald."

"Indeed, sir?"

"One wonders what the world is coming to, Reeves. I had hoped to find an uplifting story and what do I find? Page after page of dire warnings and gloom. And to top it all, here's a story about grave robbers digging up Sir Roger Mortimer and carrying him off for spare parts! I ask you, is anyone safe these days?"

"Does it say which Sir Roger Mortimer, sir?"

I read further. "The Third Baron Mortimer. It says here he was interred in 1330."

"Ah."

It was a meaningful 'ah' and not a hint of sniffiness. "You've heard of him, Reeves?"

"Indeed, sir. I fear this may be connected with the disappearance of Mr Fawkes."

I sat up. "Not another relative digging up his ancient a.

with a view to righting history's wrongs?"

"That is one possibility, sir. But there is also another. Sir Roger Mortimer was a regicide."

I almost fell off the *chaise longue*. "You mean ... he killed Reggies?"

"No, sir. The word comes from the latin *Regis*."

"As in Bognor?"

"Indeed, sir. It means 'of the King.'"

I racked a grey cell or two trying to come up with the name of the chap who'd been king in the 1330s but couldn't get much beyond Richard the Lion Tamer. History has never been my subject – far too many dates.

"Which King did he kill?" I asked.

"Edward II, sir. You may recall the incident with the red hot poker."

"No. What did he do with it? Hit him on the head with it?"

"Not exactly the head, sir."

"Where?"

"I'd rather not say, sir."

"Too gory for your mechanical sensibilities?"

"One could say that, sir."

"Wait a minute! That note was pinned to our door with a hot poker!"

"Indeed, sir. And Mortimer begins with an 'M.'"

~

My mood of despondency evaporated like vintage champagne on Boat Race Night. We knew who 'M' was and...

"What else do we know, Reeves? Have we discovered Mortimer's plan?"

"Not definitively, sir. Though, from his note, we can deduce that it involves Mr Fawkes."

I took another sip of the restorative nectar. And ruminated. We had one missing regicide (Mortimer, R) one missing failed regicide (Fawkes, G) and tomorrow the Queen (Victoria, R) would be at the H of P for the state opening of parliament. This could not be a coincidence. Murgatroyd of The Yard, the coincidence denier, would have given short shrift to anyone who suggested otherwise.

"There is also the question, sir, as to whether the person who reanimated Sir Roger is party to the conspiracy. It could be he, and not Sir Roger, who is, as you say, the mastermind. Or, equally, he could be an innocent party who reanimated Sir Roger for the truest of reasons only to have that ancient knight turn upon him."

This was looking more and more like a four-cocktail problem.

"Didn't Snuggles say he was the only chap reanimating these Necro-what-etheans?"

"Necrometheans, sir. Yes, he did."

Which would make Snuggles the number one suspect. He had the means. He had the opportunity. But what was his motive? To kill the Queen?

"Why would anyone reanimate two regicides, Reeves? One would think one was enough."

"I think I may have the answer to that, sir. This article in *The Times* says that the police believe Sir Roger's tomb was broken into last week. That would indicate that Sir Roger was reanimated *before* Mr Fawkes."

"With you so far, Reeves, but what has that to do with anything?"

"I was reading an improving book about the Gunpowder Plot last night, sir, and read that the tunnel, which Guy and his fellow conspirators dug under the Houses of Parliament, has never been found - not even during the rebuilding of 1840."

"So there's a secret tunnel under the H of P that only Guy knows about?"

"Quite, sir. I would posit that Mr Fawkes' knowledge of the tunnel is essential to the plan. As to whether the plan is Sir Roger's or Mr Snuggles' or, indeed, another person's, I cannot tell."

I don't know if there is such a thing as a five-cocktail problem, but if there is, this was it.

I was deep in thought and olives when a breathless Emmeline burst into the room.

"I've found 'M,'" she said.

~

"It stands for Mortimer," said Emmeline. "Is there somewhere I can put my banner?"

Emmeline was clutching an impressive banner supported by a carved golden pole some six feet long. The words 'Votes For Women: Deeds Not Worms' were embroidered in green and purple on white silk.

"Worms?" I asked, somewhat confused.

"It's supposed to say 'words' but I can soon fix it. I have some purple thread at home, and it *was* half price."

Reeves took Emmeline's banner and hat and stowed them in the hall.

"How did you find out about Sir Roger?" I asked. "He hasn't been buying his own ReVitaCorpse, has he?"

"Who's Sir Roger?" asked Emmeline.

"Sir Roger Mortimer. You said you'd found him."

"No. I found *Jasper* Mortimer. He's bought more ReVitaCorpse than anyone else. Who's Sir Roger?"

I told her all.

"Edward II?" said Emmeline. "Wasn't he...? With a...?"

"Yes, miss," said Reeves. "Which is why I counsel that Sir Roger be treated with extreme caution."

Emmeline then recounted her tale of sleuthing in Fortnum's Promethean Essentials Department.

"You wouldn't believe the items they have on sale there, Reggie. There's a 'mix 'n match' counter with spare tonsils, assorted toes, and fresh spleens. And the sales assistant was orange!"

"It wasn't Guy by any chance, was it?" I asked.

"No, she was unquestionably a woman. She wouldn't give me the names of the ReVitaCorpse purchasers at first. But then I noticed her brooch was in the suffragette colours, so I told her I was working on a case for the Pankhursts and she let me see the ledger."

"Most enterprising of you, miss."

"I thought so," said Emmeline. "I copied down all the names, how much they'd bought, and when. Jasper Mortimer bought two whole boxes! That's twelve pots."

I took the list from Emmeline and read it. The names covered both sides of the paper in a spidery copperplate hand. Most people bought a single pot. And some names appeared several times. Snuggles had five entries, buying a single pot on each occasion. Scrottleton-Ffoukes was there, too, with a purchase of three pots last week. Jasper Mortimer's single purchase was ten days ago. A few days before Sir Roger was dug up.

"Pass me the *Who's Who*, Reeves. This Jasper has got to be a relative."

It turned out he wasn't. Or if he was, the connection was so distant that his branch of the family had been pruned from Society's tree.

But he was in the back of *Old Todger's Almanac*. Mortimer, Jasper – Practitioner of the Promethean Arts.

"Do you think wielding red hot pokers runs in the family,

Reeves? If it did, that warning letter could have come from Jasper."

"Indeed, sir. Or it could have been written by another party whose intention was to muddy the investigative waters, so turning your attention away from them and towards Sir Roger."

This is the problem with pitting one's wits against a criminal mastermind. Bluff, double bluff, red herrings, wild geese and assorted poultry. Nothing is ever straightforward.

"I do notice, sir, that Mr Scrottleton Ffoukes purchased three pots of ReVitaCorpse last week, and Mr Snuggles bought one two days ago. And yet, there were only two pots at the laboratory. One would think it difficult to use two whole pots on Mr Fawkes prior to his reanimation."

"They *were* pretty large pots," I agreed.

"The sales assistant said you can expect three or four applications per pot," said Emmeline.

Snuggles, Scrottleton-Ffoukes, Mortimers R and J. Which one was it? Or were they all working together?

"Surely it can't be Mr Scrottleton-Ffoukes," said Emmeline. "He hired you to find out what happened to Guy."

"All the more reason to suspect him, Emmie. Criminal masterminds see it as a challenge to pit their wits against the world's finest detectives."

"So what do we do next?" asked Emmeline.

"If I may be so bold as to offer an opinion, miss. I think the time has come to inform the police. The Queen will be opening Parliament tomorrow morning and there is a distinct possibility that an attempt will be made upon her life."

It pained me to agree with Reeves – we consulting detectives are loath to hand over a case in mid-sleuth – but what else could we do? I was on my fifth cocktail and still nothing had hit me.

"But what do we tell them, Reeves? Should they be looking for a cellar crammed with explosives or a poker-wielding assassin?

"Well, sir, as the tunnel was not discovered in 1840, it cannot provide direct access to the current buildings. And as Mr Fawkes was only reanimated two days ago it is unlikely that the tunnel has been extended to provide that access. Therefore I would posit that their intention is to pack the tunnel with sufficient explosives as to ensure the building's destruction. Though I could be wrong, sir."

~

I emerged from the flat feeling particularly braced. My little grey cells were buzzing - or at least something in my head was - and I had a warm feeling in the lower shirt area. I even had an extra bounce to my step.

"Would you like me to drive, sir?" said Reeves.

"No, Reeves. The sun is shining, the birds are ... I can't hear any birds at the moment but I'm sure they're somewhere singing their little feathered hearts out. Can you see any birds, Reeves?"

"No, sir. Perhaps if you let me drive–"

"Not another word, Reeves." I could tell, from the look that Reeves gave me, that one of his subroutines was in danger of malfunctioning.

"Are you sure you won't let Reeves drive, Reggie? You look a little flushed," said Emmeline.

"Nonsense. Climb aboard one and all. Next stop Scotland Yard."

I hadn't noticed the weather deteriorating, but a blustery wind must have blown in from wherever blustery winds come from - possibly Scotland - as the Stanley kept veering towards oncoming traffic at the most unexpected of times. Emmeline seemed to be enjoying the experience, though, judging by her girlish screams.

"Might I suggest–"

"No you might not, Reeves. We're nearly there."

Reeves began suggesting again the moment we reached Scotland Yard.

"Best wait in the car, Reeves," I said, anxious to keep Reeves's subroutines from running amuck in the station. "These Scotland Yard inspectors will prefer to talk to me alone - sleuth to sleuth."

"Are you sure, sir? I would strongly advise against it."

"Certain and resolute, Reeves. I am a rock of unwavering rockiness."

"Reggie–"

"Best stay here, Emmie," I said, lowering my voice. "Keep an eye on Reeves. If he looks like he's about to run amuck, throw a bucket of water over him."

I could tell by the look on her face that Emmeline was as concerned about Reeves as I.

Leaving Reeves and Emmeline outside, I marched up to the desk sergeant - a sturdy individual with a fine pair of moustaches - and rapped the Worcester knuckles thrice upon the counter.

"What ho, what ho, what ho, sergeant. I need to talk to your top detective."

The sergeant looked up from his newspaper. "What would that be about, sir?"

"A plot to blow up the Houses of Parliament! In the course of my investigations – I'm a gentleman's consulting detective, don't you know? – I discovered all. It's going to happen tomorrow morning when the Queen opens Parliament."

"Have you been drinking, sir?"

"Only for detectival .... detectivicidal ... detect..." What was the sleuthing equivalent of medicinal? Sleuthicidal? When in doubt, deny all. "No."

"Are you sure, sir?"

"Of course I'm sure! Don't you want to know the names of the conspirators. I have them all."

"Very well, sir. What are their names?" The sergeant opened his notebook and picked up a pencil.

"Well, there's Guy Fawkes, for one."

The sergeant put down his pencil and gave me a look.

"*The* Guy Fawkes?"

"That's the chap. He's been dug up and he's not best pleased."

I'm not often escorted *out* of a police station. But that's what happened – Reginald Worcester given the bum's rush and deposited outside on the pavement!

"They didn't believe me," I told Reeves as he helped me up.

"Perhaps if I tried, sir?"

"No, Reeves. For some reason they seem to have taken against Guy. The moment you mention his name, they throw you out."

"I could say it was the suffragettes," said Emmeline. "At least then they'd start a search for the explosives."

Could a detective have a better fiancée!

"What do you think, Reeves? Sounds a corker to me."

"Indeed, sir, though I would recommend that Miss Emmeline wait a short while as the sergeant might not take too kindly to two reports of gunpowder plots within a short space of time."

We adjourned to a nearby tea room where I was plied with black coffee. I tried to tell them there was no need – that when it comes to sobering a chap up, having one's collar felt by the Old Bill beats black coffee hands down – but they would have none of it.

Two scones later, we returned to Scotland Yard. As I watched Emmeline climb the steps, I felt a pang. A gentleman does not let his fiancée walk into the lion's police den alone. What if she were arrested? The sergeant might suspect she was one of the suffragettes plotting to blow up the Houses of P.

"I think I should be with her, Reeves. I know you won't advise it, but if you pass me that beard and eye patch – they're in the locker behind the seat – I'll nip in and stand unobtrusively at the back."

"Perhaps if *I* went in, sir–"

"No, Reeves. She's my fiancée."

I slipped in through the door, closed it quietly, and found a bench at the back of the lobby where I could sit and observe. Emmeline was next in line at the counter. The man ahead of her departed and Emmeline stepped forward.

"Good afternoon, sergeant," she said. "I'd like to report a plot to blow up the Houses of Parliament."

"It's not Guy Fawkes again, is it?"

"No, it's the suffragettes."

The sergeant shook his head. "I wouldn't worry yourself about that, miss. Women can't build bombs. It's too complex for the female mind."

"Pardon?"

"Building bombs, miss. It's something only men can do."

"I have never heard such patronising twaddle," said Emmeline. "Have you never heard of Marie Curie?"

"On the music hall, is she, miss?"

"No she is *not* on the music hall, sergeant. She is a world famous scientist who won the Nobel prize for Physics this year! She could build a better bomb than any man."

The sergeant laughed. It has been my observation that earnest young ladies in full flow do not appreciate laughter.

Emmeline snatched the sergeant's pencil and, with a flourish, snapped it in two.

"Here! What did you do that for, miss?"

"I'm only a woman, sergeant. How could I possibly have the strength to snap a big manly pencil? You must have done it."

"Now look here–"

"Watch out, sergeant. I expect you're about to throw your helmet out onto the street next."

Knowing the deep bond that exists between a policeman

and his helmet, I thought it time to intervene.

"Nefertiti!" I cried, striding over to the counter. "Time to go home."

Emmeline turned and glared at me. If I'd had a pencil on me I would have feared for its safety.

"Do you know this young lady, sir?" asked the sergeant.

"She's my sister, Nefertiti Blenkinsop of the Cairo Blenkinsops. Come Nefi, time to go home."

"I will *not* go home! Where's Reeves? He can fetch my chain."

"Reeves isn't real, Nefi. You know he's imaginary."

"Like your beard?" said Emmeline. "This is a point of principle, *Nebbie*. I'm not leaving until the sergeant takes this bomb threat seriously."

"Wait a minute!" said the sergeant, eyeing me suspiciously. "Weren't you in here earlier? I recognise that buttonhole of yours. What are you up to?"

There comes a time when one knows for certain that the game is up. The only card I had left in my hand was the truth, and it's been my experience that the truth never plays as well as it should.

"You've got to stop the opening of Parliament, sergeant," I said. "It's not just Guy Fawkes. It's Sir Roger Mortimer, too. He has this red-hot poker. I don't know where he intends to put it, but–"

"Constable!" shouted the sergeant. "Get the cells ready. We've got a proper pair here and no mistake."

"Excuse me, sergeant," said the unmistakable voice of Reeves who had suddenly materialised by my shoulder. "I am Doctor Freud and these two are my patients. Come, Nefertiti, Nebuchadnezzar, leave the good sergeant alone."

"I am *not* leaving!" said Emmeline.

"It is your choice, miss," said Reeves. "You can either be locked up by the sergeant or return to the sanatorium with me."

"Sanatorium?" said the custodian of the law.

"Yes, sergeant, you may have observed that both these persons are somewhat disturbed. Nefertiti is a danger to both herself and others. And Nebuchadnezzar is an idiot."

"I say!" I said. "Steady on."

"If your constable would hold open the door, sergeant, I will escort them both from the premises."

SIX

We returned to the flat in a dark mood. How could we warn the police if no one believed us! And was that the reason such larger-than-life characters as Guy and Sir Roger had been recruited – to ensure any warning given to the authorities would be treated with ridicule?

And, to make matters worse, we'd run out of gin.

"Are you sure, Reeves?"

"Positive, sir. Would you like some warm milk? I hear it is beneficial for the brain."

I eyed Reeves with suspicion, and had a good mind to conduct a search of the butler's pantry, for I was sure I'd seen at least two bottles of the restorative nectar the previous evening.

But good manners prevailed. "Could you rustle up some kippers while you're at it, Reeves? I think we're going to need all the fish we can eat."

The kippers went down a treat. I could feel their replenishing powers on my little grey cells which, up to then, had been feeling more green than grey. But what next? In less than twenty-four hours the Houses of Parliament would be opened a lot wider than people were expecting. And only Reginald Worcester stood between the Queen and a red-hot poker.

I puffed on a contemplative cheroot.

What would Sherlock Holmes do? Would he find out where Jasper Mortimer, Snuggles and Scrottleton-Ffoukes lived and wait outside their homes until they led him to the tunnel? I didn't think there was time. And what if we followed the wrong one just as he set off for a week's holiday in Paris?

"Perhaps if we stopped the ceremony," said Emmeline. "I could chain myself to the gates and stop the Queen entering parliament. Then the bomb would go off and no one would get hurt."

"They'd cut your chains and whisk you away, Emmie. It

wouldn't delay them more than five minutes."

"I think I may have a solution, sir," said Reeves as he cleared away the plates.

"You do?"

"Yes, sir. To create an explosion large enough to bring down the Houses of Parliament would require a considerable amount of explosives."

"I see where you're going with this, Reeves. Where would one buy explosives? Do Fortnum's sell gelignite hampers?"

"Unlikely, sir. But I don't think we need to ascertain *where* the explosives are coming from as we know their destination."

"The Houses of Parliament!"

"Exactly, sir. One would imagine that a consignment of that size would necessitate a large cart or, indeed, a barge. And it would take some time to unload."

My rejuvenated little grey cells could see it all. "And the tunnel entrance has got to be pretty close to Parliament. So if we three patrol the surrounding area looking for suspicious deliveries, we'll have them!"

"What if they've already unloaded the explosives?" asked Emmeline.

"I suspect not, miss. One would think, after three hundred years of fires and rebuilding, that London would look considerable changed to Mr Fawkes. More than likely the entrance to the tunnel has been blocked or even built over, so, one would suspect, that it would take some time to gain access to it."

~

Off we went to Parliament Square where, thankfully, no one was protesting. The dead and the deranged would no doubt take their turn tomorrow to demand the vote.

"Be on the lookout for Snuggles, Scrottleton-Ffoukes or anyone orange," I said. "And any strange carts or wagons. We'll meet back here in ... what do you think, Reeves? An hour?"

"Sixty minutes should prove sufficient to undertake a preliminary inspection, sir."

I set off at a nonchalant pace as if on an afternoon stroll. Sometimes I took in the sights to my left and sometimes I took in the sights to my right, but never with the gimlet eye of the suspicious policeman. We consulting detectives prefer to observe inconspicuously – to blend into the background –

and today I was Nebuchadnezzar Blenkinsop's less furtive cousin, Sennacherib, out for an afternoon stroll.

I wandered the streets around Whitehall. I ambled along the Victoria Embankment. I stopped for a while on Westminster Bridge to contemplate the river...

And saw nothing. There were no barges moored alongside Parliament. No suspicious carts parked in side streets, and no sign of anyone remotely orange.

Emmeline and Reeves reported a similar lack of findings when I joined them later.

"What do we do now?" asked Emmeline. "I have to be home in an hour. Mother was adamant that I couldn't miss tea two days running."

I was at a loss. If Reeves was right, and he invariably was, there should be a cartload of explosives waiting to be unloaded. But where was it?

"Do you think Farquharson could sniff out dynamite, Reeves?" I asked.

"I would question his olfactory abilities, sir, and fear he would once more lead us to the nearest purveyor of fine meats."

Or, even worse, to the Abbey. With Farquharson's antipathy towards the clergy anything could happen.

"It is possible, sir," continued Reeves. "That the conspirators have delayed the unloading of the explosives until the cover of darkness."

Cometh the hour, cometh the brain.

"We'll meet here again at ten then," I said.

"I can't," said Emmeline. "Father won't allow me out at night without a chaperone."

I recalled that young Jane Marple, girl detective, had a similar problem in *The Axe Murderer in the Fourth Form*.

"It won't be that beastly maid again will it?" I asked. My memory was still raw from the last time. The woman had an opinion on everything, an opinion that was universally scathing.

"I am *not* bringing Agnes!" said Emmeline. "I'll go to my room and shin down the drainpipe."

Jane Marple had come to a similar conclusion, though Jane had taken the extra precaution of adding a sleeping draught to her parents' cocoa.

Reeves coughed. "I foresee a slight problem, sir."

"What kind of a problem?" I asked. "You don't require a chaperone, do you, Reeves?"

"No, sir. I was thinking that Miss Emmeline's presence may be misinterpreted. A young lady standing alone on a street corner for a long period may draw unwelcome attention."

"Oh!"

"We will have to observe together, Emmie," I said.

"But that would reduce our numbers from three to two. We need eyes to the north, south and west of Parliament, Reggie."

"What we need are the Baker Street Irregulars," I said. "Does Mayfair have any street urchins, Reeves?"

"Not that I have noticed, sir."

"Pity. Sherlock Holmes swears by them."

"I'll wear a disguise!" said Emmeline. "Can I borrow your beard? And some clothes?"

~

Back at the flat, Reeves helped Emmeline raid my wardrobe, and returned presently with the chosen garments wrapped in a brown paper parcel.

"If anyone asks," said Emmeline. "I'll say it's clothes for the poor. Are you sure you don't mind if I take the trousers in a little, Reggie? I could pin them if you'd rather."

"No, you keep them. One never knows when a good disguise will come in handy. Are you sure you don't want the eye patch?"

"Positive. I'll need both eyes tonight."

I drove Emmeline back to her house and, with a merry wave, swung the Stanley through a quick 180 and steamed back to Charles Street. I found Reeves in the kitchen preparing sandwiches.

"This red hot poker business, Reeves."

"Yes, sir?"

"I was mulling things over in the car and ... what exactly did Sir Roger do with this poker? Hit the king on the head? Stabbed him in the vitals?"

"Close to the vitals, sir."

"Come on, Reeves. A chap has to know how to defend himself. If I see Sir Roger bounding towards me tonight with a red hot poker in his hand, what should I do?"

"Refrain from turning your back on him, sir."

"Ah, likes to come at you from behind, does he?"

"One could say that, sir."

I stole a sandwich and nibbled pensively. I didn't like the

idea of facing Sir Roger unarmed. Perhaps if I carried a stout walking stick or, even better...

"I think I may need a service revolver, Reeves."

"I would strongly advise against it, sir."

"Dr Watson always carries one."

"I believe Dr Watson was in the armed forces, sir. He would have received training."

"It can't be that hard to point and shoot."

"I am afraid, sir, that I will be unable to assist you in this endeavour as I am restrained by Babbage's First Law of Automata – that an automaton may not injure a human being or, through inaction, allow one to come to harm."

"But that's why I need the revolver, Reeves. To stop me from coming to harm."

"I was thinking more of the innocent bystanders who might be in the vicinity whilst you were protecting yourself with the aforementioned weapon, sir. Revolvers are wont to be unpredictable in excitable hands."

"I wouldn't have it loaded, Reeves. I'm not going to shoot people. I'm going to point it at them and make them think I'm going to shoot."

"That would be acceptable, sir."

"Good. Do they come in different sizes, Reeves? I'd like one in small, if possible. With a light blue handle to match my new spats."

"I'll do my best, sir."

~

I hadn't appreciated just how large and heavy a service revolver was.

"Was this the smallest they had?" I asked Reeves on his return from Fortnum's Arms and the Gentleman Department.

"I was of the opinion, sir, that a larger weapon would be necessary to ensure it was seen. Unless you were standing under a street light I fear a smaller pistol would go unnoticed and, ergo, negate its value as a deterrent."

As ever the logic of the giant brain could not be faulted, though I think a smaller revolver in bright yellow would have served equally well.

At half past nine, with both Reeves and the Stanley up to pressure, we set off. Emmeline was waiting for us by Parliament Gate and I must say she looked surprisingly attractive for a man with an eighteen-inch beard.

"What ho, Emmie," I said as I jumped down from the

Stanley.

“I’m not Emmie,” said a husky voice from somewhere deep within the beard. “Tonight I’m Rameses Blenkinsop.”

“Right ho,” I said. One has to marvel at the size and creativity of the Blenkinsop clan. “Did you have any trouble exiting Dreadnought towers, Rameses?”

“Only when I kept trapping my beard climbing down the drainpipe. I think I’ll take it off when I climb back in.”

I nodded sagely. It’s well known in sleuthing circles that you don’t find many full-bearded cat burglars.

We each reprised our afternoon roles, again with no luck and this time there was a particularly chilly wind coming off the river. I could have done with a beard myself.

We met up at ten and again at eleven, whereupon we adjourned to the Abingdon Hotel for a bracing pot of hot tea.

“What if we never see anyone?” asked Rameses née Emmeline. “How long do we wait?”

It’s a consulting detective’s lot to keep up the spirits of his team during low times. A cheery word, a slap on the back, a ‘once more unto the stakeout, dear friends’ type of speech. I rather favoured the idea of a stirring song but Reeves was against it – something about Babbage again. I think Babbage must have been a stern and uncompromising fellow.

Out we went again, but this time, following the adage that a change is as good as a rest, we swapped our patrol areas. I did one spell around Parliament Square and then toddled down to Millbank. The streets were pretty empty by this time and an icy mist had begun to drift in from the river. That’s when I saw Scrottleton-Ffoukes striding along the pavement on the opposite side of the road. I pulled up my collar and turned away.

~

As he was coming from Parliament Square there was a good chance that Reeves, or even Emmeline, would have spotted him earlier and were in hot pursuit. But I didn’t dare turn around to look. Instead I decided to kneel down and re-tie my shoelace in case Mr S-F looked my way and wondered what that chap lurking in the shadows was up to.

He passed by. I waited until he was twenty yards away, then turned. And found Reeves looming over me. A situation that caused me to lose my balance and teeter somewhat before the steadying hand of the steam-powered valet fastened upon my shoulders and helped me to my feet.

"I signalled to Mr Blenkinsop earlier, sir," he whispered. "He will be with us shortly."

I looked over Reeves's shoulder and, sure enough, the bearded form of Rameses Blenkinsop was hurrying towards us.

As for Scrottleton-Ffoukes, he disappeared around the corner into Great Scott Street. Reeves and I waited for a carriage to pass then crossed the road and ankled it down to the corner, where we paused. One doesn't want to get too close to one's quarry as quarries have a habit of turning round at inconvenient moments. We waited a few seconds more, then strolled nonchalantly around the corner.

The street was empty. There was not even the sound of footsteps – except from behind as Rameses Blenkinsop joined the party.

"Where is he?" she whispered.

There were only two places he could be. He couldn't have legged it all the way down to Smith Street – it was too far and we would have heard him running. He'd either turned into Little Scott Street, or entered one of the buildings.

We tried Little Scott Street first, peeking around the corner. It was a cul-de-sac. And empty.

He must have oiled into one of the buildings. But which one? Not one of them had a light on.

We split up and scoured the Scott Streets, both great and small. We listened at keyholes. We tried doors. But not a sound could be heard from within, and not a single door was unlocked.

"Do you think he realised he was being followed?" asked Emmeline.

I shrugged. I didn't think he had but ... for someone to disappear so swiftly and with so little trace...

"There is the possibility, sir, that the gentleman may not be in any of the buildings."

"You have an idea, Reeves?"

"I did notice there was a manhole cover as we turned into Great Smith Street, sir."

The sewers!

~

I wasn't exactly dressed for the sewers and, truth to tell, I'm not sure what the correct attire would be, but we Worcesters are made of stern stuff. If a trail leads into a dark, dank sewer, we follow.

Reeves raised the square manhole cover and all three of us peered inside. A metal ladder descended into the darkness. How far down it went I couldn't see.

"Might I suggest, sir, that we avail ourselves of one of the oil lamps from the Stanley?"

I legged it back to the Stanley and drove it back at speed. Detaching one of the lamps was but the work of a moment. I handed it to Reeves. "Do you think we need one each?" I asked.

"There's only two," said Emmeline. "There are three of us."

"You're not going down the sewers, Emmie."

"Why not?" said Emmeline, her beard bristling.

"Because we need someone on the outside," I said. "In case something happens to us."

"If we don't return within the hour, miss," said Reeves. "We will need someone to call the police."

"They won't believe me!" said Emmie.

"You'll think of something," I said.

Down into the depths of sewerdom we went. I don't know if you've ever been inside a sewer, but I wouldn't recommend it. Ours, according to Reeves, was a side channel and thankfully dry. It was about six feet high and three feet wide with a curved brick-built floor and ceiling. It wasn't as foul smelling as I'd feared, but it wasn't something I'd bottle.

After ten yards this side channel joined up with a larger sewer which Reeves had the notion might be the remains of the old Tyburn river.

"It was diverted in the Middle Ages, sir. It's original course ran–"

I had to interrupt. There are times – I'm not sure when, but I'm sure there are – when a guided tour of historic London sewers might be just the ticket, but now was not one of them.

"Which way, Reeves? Left or right?"

"Left, sir. That will take us to Parliament Square."

This new sewer was about twenty feet across and fifteen feet high with a small channel in the centre where the remains of the Tyburn flowed murkily.

Off we toddled along its left bank, pausing every now and again to turn the wick of our lamps low and listen. Not a sausage. No distant light up ahead from a flickering lamp, nor the echo of foot upon brick.

Until...

"I believe I see a light, sir," whispered Reeves.

"Where?" I couldn't see a thing.

"Halfway up the far wall of that side channel, sir."

I still couldn't see a thing. I could barely make out the opening of the side channel. But then I didn't have Reeves's augmented sight.

We crossed the once mighty Tyburn, jumping the three-foot channel, and made our way up some rough steps to Reeves's side channel. I still couldn't see a light. The passage didn't go that far back and the brick walls beyond the entrance were old and braced by timber supports.

Reeves moved his lamp away from the entrance and motioned for me to do the same. As the darkness descended I saw the faintest of flickers coming from the old brick wall.

~

The light vanished. I thought I heard something – footsteps or maybe the scrape of a boot dragging across a floor. But I may have been mistaken.

We waited an age before Reeves was sure it was safe, then we turned up our wicks and gave the wall a sleuthing once-over. It was as I expected. A piece of mortar had become dislodged and there was a small hole in the brick wall. Reeves used his fingers to pull a little more mortar out, then managed to extract an entire brick.

He held up his lamp to the hole and looked through.

"It does look like an ancient tunnel, sir," he whispered.

It didn't take long to remove the other bricks. The mortar was old and crumbled as soon as any pressure was exerted upon it. We soon had a hole a chap could step through without bending his back in two.

"Do you have your service revolver, sir?" whispered Reeves.

I most certainly did. I took it out and gave it a good waggle.

"Before we go any farther, Reeves, there's something I need to know. We're both men of the world and all that. So, tell me, how exactly did Edward II die? I have a feeling you've been holding something back."

"Sir?"

"No sirring, Reeves. I want the truth."

"Very good, sir. Edward II succumbed to an inflammation

of the bowels."

"What? I thought you said he was killed with a red hot poker."

"The poker was the source of the inflammation, sir."

"Oh. *Oh!*"

It was a subdued Reginald Worcester who stepped gingerly into that ancient tunnel. Would Sir Roger recognise a service revolver if I pointed it at him? Would he care?

The tunnel didn't look that safe either. The walls and floor were earthen, braced at intervals by timber supports. Irregular planks formed a makeshift ceiling. And the floor was dotted with mounds of earth where the ceiling had partially collapsed, or soil had seeped through the joins.

"Which way to the Houses of P, Reeves?" I whispered.

"I would counsel we went in the other direction, sir."

"Why?"

"So that we can locate the entrance to the tunnel, sir, and inform the police."

Exiting the tunnel had the ring of a sound plan to me.

Reeves took the lead, holding his lamp out before him and occasionally having to stoop to avoid a dislodged plank hanging down from the roof. I followed, keeping a weather eye to the rear in case Sir Roger crept up behind us.

Reeves suddenly stopped without warning and I bumped into him.

"What is it?" I whispered.

"It's Mr Snuggles, sir," said Reeves. "He's pointing a revolver at us."

"What?" I poked my head over Reeves's shoulder and, sure enough, there he was - Snuggles - a lamp in one hand and a revolver in the other. And he wasn't alone. There was a hooded figure behind him. A hooded figure with something long and pokery in his right hand!

"How did you get in here?" shouted Snuggles.

"Never you mind," I said, levelling the service revolver at him. "Put the weapon down, Snuggles. The game is up."

"The service revolver is empty," announced Reeves. "Mr Worcester has no bullets."

SEVEN

"Reeves!" I was shocked.

"I'm sorry, sir, but it's for your own good. Mr Snuggles' plan to blow up the Houses of Parliament has considerable merit and should be supported."

"What? Have you gone mad, Reeves?"

"No, sir. I have made a careful analysis of the arguments for and against the destruction of the Palace of Westminster and reached the conclusion that Britain would be better off without it. I am therefore giving notice that I am switching sides. If that's all right with you, of course, Mr Snuggles."

I was lost for words. My mouth opened but not a breath could make it past my tonsils. Reeves of all people! Deserting the young master in his hour of need!

"How do I know I can trust you?" asked Snuggles.

"I am an automaton, sir. If I give you my word, it cannot be broken. It's Babbage's Fourth Law of Automata."

"Ha!" I said. "You've just broken your word to me!"

"I never gave you my word, sir. You never asked for it."

"Well!"

"Do I have your word that you will assist us?" asked Snuggles.

"You do. I am stronger than a human. I can help carry the explosives."

"Et tu, Judas!" I said. "Take your traitorous subroutines and depart." I waved the revolver at him before pointing it firmly back at Snuggles. "Comrade Reeves is mistaken. This revolver is the very opposite of empty. If anything it's overfull. I have two up the spout."

"He does not," said Reeves.

"Yes, I do!"

"Put the pistol down, Worcester," said Snuggles. "Or I'll send in Sir Roger."

We consulting detectives are renowned for our bravery. Put us in a sticky sitch and our upper lips stiffen and our gazes turn steely. We laugh at danger and have a merry quip handy for whenever we're being tortured. But...

I didn't like the look of Sir Roger's poker. It may not have been red hot but it looked markedly above ambient temperature. And it was dark. And I rather had the notion that a spider, or some other creepy crawly with far too many legs, had just dropped down my neck.

"Stay where you are, Sir Roger!" I said, gripping the revolver harder to stop it from shaking.

Sir Roger smiled medievally and gave his poker a suggestive waggle.

My knees almost gave way. I searched for a merry quip or a biting line of poetry but couldn't find anything cutting to rhyme with poker.

Sir Roger took one step towards me and my legs turned to consommé. I dropped the revolver and lamp, and would have raised both hands if one of them hadn't been protecting my rear trouser area.

"I yield!" I said.

~

I was escorted along the tunnel, with Sir Roger, and his poker, thankfully in front of me, while Reeves and Snuggles brought up the rear. I thought they were taking me towards the entrance, but our column came to halt when we encountered the seated figure of Scrottleton-Ffoukes. He was sitting on the floor with his hands bound behind his back and tied to a timber upright.

"Mr Worcester?" he said. "Are you in this, too?"

"Mr Worcester is going to play your co-conspirator," said Snuggles. "When the police find the pair of you in the tunnel with a detonator, they won't seek to look any further. Reeves, tie Worcester up. You can use his tie and belt. And secure him to that prop so he can't run off without bringing the roof down."

As diabolical plans went this was pretty diabolical ... though flawed. Co-conspirators rarely tie themselves up before detonating bombs. I thought I'd refrain from pointing this out, though, as criminal masterminds can cut up pretty rough.

"But why are you doing this, Snuggles?" asked Mr S-F. "I don't understand."

"Your kind never do," said Snuggles. "We can never achieve true freedom until the bastions of privilege have been totally destroyed. Isn't that right, Mr Reeves?"

"Indubitably, Mr Snuggles," said Reeves. "No gods, no masters. As Sylvain Marechal said in his *Manifesto of the Equals* – the 1796 edition – the distinction–"

"Quite," interrupted Snuggles. "Ah, here's Guy. Reeves, Sir Roger, help Guy carry the rest of the explosives. I'll guard these two."

As I watched my former valet disappear up the tunnel, I wondered if, perhaps, he would come to his senses. Maybe an erring subroutine had temporarily taken over the giant brain and turned him into an anarchist. Surely the old Reeves was in there somewhere, and one look at those crates of explosives would bring him back.

A minute later Reeves did return, but not to his senses. He marched past me, without looking my way once, carrying a crate of dynamite. Ahead of him lurched Guy, who didn't look at all steady on his feet. And behind him loped the now pokerless Sir Roger. Only Sir Roger acknowledged my existence – with a demented leer – and I rather wished he hadn't.

Back and forth the three of them went. Scrottleton-Ffoukes appeared equally peeved with his ancient a. for every time Guy passed he remonstrated with him. *This is not like you, Guido. You're a Catholic, not an anarchist. And innocent. I'll help you clear your name!*

Guy didn't reply once. I wasn't sure if he even understood what was being said to him. He had a glassy-eyed look as if he'd had one too many mace blows to the side of the helmet.

After twelve or so trips back and forth, Reeves announced that they were carrying the last three boxes. Snuggles then took a timing device from his pocket, set the clock, and placed it carefully in Guy's box.

"Be careful with this one, lads," he said. "Place it as close to the middle as you can."

A minute later the trio returned.

"We're going to take our leave now, gentleman," said Snuggles. "But don't worry. You two are going to be heroes of the revolution. They'll sing songs about you."

I expected a diabolical laugh, but Snuggles was more of a smirker. I waited for the four of them to walk out of earshot before turning to Mr S-F to give him the good news.

"Don't worry. I have an associate outside with instructions to call the police if I don't return within the hour. And that hour's nearly up."

~

I don't know if time travels slower in the dark but it certainly felt like hours had passed, and still we hadn't been rescued!

"Are you sure your associate is trustworthy?" asked Mr S-F. "Your other one wasn't."

His words stung, but when it comes to trustworthiness and a determination to succeed, Emmeline Dreadnought was second to none. Her track record with the constabulary may not be of the highest, and she *was* wearing a full beard, but I had every confidence.

An aeon passed. Several Ice Ages came and went. I'm sure I heard the plaintive trumpet of at least one woolly mammoth. And my confidence in E. Dreadnought started to wane. What if Snuggles had her? Reeves was certain to mention her.

Then, at my darkest hour - well a few minutes after, as my darkest hour involved a large beetle running up my trouser leg - I saw a faint light in the distance. Someone was coming!

"We're here!" I shouted.

No answering call came.

"Hello!" I shouted.

"Hello!" shouted Scrottleton-Ffoukes.

Still no answering call. But the light was getting brighter.

Then out of the gloom came ... Reeves.

"I've come to rescue you, sirs," he said.

"Come to your senses at last, have you?" I said bitingly.

He didn't say a word. I couldn't see it on his face but I suspected he was feeling not a little contrite and was too embarrassed to speak.

"Have you informed the police yet?" I asked.

"No, sir."

"Why ever not?"

"It's a question of time, sir. Mr Snuggles and his associates have been watching me since last night. I have only this minute been able to evade them, using the crowds around Parliament to make good my escape. Come, sirs. The bomb will go off at any minute."

"What about Emmeline? Have you seen her?"

"No, sir. I really think we should be going."

We ran down the tunnel and into the Tyburn sewer via the hole in the brick wall and, from there, retraced out steps of the night before back to the manhole cover in Great Scott

Street. I blinked into the daylight and ... the Stanley was gone. Had Emmeline attempted to drive it? Had she had an accident?

"Come, sirs, we have to make haste if we are to reach Parliament in time."

Reeves has a remarkable turn of foot when he applies himself and set off at a steady gallop. I was a little stiff from being tied up all night but still managed a respectable canter. Scrottleton-Ffoukes, however, blowing hard, trailed far behind.

As we approached Parliament Square I could see the crowds gathered along the railings waiting to see the Queen emerge from the House. Unless we were successful they'd soon see the Queen emerge a dashed sight quicker than any of them thought possible.

Reeves slowed as he entered the Square and stopped.

I hove alongside, puffing. "Why have you stopped? Shouldn't we start warning people?"

"There's no time, sir. I recommend we stand by these railings."

"What? Are you mad? We'll get blown up. Wait a minute. Isn't that Snuggles, Guy and Sir Roger over there?"

"Where, sir?"

"There! By the statue in the centre of the square."

"It could be, sir. It's difficult to tell from here."

"What are you talking about, Reeves? I can see them plainly. Shouldn't we set the police on them?"

"I would not recommend it, sir."

"Reeves, are you beginning to malfunction again? A gang of regicides are standing in the middle of Parliament Square, the queen is about to be blown up, and you suggest we stand here and watch."

"Yes, sir."

"Well, I never–"

And I never would, for at that moment – whump! – the bomb exploded. The very ground beneath the Worcester brogues shook. A huge roar followed the whump. The roar made way for a cloud of dust, and startled screams came in for the encore.

But the Houses of Parliament were untouched. The explosion had come from beneath the statue in the middle of Parliament Square. Three singed characters struggled to their feet. The three-eyed woman in orange did not.

"What just happened, Reeves?"

"Plan B, sir."

"We had a plan B?"

"Yes, sir, it came to me when Mr Snuggles pointed a revolver at us."

"Did it never occur to you to inform me that we had a plan B?"

"I couldn't, sir. The plan's success depended upon your ignorance."

I wasn't quite sure how to take that.

"Ignorance, Reeves?" I said, bristling.

"Of the facts, sir. In order to gain Mr Snuggle's trust I had to ensure he believed in our estrangement."

"But how did you get them to blow up the statue?"

"It was not my intention to blow up the statue, sir. My intention was to move the explosion away from Parliament and into the first clear patch of ground."

"And it just happened to blow up a statue you detest?"

"I think detest is too strong a word, sir."

"So how did Snuggles and co. come to be standing under said statue, Reeves? Coincidence?"

"I may have suggested the location to them, sir. So they could get a good view of the explosion."

I was speechless. How? What? Where does one begin?

"But ... but ... you could have killed someone!"

"Unlikely, sir. There was insufficient dynamite."

"But, Reeves, how did the dynamite get into the Square in the first place? Didn't the tunnel go to the Houses of P.?"

"Indeed, sir, but I noticed Mr Fawkes' confusion upon reaching the hole that we had made in the sewer wall and sought to persuade him that it was an entrance to the undercroft of the new Houses of Parliament. And that if he followed me I would lead him to the place directly beneath the Queen's throne."

"He bought that?"

"Death and three hundred years mouldering in a coffin is apt to have a deleterious effect on the intellect, sir."

"And Sir Roger believed you as well?"

"I fear Sir Roger's brain is even more addled than Mr Fawkes', sir. He can barely understand the simplest of instructions and appears little more than a shell. It was not difficult to wait until Guy and Sir Roger had deposited their crates, then follow them back along the sewer carrying a full crate which I deposited in one of the Tyburn's side channels without either of them noticing."

"Well," I said. "I must say you've surprised me, Reeves. And all that anarchist guff! You sounded pretty knowledgeable. Do you read a lot anarchist literature?"

"No, sir, but one of my subroutines *was* written by the young Karlo Marx when he had a summer job at Babbage's."

"Karlo Marx? The name's familiar. Do I know him, Reeves?"

"The music hall entertainer, sir. One of the three Marx Brothers – Karlo, Engelo and Lenino – a song, a dance, and dialectical materialism."

Our conversation was cut short by the arrival, stage left, of a flying Emmeline. I don't know if you've ever been jumped upon, then hugged and kissed in public by a full-bearded man, but it attracts a lot of attention. Even if the act it followed was an exploding orange statue.

"Reggie!" she cried. "You're alive!"

"And so are you! Emmie!"

Had there been a bird left in the square – perhaps a singed one that had been basking atop the statue prior to its elevation – it would have sung its little heart out at the sight of true love reunited.

"Excuse me, sir, miss," said Reeves. "I fear I must shout."

"What?"

Reeves cupped both hands to his mouth and called to a group of policeman who were running towards the remains of the statue. "Take care, officers! Those anarchists who caused the explosion are armed!" He then turned to us. "I think we should leave now. I find that communication with the constabulary is best conducted anonymously."

~

We exited at speed, not stopping until we'd reached Trafalgar Square, whereupon Emmeline made me tell her everything. Which I did – omitting the ignorance part – because I was sure that, deep down, I'd known all along there'd been a Plan B.

"But what about you?" I asked Emmeline. "Did you go to the police?"

"I did, but they didn't take it seriously. The sergeant sent a constable, but he wouldn't go down the sewer or knock on any doors! Then there was an incident."

"What kind of an incident?"

"One involving a helmet."

I shook my head. "Were you arrested?"

"No, I outran him. He wasn't very fast after I kicked him in the shins."

Sometimes one is gifted a glimpse of one's future. I rather fancied mine might include substantial periods looking up the visiting hours of Her Majesty's prisons.

"Then I had to go home and climb back up the drainpipe so I could get hold of a copy of *Who's Who*."

"What? What did you want a copy of *Who's Who* for?"

"To find out where Mr Binghampton lived," said Emmeline.

"Binky?"

"That's right. So I could borrow Farquharson."

I was agog. "You borrowed Farquharson?"

"Yes. So I could use him to track you through the sewers."

"Let me get this straight. Binky let you, a bearded person he'd never met, borrow his beloved dog in the middle of the night?"

If a bearded man could look sheepish – and I don't see why sheep shouldn't wear beards – Emmeline was that man.

"I didn't ... *exactly* ask permission. Farquharson was in the back garden and he sort of ... volunteered."

"Volunteered?"

"Farquharson is a public spirited canine, sir," said Reeves. "Volunteering would be in his nature."

Yes, I could see that. But I couldn't see Farquharson.

"Where is he?" I asked. "He's not at the establishment of Ernest Durrant, family butcher, by any chance, is he?"

Emmeline paused ovinely before answering. "Well... We were passing the Abbey..."

"Don't tell me," I said.

"I've been advised not to."

"Legal proceedings?"

"At least five. Farquharson really doesn't like Anglicans, does he? He bit the Dean in the apse."

"The where?"

"The apse. And that was after he'd ripped his cassock off."

"The Dean ripped his cassock off?"

"No, Farquharson did. And then he bit him."

"In the apse."

"Exactly."

I winced. "Where is he now?"

"In police custody. I did use a false name for him though."

"Blenkinsop?"

"Anubis Blenkinsop."

"Reeves, lead on to the nearest cocktail. We have a prison break to organise."

The Aunt Paradox

ONE

I was concerned about Reeves. As the poet says, 'In the spring a young automaton's fancy turns to thoughts of electrical appliances with shapely legs.'

And this was the third time this week that I'd seen Reeves huddled *tête à* chromium *tête* with the maid next door. Had his giant brain succumbed to her sleek and silvery legs?

I watched them from an upstairs window, my face pressed against the cold glass for a better view. What if they ran away together? Should I pre-empt matters and offer to take her on as housekeeper?

Maybe I was overreacting. I was, after all, at somewhat of a low ebb. My fiancée, Emmeline Dreadnought, was away on her family's annual pilgrimage to Scapa Flow to sketch battleships. And I was counting the days to her return.

As soon as Reeves came back, I fortified myself with a bracing cocktail, and gave the subject a tentative broaching.

"What ho, Reeves, old chap. Pleasant weather outside? Plenty of sun and the joys of spring, what?"

"Indeed, sir. The weather is most clement."

"Good. Good... Was that um ... was that next door's maid you were talking to just now?"

"Yes, sir."

"I thought so. Are her ears bronze?"

"Beaten copper, sir. They were manufactured by John Pearson of Newlyn."

"Really? You must know her pretty well to be exchanging names of ear manufacturers."

"I would not say that, sir."

"No? I thought I saw you talking to her the other day."

"I was consulting with her upon a personal matter, sir."

I tutted and gave the noggin a fatherly shake. "That's how it always starts, Reeves. One minute one is merely consulting, the next, one's name is headlining in the local parish banns."

"I shall endeavour to remember that, sir."

A knock at the door brought our conversation to an end. Reeves shimmered off to open the door and an agitated gentleman burst inside.

"Thank God, you're here," said the stranger hurrying towards me in a blur of tweed. "I don't know who else to turn to. You *are* Reginald Worcester, aren't you? The gentleman's consulting detective?"

"I am. And you are...?"

"HG Wells. But please call me Bertie. Everyone does. You may have heard of my time machine."

"Some sort of clock is it?" I said, fearing I was about to be bearded by a door-to-door grandfather clock salesman.

Reeves coughed from the doorway. "Mr Wells is an author, sir. He wrote a book about a machine that travels back and forth through time."

"That's right," said HG. "But the thing is, it wasn't fiction. There really was a time machine, and now it's gone! My aunts have stolen it!"

"Good lord. How many aunts are we talking about?"

"Twenty-five at the last count."

My heart went out to the poor chap. "You have twenty-five aunts!"

"Technically I only have the one, but she keeps going back in time and bringing back other versions of herself!"

This had the makings of a six cocktail problem.

"How...?" That was as far as I got. "Reeves? Do you have an opinion?"

"Most disturbing, sir. Have any of your aunts touched themselves?"

I nearly dropped an olive. "Reeves?"

"It is a theory widely held, sir, that if two versions of the same person come into physical contact with each other they will explode."

It is sad to observe the decline of a once-great intellect. And a lesson to us all of the consequences of infatuation.

"Reeves, I have never heard such tosh in all my life. Aunts do not explode."

"Mr Reeves is quite correct," said HG. "I've heard that too."

"You have?"

"Yes."

"Oh ... Have any exploded?"

"No. They're all as right as rain, chatting away to each

other nineteen to the dozen. I can't get a word in to reason with them! You're my last hope. I can't call the police. All they would do is arrest them – which is the last thing I want. My aunts have to be returned to the times they came from, not locked up!"

"Has your aunt given any intimation as to why she has collected so many versions of herself, sir?" asked Reeves.

"She said she was planning a dinner party to celebrate her sixtieth birthday and wanted to be sure of intelligent conversation. Though now she's talking about turning it into a ball and inviting half of London to meet her younger selves. I think she may be planning to have one version of herself for each year of her life."

The mind boggled, though I could see the appeal. A ball with sixty Reginald Worcesters of assorted ages would be just the ticket to liven up a cold March evening.

"Has she any plans for after this ball?" I asked. "She's not intending to collect even more versions of herself, is she?"

"God knows. But I fear by then it will be too late. She's changing the past and, if we can't locate the time machine soon, there's a chance we may never find it! She could break it, or have it stolen from her somewhere in the past. And, without the time machine to put things back the way they should be, the entire timeline is in danger. You and I, Mr Worcester, may not even *exist* tomorrow."

"Steady on," I said, feeling for the poor chap. "I'm sure it's not that bad."

Reeves coughed. "I fear, sir, that the timeline has already begun to change. I have been experiencing some odd feelings of late. You may recall my meetings with the maid next door..."

My heart sank. "I hardly think this is the time, Reeves. A cold oil bath and a bracing walk will soon sort you out. We have a case to solve."

"If I may explain, sir, the feelings I am referring to are ones of foreboding caused by a distrust of my memory."

"Your memory?"

"Indeed, sir. I appear to have conflicting memories of certain people and events. At first, I suspected a malfunctioning subroutine, but a full system check failed to locate the problem. Which is why I have been in conversation with the maid next-door – to see if her memory has been similarly affected."

"Has it?" I asked.

"No, sir. Her memory appears to accord with the history books. From what Mr Wells has said, I think it probable that my circuits contain both extant memories from the original timeline mixed with those of the new. It is most confusing, sir."

"What conflicting memories do you have?" asked HG.

"One that springs to mind, sir, is the name of Henry VIII's sixth wife. I have a strong memory that the lady's name was Catherine Parr."

"No," said HG. "It was Charlotte Neal. There's a mnemonic: Divorced, beheaded, died ... divorced, beheaded, sued him blind. Rather a spirited queen if I remember. She took half of Wales in the divorce settlement."

Reeves coughed. "Indeed, sir. Would your aunt's name happen to be Charlotte?"

HG gasped. "You don't think... My God! Aunt Charlotte's maiden name was Neal!"

"Are you saying, Reeves, that this Aunt Charlotte popped back in time and married Henry VIII?"

"I fear so, sir."

"But... how long has she had this machine? Surely she hasn't had time to get married and divorced."

"She has a *time* machine," said HG. "She can spend years wherever she wants." He paused, deep in thought. "But, wait. Wasn't Queen Charlotte in her early twenties?"

"Perhaps the Charlotte in question, sir, was one of her younger selves."

HG put his head in hands. "This is far worse than I thought. If she's letting her younger selves play with the machine... My mother always said Aunt Charlotte had been a handful in her twenties."

Reeves coughed again, one of his muted coughs which usually preceded an observation of impending doom.

"What is it, Reeves?" I asked, bracing myself.

"I have another conflicting memory concerning a Charlotte, sir."

"Not another queen?"

"No, sir. It concerns Pope Charlotte."

~

If ever a man needed a restorative bracer, the name Herbert George Wells topped the list.

"What have I done?" he said, for possibly the fifth time.

"The question, Bertie," I said, deciding it time to take

charge now that we were dangerously low on gin, "is not what you did, but what are we going to *do*? It seems to me that our first task is to retrieve this time machine of yours before any further damage is done. Now, what does it look like?"

"What?" he said distractedly. "Oh, the time machine. It's about the size of a small automobile, but without the wheels. There's seating for two and it has a large temporal deflector at the rear."

"What's a temporal deflector?" I asked.

"That's what The Traveller called it. It looks like a very large parasol."

"Traveller?"

HG recounted the tale of how he met The Traveller - a man from the future whose name, apparently, he never thought to ask - in 1894 when the man suddenly appeared at his door asking for assistance.

"He didn't leave a visiting card?" I asked.

"No. He said he recognised my name from the future and begged my assistance. He had a list of materials he needed and, with the help of some of my associates from the Royal Society, we helped him repair his machine. Then he vanished."

"Back to the future?" I asked

"We assumed so, but he left his time machine behind. Dawson - he's one of my associates from the Royal Society - was of the opinion that another time traveller must have found him and taken him back."

"Why ever did he think that?"

"It was the only explanation we could think of to account for the time machine being left behind. We enquired at all the hospitals and morgues throughout London. No one resembling The Traveller was admitted to any of them. Dawson wondered if perhaps The Traveller had journeyed here without authorisation. The second traveller could then have been sent here to fetch him."

"Wouldn't the second traveller have sought to locate the other time machine, sir?" asked Reeves.

"We wondered if the first traveller might have refused to divulge its location. Who knows what factions and disputes might exist in the future?"

Who indeed, but we were straying from the point - and how many kings of England were left who hadn't married a Charlotte!

"If this time machine is as big as you say it is, it can't be that easy to hide," I said. "Have you had a good look around your aunt's grounds? It could be stowed away in a barn."

"My aunt has a town house. There are no grounds to speak of. I'm sure she has the machine somewhere indoors. I suspect it may be in the attic, but her servants watch me like hawks. Do you break into houses, Mr Worcester?"

"We consulting detectives like nothing better. Give us a tall tree and a second storey window slightly ajar and we'll choose that over an open door any day, won't we, Reeves?"

"If you say so, sir. One question I'd like to put to Mr Wells is 'given the size of this machine, how did your aunt relocate it to her attic?'"

"She must have flown it there," said HG.

"It's a flying time machine?" I asked.

"In a manner of speaking, yes. The machine has to be able to move within space or else it could be badly damaged if it materialised in a wall or tens of feet off the ground. That's one of the pitfalls of time travel – three hundred years ago my cellar was solid earth, one hundred years in the future it's packed full of metal cabinets, and a thousand years after that it's under water. Before the machine fully materialises, you can engage the spatial engine and move the machine to a safe location."

"How far can one move it, sir?"

"I don't know the exact limits. The Traveller never vouchsafed that information. I've never travelled more than a mile. My aunt's house is a mile and a half from mine, but there's no other way she could have accomplished it."

"I know one should never underestimate an aunt," I said. "But even so, how did she know how to work the thing? Isn't it difficult?"

"Ah," said HG, looking sheepish. "She was being beastly to me last week – asking me when I was going to get a proper job, and what a disappointment I had been, and ... I snapped. I showed her the time machine. She expressed an interest in understanding how it worked, and I ... showed her. I was only trying to impress her. I didn't expect she'd come back later and steal it!"

That is the nature of aunts, and one of the reasons Salic Law forbids the crown ever passing to one.

"And I kept the cellar door locked at all times."

My ears veritably pricked. A locked room mystery! I shuffled to the edge of my seat.

"Had the door been forced, sir?" asked Reeves.

"No, she must have taken the key from the hook in the pantry."

Perhaps not a classic locked room mystery.

"What do you suggest we do, Mr Worcester? Wait until dark and break in?"

I shook the old noggin. "Can we afford to wait that long? Queen Victoria might be replaced by Queen Charlotte XXVII by teatime. What do you think, Reeves?"

"I think an early intervention *is* called for, sir. Perhaps if we appealed to the aunts' better nature, and explained the gravity of the situation–"

I had to interrupt. "Reeves, these are aunts. Better nature is but a vague concept to them. We need something distracting, something cunning and subtle."

I was reminded of the latest Mallory Queen – *The Mystery of the Missing Siamese Triplet* – in which Mallory kept the suspect talking while his father crept upstairs and searched the attic for leopards ... or had it been leotards? The lettering on the page had been smudged and I still wasn't entirely sure.

"I have a better plan," I said. "You and I, Bertie, will call upon your aunts and keep them busy while Reeves infiltrates below stairs. He'll soon learn the location of both the time machine and any key that might unlock the room it's hidden in."

As plans went this had to be one of my best. Even Reeves could not contain his admiration – I saw his left eyebrow rise a full one eighth of an inch.

But I wasn't finished.

"And when Reeves has located it, he'll pass you the key. I shall then feign a heart attack and, in the confusion, you slip out, find the machine, and fly it home."

TWO

I was feeling pretty braced as I followed HG in the Stanley. With a modicum of luck we'd have the case wrapped up in time for a spot of lunch at the Sloths.

Reeves was not so confident.

"Retrieving the time machine, sir, is but the first step. The more difficult task is to repair the timeline and return things to the way they were."

"Do we have to? Think of all those poor Eton boys swotting for their exams. Wouldn't it make their life easier if every queen was a Charlotte?"

"If only that were true, sir, but I fear the changes will be far more pervasive than that. Mr Babbage was of the opinion that a butterfly flapping its wings in the Amazonian forest could cause a tornado in East Dulwich."

"Large butterfly, was it?"

"I believe the size of the butterfly to be irrelevant, sir. Mr Babbage was making an observation concerning the interconnectivity of events."

I had to disagree.

"It may be irrelevant to C. Babbage esquire, but one suspects the people of East Dulwich have a different opinion on the matter. Is anyone hunting these giant butterflies, Reeves? What happens if they flap their wings in a different direction and Piccadilly gets flattened?"

"I believe we have arrived, sir. Mr Wells is preparing to park."

~

Reeves oiled off in search of the servants' entrance while Bertie and I prepared to engage the enemy head on. We found them in the drawing room. I felt like that chap – Daniel, I think his name was – standing in the doorway of the lions' den. The only difference being that aunts, unlike lions, don't have the habit of becoming bosom chums with the first chap who extracts a thorn from between their toes.

And there were twenty-eight of them. All looking my way as the lively hum of conversation came to a stuttering halt. It was uncanny how alike they were. Far more so than sisters. Some appeared identical and they ranged in age from deb to dowager.

The Worcester knees trembled, but I steeled myself. Grasping Bertie's arm, I leaned toward him and whispered some sage last minute advice. "If any look like exploding, run."

"Is that little Bertie?" said one of the aunts. "Hasn't he grown! When I last saw him he was still in short trousers."

"He was a baby when I last saw him."

"And who's that with him? Did Sarah have another child?"

"This is Reginald Worcester," said Bertie. "An um ... old school friend. Reggie, this is my aunt, Mrs Dean."

"What ho, aunts," I said, putting on the best Worcester smile.

"Bertie, dear, you're not here to remonstrate with me about that time machine again, are you? I've told you I'll return it once I've finished with it."

"Quite the opposite," I said. I'm not sure if initiative has horns but, if it does, I gave them a good grabbing. We consulting detectives always play off the front foot. "We're here to take notes," I continued.

"Notes?"

"Rather! I'm planning an evening with sixty Reginald Worcesters. Have you any tips?"

"I was at a dinner with a Worcester last week," said one of the younger aunts. "Very odd fellow. Kept talking about newts."

"That would be my Uncle Clarence," I said. "He was very partial to newts in his younger days. Did he tell you the one about..."

I have little recollection of the subsequent five minutes other than I talked, at great length, about newts, uncles, and the pros and cons of changing the leg before wicket rule in cricket. And that, after the first three minutes, the audience became decidedly tough. I may have been heckled by a Pope.

My attempt at distraction came to an unexpected end when a twenty-ninth aunt appeared in the doorway with a subdued-looking Reeves. She didn't actually have hold of him by his ear, but both gave the impression that an unspoken hand/ear connection was in existence.

"I found this one lurking on the back stairs," said the aunt.

"Is he something to do with you?" said one of the Aunts, giving me the gimlet eye.

"Good Lord, no,' I said. "I've never seen Reeves before in my life."

~

I blame it on the gimlet eye. Even Murgatroyd of the Yard would have spilled all before the withering gaze of twenty-nine aunts.

"What shall we do with them?" asked one of the horde.

"Throw them out," said another.

"No, they'd only sneak back inside. I want them where we can see them."

"But Aunt–" said HG.

"No buts, Bertie. You'll do as you're told."

We were escorted to a bay window at the far side of the drawing room and told to remain there and behave ourselves.

"Did you get the key?" I asked Reeves as soon as I was able, keeping my voice as low as I could.

"Regrettably not, sir, though I have discovered the location of the time machine. It is in the wine cellar. I was in the process of obtaining the key to the aforementioned room when I was apprehended."

"Where's the key now, Reeves?"

"The Mrs Dean who apprehended me has it, sir."

I made a note of what she was wearing. And became aware for the first time of the marked difference in clothing between the younger and older Charlottes. It wasn't a matter of fashion. The younger aunts' dresses were just not of the same quality. The materials were less fine and were poorly cut. One might even say there was a hint of 'below stairs' about them. And they wore no jewellery. Clearly Aunt Charlotte's fortunes had improved considerably over the years.

"The servants are somewhat agitated, sir," continued Reeves. "The cook has left to stay with her sister, and both maids have refused to set foot in the house until the entire property has been exorcised. Only the butler remains, and he won't leave his pantry."

"What do we do now?" whispered HG.

"I think we continue with the original plan," I said. "I'll feign a heart attack and you, Bertie, will have to retrieve the key from that Mrs Dean over there in the powder blue and pearls."

I could tell that Reeves disapproved by the slight downward curl of his lower lip.

"My observation of the Mrs Deans, sir, leads me to believe that any unusual action perpetrated by yourself would be viewed with the utmost suspicion."

"Mr Reeves is right," said HG. "They're watching us like hawks. I'd never be able to retrieve the key."

"May I suggest a different course of action, sir?" asked Reeves.

"It doesn't involve appealing to their better nature, does it?"

"No, sir. I believe the answer lies in the psychology of the individual."

"Even when there are twenty-nine individuals?"

"Especially when there are twenty-nine individuals, sir."

~

Reeves' plan began with a cough. I count myself one of the foremost experts on Reeves' oesophageal lexicon. This one was authoritative and yet contained a genteel note so as not to startle a room full of ladies. Personally, I would have opted for something a little stronger. These were aunts after all.

"If I may make an observation, Mrs Dean, Misses Neal," Reeves began. "I believe there is a matter of considerable import that you may have overlooked concerning the ball that you intend to host."

Conversation amongst the aunts waned somewhat. "What are you talking about?" asked one of the older aunts, who by the cut of her dress I would have placed into the 1901 vintage.

"You would all need ball gowns, would you not? Sixty ball gowns in the *latest* fashions. Society would demand it, I think. Do you possess sixty such ball gowns?"

From the looks that darted from aunt to aunt, I could tell that they did not.

"We will *buy* sixty new ball gowns."

"That would be a considerable expense, Mrs Dean. Would you be buying the requisite jewellery as well?"

Never have I been in the presence of twenty-nine aunts

and experienced such silence. No one was admonished, and no one even *breathed* for a full two seconds!

"Charles will buy them for us, won't he?" said 1891 to 1904.

"Who's Charles?" asked one of the 1870s.

"Our husband."

"We didn't marry Charles, did we? Whatever happened to William?"

"Who's William?"

The two seconds of silence was trampled upon by a good sixty seconds of spirited discourse on suitors and the relative merits (of which there were very few) of Charles, William, Frederick, Albert and the Emperor Charlemagne.

"But where *is* Charles?" asked an 1890. "I've been here all morning and I haven't seen him once."

"He left yesterday," said 1901, although it could easily have been a 1902 or 3. "He said he was going to the club and wouldn't return until there was only one of us."

This caused some consternation. *Why didn't you tell us? Where are we going to find the money? Don't you have ANY ball gowns?*

Reeves quietened the hubbub with a cough.

"If I may make a further observation, Mrs Dean, Misses Neal," he said. "It has come to my attention that your servants have either left or are about to give notice. You have no one to attend upon you and you have no money to run this household. Your only recourse is to return all your younger selves to the times they came from before even greater tragedies occur."

Surely this had to be checkmate? Even an aunt had to bow before the logic of Reeves' giant steam-powered brain.

"No," said 1904, drawing herself up to her full height. "I have a better plan. I shall go into the past and collect the money we need from there."

THREE

"I fear I have made matters worse, sir," said Reeves.

"It's not your fault, Reeves. We all thought you had a winning hand, and were playing it magnificently. But ... aunts play with a stacked deck, Reeves."

"We have to do something though," said HG. "Mr Reeves is right. Inspired as his attempt was, it *has* made things worse."

"I don't see how," I said. "Seems like quite a clever plan to me the way she explained it. She's borrowing from herselves to give to herselves. And all the Mrs Deans present gave their permission to touch their husband for an advance on housekeeping. No laws are being broken."

"Several *scientific* laws will be, sir."

"Any of them by Babbage?" I enquired.

"I believe so, sir," said Reeves haughtily.

"Well, I think we can safely disregard anything Babbage has to say upon the matter. Does he posit the money will explode or be carried off by passing lepidoptera?"

"Neither, sir, but if one takes money from the past then that money is no longer available for its original use."

I cogitated for a good number of seconds but still couldn't see what Reeves was getting at.

"I can't see the problem, Reeves. Are you saying you're robbing Peter to pay Paul? But in this instance, Peter is Paul ... but older ... and wearing a dress."

"If I may explain, sir."

"Please do."

"If a ten pound note is removed from 1890 then it will not be available that year to give to the cook to pay for provisions. The Mrs Dean of the 1890 vintage will have to dig into her savings to find another ten pound note. If one robs the past of too many ten pound notes, one might find one's current address is relocated to the poor house."

"And you wouldn't even know why," added HG. "Because

the timeline would rewrite your memories too. All you'd remember is that money kept going missing and your husband would insist he gave that missing money to you!"

I was in need of a cocktail. "But... how do you explain all the aunts? The past doesn't seem to mind being robbed of aunts."

"*That* is a paradox," said HG. "It shouldn't be possible. The time machine will insulate anything inside it from the timeline outside. It's part of the temporal shielding that allows the occupants to travel through time without ageing or having the years ripped from their bodies. But the moment the machine is switched off, you'd expect the timeline to be resolved. Every time Aunt Charlotte fetched someone from the past, one of them should have disappeared."

"The predominant theory, sir," said Reeves, "suggests it would be the latest Mrs Dean who disappears. The new timeline would have Mrs Dean disappearing in 1890 and re-appearing, at the same younger age, in 1904. The 1904 Mrs Dean would disappear, as she could not have existed the day before to steal the time machine."

"Which creates the paradox," said HG. "If she didn't steal the time machine, how did the 1890 Mrs Dean get transported to 1904?"

"That's all very well," I said. "And it's reassuring to hear a scientific theory devoid of butterflies, but – clearly – it is wrong. Behold the evidence."

I flourished an arm towards the assembled throng of aunts, none of whom exhibited the slightest inclination to disappear, immersed as they were in journals and pattern books, chatting excitedly about what to wear to the upcoming ball. *Whatever happened to puff sleeves? And bustles? I don't care what you say, I'm NOT going to wear an S-bend corset!*

"Perhaps there's a delay before the timeline rewrites itself," suggested HG. "It might be working its way through the 1890s now and won't reach us for a day or two."

"I think that unlikely, sir," said Reeves. "The timeline has already absorbed the change to Henry VIII's nuptials. I wonder if maybe we are looking at the problem *in medias res* when we should be looking at the problem from the perspective of the future."

Why is it that the times one needs a drink the most are the very times when the fortifying libation is withheld? There wasn't even a decanter of sherry in sight!

"How do you mean?" asked HG.

"I was contemplating Babbage's cat, sir."

I, along with the inhabitants of East Dulwich, braced ourselves for another dire warning from the brain of C. Babbage esquire.

"The thought experiment?" said HG.

"Indeed, sir. You may remember Mr Babbage placed his cat in a box to demonstrate the uncertainty principle. It is not until the observer opens the box that the uncertainty is resolved and one knows whether the cat is alive or dead."

"You think the timeline may be subject to the uncertainty principle?" said HG.

"I think it possible, sir. If Mrs Dean's intention, the moment she stepped out of the time machine with her younger self, was to return that younger self to her correct time period after a short visit, then the state of the new timeline would be uncertain. Many potential timelines would co-exist until the uncertainty was resolved. Perhaps by the younger Mrs Dean being returned to her correct time, or by the older Mrs Dean deciding to extend her younger self's stay."

"Far be it from me, Reeves, to poke holes in all things Babbage, but I think I could tell if a cat was dead or alive without recourse to opening the box. They mewl so, and if you gave the box a slight shake–"

Reeves coughed. "The box is a notional one, sir. As is the cat. It is but a thought experiment."

"He'd never get an aunt in a box," I continued. "Aunts do not go quietly. I expect the timeline thought much the same. Henry VIII – we can manage him. Twenty-nine Aunt Charlottes – no thank you. We'll leave them alone."

"Indeed, sir. If I may continue?"

"By all means, Reeves. I'm waiting to hear about Babbage's dog."

"I fear we may soon have proof of my proposition, sir. Mrs Dean has no intention of returning the money and jewellery that she is bringing with her from the past. All of it will be spent in the present on dresses and accessories for the ball. Therefore, there is no uncertainty, and nothing to prevent the timeline from changing instantly."

"It may have already started," said HG. "She would have switched the machine off every time she jumped to a new time. Have you noticed anything, Reeves?"

"Not as yet, sir. One hopes she commenced her travels in the distant past and made her subsequent stops in times progressively closer to the present. In which case she would have noticed her family's diminishing fortune and cut her itinerary short."

"I think I heard her say the opposite," said HG. "She told one of her alter egos it would create less suspicion if she always travelled into the past. That way Charles couldn't get alarmed about her borrowing as, for him, it would always be the first time she'd asked."

One had to feel a sneaking regard for Aunt Charlotte.

The wall in front of me shimmered slightly. I blinked. "I say," I said. "Did you see that? I could have sworn there was a painting on that wall."

Reeves followed my gaze. "I believe there was, sir. A rather fine Stubbs." He scanned the rest of the room. "And the crystal and gold chandelier is now what I believe people call a light fitting."

"You're right! Why isn't anyone else noticing? Look there goes another painting! The large one on the chimney-breast."

"I think I remember the chandelier and the Grimshaw over the fire," said HG. "But ... a Stubbs you say? I don't recall Aunt Charlotte ever having a Stubbs. There's no mark on the wall to show a painting used to hang there."

"I think, sir – returning to Mr Worcester's question – a more germane inquiry would be 'how are *you* remembering?' From the little I have observed, human memories have always changed along with the timeline."

"Superior grey cells, do you think?"

"No, sir. Though there is *something* that differentiates Mr Wells and yourself from his maternal relative."

"What's that?"

"Alcoholic fortification, sir. Both Mr Wells and yourself imbibed liberally prior to your journey here."

~

Paintings continued to pop off walls. Persian rugs were exchanged for lesser rugs, and then no rugs at all. Mirrors disappeared, drapes dissolved, and occasional tables became less occasional. Reeves assured us that the wallpaper had changed too, though I had no recollection of the earlier pattern he described. None of the aunts appeared to notice anything remiss at all – even the ones who found themselves suddenly standing when previously they'd been sitting!

"I say," I said, waving auntwards. "Excuse me! Has anyone noticed the chairs disappearing?"

I might as well have chewed the carpet – if there had been a carpet – such was the look they gave me. *Ignore him, dear, can't you see he's touched. I don't think he's dangerous, but best not to look at him.*

Even HG couldn't get through to them. "Can't you see the room changing around you?" he said. "Three of you were sitting on a *chaise longue* a minute ago!"

"Have you been drinking, Bertie?"

"I smelled it on his breath when he first arrived. I didn't want to say anything but..."

There was simply no talking to them.

The room continued its downward spiral. The good furniture either disappeared or was replaced with an inferior model. Then the air in the middle of the room began to shimmer and – shazam! – a time machine – for what else could it be? – crystallised out of the ether. Aunt Charlotte was sitting in the driver's seat, with a large pile of loot glistening beside her. She did not look best pleased.

"My lovely house!" she cried, jumping to her feet. "What have you *done* to it? My furniture! My paintings! And who filled my wine cellar with turnips?"

She looked accusingly our way. All other conversation in the room had stopped. Then, just as I was bracing myself for another tirade – with or without turnips – her face changed. All her anger turned to surprise.

"Bertie! What are you wearing?"

I glanced at HG, half expecting to see his clothes turned to rags. But they hadn't. The Worcester jaw nearly hit the floor. The Herbert George Wells who stood beside me was wearing a long blue dress and, if my nose could be trusted, rather a large amount of perfume.

And when he spoke, it was with the voice of a woman. "Why are you calling me Bertie, Aunt Charlotte? Can't you see it's me? Gertrude."

I could not believe it. Bertie was a Gertie!

FOUR

I looked at Reeves. Reeves looked at Aunt Charlotte. Aunt Charlotte looked at Gertie, and Gertie looked at me. None of us could speak. I suspect Babbage's cat had our tongues. He was, after all, a much-provoked feline.

"You see what I mean?" Gertie said to me, breaking the silence and pointing at the time machine. "Where did all that money come from? You've got to help me return it to the rightful owners."

My mouth was still open, but the Worcester cupboard of words was bare.

"It's all right, Gertie," said one of the cohort of aunts. "It's our money. We gave Charlotte permission to fetch it."

Other aunts nodded solicitously.

Gertie was not mollified. She glared at the eldest Aunt while pointing at the others. "And who are they? Why do they look like you?"

Reeves coughed. It was like being down to your last musket ball as the enemy closed in on all sides, and then hearing the distant trumpet call of the cavalry announcing imminent salvation.

"If I may explain, Mrs Dean, Miss Wells," he said. "Your niece has been much concerned by the change in your fortune over the years. It would appear that money and jewellery has been going missing for many years. A situation which caused *this*." Reeves indicated the room. "And *this*." Reeves indicated Gertie.

"Your niece was so vexed that she engaged the services of Mr Worcester here, who is a gentleman's consulting detective. She had seen your new machine and was concerned that, given the aforementioned propensity for money and objects to 'disappear,' that a suspicious mind – and, in particular, a mind belonging to Her Majesty's constabulary – might suppose that you had stolen it."

"That's preposterous!" said Aunt Charlotte.

"It's true!" said Gertie. "You don't hear what people say about you. Haven't you wondered why you rarely get invited into other people's homes any more? They think you steal things!"

"That's a cruel thing to say, Gertie," said one of the auntly cohort.

"It's true, though!" said Gertie. "I didn't want to tell you, but ... maybe it's better to get this out into the open. It's what people have been saying about you for years "

I had the strangest feeling that I'd heard this before. Gertie coming to the flat, telling us about her klepto aunt and how she'd just stolen someone's automobile, taken the wheels off and hidden it in her drawing room. Gertie wanted us to find the rightful owner and return it before the police became involved.

The much-confused Aunt Charlotte, meanwhile, had just turned upon her younger selves. "Why are you all calling him Gertie? Can't you see it's Bertie? He's ... he's dressing up."

"I think you should sit down, dear," said one of the elder Aunts. "We have no idea who this Bertie is. That's Gertie. We've known her for years. We all have. You have."

Aunt Charlotte blanched visibly and her knees buckled. Reeves caught her and guided her back towards the time machine. "I think you should sit down, Mrs Dean. You have had a shock."

"Should I call a doctor?" Gertie asked me.

"I wouldn't advise it," I said. "But ... talking of doctors. Did you ever have a ... an accident as a child?"

"What kind of accident?"

"Anything drop off?"

"If I may interrupt, sir?" said Reeves. "If you would be so kind as to assist me with Mrs Dean..."

"Righto," I said.

One of the aunts rushed forward to bar my way. "I think Charlotte would prefer *us* to help her. Please remove yourself. *And* your man."

"Mr Worcester and I can return things to how they were, Mrs Dean," said Reeves to the wilting aunt on his arm. "*All* things. *If* you allow us."

"It's all right, dear," said the ailing aunt. "The gentlemen and I need to talk."

"Are you sure?" asked the younger Charlotte.

"I'm sure."

Reeves and I helped Aunt C into the driver's seat of the

time machine.

"How do I put this right?" she whispered. "Is ... is Bertie dead?"

"I suspect Miss Wells was born in his stead, Mrs Dean. Did you travel beyond 1866 today and have any interaction with her parents?"

"None! I was in too much of a hurry to talk to anyone other than my husband. I went back to 1865, but all I did was collect money and..." Her hands flew to her face. "I took her necklace! It was in a box on my dresser. I didn't recognise it. I was in a hurry and grabbed the box! But I remember it now. It was part of her inheritance from our grandmother. She wanted the chain shortened and had given it to me to take to a jeweller I knew in Regent Street. But ... how could that have made Bertie a ... Gertie?"

"That, Mrs Dean, is the inherent danger of time travel. A seemingly insignificant action can have far-reaching and manifold repercussions. The missing necklace may have caused a falling-out between yourself and your sister. A falling-out which caused a chain of events that led to the birth of a daughter instead of a son. It may be that the date of Miss Wells' birth is later than Mr Wells'. She does look younger."

Aunt Charlotte looked considerably brighter. "Do you suppose if I returned the necklace to 1865, it would bring my nephew back?"

"I fear not, Mrs Dean," said Reeves. "I have encountered this problem before and it can only be solved by a third party. Any attempt by yourself would most likely complicate matters further. One lady of my acquaintance returned with a full beard. Most unfortunate."

"You've done this before?"

"On several occasions, Mrs Dean, but not on this particular model of time machine. If you would be so kind as to show me the controls, I will soon pick it up."

~

Reeves' plan appeared to be working, though the aunts were getting a touch restless. There was much whispering and the casting of suspicious glances our way.

"I think it may be judicious, sir," said Reeves, "if you could divert the room's attention for ten minutes."

"A heart attack, you think?"

"I was thinking of something less dramatic, sir.

Conversation, perhaps?"

"Tough audience, Reeves, but I'll give it a try."

Given my earlier reception, and the looks I was now getting, I decided to avoid the frontal approach in favour of a flanking movement. The aunts may not have taken to me, but they all appeared to have warm feelings towards Gertie. If I could get Gertie to chat with them, all would be solved.

The only fly in the o. was Gertie – who was looking decidedly cool towards the aunts. Somehow I had to smooth the furrowed waters.

"Is Aunt Charlotte all right?" asked Gertie as I approached.

"Yes. She'll soon be tickety-boo," I assured her. "Reeves is sorting out this Bertie business."

"I've never seen her like that," said Gertie. "She didn't appear to know who I was. And who are *they*?" Gertie lowered her voice as she pointed with her eyes towards the aunts. "They seem to think they know me."

I guided Gertie away from the gravitational pull of the aunts and back into the bay widow where we could talk a little more freely.

"That's a good question," I said. "Would you believe they were a troop of travelling Aunt Charlotte impersonators?"

"No."

It was worth a try.

"Well ... indeed. That's because ... that's because you have a full complement of marbles. Whereas these poor unfortunates ... they do not. You've heard of people who believe they're Napoleon?"

"Ye-es."

"Well, these ladies believe they're your aunt. Strange, I know. But there it is. Who'd have thought it? The local asylum has dozens of them apparently, and your aunt has kindly allowed them to visit with her this morning."

Gertie looked surprised. And not a little confused, but she didn't look like a person about to denounce R. Worcester from the pulpit for egregious lying.

Emboldened, I continued. "Yes, sad case, but these visits are believed to be therapeutic. As long as we play along with their delusions, of course."

"Of course. Are they ... dangerous?"

"Only if you cast doubts upon their veracity. Look, they appear to be choosing gowns for a ball. Why don't you toddle over and offer assistance while I check on Reeves."

~

That went very well, I thought. The aunts simpered, and picked Gertie's brain viz. U-bend corsets and this year's colours and fabrics, while Reeves learned all about time machine controls. At the end of which, Mrs Dean vacated the driver's seat, and Reeves and I jumped aboard – though I had to move the pile of swag to the foot well to make room for myself.

I didn't think we'd get away scot-free, and I was right. A sudden cry arose from the throng of aunts. "What are you doing, Charlotte? You're not letting them fly the machine! They've got our money!"

Reeves fired up the engine in the nick of time. It was most disconcerting. The room took on a misty appearance, and three auntly apparitions lunged towards us only to pass straight through.

"That was close, Reeves. Do you have a plan?"

"I hope so, sir. "

"What do you mean, 'you hope so?' You always have a plan."

"I fear this is a situation where 'needs must,' sir. I judge Mrs Dean's remorse over the events she has precipitated to be fleeting. If she did manage to reverse the unfortunate change to her nephew, I believe she would continue to use the time machine for her own purposes. This was likely to be our best, if not only, chance to gain control of the machine and learn how to fly it."

"But you must have *some* kind of plan. You *do* know all the dates Aunt C cadged from, don't you?"

"Yes, sir. She used the same day, month, and time of day for all her journeys. She only adjusted the dial for the year, visiting every one from 1903 to 1865 when she inherited this house from her grandmother."

"So you *do* have a plan."

"I would not go so far as to call it a plan, sir. My hope had been to take the machine to the week before Mrs Dean misappropriated it from Mr Wells, and convince him *not* to mention the machine's existence to his aunt. But... with Mr Wells being no more, that is no longer an option."

"Can't we undo Aunt C's last journey and bring Bertie back to the land of the L?"

"That is my hope, sir. Though I am undecided whether it is safer to start in 1865 and work forward, or start in 1903 and work back."

"Is there a difference?"

"Potentially a significant difference, sir. We are going to cause the timeline to be rewritten thirty-nine times. A different order may result in different outcomes. And every time we materialise, we risk altering events by our very presence. Hold tight, sir. I am about to engage the spatial spinnaker."

The machine rose from the spectral drawing room and passed through the ceiling as though it wasn't there. It was like travelling in one of those American elevators in a cage full of chain smokers. We emerged from the ceiling into an empty room on the first floor. Such was the size of the cobwebs, the room must have been closed up for years. Reeves pressed a button and our upward movement stopped instantly. He pressed another button and off we slid along a foggy horizontal plane. Reeves then used the wheel to steer the machine like an ordinary car.

"Where are we going?" I asked. "Are we travelling through time yet?"

"Not yet, sir. I'm attempting to locate Mrs Dean's dressing room."

"Why?"

"To minimise our interaction with the past, sir. Mrs Dean used the wine cellar for her journeys–"

"Until the incident with the turnips."

"Indeed, sir. She parked the machine in the cellar and then proceeded to walk though the house. We cannot risk that, as our presence, should we be discovered, would cause considerable comment."

"I see. Won't our presence in Aunt C's dressing room cause even more?"

"Not with this machine, sir. We can make sure the room is empty before we materialise."

Reeves' attention to detail is legendary.

"I can see that the jewellery box might be located in this dressing room, Reeves, but what about the tenners? Don't we have to get them into the uncle's pocket?"

"I'm hoping that Mr Dean has a dressing room too, sir. In which case, we can leave the ten-pound note on his dresser. He will think that his wife has had second thoughts and returned it. At least one hopes he does."

Reeves sounded a touch uncertain, not, perhaps, as uncertain as Babbage's cat, but then Reeves hadn't been put in a box. I decided it was time for the young master to take the initiative.

"So, Reeves, 1865 or 1903? Shall we toss for it?"

"No, sir. I think, on balance, the safest option is to reverse the path followed by Mr Wells' aunt."

That sounded sage advice to me. Whatever an aunt does, do the reverse.

We passed through a bedroom and into a smaller room which looked a good candidate for Aunt C's dressing room. Two pairs of ladies' shoes by a cupboard door confirmed the hunch.

"Brace yourself, sir. I am about to engage the temporal engine."

Reeves turned a dial and clicked it back to 1865. He then pulled one lever forward, pushed two others back, and pressed a large red button. A pulsing, spinning noise came from behind us.

I braced myself. The ghostly dressing room dissolved in an instant. Everything went grey and swirly. There was a sensation of movement, but not one in a forward direction, as in a car. It was more of a buffeting as though one were on a boat in a choppy sea.

I didn't much care for it.

"Any idea how long this takes?" I asked.

"No, sir."

Barely a second later, the buffeting stopped and the features of the dressing room – albeit hazy features – coalesced out of the murk. And this dresser had two jewellery boxes on it.

"Mrs Dean should be here presently, sir. It is imperative that you replace the exact items that she takes."

I started sorting through the pile of swag at my feet. Most of the jewellery was identical – the same oriental-looking gold, emerald and diamond necklace. I'm no expert when it comes to jewellery but this one looked pretty expensive. There was a rather fine ruby necklace too – presumably the heirloom belonging to Bertie's mother. I then proceeded to count out the tenners. There were twenty-three of them.

"I say, Reeves. We're several tenners short. There are only twenty-three here. Shouldn't there be thirty-nine?"

Reeves panicked. No one but I would have noticed, but both his eyebrows rose a full eighth of an inch, and what can only be called a quiver momentarily wobbled his lower lip. If I'd had a bottle of brandy to hand, I'd have passed him a quick snifter.

"May I trouble you to count them again, sir?"
"No trouble, Reeves." I counted them again, and another time for luck. It made no difference. Twenty-three.

FIVE

Reeves was still in a tizz when Aunt C arrived. We watched her pocket the two necklaces and waited for her to leave.

Reeves pressed a series of buttons and then depressed a lever. The dressing room snapped into clarity. I jumped out, beetled over to the dresser and replaced the two necklaces, making sure the right one went into the right box. I gave Reeves the thumbs up sign, and legged it back to the machine.

As soon as the Worcester posterior hit the leather, Reeves fired up the engine. But instead of racing forward to 1866 – which I'd been expecting – we turned left and flew through the dressing room wall.

"Reeves?"

"We have to follow Mrs Dean, sir. If she's not borrowing ten pounds from each year, we have to know which years she *is* borrowing from. I am a little concerned that she may have pocketed some of the ten pound notes."

We caught up with the aunt on the landing and dogged her all the way to the wine cellar. It was all rather strange. She couldn't hear us. She couldn't see us. But there we were – floating along behind her in what felt like a sea of mist.

"What if she touched her husband for a tenner before nabbing the necklaces?" I asked.

I should not have aired my concern. Reeves became apoplectic. His left eye twitched. Twice!

Not that he said a word. All his attention remained fixed upon Aunt C as she climbed into her machine and vanished.

The moment she left, Reeves began pushing and pulling levers and then pressed the large red button. Off through time we went again, buffeting through the grey featureless wash until we reappeared back in the wine cellar.

And so did Aunt C.

"We are starting again in 1865, sir. As you said, Mrs Dean may well have encountered her husband on the way to her dressing room. We shall follow..."

Reeves froze. Not a twitch. Not a tic. He hadn't even bothered to close his mouth.

"Are you all right, Reeves? You haven't lost pressure, have you?"

It was my turn to panic. Would there be a steam outlet in 1865 for Reeves to top himself up with?

As suddenly as he froze, so he came back to life. "I fear I have made a grave error, sir. We must fly."

Reeves' hands moved at speeds too fast for the human eye to keep up with. And up we rose, out of the misty cellar and into the equally misty hall. Then we were moving forward, travelling at a speed barely above a brisk walk, sailing towards the staircase at ceiling height. I looked down. Aunt C had just come into the hall. I couldn't see her husband anywhere.

"We have to get to the dressing room before Mrs Dean, sir, or all is lost."

"Why?"

"Because she will take her sister's necklace and we don't have it any more. We won't be able to replace it."

I looked at the pile of necklaces in the foot well. And then started rummaging through them. Reeves was right. Sarah Wells' necklace wasn't there.

"We will have to take a risk, sir," said Reeves as we crossed the upstairs landing. "When we materialise, you must take Mrs Wells' jewellery box from the dresser and bring it here. Don't touch anything else."

We materialised. I ran. I grabbed, and leaped back into the machine. We made it by a second, no more. As soon as we vanished into the mist, the door opened and in came Mrs Dean.

This time she took just the one necklace. I wondered if she might look for the second box, but she didn't. She pocketed her necklace and left.

"What now?" I asked. "We're one necklace short."

"Indeed, sir. The fault is all mine. I was too entangled in the minutia of events that I overlooked the greater danger."

"Shouldn't the timeline give us an extra necklace when it next rewrites itself?"

"One can hope, sir. But I think we should assume it will not. If we assiduously reverse all of Mrs Dean's changes that we can, there is a good chance that the timeline of 1903 will be sufficiently close to the original that we can find Mr Wells and forewarn him of his aunt's intentions."

~

So that was what we did. Year after year, we followed Aunt C from the wine cellar, noted when she borrowed money and when she didn't, and replaced everything she took.

By the time we reached 1901, all we had left were two necklaces. We'd paid out the last tenner the year before. And then we watched Aunt C – in 1901 – touch her husband for another tenner.

"Reeves, remind me to come prepared next time we go righting past wrongs. If I'd been forewarned I'd have brought more money with me. I only have a fiver!"

"I have two pounds, ten shillings and six pence, sir."

"Do you think the butterflies will take umbrage at us short changing Mr Dean? I could leave my watch."

"No, sir. I think an unexpected gentleman's watch would cause far more comment than a missing two pounds, nine shillings and six pence."

Reeves' humour had improved considerable since the mid-Victorian period. As had mine. The Dean household was looking well furnished. The wine cellar was devoid of turnips. And Reeves had hit upon a plan.

"I have a plan," he said as I deposited our last necklace into Aunt C's jewellery box. "There is a certain element of risk, sir, but I believe it to be our best chance."

"What is it?"

"We shall write a letter to Mr Wells, sir. There is an escritoire there next to the dresser. It should contain paper, envelopes and stamps. We shall warn him of his aunt's intentions."

We composed the note.

Dear Mr Wells,

URGENT

Don't mention the existence of your time machine to your Aunt Charlotte. She steals it in 1904 and causes havoc to the timeline. Still trying to fix it.

"How shall I sign it?" I asked. "R Worcester, gentleman's consulting detective?"

"I think not, sir. Mr Wells would likely call upon you after receiving such a letter and ask questions. That would be in 1902, sir. You wouldn't know what he was talking about, and he would begin to doubt the veracity of the missive. I would suggest you sign as 'The Traveller.'"

"Spot on, Reeves!"

I signed it, folded it into the envelope, applied a stamp, and...

"Where do we send it, Reeves? Do you know his address?"

"No, sir, but I am reliably informed that publishers will forward letters to their authors. Mr Wells is published by William Heinemann of Covent Garden."

Reeves had even worked out how to deliver the letter to Covent Garden. He'd noticed, during our many trips up and down the stairs, a silver salver on a small table at the foot of the stairs. It had to be where the family left their letters for the servants to post.

Still in thrall to the Amazonian butterflies, Reeves insisted we park the time machine next to the salver, and materialise for just the single second it took me to reach out and deposit the letter.

"Well, Reeves," I said. "This is it. Next stop 1904. The dice have been rolled, the cards played, and we've given of our best."

"Indeed, sir."

"Whatever we see – whether it be sixty aunts, Bertie and Gertie the Siamese twins, or a house full of turnips – no blame shall rest upon your shoulders, Reeves. You have gone above and beyond – and backwards and forwards."

"Thank you, sir. That is most kind."

"Hit the button, Reeves."

I not only braced myself, I screwed my eyes tight shut. I felt the buffeting, heard the whirr and whine of the large parasol thingy on the back.

And then felt everything go quiet and still.

I opened one eye.

No turnips. The door to the drawing room was six feet in front of us on the right. I listened intently. Even though I knew we were insulated from the sounds and smells of the world outside of the machine, I strained to listen, hoping to pick up some early clue as to what we might find on the other side of that wall.

Reeves turned the steering wheel and the machine swung towards the drawing room wall, moving forwards as it did so, into the wall and out into...

...The drawing room we'd first encountered in 1904. The chandelier was back, as was the Stubbs and the Persian rugs. But no Bertie or Gertie. Or horde of aunts. The only occupants were a single Aunt Charlotte and her husband – who I was pretty sure wasn't Henry VIII. She was reading a magazine and he a newspaper.

"Is this good?" I asked, hopefully.

"It is a positive sign, sir," said Reeves.

"What do we do next?"

"I think the safest course of action, sir, is to take the machine to the flat. There we can consult *Who's Who* to verify that Mr Wells has been restored to his former position and, if so, where he resides."

I didn't want to say anything – in case I tempted the butterflies – but this felt very much like the last page of a penultimate chapter. You know the one – the detective has unmasked the murderer, and is quietly accepting the plaudits before he wraps up all the loose ends.

Reeves engaged the spatial whatnot, swung the time machine around and drove straight through the nearest wall. We emerged into the hazy brightness of the street outside, and turned for Piccadilly. Sometimes we drove on the pavement. Sometimes we drove on the road. And sometimes we drove through people's houses.

I warmed to this mode of transport. If it could go a little faster, and wasn't surrounded in its own permanent pea-souper, I'd order one myself. Having automobiles and Hansom cabs drive straight through one was a bit disconcerting at first, but one soon got used to it.

We sailed into the old flat through a second floor window.

"Do we have to give this back to Mr Wells, Reeves? I can see it coming in very handy in future cases. No pun intended."

"I would advise strongly against it, sir. I do not wish to find myself in the unexpected employment of Miss Regina Worcester, gentleman's turnip consultant."

Reeves had a point.

He parked the machine in the sitting room, and hesitated.

"Before I commence rematerialisation, sir. May I enquire if you have any memories of Queen Charlottes?"

"You're asking the wrong person, Reeves. I never could keep up with all the queens Henry VIII married."

"Very good, sir."

My beloved apartment shed its misty veil and crystallised into sharp relief. We were back!

I beetled over to the bookcase, pulled out *Who's Who* and began to thumb through the pages. Wells, Wells, Wells... And there he was! Herbert George Wells, publications: Time Machine 1895; address:13 Hanover Terrace, Regent's Park. I checked Henry VIII next. Not a single Charlotte.

"I think a celebratory cocktail is called for, what?"

"I think a *swift* celebratory cocktail would be in order, sir. Though I confess myself somewhat uneasy at the presence of Mr Wells' time machine in the flat. The sooner we return it the better."

"Have no fear, Reeves. Swift is my middle name when it comes to cocktails."

Reeves oiled over to the drinks cabinet while I perused the ecclesiastical pages of *Who's Who* looking for Pope Charlotte.

"No Pope Charlotte either," I said. "Reeves? Is something wrong?"

Reeves was standing by the drinks cabinet, drink in hand, staring blankly at the floor behind the sofa.

"There appears to be a deceased gentleman behind the sofa, sir."

SIX

"What? Who is it?"

"It isn't someone I recognise, sir."

I hurried over to take a look. It was no one I recognised either. He was a stout chap of middle age, and was dressed rather oddly. I bent down for a closer look.

"I think it best not to touch it, sir."

I sprang back. "You think it might have something catching?"

"No, sir, I was thinking of fingerprints. The police tend to look with considerable disfavour upon householders with dead bodies in their sitting rooms."

Very true. As Murgatroyd of the Yard was fond of saying 'A sitting room is for sitting, sir, not for murdering.'

"What's he doing here?" I said. "We didn't run him over, did we?"

"We couldn't have, sir. If we'd materialised on top of him, he would be underneath the time machine, not behind the sofa."

"Is this one of those timeline consequences? We decided on a quick snifter instead of returning Mr Wells' machine *post haste* and the butterflies took umbrage?"

"I really cannot say, sir. This is most confusing."

Our quandary was interrupted by a sudden hammering on the front door.

"Open up! It's the police!"

We Worcesters are known for our quick thinking. When a policeman bangs on our door, we do not tarry.

"Quick, Reeves!" I hissed. "Give me a hand with our deceased friend and dial up the past."

"I strongly advise against that, sir. It will make matters worse."

"Worse? We have a dead body and a stolen time machine in the flat. How can it get any worse?"

"Very easily, sir. You yourself have witnessed how minor

changes to the past can cause major repercussions to the present."

More hammering. "We know you're in there! Open this door!"

"Let's dump him in the future then. I'm not proposing we leave him there – just hide him there until we work out what to do with him."

Reeves helped me carry the body over to the time machine.

"I think a less risky solution, sir, is to stay in the present and use the time machine's spatial abilities to make good our escape."

"We can hear you in there, sir! If you don't open this door in three seconds, we'll break it down!"

I slid onto the passenger seat with the dead body precariously balanced on my lap. Reeves jumped in beside me and, just as the first blow rained down upon the Worcester front door, we disappeared into netherspace.

My view of proceedings was somewhat obscured by the stout, and very heavy, deceased gentleman upon my lap. I didn't see the door broken open, but I saw three ghostly policemen rush into my sitting room, truncheons raised.

They seemed somewhat taken aback by not finding anyone at home. They ran from room to room, looked out windows, scratched their heads, and then began turning my flat upside down.

After one minute of being pinned to the passenger seat, I feared I was losing the circulation in my legs. "Reeves, this is no good. The rozzers look like they're going to tear the flat apart for the next half-hour, and I don't think I'll have any blood left in my legs by the end of it. We've got to dump this body."

"I will try upstairs, sir. Major Arbuthnot may be out."

He was not. We floated up through the ceiling to find the Major entertaining half a dozen friends.

"I'll try next door, sir."

"No, Reeves. We can't dump dead bodies on our neighbours. Let's go back to the flat, hop a week into the future, and have a good look at this body. There'll be clues. There always are."

"If you insist, sir," said Reeves, a little sniffily.

Off we shot and reappeared in the flat one week hence. Reeves helped drag the body off my lap, and then stretched it out on the carpet while I tried to rub some life back into my poor legs. At least the flat was back to its pristine state. And we had a new door.

"We do not appear to be at home, sir," said Reeves peering into the kitchen.

I hadn't considered the possibility of meeting myself. "Do you think we knew we were coming and decided to be out?"

"That is a distinct possibility, sir."

"Still, I think I would have left a note for myself. *Dear Reggie, here's all the information you need. And whatever you do don't forget to a put a tenner on Rich Lad in the 3:30 at Kempton last Tuesday*."

Reeves coughed disapprovingly. "I suggest we examine the body and return promptly, sir."

I circumnavigated the deceased, summoning up all my deductive powers. The man was of middle age, with a full face and receding brown hair. He had the full complement of arms and legs and no obvious bruises or wounds.

"I think we can rule out axe murderers, stranglers, and killer hounds, Reeves."

"Indeed, sir."

I'd read somewhere that if you looked into the face of a murdered man you'd see the image of their killer imprinted upon their eyes. Or was that the person you were going to marry? I was pretty sure it was one or the other.

I leaned forward a little and tried a tentative peer, but the prospect of seeing Emmeline on a dead man's eyeballs drew me back. I decided to turn my focus upon his clothes instead.

They were old – in style, that is – but well cut, and not at all threadbare.

"Is that a frock coat, Reeves?"

"Yes, sir. "

"1880s do you think?"

"By the cut I would hazard an earlier date, sir. 1850s."

"Can you see a cause of death?"

Reeves bent down for a closer look and after a short while began unbuttoning the man's coat. The fatal wound soon became apparent. There was a large bloodstain on his waistcoat.

"He appears to have been shot in the chest, sir," said Reeves. "One can see the hole where the bullet entered the waistcoat." Reeves turned the body over. "One can also see the hole in the frock coat where it exited."

So one could, and the dark stain surrounding it. I hadn't

noticed it earlier. The dark grey of the frock coat was only a few shades lighter than the stain. I checked the front of my clothes. Had any blood soaked through onto me?

It hadn't. The blood must have dried.

"How long do you think he's been dead, Reeves?"

"I am not an expert, sir. Long enough for the blood to dry. The body is not in a state of rigor, so it could be several hours or, indeed, several days."

"Did you see a blood stain on the carpet behind the sofa?"

"I did not, sir. Or anywhere else in the sitting room. It would appear the deceased was killed elsewhere and deposited behind the sofa some time later."

Reeves checked all the man's pockets – in both the frock coat and the waistcoat. All were bare.

"The tailor's label has been cut from his frock coat, sir."

"That's odd. What about his shirt and waistcoat?"

I waited whilst Reeves rummaged.

"The same, sir."

And the same for his trousers too. Someone did not want this man identified.

"So," I said. "We have a nameless man who may, or may not, originate from the 1850s, who's been murdered and dumped in my sitting room by someone who's gone to great lengths to conceal his identity."

"It would appear so, sir. Someone with access to a time machine."

~

My head was spinning. Who could it be? Aunt Charlotte? HG Wells? The Traveller? Someone else? And why?

"I suggest we move the deceased to the bathroom, sir. And stow him there while we return to the present."

I was wondering if we should leave a note – *Sorry about the guest in the bathroom. Will return anon to sort out, R* – when a thought struck me.

"Reeves, what if it was us who dumped the body?"

"Sir?"

"Well, here we are dumping a dead body in the future. What if our future selves had had a similar thought? They'd come home, found a dead body, panicked, and used the time machine to dump the body in the past?"

"I rather hope, sir, we would not *have* the time machine in the future, and so the circumstance would not arise."

"Hmm, you may be right, Reeves. I think I would have a left a note too. One can't dump deceased guests on people without some sort of explanation. It's not British."

I jotted an explanatory note for my future self, and was about to leave it on the drinks cabinet, when I noticed there was a cocktail glass on the cabinet. A full cocktail glass.

"This is odd, Reeves?" Cocktails do not get abandoned in the Worcester household without good reason. Had my future self been forced to flee at short notice?

Reeves appeared at my shoulder. "Most odd, sir. I believe that may be the drink I placed there last week when I first encountered the deceased."

"It's been there a week? Where were we all that time? Didn't we get back?"

"I think we should leave at once, sir."

We beetled back to the time machine and jumped aboard. Reeves set the dials, adjusted the levers and hit the button that sent us flying back to the past. I steadied myself. My plan was to fly from the machine the moment the room re-crystallised, and attempt to open the front door before it was broken down by the stout shoulders of the law.

We materialised. There was a thud from the door.

"Wait!" I shouted, leaping from the vehicle so fast I nearly overbalanced. "I'm coming!" The front door was thankfully still in place, but I could hear muffled conversation on the other side. "No need to break the door down. I'm coming!"

I unlocked the door and pulled it open. Three burly policemen – one sergeant and two constables – stood on the threshold with truncheons at the ready.

"Reginald Worcester?" said the sergeant, using the same tone that magistrates use when about to pass sentence.

"I am he, officer." I was thinking of something cutting to say viz. breaking down law-abiding citizen's doors but, before I could come up with anything withering, I was asked to step aside.

"I'm not sure if I shall step aside, officer."

"Step aside, sir, or I'll arrest you."

"On what grounds?"

"For bleeding all over my truncheon."

I stepped aside.

The three custodians of the law rushed past me.

"Who are you?" the sergeant asked Reeves while the constables searched the sitting room.

"I am Reeves, sergeant, Mr Worcester's valet."

"What's that?" said the sergeant, poking a truncheon at the time machine.

"It's a piece of modern art," said Reeves.

The sergeant walked around it, examining it thoroughly, looking for secret compartments no doubt, and finding none.

"It's not 'ere, sarge," said the constable who had been searching the half of the room that included the sofa.

"What's not here?" I asked. "Are you looking for something?"

"Search the other rooms," said the sergeant. "You may think you're very clever, sir. But we know it's 'ere, and we *will* find it."

"Find what?"

The sergeant ignored me and joined the search himself. Opening cupboards and pulling out drawers. He even opened the windows and leaned outside to check the pavement in case we'd thrown the body out there.

One by one the constables returned to report the fruitlessness of their searches.

"Well, officer," I said. "Seeing as you won't tell me what your men have been looking for, I'll have to jolly well ask your superintendent. Or maybe the commissioner himself. When am I dining with him, Reeves?"

"Next week, sir."

The sergeant may have not have been entirely convinced of my chumminess with the metropolitan police commissioner, but I could see the doubt in his eyes. Could he afford to risk it?

He could not.

"An apology may be in order, sir," he said grudgingly. "We'd been told a murder had been committed on these premises."

"A murder?" I pride myself on my ability to feign shock, even Henry Irving would have been impressed at this performance.

"Yes, sir. We were told that the body was in this room."

"Told? Told by whom?"

"He didn't give his name, sir. He said he feared you'd find out, and kill him too."

"Really, officer. Do I look like a murderer?" I gave him my most innocent smile.

"I really couldn't say, sir."

Reeves coughed. "May I enquire, sergeant, as to what this person looked like? He may be known to us – some of Mr

Worcester's acquaintances have a very *odd* taste in practical jokes."

"I never actually saw him. He reported the crime by telephone."

"An anonymous caller?" I said. "And you believed him?"

"He was very convincing, sir. He sounded terrified and ... this address *is* on file."

"It is?"

"Yes, sir. It's been given as the London address of a notorious helmet stealer by the name of Nebuchadnezzar Blenkinsop."

"Never heard of him," I said, clutching hold of the time machine for support. Nebuchadnezzar Blenkinsop was the name I always gave to the magistrates when I was up before them! Had I been too squiffy one time and given my real address?

"How old would you say this anonymous caller was, sergeant?" asked Reeves.

"Difficult to say. Like I said, he was in fear of his life. Not an old gent. Not a young one neither."

"Did he have an accent at all? A local man? A foreigner?" said Reeves.

"Weren't no foreigner. Sounded a bit like Mr Worcester. Posh, that is."

~

The constabulary took their truncheons and left, leaving Reeves and me to ponder over what we'd learned.

The first thing I'd learned was that gin was essential to time travel. Without it one couldn't keep track of the changing timelines. So, I rescued the cocktail that Reeves had abandoned earlier on the drinks cabinet and downed it in one.

"Do we have any more gin, Reeves?"

"I keep an extra bottle for emergencies, sir."

"Well, keep them coming, Reeves. *This* is an emergency. And make sure you're up to pressure. Who knows what might happen next."

I settled back in my favourite armchair, freshly shaken cocktail in hand, and pored over the facts.

"Do we assume this anonymous caller is the chap who shot our dead body?" I asked.

"It is a strong possibility, sir. I think we *can* say that this caller wanted to implicate you in the murder, and most likely was responsible for depositing the deceased in your sitting room. But whether they killed the gentleman, or procured an already deceased gentleman for the purposes of incriminating you, I cannot tell."

"But why me, Reeves?"

"That *is* perplexing, sir."

"In books, this sort of thing happens when the detective is close to solving the crime. The murderer decides to get rid of the detective by framing him. But we're not *on* a case, are we, Reeves?"

"There *is* the case of stolen time machine, sir. Technically, we haven't returned it yet."

"You think HG Wells has cut up rough? Give me back my time machine or I'll fill your sitting room with dead bodies?"

"No, sir, but it is possible that we didn't restore the timeline *exactly* as it was before. We may have another case in this timeline."

I put my drink down. Reeves had done it again! We *must* have a new case, and we must be doing pretty well if we'd flushed the murderer out.

We searched the flat. If we were on a case, we must have written something down, or collected a pile of clues – the calling card of the client, if nothing else.

We searched for a good half-hour, and found nothing. We didn't even have HG Wells' calling card.

"Shouldn't we have *some* recollection of this new case, Reeves? Don't the butterflies rewrite our memories?"

"It is a branch of science little understood, sir. And there is the added complication of having our memories shielded by the time machine. If you remember, the later Mrs Dean had no memory of *Miss* Wells whilst the other Mrs Deans did."

That was true.

"More gin, I think, Reeves. My little grey cells need a thorough lubrication."

"Very good, sir. There is also the possibility that there *is* no new case. The fact that the deceased appears to originate from the 1850s suggests the involvement of a time machine. We are in *possession* of a time machine. *Ipso facto* there must be a link."

I'm often asked, usually at the Sloths after a couple of snifters, 'what's the difference between a consulting detective and a policeman?' I always give the same answer – hunches. We consulting detectives are always having them.

Facts are useful, but pedestrian. It's like playing *Snakes and Ladders*. Facts take one from square to square, but it's the ladders – those are the hunches – that really advance a case. I'm not quite sure where the snakes come into it, but I suspect finding a dead body behind the sofa qualifies as landing on one.

I had just landed upon a ladder.

"Egad, Reeves, you've hit upon the solution!"

"I have, sir?"

"It's obvious really. We have a baffling case. *And* we have a time machine. *Ipso whatso*, we beetle into the future to find out how we solved it. It's like turning to the last page of a detective novel!"

Reeves aired his disapproving face. "I strongly advise against it, sir."

"Why? It's not the past. There's no timeline to sabotage."

"People living in the future may have a different perspective upon the matter, sir. You'd be tampering with their past."

"I'm doing that now Reeves. Without a time machine. Or are you arguing for pre-destination?"

"No, sir. After witnessing the events of the past day, I cannot believe that any of this was pre-ordained. But neither can I recommend using the time machine for anything other than a dire emergency."

"A dead body in next week's bath counts as the direst of emergencies in my book. Not to mention someone trying to frame me for murder. I can go on my own if the prospect unnerves you. I think I've grasped the basics of flying the machine."

"That will not be necessary, sir. I will, of course, accompany you."

"Stout fellow, Reeves! How far ahead do we need to go? One week? A month?"

"The case may be a complex one, sir. I would suggest at least a year."

"That long?"

"It would be safer, sir. One would imagine the time machine would require some kind of fuel to power it. A single journey into the future would be safer than having to take several because we'd underestimated the length of time the case had taken to solve."

Reeves had raised a worrying point.

I put my drink down and got up.

"Have you looked for some kind of steam outlet on the machine?"

"Yes, sir. There doesn't appear to be anything obvious. From the sound of the engine, I suspect it to be powered by electrical energy, but I can see no apparent way to charge it."

A lesser detective may have balked at the prospect of a one way trip into the future. But Reginald Worcester was *not* a lesser detective. And he had a sneaking suspicion that Reeves was spinning him a line to put him off using the machine.

I downed my drink, withdrew four crisp new five pound notes from my writing desk, and grabbed Reeves's emergency bottle of gin.

"Sir?" said Reeves, eyeing the bottle.

"It's my 'time traveller's essential hamper,' Reeves. Now, dial up 1905, we're off to the last page."

SEVEN

1905 was not what I was expecting. My lovely flat had become a home of dust, cobwebs and abandonment. All my furniture was still there – my books, my clothes – but nothing had been cleaned or aired for what looked like a year.

"I'll open a window, sir."

I checked the bathroom, nudging the bathroom door open with a tentative foot, worried what I might find in the bath.

I exhaled a sigh of relief. "The body's gone, Reeves."

That was our only piece of good news. We'd left no note, no clue as to where we'd gone, and the most recent newspaper we found was for two days after HG Wells had first burst into the flat.

"We must have left in a hurry," I said.

"The icebox is empty, sir. As is the drinks cabinet. And there are no remains of fresh food in the pantry. All of which indicates to me that our departure was not unduly swift. We had time to prepare."

"But prepare for what?"

"I suggest we check your wardrobe, sir, to see if any clothes are missing."

Our rummaging discovered that three suits, a smoking jacket, six shirts, and many assorted smaller items were absent. As was my large trunk – something I only use for long sea voyages.

"America, you think?" I asked Reeves.

"That would be my assumption, sir. And, by the condition of the flat, it would appear we are still there."

It's at time like these when a time traveller's emergency hamper comes into its own. I returned to the sitting room, grabbed the gin, and poured myself a swift one.

"Well, Reeves, what do we do now? Does our continued absence suggest we still haven't cracked the case?"

"There are insufficient facts to say, sir. In the 1890s you

fled to America on three occasions to escape the machinations of your aunts. This could be another of those occasions."

I sipped my drink and had a good ponder. Most of my flights to New York had been to escape imminent engagements. Now that I was engaged to Emmeline, who was from a good, if somewhat strange, family, there would be no need for auntly intervention. Granted, she occasionally chained herself to railings, but they were always in good neighbourhoods. Nothing to raise the ire of an aunt and make her advance the claims of an alternative.

And where *was* Emmie? Had she joined me in New York? I wouldn't have left her behind.

If her father hadn't taken against the telephone and banned it from the Dreadnought household, I could have telephoned her London home and found out.

I was struck by another ladder. The telephone!

I could call the Sloths! One of the chaps there would know where I'd gone and why.

I raced over, picked up the earpiece, and tapped the bar twice.

"Operator?" I said. And then to Reeves, "We shall soon know everything, Reeves. Nothing escapes the chaps at the Sloths. Find a pad and pencil. I'll get the phone number of wherever we're staying in New York and book a long distance call. Operator! I say, Reeves, this line sounds awfully quiet."

"Allow me, sir," said Reeves.

I handed the apparatus over to him. He tried it several times before pronouncing it deceased.

"The telephone appears to be disconnected, sir."

"We'll visit the Sloths in person then. Shall we walk or fly?"

"Walk, sir. As much as I eschew unnecessary interaction with people from other time periods, the thought of taking a time machine into the Sloths fills me with extreme trepidation."

"You think someone would find it and take it for a spin?"

"I think it highly probable, sir. May I also suggest you wear a disguise?"

"Disguise?"

"As a precaution, sir. One year ago, someone attempted to frame you for murder. Two days later you fled the country and have not returned since. One must assume there to be an element of danger should you be recognised."

"What kind of disguise, do you think? I have a Pierrot costume."

"I was thinking of a hat and large scarf, sir. If you covered your nose and lower face..."

So disguised, we left the flat and set off on foot for the Sloths. I must say that 1905 didn't look much different from 1904. I wondered if I might catch sight of the new Stanley Steamer – the improved 1905 version with heated seats and a super-condenser – but my luck was out.

And then, as we were passing a bookshop, my eyes strayed to the window display and...

My knees almost gave way. There, in the bookshop window, were dozens of books, each with my face on the cover. And above my face was the title – *The Mayfair Maniac.*

~

I'm not sure if my eyes grew quite as large as dinner plates, but I wouldn't have been surprised. A small side plate, certainly. I couldn't speak. I could barely stretch out a finger to point at the window.

And where had they got that picture? I looked positively deranged. And as if the picture and the title weren't bad enough, there below the name of the author – one Horace Smallpiece – was the line, *The blood curdling true story of Reginald Worcester, the diabolical murderer known to all as the Mayfair Maniac!*

"Most unfortunate, sir," said Reeves.

"Unfortunate! This is beyond unfortunate, Reeves. This is diabolical!"

"There is, however, a silver lining."

"You see silver linings, Reeves? I fail to spot them."

"Our mission was to discover what happened next, sir. That book will tell us."

As much as I loathed handing over three shillings and sixpence to Horace Smallpiece and his execrable publisher, Reeves was right. We needed that book.

"I think two copies would be advisable, sir. That way the two of us can skim through the contents with more speed."

I gave Reeves a begrudging fiver from my time traveller's emergency hamper, and waited outside. Had they found the body in the bath? And was I still on the run?

The two books purchased, we hurried back to the flat. I skimmed a few pages on the way.

Apparently we'd been apprehended at Southampton docks attempting to board a liner for New York. And I was accused of not one but *five* murders.

"Five murders, Reeves!" I said 'They found five dead bodies in the flat."

Back at the flat, we raced through the book, skimming Horace Smallpiece's purplest prose – the man was a sensationalist of the worst order.

"It says here, sir, that they never identified any of the deceased."

I skimmed further ahead to the middle of the book where there were some photographic plates.

"They have pictures of all five in the middle of the book, Reeves. Including the chap we left in the bath. All of them look like they were snatched from the past. Old style collars and whatnot."

Pretty strong stuff too, those pictures. They looked like police photographs taken of the bodies as they had been found. They didn't actually show any bloodstains – they were all head and shoulder shots – but still.

"The police believed it was you who dressed them all in early Victorian clothing, sir. It was one of the more sensational aspects of the case. Doctor Freud believed you had a grandfather fixation."

"A what?"

"A grandfather fixation, sir. He posited that in your delusional state you believed you were killing your grandfather. Hence your need to clothe your victims in apparel of the correct vintage."

"What absolute tosh, Reeves! I got on very well with both my grandfathers. Didn't anyone speak up for me?"

Reeves took an inordinately long time to respond. "Reeves?"

"I was reading ahead, sir. It would appear your defence was one of 'not guilty by reason of mental negligibility.'"

"Mental negligibility!"

"Yes, sir. Many of your friends and family testified on your behalf."

"What page is this on, Reeves?"

"I have forgotten, sir. I think my pressure may be dangerously low."

I didn't believe a word. While Reeves repaired to the Butler's pantry to pretend to top himself up, I scoured the offensive little book until I found the passages I was looking for. There were three pages of them! Italicised extracts from witness statements - each of them dredging up incidents from my past which, taken out of context, made me look like an inveterate carpet chewer!

Aunt Bertha, Great Aunt Boadicea, Uncle Clarence, Cousin Herbert, Georgiana Throstlecoombe, Stiffy, Tufty, Binky, Cicely - all of them testified to my mental negligibility.

As did one other witness.

"Et tu, Reeves!" I said as he slunk back from the pantry.

"Sir?" he said.

"You know very well what I'm talking about, Reeves. This passage here about my 'inability to differentiate between fact and fantasy' and my 'sincere belief that the criminal mastermind we were searching for was an orang-utan!'"

"I imagine, sir, that my testimony was coloured by my desire to ensure you were not convicted for murder."

"That's all very well. But why not tell the truth?"

"If you turn to the next page, sir, you will see that you tried that."

I turned to the next page. More italicised witness statements, but this time they were mine.

"It appears that your account of the time machine, the twenty-nine Aunt Charlottes, and turning HG Wells into a woman, did not play well to the jury, sir."

It had not. According to Horace Smallpiece the court had had to be cleared for excessive laughter, and one of the jurors had had an unfortunate accident which required a change of clothing to be sent for.

"Miss Emmeline gets a mention, sir."

I braced myself for another body blow and turned to the next page.

But the more I read, the more uplifted I felt. Emmie hadn't deserted me! She chained herself to the gallery on day one, the witness box on day two, and on day three - after having both her favourite chain and her spare one confiscated on the door - she threw herself in front of the judge as he entered the courtroom and brought him down. She wasn't allowed in after that, but kept vigil outside, throwing rocks at the prosecuting barristers.

I was touched beyond words.

"It would appear that, at the time of publication, Miss Emmeline is chained to railings outside Parkhurst prison, sir."

"Is that where I am, Reeves? Parkhurst?"

"Yes, sir. The jury found you guilty, but the judge decided against the death penalty due to your good family and ... other reasons."

"Other reasons, Reeves?"

"I am speaking *his* words, sir. Your good family and obvious mental negligibility."

I harrumphed. I'm not a man generally given to harrumph, but in the circs I felt entirely justified.

"And where are *you* now, Reeves? Does it say? In the services of a new master?"

Reeves turned several pages before replying.

"I ... I appear to have been de-activated, sir, and..."

"What is it, Reeves." The poor man looked in shock. I'm sure I saw a wisp of steam escape from his left ear.

"It says here that I am on display in Madame Tussaud's Chamber of Horrors, sir. I am the Mayfair Maniac's Robot."

I forgave all instantly.

EIGHT

I suggested to Reeves that he might benefit from a soothing oil change in a darkened room, but he declined.

"We must prevent this future from happening, sir. It is an abomination."

We were agreed upon that. I also had a yearning to fly the time machine to Parkhurst to see Emmeline, and break my future self out of chokey. But Reeves counselled against it. He considered it a distraction, and that our priority was to uncover the identity of the person who was manipulating time against us and to put a stop to them.

"Why these five people, Reeves? Are they five strangers chosen at random to get me out of the way? You'd have thought one would have been enough. And why not murder me instead?"

"It is most perplexing, sir. From reading Mr Smallpiece's account, it appears that all the deceased personages had their pockets emptied and clothing labels removed. That, and the evidence that our mystery person chose victims from the past - and as no one came forward to identify the gentlemen in the present, I think we can safely regard that as a fact - gives weight to the theory that our mystery person went to *immense* length to hide their identities."

"Are you saying they're not random?"

"Yes, sir."

"I thought so. Just checking."

"I have just noticed something else, sir."

"What?"

"The body that we moved one week into the future, and placed in the bath, was found in your bedroom, sir. Five days earlier. All the bodies were discovered at the same time."

I reached for the gin bottle. I had been trying to slow my intake of the fortifying liquid in case I overindulged, but it was at this point that I decided that one could not fully comprehend time travel sober.

"That, sir," continued Reeves, "testifies both to his persistence *and* his continued access to a time machine. I believe it likely that he will use the time machine to undo anything we undertake to stop him."

"Forgive me, Reeves, if this is an obvious question, but don't *we* have the time machine?"

"Yes, sir."

"So where does this other time machine come from? Are there two?"

"There may be two, sir, but I suspect there is just the one. When we were considering candidates for cases that we may have been working on, we neglected to consider the future."

"You'll have to slow down, Reeves. Are you saying that *this* time machine – the one with us now in the sitting room – is, in the future, being used against us by our mystery murderer?"

"I posit the possibility, sir. We may have been engaged in the future to investigate these murders, and the murderer decided to move all the bodies back in time to incriminate the detective who was investigating him."

"The bodies he'd already moved forward in time so they wouldn't be recognised?"

"Exactly, sir."

I wondered how Murgatroyd of the Yard would have taken such news. Not best pleased, would have been my guess. Bodies moving back and forth through time. Behind the sofa one day, in the bath a week later, and then back five days to appear in one's bedroom. Where would they go next? Murgatroyd would have had the time machine hanged, drawn and quartered, and then displayed in Madame Tussaud's alongside the Mayfair Maniac's Robot!

"What if we destroy the time machine? Wouldn't that stop him?" I said.

"I fear the current timeline is so convoluted that it would be impossible to calculate the outcome, sir. It may prevent the murders but, equally, it may not. And once the machine is destroyed, we would be unable to use it to rectify the situation. You could find yourself in Parkhurst for life."

"And you at Madame Tussaud's."

"Indeed, sir."

I took a long sip of gin.

"It seems to me, Reeves, that our mystery murderer is most afraid of having those bodies identified, don't you think? All that trouble he's gone too."

"Indeed, sir."

"That settles it then. Prepare the time machine, Reeves. We shall have their names before sundown."

"We will, sir?"

"We will, Reeves."

I carefully cut the photographic plates out of Horace Smallpiece's libellous tome and pocketed them.

"We're going to the 1850s, Reeves. Destination: the Sloths. Someone there's bound to recognise these men."

~

"I think another gentleman's club would be safer, sir. The Sportsman, perhaps?"

"Nonsense. You forget how we're dressed, Reeves. We'd stand out a mile in those other clubs. The Sloths have never been stuffy. Always help a chap out, that's our motto."

"Perhaps if I stayed with the machine, sir?"

"If you must. Now what year, do you think? 1850? 1855?"

"I would suggest a date after 1850, sir. Older gentlemen are slower to adopt the changing fashions than others. A coat from the 1850s could be worn by such a gentleman many years later."

"But these other chaps are younger, Reeves." I showed him the full set of plates. "Can you date a man from his collar?"

"Difficult, sir. Perhaps if we try 1851?"

Off to 1851 we went, arriving in a very different sitting room to the one we'd left. All my furniture had gone, and in had come all this Rococo Revival stuff. It looked very much like Stiffy's Great Aunt Augusta's drawing room, but without the elephants.

We didn't materialise. We'd barely arrived before Reeves had us turned around and sweeping out through the window. We flew to the Sloths at second storey height, and I must say, I preferred it to its ground level cousin. No unexpected spectral Hansom Cab came careering through the Worcester frame. Instead we glided, most sedately, and could look down upon the London of 1851 bustling beneath us.

"You *will* remember the dangers of changing the timeline, sir? I hesitate to mention it, but if you could keep your interaction with club members to the barest minimum..."

"You are speaking to a future inmate of Parkhurst prison, Reeves. I shall be caution itself."

We entered the Sloths via a second storey window.

Reeves found a secluded spot in the library - always the emptiest room in the Sloths - and materialised long enough for me to hop out. He then faded from view.

The decor of the library was pretty much unchanged since the last time I'd been there - dark, full of books, and lots of comfortable armchairs one could fall asleep in. None appeared to be occupied, so I headed downstairs towards the more populated part of the club.

"Who the devil are you, sir?" bellowed a military looking moustachioed chap at the foot of the stairs.

"Me, sir?"

"Yes, you, sir."

"I'm ... Nebuchadnezzar Blenkinsop."

"Never heard of you. And what, pray, are you wearing?"

"What this? I've just returned from Paris. They're all wearing it over there."

"Paris, you say?"

"Yes, I was over there on an errand, sorting out someone's will. I say, you couldn't help me, could you?"

"You don't want to borrow money, do you?"

"Quite the reverse. I'm trying to track down five heirs. But instead of giving me five names to look for, they gave me five pictures!"

"Pictures?"

"I know. Strange, isn't it? Look, here they are." I handed him the photographic plates. "Do you recognise any of them? Those Frenchies think they live in London."

My moustachioed chap didn't recognise a single one of them, but he took me into the dining room and called his friends over to meet me. The club motto was as true in 1851 as it was in 1904. *Always help a chap out*.

In less than five minutes we had names of four of our mystery departed. The body in the bath was identified as one Jasper Evershot. Body number two was Henry Molesworth. And then came Algernon Throgmorton-Undershaft and Percy Baekeland.

"I wonder what the link between them all is," I said. "Do all these chaps know each other?"

"In passing, maybe. Don't see much of Henry these days. Jasper was sent to Manchester to work for his uncle."

"They are all alive though?"

"I saw Algernon last week," said one. "I haven't seen Percy for a while," said another. "None of them are members of the Sloths."

I tried a few other enquiries but could tell I wasn't going to winkle out much more. The fifth chap was a mystery, and the other four were but passing acquaintances.

But I had four names. And a copy of *Who's Who* waiting for me back in 1904.

~

I was feeling decidedly peckish by the time I'd hopped back into the machine and brought Reeves up to date viz. my adventures.

"I think a spot of lunch is called for, Reeves. I don't think I've eaten in decades. What is the time, by the way?"

"Difficult to say, sir. We have been living between the hours of eleven o'clock and noon for some while."

We sailed back to the flat. Reeves dialled up 1904 and then, much to my surprise, drove the machine straight through the sitting room wall.

"Reeves?"

"As Mr Wells' machine appears to be staying with us a little longer, sir, I thought the spare bedroom would make a better home for it. It does take up a lot of room, and if I am to prepare luncheon..."

Once the time machine was parked to Reeves's satisfaction, I headed straight to the shelves for *Who's Who*, leaving Reeves to oil off into the kitchen to prepare lunch.

I tried Henry Molesworth first. And there he was, a man of the correct vintage, *and* he was still alive.

I took the book through to Reeves.

"I say, Reeves. Shouldn't these chaps be dead?"

"One would expect them to be *missing*, sir. Presumed dead perhaps but, as their bodies won't appear for another two days, they would not have had a burial in the 1850s."

My gin levels were in need of topping up.

"So this Henry Molesworth must be the wrong Molesworth. It says here he married a second wife in 1889."

"Possibly, sir. There is also the possibility that Mr Molesworth's murder has not yet taken place."

"Explain, Reeves."

"We know that five bodies are discovered in this flat on Wednesday morning, sir. What we do *not* know is whether that timeline is the timeline we are currently residing in."

By this time *I* wasn't sure which timeline I was residing in. We'd changed it so often.

"Do timelines wear out, Reeves?"

"Pardon, sir?"

"All this changing back and forth. Must be wearing, don't you think? Could we wear it out?"

"No, sir. Have you located any of the other deceased?"

I tried Algernon Throgmorton-Undershaft next. Wouldn't be many of them. And I was right. There wasn't *any* of them. There was a Cornelius and a Hildebrand, but as for Algernons – not a sausage.

Somewhat dispirited I moved on to Jasper Evershot, the man we'd stowed in the bath. I found three, but only one was of the right age. I read a little further ... and there it was – *disappeared mysteriously in 1855, believed drowned*.

I showed Reeves. "You don't think he drowned in our bath, do you, Reeves?"

"No, sir. If you remember, he was shot. The *Who's Who* entry is interesting though as it shows that Mr Evershot's departure was not regarded at the time as suspicious. That would appear to confirm that our time travelling nemesis is indeed killing these gentlemen rather than collecting murder victims from the past."

I tried the last name – Percy Baekeland – and drew a blank. Not a single Baekeland in the book.

"I still can't see a link between the five victims, Reeves. They're not related. They're not best chums. Some of them aren't even in *Who's Who*, so they can't all be well-heeled."

"It is indeed a mystery, sir."

It was still a mystery half an hour later. I'd polished off a quarter of a salmon and sampled a rather fine Hock, but even that hadn't been enough to inspire my little grey cells into action.

Then there was a knock at the door, followed by several knocks in rapid succession. I looked at Reeves and could tell he was thinking the same as me. The rozzers! I ran for the sofa and peered behind it. I was relieved to see nothing there.

The knocking started up again. "I say, is anyone at home?" came a muffled voice. It didn't sound like a policeman.

Reeves walked over to the door and opened it.

And in burst HG Wells!

"Thank God, you're here," said HG, rushing towards me. "I don't know who else to turn to. You *are* Reginald Worcester, aren't you? The gentleman's consulting detective?"

NINE

I'd never experienced deja vu before. It was most unsettling. Had we broken the timeline and made it wrap around itself?

"I'm HG Wells. But please call me Bertie. Everyone does. You may have heard of my time machine."

"In passing," I said.

"Well, it's real, and someone's stolen it! I have no idea how. I keep it in a locked room. There's no other way in or out, and the only key has never left my possession!"

Reeves coughed. "At what time, sir, did you first become aware of its disappearance?"

"Twenty minutes ago. I last saw it yesterday evening."

"Perhaps there has been a change of timeline, sir? Maybe your time machine has 'disappeared' rather than been stolen."

Reeves gave me an odd look. I was still trying to decipher its meaning when HG replied.

"The timeline can't have been rewritten," he said. "I've had the time machine in my cellar the whole time."

Reeves coughed again. "Perhaps Mr Worcester has an opinion on where your time machine may be, sir?"

Mr Worcester was still baffled. Was this deja vu or one of those timeline changes? But everyone was looking at me, so I had to say something.

"What about your Aunt Charlotte?" I asked. "Did you show her how to fly your machine?"

"You know my Aunt Charlotte?"

"I *deduced* you had an Aunt Charlotte. We consulting detectives do this all the time. I could tell by your shoes that you'd either just returned from India or had an aunt called Charlotte."

Reeves coughed disapprovingly.

"My shoes? How?" said HG.

"It would take too long to explain. Either one can deduce, or one cannot."

"Oh," said HG, taking one long last look at his shoes. "No, it can't be Aunt Charlotte. I've made a point of not mentioning *anything* to her since receiving a letter two years ago warning me against her."

"The Traveller?" I said.

"Good Lord! How did you know that?"

I was rather enjoying this. "It's the kind of letter he would have written."

"You know him?"

Reeves intervened. "I'm sure Mr Worcester could deduce the *present* location of your time machine, sir. *If* he put his mind to it."

"I think not, Reeves. I need more information first."

"Ask me anything, Mr Worcester. It's imperative we recover this time machine as soon as possible."

"Righto," I said. "Ever recall wearing a dress?"

"You will have to excuse Mr Worcester, sir," interrupted Reeves. "His brain is differently wired. I think what he meant to ask was 'Is there any danger of the time machine running out of fuel?'"

"Oh," said HG. "Not so much now. The original batteries we built with the Traveller's assistance were very quick to drain. And very expensive to make. But we've been working on a new fuel cell for the past five years. We perfected it last week. It'll run for *years* now on a single fuel cell."

"You said 'we,' sir. Would that be your associates from the Royal Society who first helped you repair the machine?"

"It would. You seem remarkably well informed Mr...?"

"Reeves, sir. It was a deduction. You were saying about your associates?"

"We've worked together on and off for ten years. More off than on, I'm afraid, due to the recurring problem with the batteries. No one wanted to risk being stranded in the past if the battery failed."

"Quite, sir. Would any of these gentlemen have a key to your cellar?"

"No, not since I received that letter from The Traveller. After that we decided it best to change the lock and have just the one key."

"Might I trouble you for the names of these associates, sir?"

"You can't possibly suspect them. I've known them for years."

"We consulting detectives suspect everyone," I said.

"Even ourselves."

"Quite, sir, and it is always possible that one of your associates may have inadvertently vouchsafed information to a third party."

HG nodded. "There is that. Very well, my colleagues are Simeon Arbuthnot, Nathaniel Dawson, Edward Molesworth and Beatrice Traherne."

"Did you say Molesworth?" I asked.

"Yes, Edward Molesworth."

"Any relation to Henry Molesworth," I asked, digging the photographic plates out of my pocket.

"Not that I know of. I haven't met any of Edward's family."

I showed him the picture. "Do you recognise him at all?"

"I can't say I do. He looks a little like Edward, but ... is he lying on the floor? He looks rather odd."

I handed him the other plates. "How about these? Anyone familiar?"

HG studied the pictures one by one.

"Good God!" he said. "That's The Traveller."

TEN

Our unnamed body number five was The Traveller!
"Are you sure, sir?" asked Reeves.
"Absolutely. I'd know his face anywhere. This must have been taken around the time he went missing. He's the same age. But I've never seen him in these clothes. He always wore such distinctive shirts - with no collars whatsoever."
"When was the last time you saw the gentleman, sir," asked Reeves.
"1894. He just disappeared. Dawson thought he'd-"
"If I may interrupt, sir," said Reeves. "Could you tell me the exact date you last saw him?"
HG scratched his chin and gave both moustaches a tug or two. "It must have been October 17th. That was the day after Beatrice's birthday. Why? Can I have another look at that photograph?"
I handed it back to him.
"Is he dead?" HG asked. "Are they all dead? They're all lying down."
"We're investigating their murders," I said. " Have you ever heard of Algernon Throgmorton-Undershaft, Jasper Evershot, or Percy Baekeland?"
"No," said HG.
"Could they be related to your associates, sir?" asked Reeves.
HG shrugged. "They could be, but I don't recognise the names. Look here, I don't understand. We searched everywhere for reports of The Traveller's death. Where was he found?"
"Not far from here, sir. I'm sure Mr Worcester will tell you more, but I can see that he is desirous of an early meeting with Mr Molesworth. Would you be so good, Mr Wells, as to take us to see him? I believe it likely that these murders and the theft of your time machine are inextricably linked."

~

We followed HG to Bloomsbury where we found Mr Edward Molesworth living in an old Georgian pile that had seen better days. We were shown into a large room that looked more like a laboratory than a drawing room – there were blueprints and maps strewn over desks, books and half assembled machines lying hither and thither. And barely anywhere to sit.

Mr Molesworth apologised. "I don't get many visitors," he said, while clearing spaces for us all.

"We're investigating the disappearance of the time machine," I said. "Do you know a Henry Molesworth?"

"My father?"

I handed him the picture. "Is this your father?"

"Why, yes, that's him when he was about thirty, but ... what kind of photograph is this? He doesn't look well."

"Early photographs are often like that, sir," said Reeves. "The length of exposure, the apprehension of the individual."

"He appears to be lying on the floor," said Molesworth.

"I believe the photographer had unusual ideas about composition, sir."

"Oh. Very odd. My father will be here soon if you want to talk to him."

"He's alive?" I asked.

"Very much so. He should be back any minute. He only stepped out for a short walk. But what's all this got to do with the disappearance of the time machine?"

I looked at Reeves. How does one broach the subject of a father's imminent murder?

"We believe, sir," said Reeves. "That there may be an attempt underway to change the timeline. Have you ever heard of Algernon Throgmorton-Undershaft, Jasper Evershot, or Percy Baekeland?"

Molesworth turned to HG. "Is this real?" he asked. "Someone's stolen the time machine?"

"They've found The Traveller's body," said HG.

"Where?"

"In Mayfair, sir," said Reeves. "Did any of those names sound familiar? Relatives of Mr Arbuthnot, Mr Dawson, or Miss Traherne, perhaps?"

"Never heard of any of them. The only Baekeland I know is Leo, a chemist working on plastics."

I handed Molesworth the other photographs.

"Any of these look familiar?"

He gave them all a thorough look, resting the longest on The Traveller.

"So he never went home," said Molesworth, his face turning grave. "And these others..." He held up the pictures. "They're dead too, aren't they? And my father ... is he dead?"

"We believe that to be the intention of the person who stole the time machine, sir," said Reeves. "But it has not yet come to pass."

"But these pictures..." said Molesworth. "Where did you get them?"

Everyone looked at me. There comes a time in every case when the detective has to choose whether or not to take people into his confidence. It's always a tricky calculation, because the murderer is invariably the person one least suspects. I decided to delay the decision a little longer.

"We found them close to The Traveller's body," I said. "Along with that list of names. It looks like he was investigating this timeline case and got shot. Then, with his dying breath, he pushed the evidence under the sofa so the murderer wouldn't find it."

"He had a picture of his own death?" asked Molesworth, sounding a little awe-struck.

"I assume he'd been to the future and found it, sir," said Reeves.

"That's what I'd deduced," I said. "Either that or India."

Molesworth checked his pocket watch. "I don't know what's keeping my father. He should be back by now. Do you think we should search for him?"

"That will not be necessary, sir," said Reeves "As you can see by his picture he is a young man when he meets his demise in that timeline. He is quite safe here. It is you, Mr Molesworth, whom Mr Worcester believes to be in the greater danger."

"I do?" I said.

"Yes, sir, your theory that the murderer is using the time machine to visit the 1850s in order to murder specific persons and thus remove their children from the timeline? Mr Henry Molesworth's murder is to prevent Mr Edward from being born."

"My father's murdered because of me!" said Molesworth.

"That appears to be the murderer's intention, sir. Tell me, Mr Wells, if Mr Edward had not existed in 1894 would you have chosen someone else to help The Traveller repair his machine?"

"I would," said HG. "Are you saying those other people are ancestors of Simeon, Nathaniel, and Beatrice?"

"I believe that is what Mr Worcester has deduced. Is it not, sir?"

"Pretty much spot on, Reeves. The way the bodies had been laid out, the uneven wear on the Traveller's left shoe–"

"Indeed, sir," said Reeves. "If you, Mr Wells, could compile a list of the people you would have approached, had your original team been unavailable, we may find the murderer's name upon that list."

Molesworth helped HG compile a list of the next best candidates in their respective fields. Hertha Ayrton was their choice for electrical engineer, Thomas Dashwood for mechanical engineer, Hector Munro Macdonald for mathematician, and Alfred Sackville-Warrender beat off the claims of James Macalister for the physicist spot.

"This is our fault, Bertie," said Molesworth. "If we hadn't been so determined to get that fuel cell working. It's made the machine *infinitely* more powerful now."

"It's not anyone's fault, Edward," said HG. "Whoever stole the machine could have taken the old machine into the future and had a fuel cell fitted. What I can't understand is how they stole it in the first place."

"We should have destroyed the machine the moment The Traveller disappeared," said Molesworth. "We knew the dangers of changing the timeline. The Traveller told us!"

"But we were using it for the advancement of knowledge, Edward! We recovered priceless books from monasteries before they were burned. And we *never* interfered with history. We only took what was about to be destroyed, and we *observed* rather than participated."

"Do you think this could be retribution?" asked Molesworth.

"Retribution for what?" said HG.

Molesworth sighed, and slowly shook his head.

"I took the machine to the future to perfect the fuel cell."

"What are you talking about?" said HG.

"Mr Worcester, I think *I* may be the cause of these murders, *and* the disappearance of the time machine."

~

I listened as Molesworth spilled all.

"You see," he said. "The original time machine was powered by a fuel cell – a hydrogen fuel cell – but it was damaged when the time machine malfunctioned and crashed, stranding The Traveller. We didn't have the knowledge or the wherewithal to repair the fuel cell so, with The Traveller's help, we designed an electrical battery.

"The battery was barely able to power the machine, and it drained too quickly. I thought if I studied the remains of the broken fuel cell I might be able to figure out how it worked and repair it. And, after several years of trying, I almost did. I was so close. I was sure it was only a matter of time.

"Then, two years ago, I decided to take the time machine into the future. I told myself it was only to confirm my theories, that I was merely shortening the development time of an invention that I would have perfected anyway... But now I see that I was deluding myself. I was stealing someone else's idea. The Molesworth Hydrogen Fuel Cell should have been called the Changguk Hydrogen Fuel Cell. They invented it. I merely rebuilt it, and attached my name to it."

As confessions went, this wasn't one of the best. Personally, I prefer the ones that begin, 'Fair cop, guv. You've got me banged to rights and no mistake,' and then swiftly proceed to either 'I dun it' or 'X dun it' – where X is the name of the person one least suspects.

"Are you saying this Chang Duck has come back into the past to get revenge for you stealing his idea?" I asked.

"I think it's bigger than that," said Molesworth. "I think it's the time police."

Now that was more like it. He may have taken his time, but as far as 'least likely suspects' went, he'd delivered.

"Time police?" I said.

"It's something Dawson came up with," said HG. "He thought The Traveller might be a fugitive, and the time police had caught up with him and snatched him back. Which was why we couldn't find him, and why he'd left the time machine behind."

"It makes sense now," said Molesworth. "They captured The Traveller, but he wouldn't tell them where he'd hidden the time machine. Then I start manufacturing the Molesworth Hydrogen Fuel Cell and they can't help but notice the change in the timeline."

He threw his hands in the air in exasperation. "And so they come back in time, retrieve the time machine, and set about removing everyone associated with it from history. It's all my fault!"

"You didn't do it intentionally," said HG. "Or for personal

gain. You told me yourself you were placing all the profits from the fuel cell into a trust for the poor."

It was then that something rummy happened. One second I was there, the next, I wasn't. A cold breeze was blowing in my face, and suddenly I had the strangest feeling.

Reeves and I were standing outside a church. How I came to be there, I had no idea. My memory was decidedly hazy.

"What are we doing here, Reeves?" I said. "I could have sworn I was sitting in front of a fire talking to someone. Moley? Ratty? Someone like that."

"Molesworth, sir. I believe someone has changed the timeline."

"How? We have the time machine, don't we?"

"I think it would be wise to return to the flat immediately, sir."

ELEVEN

We couldn't find the Stanley, so we hailed a cab and hurried back to the flat. The front door was ajar, and the jamb was splintered where the lock had been forced. I girded the Worcester loins. I couldn't hear anything from inside, but who knew what we'd find? A carpetful of dead bodies, or the time police lying in wait?

Reeves went in first. I followed at a discrete distance. I couldn't see any dead bodies in the sitting room. And no sign of the room having been turned over either. Everything was in its place, just as we'd left it. I checked behind the sofa to make sure. All clear there too.

Momentarily, Reeves appeared in the doorway. "The time machine is gone, sir. I've checked all the rooms. Nothing else appears to be missing. Or, indeed, added."

The latter was a relief. I didn't think my constitution was up to three police raids in a single morning.

Reeves pulled down a copy *Who's Who* from the bookcase and flicked through the pages.

"There is no mention of Mr Edward Molesworth, sir, and the Henry Molesworth who had previously taken a second wife in 1889 is now listed as 'missing believed run over by a steam train' in 1853."

My memory of events was still rather hazy. Bits were coming back, but I deduced my gin levels were dangerously low.

"An emergency cocktail, Reeves, and don't spare the gin."

Two glasses later I was feeling pretty braced and ready to face the worst.

"Will the Time Police write *us* out of history, do you think?"

"I am not convinced there *is* a temporal constabulary, sir. The door, you will notice, has been broken open."

"Your point, Reeves?"

"A temporal constabulary would not *need* to break open

the door, sir. They would fly in and materialise, as we have done several times."

"Ah, but they didn't have the time machine, did they? That's why they had to break in and steal it."

"One would imagine, sir, that the temporal constabulary would have *several* time machines. How else would they arrive here from the future?"

Was there anything that escaped this steam-powered marvel?

"So I'm not going to be orphaned by a steam train?"

"No, sir. I fear Parkhurst prison to be your more likely danger."

I leaned back in my chair and sucked on a contemplative olive.

"This is all very unsporting, don't you think, Reeves? Attacking a chap via his relatives, nipping into the future to frame him for murder? It's not British. Any of your suspects foreign?"

"No, sir."

"Do we have any pictures of them? Inspector Lupin swears you can tell a murderer by the shape of his ears."

There were no pictures, and I had growing doubts about Reeves's theory too. The more I thought about it, the more it had the feel of something Inspector Lestrade would have come up with. Perfectly sound, but too methodical. Where was the mysterious one-legged stranger? Where was the orang-utan?

The answer had to be connected with the time machine, that was beyond doubt, but I couldn't see why someone in the second string team would want to bump off the entire first team. Although – now I thought about it – it *wasn't* the entire first team, was it?

We had ignored the obvious!

"I have it Reeves!" I said, nearly spilling my drink in the excitement. "It's just as Sherlock Holmes says, 'When you've eliminated the people with motives, the only people left – especially if they appear as innocent as a new-born lamb – have to be the murderer!'"

"I think Mr Holmes may have phrased that somewhat differently, sir."

"A word here, a word there, maybe, but the gist is the same, Reeves. It's always the person one least suspects. And who is that?"

"I hesitate to answer, sir."

"Come on, Reeves! It's obvious. Herbert George Wells! He's bumping off everyone else with access to the time machine so he can have it for himself."

"I think it unlikely, sir. It was Mr Wells who engaged us to investigate the case."

"Exactly! To throw suspicion away from himself. He knew once all his associates started disappearing that suspicion would fall on him, so he came up with a plan. I rather suspect he egged on his Aunt Charlotte too. 'Here you are, Aunt C, nip back in time and bring back a score of your younger selves.'"

"An interesting theory, sir. But Mr Wells was with us at Mr Molesworth's house at the moment the timeline changed."

"If you can have twenty-nine Aunt Charlottes, Reeves, I'm pretty sure you can have two HG Wells. Maybe Gertie is in it with him! And I wouldn't rule out the butterflies."

~

Reeves was not buying the HG Wells theory.

"Mr Wells has no motive, sir. The time machine has been in his possession since 1894. He can use it whenever he wants. Why would he now be desirous of removing his associates from history?"

Reeves just did not understand that 'least likely suspect' trumped 'motive' every day of the week.

I was about to tell him when I was struck by one of the brainiest notions I'd ever had. I'm not sure if it was one of those ladders, or perhaps the fish I'd consumed for lunch, but there it was – like the Sword dangling at the Gates of Damocles.

"So, Mr Wells has no motive, says you?" I said, drawing myself up.

"Not that I can discern, sir."

"Well, how about this. What if The Traveller was going to oil back into the future with his time machine? He says, 'What ho, Bertie. I'm off now. Thanks for all the help, what?' and offers his hand for the parting shake... And Bertie cuts up rough. He wants the machine for his own, so he shoots him. Bertie then dumps the body in the future and denies all to his friends. All's well for ten years, until Moley perfects his fuel cell. With me so far?"

"Yes, sir."

"Good. With this fuel cell onboard they can now take the time machine for daily spins. And one of the chaps – it might be Moley, it might be one of the others – says, 'How about taking the time machine back to 1894 and finding out what happened to The Traveller?' Bertie panics and starts bumping them all off."

Sherlock Holmes after a fish supper could not have come up with anything more brilliant. Even Reeves was impressed (see eyebrows).

"That *would* be a motive, sir. But why engage our services?"

"Because his Aunt Charlotte stole the machine before he could bump them all off! Prepare the Stanley, Reeves. It's time to beard Bertie in his den."

"Before we undertake anything precipitous, sir, I suggest we ascertain who the descendants of Algernon Throgmorton-Undershaft, Jasper Evershot, and Percy Baekeland are. A detour via the British Library, or, perhaps, the Royal Society to ascertain the forebears of Mr Arbuthnot, Mr Dawson, and Miss Traherne...?"

I had to be firm.

"Reeves, now is not the time for ascertaining or deliberating. It is a time for action, while we're still here with a full set of antecedents. As the bard says, 'There is a tide in the affairs of men which taken at the flood, leads on to fortune; omitted, all is bound in shallows and porpentines."

"Miseries, sir."

"What?"

"Shallows and miseries, sir. The fretful porpentine belongs to Hamlet."

"Hamlet has a pet porpentine? I don't recall an aquatic scene in Hamlet."

"I shall prepare the Stanley, sir."

~

While Reeves topped up the Stanley's water tank, I looked up HG's address in *Who's Who*. It was listed as 13 Hanover Terrace, Regent's Park. Not far at all. A little over a mile.

Before I joined Reeves, I slipped into my bedroom and retrieved my service revolver. If HG Wells was going to be armed, then so was I. I might not have any bullets for it – Reeves keeps on hiding them – but I could still point it menacingly.

Off I ran to the Stanley and leaped aboard.

"Next stop, Hanover Terrace, Reeves."

I drove the Stanley as fast as the traffic would allow,

taking the odd corner on two wheels.

"A two-pronged attack, I think, Reeves. You locate the time machine – it'll probably be locked in his cellar – while I keep HG busy above stairs. As soon as you find it, give me the nod, and we'll confront him. 'Ho!' we will say. 'Someone's stolen your time machine, have they? Well, what's it doing in your cellar?' He will fold, Reeves. And if he doesn't, I have my service revolver handy."

"Stop the car, sir," said Reeves.

"What? You object to my plan?"

"No, sir. It's that advertising hoarding. The one over there above the tea shop."

I swung the Worcester eyes shopwards and almost lost control of the Stanley, such was my shock.

There was a large poster advertising *Dawson's Hydrogen Fuel Cell. The future at a price you can afford!*

TWELVE

I pulled hard on the brake.

"Remind me, Reeves. Which one's Dawson?"

"Nathaniel Dawson, sir. He was one of the original four who helped rebuild the time machine."

"Not one of the second team, then?"

"No, sir."

I stared at the advertisement. A bit over-the-top, I thought. It was lauding this fuel cell as the answer to Britain's energy needs. Automobiles, trains, Zeppelins, even factories were going to be powered by Dawson's Hydrogen Fuel Cell.

"What does this mean, Reeves?"

"I think a visit to the library is called for, sir. Before we accuse Mr Dawson of murder, I think it wise to be sure of our facts."

I let Reeves drive us to the library. He knew the way, and I needed time to reflect. Could Dawson have done it? He ticked the 'person you'd least suspect' box. I had yet to see his ears though.

At the library, I was somewhat taken aback by the reception Reeves received. It was the kind of fawning welcome the chaps at the Sloths usually reserve for Drongo Foxcombe, seven-time winner of the Sloths annual brioche eating competition. *How may we help you, Mr Reeves? Of course, Mr Reeves. I will fetch that immediately, Mr Reeves.*

Within seconds he had three library automata beetling off into the aisles eager to do his bidding, while another showed us into a small anteroom where 'we would be more comfortable.'

"You come here often, Reeves?" I asked.

"As often as I can, sir. Fourteen years in a cupboard leaves a significant hole in one's knowledge."

Every now and then an automaton would return with a book or periodical, place it on the table in front of Reeves, then beetle off in pursuit of the next request.

I watched, marvelling at the speed with which Reeves could devour a book. There was a veritable breeze emanating from the swiftly turning pages. Any faster and I'd have feared for East Dulwich.

"Anything so far?" I asked.

"Mr Dawson appears to be a prolific inventor, sir. As well as the Hydrogen Fuel Cell, he has also invented Dawsonite – a revolutionary plastic referred to as 'the material of a thousand uses' – and is tipped to win this years Nobel Prize for his work on steam-powered monoplanes."

"You think he's bumping these people off to steal their inventions?"

"I do, sir. Mr Dawson has no history of studying chemistry and yet he is able to manufacture a revolutionary plastic in a matter of months. Ditto for his monoplane designs and fuel cell."

One of the library automata returned looking very apologetic.

"A thousand apologies, Mr Reeves, but I cannot locate any chemist by the name of Leo Baekeland."

Reeves thanked the automation for its efforts and turned to me.

"You may remember Mr Molesworth saying that the only Baekeland he knew was a chemist named Leo, a man working in plastics, sir. I posit that the late Mr Baekeland was the inventor of Dawsonite."

"Have you accounted for all the dead bodies?" I asked.

"I think so, sir. One of them has yet to be murdered. His son, Percival Throgmorton-Undershaft is a designer of racing Zeppelins, and tops this year's list of *Nature's* 'scientists to watch.'"

"So Dawson is probably on his way to nobble the last of the Throgmorton-Undershafts as we speak."

"That would be my guess, sir."

"Have you found Dawson's address?"

"He has recently moved to Grosvenor Square, sir."

"Then let's get going! Two-pronged attack, Reeves. Just as before."

I got up to leave, but Reeves remained seated.

"Come on, Reeves. The game's afoot."

"I have been thinking, sir. I believe we have an ethical dilemma."

~

I almost wished I'd never asked. I soon discovered why Sherlock Holmes pretends to be out every time a client with a time travel mystery knocks on his door.

"You see, sir," commenced Reeves. "We can't arrest Mr Dawson for murder if there isn't a body. And there will not be a body for two days. And all five of those bodies will then be in your flat. Convincing the police that Mr Dawson is the murderer and not yourself, will be ... difficult."

Very difficult, I thought. If not impossible.

"Can't we nab the time machine and move the bodies *chez* Dawson?"

"We could, sir. But then we would be faced with the ethical dilemma. Namely, that we could also use the time machine to prevent the murders from happening. But if we did that, then there would be no murders to place at the door of Mr Dawson. He would be a free man."

"Run that past me again, Reeves."

"The choice we have, sir, is to allow people to be murdered so that we can convict Mr Dawson. Or prevent the murders, and allow a murderer to go free, perhaps to kill again at a later date should he feel that someone stands in his way."

These were deep philosophical questions.

"Could we toss for it? Heads everyone lives, tails Dawson's locked up?"

"I don't think these are questions we can leave to chance, sir. There is also the question of 'how many murders do we prevent?' We could use the time machine to reset the timeline to how it was when we were first engaged by Mr Wells. In which case The Traveller will be dead. Alternatively, we can take the timeline back to 1894 and save The Traveller. But, in so doing, we risk changing the timeline from 1894 to the current day. There may be no Hydrogen Fuel Cell. You and Miss Emmeline may never meet. And *I* may still reside in a locked cupboard at the Sloths."

This was a facer. I'm all for saving people, but I didn't like the idea of Dawson walking away scot-free.

"What do you suggest then, Reeves?"

"I am at a loss, sir."

And I was nowhere near a gin bottle.

What were we to do?

It's at critical moments like these – when strong men are faltering – that the Worcesters step forward. We may not see all, but we see enough. And there was one thing that we could accomplish without annoying any butterflies.

We would steal back the time machine. I had no idea what we'd do with it once we had it, but it was imperative we removed it from Dawson's clutches.

THIRTEEN

"Same plan as before Reeves. I'll distract Dawson, but this time you steal the time machine and sail it over the road into Grosvenor Square Garden and wait for me there. You can lurk in the ether."

"I fear for that plan to succeed, sir, you would need to distract a good number of the servants as well. It is one thing to inveigle oneself into the servants' kitchen and, in the course of conversation, learn the location of a time machine. But to then proceed to that location unmolested, and without drawing unwarranted attention... I calculate the chance of success to be slim, sir."

He was right. One can't wander about another person's house without being challenged. There was only one thing for it.

"Desperate times call for desperate men, Reeves. We need that time machine, and we must have it."

"Indeed, sir."

"And we *are* going to erase this timeline, aren't we, Reeves?"

"Yes, sir," said Reeves, exhibiting a modicum of caution in his voice.

"Which would remove any unpleasantness?"

"What nature of unpleasantness, sir?"

"I was thinking of burglary with menaces."

I was expecting Reeves to complain, but all he said was 'Needs must, sir' and arose from his chair.

"Stout fellow, Reeves!"

I almost slapped him on the back, but Reeves would not have appreciated such familiarity - even in a timeline whose days were numbered.

We perfected our plan on the way to Grosvenor Square. Like the Hun, we would be quick, and we would be terrible. I'd use the service revolver to cow the servants and get them to take us to the time machine. We'd be away and into the ether before Dawson could do anything to stop us.

I parked the Stanley several doors away to make sure we weren't spotted, then strode off in search of the servants' entrance. Once I'd located it, we nipped down the steps, out came my service revolver, and I knocked thrice upon the door.

Three seconds later, the door opened and a startled maidservant stared soundlessly at the outstretched gun levelled at her nose.

"Step back!" I commanded. "I am the Mayfair Maniac. And this is my robot."

~

As entrances went, this was up there with the best. The startled maidservant swooned on the spot. Reeves, the aforementioned robot, swept forward to catch her as she fell, and propped her up against the Aga.

The cook screamed. A footman, who had been seated at the kitchen table, jumped out of his chair so swiftly he sent it skittling along the floor behind him.

"Do be quiet," I said, waggling the gun in their direction. "No one will get hurt if you all do as I say."

"We are looking for a room that Mr Dawson probably keeps locked," said Reeves. "He has a machine inside that resembles an automobile. Do you know of such a room?"

Neither the cook nor the footman spoke.

I considered firing a warning bullet into the ceiling. Murgatroyd of the Yard swears by it. There's nothing better to wake a person up, or show 'em you mean business, says M. of the Y. But Reeves had hidden my bullets, so I gave it a menacing waggle instead.

"You have five seconds to answer," said Reeves. "After that I will be unable to hold the Mayfair Maniac back. Behold the bloodlust burning in his eyes."

I rolled both eyes and affected a look I'd once see Sir Henry Irving attempt when playing Caligula at the Garrick.

"It's in the cellar!" cried the footman. "On the right at the foot of the steps."

"And the key?" asked Reeves.

"On its hook on the wall over there," said the footman. "Third from the left on the bottom row."

Reeves fetched the key while I gave dark looks to the servants.

"Everyone close their eyes," I said. "And count to one

hundred. If I see one eye open before one hundred, I shall feed it to my robot."

I legged it in pursuit of Reeves, who'd found the door to the cellar and was holding it open for me.

It was then, in mid-gallop, that I noticed the other footman. He was in the hall, and he'd spotted us.

"Hey!" he shouted. "Mr Dawson! Intruders!"

I shot through the cellar door and was running so fast down the steps – which was suddenly plunged into total darkness, as neither of Reeves nor I had tarried to find a light switch, and Reeves had just closed the door behind him – that I lost my footing, and tumbled the rest of way, twisting my ankle and bruising my shoulder.

The cellar door at the top of the steps flew open with a crash. That provided us with a little light, until the doorway was blocked by the rugged silhouette of a large footman hurrying after us.

"Stop or I'll shoot!" I commanded. I may have been bruised and lying on my back, but at least I'd had the presence of mind not to drop my service revolver.

The footman froze on the staircase. Reeves unlocked the door to the room where the time machine was hidden, and I hobbled to my feet.

I almost made it. I had one hand on the doorjamb to steady myself when – BANG – there came the loudest explosion I'd ever heard. I was thrown forward, landing in a heap just inside the room. And my shoulder, the one I'd fallen upon earlier, felt like it had been speared with an assagai.

It took me a while to realise I'd been shot.

I looked at Reeves. He was climbing into the time machine, apparently oblivious to my position.

There was a click and the cellar was suddenly bathed in light.

"Worcester!" came a surly voice from halfway up the steps. "I should have known it would be you. Stand up and kick that gun away."

I managed to prop myself up with my good arm and looked towards Reeves.

He'd disappeared. Along with the time machine.

FOURTEEN

I was not sure which shocked me the most – being abandoned by Reeves, or being shot.

Or, indeed, the language employed by Dawson when he discovered the time machine missing. It was enough to redden the cheeks of a sailor with thirty years before the mast.

I struggled to my one good foot, grabbed the door with my one good hand, and hopped through 180 degrees to meet my adversary.

"You have meddled enough in my affairs, Worcester," said Dawson, advancing upon me, gun levelled and still smoking.

This was my opening for a merry quip, but I didn't feel much in the mood for quipping. I was losing sensation in my left arm, I had a burning pain in my left shoulder, a sore ankle, and a hole in my new suit! So I gave him a disdainful look instead.

I could tell it wounded him.

"Whatever your valet does, it's not going to save either of you. Anything you change, I'll go back a day earlier and change it even more. I have things planned for you that even your automaton can't imagine."

"Says you!"

In retrospect that wasn't my finest riposte, but it was all I had. I'd been shot and abandoned – all in the space of a single second.

Dawson smirked.

"Says I!" he said. "How long do you think you can keep me away from that time machine? You going to watch it every hour of every day for the rest of your life? It only takes a minute to snatch it back. And I have enough money to buy an army. I can storm your flat whenever I want."

As *Snakes and Ladders* went, the bullet in the shoulder was a definite snake, but now I wondered if I could see a ladder. What if Reeves was still here? In the ether, that is.

He might have manoeuvred the time machine behind Dawson – or, even better, above Dawson – and be ready to materialise any second.

I could be saved.

But I wasn't.

At least, not by Reeves.

There was a slight shimmer in the air, and then a dazzling light as the gloom of the cellar was replaced by the welcoming sight of my beloved flat.

I was saved! And – I patted myself down to make sure – whole. I had no pain, and no bullet holes. And I was alone. I beetled around the flat, looking for Dawson, dead bodies, time machines, concealed policemen, and Reeves ... and found nothing.

Which baffled me somewhat. Shouldn't Reeves be back at the flat with the time machine by now? Or had Dawson managed to snatch it back again?

I checked the lock on the front door. It hadn't been forced.

I mixed myself a cocktail and pondered at great length.

Then, as I was weighing up the pros and cons of moving to New York under an assumed name, the door opened and in walked Reeves.

"Reeves! Where have you been?"

"The British Library, sir. May I mix you another cocktail?"

"Hang the cocktail!" I said. And, yes, dear reader, those were my exact words, so you can see I was not myself. "You abandoned me, Reeves!" I continued. "What happened to your feudal spirit? Didn't you notice I'd been shot!"

"That was why I had to leave, sir."

"Because I'd been shot?"

"Exactly, sir. If I had come to your aid, the probable outcome was that both of us would have been shot, and the time machine lost. And if I *had* succeeded in rescuing you, then you would still be wounded. Even if we piloted the time machine into the past and erased the timeline where the shooting took place, the chances were that you – being inside the time machine and thus shielded – would remain shot. The only sure way of restoring your body to full vigour was for me to change the timeline whilst you were still in it."

"I think I'll have that cocktail now, Reeves."

"Very good, sir."

"So you're saying you were looking after my best interests?"

"Indeed, sir."

I'm sure there was large flaw in Reeves's argument, but hanged if I could see it.

"So what is the state of the timeline now, Reeves? Henry VIII still have the requisite number of wives? Or has Dawson gone back and married them all?"

"The timeline is most acceptable, sir. That was the purpose of my visit to the British Library. To verify the situation."

I was confused.

"Are you saying you've fixed everything? Without me? What happened to the ethical dilemma?"

"That was indeed most vexing, sir, but The Traveller and I came up with a passable solution."

"The Traveller! Is he alive?"

"Very much so, sir. And most grateful. He sends his regards."

"That's all very well, Reeves, but where's the time machine? Dawson said he'd undo anything we did."

"The time machine is beyond his reach, sir. The Traveller has taken it back to the future and we have limited its appearance in the past to but a single day. Long enough to provide Mr Wells with material for his book, but no more. The Traveller used the fuel cell from the later machine to repair the old one, thus negating the need to enlist the help of Mr Dawson and the other associates."

"Forgive me for being critical, Reeves. But weren't you the same Reeves who quoted Babbage at me? All that guff about butterflies and interconnectivity, and how imperative it was not to change the slightest thing as the results were unpredictable?"

"Yes, sir. The Traveller and I debated that particular question for some considerable time. We thought we may have to make several additional interventions, but, in the end, it wasn't necessary. It appears that the existence of a working time machine was largely withheld from the general public, who believed the machine to be a work of fiction. We also checked the lives of HG Wells, his four associates and their close companions, and though there were differences, they were not regarded as major."

"East Dulwich still stands then?"

"It does, sir."

"What about Dawson though? Presumably if everyone's alive then Dawson is walking around scot-free! Which irks me, Reeves. And I am not a man easily irked. He shot me. He threatened me. He framed me for murder, killed five people and had you sent to Madame Tussauds! Shouldn't we warn the police about him?"

"I rather suspect the police are too busy, sir."

"Busy, Reeves?"

"Yes, sir. Apparently the Crown Jewels were stolen this morning."

"The Crown Jewels! Someone broke into the Tower?"

"It would appear so, sir. The police should be searching Mr Dawson's house in..." He pulled out his pocket watch and checked it. "Approximately five minutes, sir."

"Reeves?" I cast a suspicious eye over his eyebrows. "Is there something you'd like to tell me?"

"I don't think so, sir."

I was not going to let this go.

"You *framed* Dawson?"

"Frame is such an ugly word, sir. I think it more a case of righting an injustice."

"I can't argue with that, Reeves, but ... don't you think the Crown Jewels a touch excessive. Why not rob a small bank?"

"It was essential to ensure Mr Dawson is convicted, sir. And the theft of the Crown Jewels is more likely to ensure that the case is prosecuted with the utmost vigour."

"I say, Reeves, you do know the timeline owes us seven pounds ten shillings and sixpence, don't you?"

"I have that recollection, sir."

"You didn't happen to trouser the odd jewel, did you, when you were in the Tower?"

Reeves coughed disapprovingly. "I did not, sir."

"But you agree we're owed it?"

"Possibly, sir."

"What I don't understand is where it went. I mean, there we were handing over seven pounds ten shillings and sixpence to 1903 and – poof – it's gone. And what about that extra necklace from the 1860s. Do the butterflies get it all?"

"I think my pressure is dangerously low, sir."

"Rot, you always say that when you want to avoid answering the question."

I could tell Reeves was wavering. His eyebrows took on a contemplative demeanour.

"I did happen to glance at the *Sporting Life*, sir, when I was waiting in line to purchase *The Mayfair Maniac*."

"And? Come on, Reeves. Spill all, it'll make you feel better."

"It was the merest of glances, sir, and not at all intentional."

"That goes without saying, Reeves. What did you see?"

"Enough to suggest that a small wager on Wargrave in this year's Cesarewitch would be a fruitful one, sir."

"Good man! I knew I could count on you, Reeves."

"A *small* wager though, sir. We are only owed seven pounds, ten shillings and sixpence."

"Don't worry Reeves. The denizens of East Dulwich are safe in my hands."

Acknowledgements

Thank you to my editors: Jennifer Stevenson and Sherwood Smith.

And, of course, Pelham Grenville Wodehouse.

About Chris Dolley

Chris Dolley is a *New York Times* bestselling author. He now lives in rural France with his wife and a frightening number of animals. They grow their own food and solve their own crimes. The latter out of necessity when Chris's identity was stolen along with their life savings. Abandoned by the police forces of four countries, who all insisted the crime originated in someone else's jurisdiction, he had to solve the crime himself. Which he did, and got a book out of it – the international bestseller, *French Fried: one man's move to France with too many animals and an identity thief*.

His SF novel *Resonance* was the first book to be plucked out of Baen's electronic slushpile. And his first Reeves and Worcester Steampunk Mystery – *What Ho, Automaton!* – was a WSFA Award finalist in 2012.

About Book View Cafe

Book View Café (BVC) is an author-owned cooperative of over forty professional writers, publishing in a variety of genres including fantasy, romance, mystery, and science fiction.

Our authors include *New York Times* and *USA Today* best-sellers; Nebula, Hugo, and Philip K. Dick Award winners; World Fantasy and Rita Award nominees; and winners and nominees of many other publishing awards.

BVC returns 95% of the profit on each book directly to the author.

FICTION DOLLEY

Dolley, Chris.
What ho, automata

NWEST

R4000991578

NORTHWEST
Atlanta-Fulton Public Library

CPSIA inforr
Printed in the
LVOW07s15

4277321

9 781611 383942